WHEN SNOW FALLS

BOOK I OF THE WHEN LIGHTNING STRIKES SAGA
B. NOVA KARDINALIS

Book Cover by ANKBookDesigns

Editing by Morgan Waddle and Jessica Harden

Map Illustration by Virginia Allyn

1st edition 2025

CONTENTS

TRIGGER WARNING

This is a dark urban fantasy series with a mafia-like structure and Demons who eat humans to survive.

This series contains, alludes or mentions violence, murder, death, blood, anti-social behaviour, corruption, disownment, racism, sex work, amnesia, sleep disorders, scars, gang violence, human trafficking, torture, stalking, imprisonment, homelessness, drugs, alcohol, war, genocide, animal deaths, animal cruelty, natural disasters, climate change, riots, police brutality, disappearance of a loved one, kidnapping, medical experimentation, child abuse, cannibalism, infertility, addiction, anxiety disorders, post-traumatic stress disorder, self-harm, alcoholism, infidelity, domestic violence, foster care, abandonment, sexual assault, grooming, hate crimes, bullying, classism, depression, hallucinations, suicide and dissociation.

Please do not continue to read if you are uncomfortable with any of these topics.

Your mental health matters.

To Teodor, my entire heart and soul

To Kasper, my baby

To Victoria, who pushed me to publish

And finally, to Marius, who believes he inspired Hyacinth.

DEFINITIONS, PHRASES AND SLANGS

- **A.D.** – After Demons. Used to mark the years following the Reckoning.

- **Apex** – A group of individuals who have earned titles from the Underworld. Considered the highest-ranked and respected in the realm.

- **Blood**

  - A sacred promise among Stygians. If broken, the offender must shed blood as punishment.

  - End of a prayer to Phobus. The final word in a prayer to Phobus

  - Curse word, equivalent to 'fuck'. e.g: for blood's sake, bloody hell, ect.

- **Clan** – A group united by shared objectives or religious beliefs. The two largest clans are Stygians and Etherians.

  - **Corpse Killers** – An Etherian clan known for their extreme violence and brutality.

  - **Galazio** – Corrupt law enforcement; a rogue faction within the system.

  - **Stygian clans**

    - **Kokkino** – 'Red' clan. Protects using violence.

- **Hriso** – 'Gold' clan. Politicians and power brokers.

- **Mov** – 'Purple' clan. Traffickers of humans, drugs, and weapons.

- **Prassino** – 'Green' clan. Experts in surveillance and electronic control.

- **Aldring** – A Demon's coming-of-age ritual.

- **Ether** – The realm above the clouds where Angels live.

- **Etherian** – The language, religion, and culture associated with Angels.

- **Kynigos** – An alliance of four ancient families who were once Demon hunters.

- **The Reckoning** – The event that ended the recent war between Demons, Humans and Angels. Nearly caused Demon extinction.

- **Swears phrases and exclamations**

  - **Oh my gods** – General exclamation used by most people.

  - **Angels above** – Commonly said by Etherians.

  - **Demons below** – Commonly said by Stygians.

  - **Stars above** – Used by Angels, Poiesis, Moira, and Arcacia.

  - **Bloody hell** – Used mainly by Demons and Phobus.

- **Slurs and insults**

  - **Corpse** – A slur used to describe Demons; derogatory and dehumanising.

  - **Dog** – An insult implying someone is submissive, pathetic, or beneath others. Similar to "bitch" or "lapdog."

- **Feathers** – Insult towards Angels. Dismisses them as delicate, defined only by their wings.

- **Hollow** – A slur used to describe Angels; holy outside, empty inside.

- **Skykisser** – A slur directed at Etherians; often used by Stygians.

- **Stygian scum** – A slur directed at Stygians; often used by Etherians or humans.

- **Vampire** – Used by Demons to insult other Demons, implies weakness and imitation. Refers to demons who are seen as watered down or pathetic.

- **Soulesity** – Northernmost country in the realm.

- **Stygia** – A subterranean region beneath the mountains. Home to demons.

- **Stygian** – The language, religion, and culture associated with Demons.

DEMONS
SELKIES
SOUL
WAREHOUSES
ICE RINK
BERNADETTE'S
FACTORIES
THE UNDERWORLD
NEON NIGHTS
WEST SOULESITY SQUARE
SKOL
KYLO'S
CITY PRISON
JEROME'S
THE LIGHTHOUSE
ETHER KINGDOM

STYGIAN TERRITORY
"ANGELS"
...ESITY
GATED MANORS
KOLDEN'S
...OULESITY ETHERIAN SCHOOL
NIKO'S DOJO
CITY HALL
PYRAMID OF CONVERGENCE
...AST SOULESITY CIRCLE
CITY LIBRARY
...CITY MUSEUM
POLICE STATION
EAST SOULESITY SCHOOL
...RENEE'S FLORIST
KOKKINO CLAN ESTATE
THE DOCKS
"HUMANS"

HYACINTH

I need a distraction, something to replace

This creeping boredom, this endless chase.

One day, it will drown this fragile realm,

As chaos rises to take the helm.

Soon, I'll find her, the one who embraces the night,

So beautifully broken, a corrupt light.

My childhood friend, my soulmate, my nightmare, my dream,

I'll love her, then lose her—it's all fate's cruel scheme.

Again and again, the cycle's the same,

Maybe if I don't love, I'll escape this game.

But our minds entwine in an endless twist,

These Penrose steps, too tempting to resist.

PART 1

DO YOU WANT TO PLAY A GAME?

I

THIS BLOODY CITY

June 70 A.D.

They say the most painful thing in the world is a broken heart. Whoever said that had obviously never broken a bone.

With one foot pressed onto the centre of the man's back, one hand holds his shoulder, the other clasped around his wrist. I lean in close and his head turns, eyes locked with mine. Fat beads of sweat rolled down his forehead, his eyes bulged out of his skull and his mouth opened wide, wrinkling and creasing the skin on his face. With a bit of a pull to the side, the bone and ligaments in his arm snapped with a satisfying crack.

His screams echoed around us, louder than any broken heart ever could.

"Cinth," Niko's sharp voice sounded behind me, but I didn't turn to look at him, intrigued and relished in the agony of the man before me. Niko's presence cautiously approached me, but his voice held firm. "Enough."

The man's screams had stopped by now, whimpering, trembling, and weeping. Tears mixed with sweat, mucus, blood, and drool stained his face.

They're always the same.

Pathetic.

And it's become exponentially boring.

I licked the front of my teeth, clearly showing Niko my annoyance for his interruption, before finally releasing the man.

The man scurried away, his unnaturally bent arm dangling at his side. He spat a bit of blood from his mouth and turned. "You're insane! You're actually insane!"

I rolled my eyes, shoving my hands in my pockets.

"Why this one?" Niko asked, his jaw tight.

Nikodemus Kolden was a man in his late forties, fit and intimidating–to other people I guess. A classy man, only seen wearing suits and always disapproving of my style, which was entirely opposite to his. I much preferred my oversized hoodies and black track pants to allow more movement. Though we have similar almond skin and dark brown, nearly black hair, his is cut short and styled neatly, with a clean stubble beard. Whereas, I left my hair a mess, long enough to go over my eyes, which are two different colours. Bright green and dark enough to call black.

I finally turned my attention away from the man and to my mentor. His dark brown eyes used to look at me with pride, but now they only reflected fear and disgust of what I had become and what I am becoming. He's kept me on a tight leash, but I'm growing much too big for my collar.

A few bystanders assisted the man, attempting to stop the bleeding in his nose, most likely calling the police and ambulance. Still, we'll be gone before they arrive.

"And in daylight?" Niko stated through clenched teeth.

I looked up at the setting sun, not that anyone ever really sees the sun, the constant grey clouds block us from it.

"I don't know." I shrugged. "His shirt pissed me off I guess." He was just a regular button-up, probably on his way home from work.

Niko took the collar of my hoodie and pulled me toward him. "I have had it up to *here* with you. You no longer look for an excuse anymore when you get into fights–"

"Does it look like he could even fight me back?" I chuckled. "Call it what it is, Niko." I shifted my gaze back to his. "Attempted homicide."

Niko tries really hard not to show his horror for me, but he's been locking the door to his bedroom since I was ten. His grip on my collar loosened as he backed away. "Get in the car"–his eyes hardened–"now."

I shook my head and walked towards the carelessly parked car half on the sidewalk.

He really wasted no time stopping me from my boredom.

We climbed into his car and just as we strapped our seatbelts on, a loud thud followed a man, now groaning on the hood, and I jumped in my seat.

Of all the things to fall from the sky, I don't usually expect it to be a person.

He wore a suit, his dark hair gelled back. Eyes squeezed shut, he reached up to grip the back of his head, now dripping blood. When he opened his eyes, he lifted his head up and let out a shout, as a tiny girl dropped down. Her feet landed on either side of his torso, making the car jerk again.

Her dark, cedar-brown hair was straight and long, the light wind picking up the ends of it down by her hips. The black turtleneck, long-sleeved top, short dark red skirt, black thigh high socks, and black shoes made it obvious which clan she was a part of.

Kokkino clan.

The girl eased herself down onto his stomach, her hand resting lightly on his chest. Slowly and soothingly, she traced her fingers up past his neck to the back of his head, then gripped his hair firmly, holding him in place. His eyes went wide and stunned, mouth slightly parted, almost as if he were yearning for her touch. Extending my neck, I attempted to catch a peek of her face, but it was curtained by her hair.

Her movements were slow, taking her time, as though savouring the moment. She lifted the side of her skirt to reveal her thigh strap, packed with small throwing knives, taking one of them into her slender hands. She pushed the tip of the blade all the way into the man's eye until he eventually stopped convulsing.

Bloody hell.

The girl yanked the knife out and slipped it back into her thigh strap. She flipped her hair out of her face as she sat back up, giving me a slight glimpse of a red bandana covering the bottom half of her face. Her chest heaved, the muscle in her legs trembling as she stood from her position and stepped toward the edge of the hood, scanning the area, seemingly waiting for something.

Her head snapped toward the audience from my rampage, watching with utter fear and disbelief. They were frozen with dazed expressions. Even the man I injured seemed to be entranced.

I turned to Niko, wondering if he could see this weird behaviour, but his expression mirrored the others.

The girl hopped off the car, leisurely walked away, and disappeared deeper into the city.

"My... My car..." Niko groaned, dropping his face in his hands. "My bloody car."

Releasing a breath, I exited the car, Niko too devastated to move. I pushed the corpse off the hood, revealing the beating the car had taken, ignoring the shrieks and gasps of bystanders.

Oh, now they react.

I got back inside to see Niko slamming his forehead on the wheel, cursing under his breath. "My car. My car."

"Just get a new car. It's time for one anyway."

It's not like he couldn't easily pay for a new car–a million new cars–and still have enough money to live the rest of his life comfortably without lifting a finger.

He slowly turned his head towards me. "You don't understand, Cinth, it's not about the physical damage–" he gently caressed the wheel "–my baby has been through so much."

"Does Renee know you love your car more than her?"

"Yes. And she respects us," Niko spat, finally turning the engine as the sirens approached.

"Us," I mocked. "Gods, you're embarrassing."

He laid on the throttle and swerved the car away from the area with a jerk. "It's my job to embarrass you."

After a bit of driving, I looked over at him. "Are you going to tell Silias one of his clansmen damaged your car?"

Niko knitted his brows in confusion. "Why would I do that?"

"Because the person who did that was obviously from the Kokkino clan."

There was a long silence.

"What's the point?" he muttered under his breath. "Doesn't matter if he had seen it with his own eyes. I'm not getting anything from that greedy bastard."

I shrugged, picking at the dried blood under my nails.

That girl stabbed the man in the eye, a signature kill of the Kokkino clan's Grim Reaper. But she looked really young, too young to be in the Kokkino clan. All the stories I've heard, Reaper seemed to be in her twenties.

The first whispers began right before summer and the rumours about her have only continued to grow and spiral. The woman was a menace, never leaving a soul alive in her wake. No one's ever seen her before, but maybe, now that she's been named by the streets, she doesn't care if she's seen. Perhaps it's pure amateur sloppiness.

I shook my head. It wouldn't do anyone any good to snitch on her, especially if she wasn't a part of the clan.

She shouldn't have worn Kokkino's colours if she's going to be causing problems. No matter what unwritten laws the Underworld unspokenly agreed upon, Silias didn't have any limits to what he would do and no one had the guts to stand up to him anyway. You don't cross the most powerful man in the city, especially after what he did to get there. It made him a particularly dangerous and vexing man.

I sat further back in my seat, staring mindlessly out the window.

Gods, I hate this bloody city.

Soulesity, the Northernmost city on the planet, with ten months of winter and about two months of warmth. Although, it never gets warmer than twenty-five degrees. It's isolated, surrounded by the sea and everything North of it is large, deep canyons. After that, an endless cold desert, monstrous mountains and from there... Well, no one had returned from the mountains and the massive glaciers make it impossible to take a boat. Stygia, Demon territory, was located somewhere in the mountains. Though Demons were technically extinct, no one had the courage, or the stupidity needed to explore the area and check.

My eyes fell to the North. There used to be a tall stone wall there, spreading the border between the North of the city and the canyons. Built to keep Demons out. Once heavily monitored and guarded, now abandoned and mostly destroyed from the war seventy years ago.

We drove over the only bridge connecting the West and East side, crossing a large, raging river that divides the city into two parts. There have been talks of building a dam to help control the water and create clean energy to power Soulesity. However, they've been discussing it for years and nothing has come of it.

After the war, the neon lights of the West were no longer thought of as high-tech. Now they casted shadows for gang violence, drug dealings, and the homeless. The quiet side of the East held old buildings that were now considered elegant.

I tilted my head back, looking through the sunroof of the car. Above Soulesity, somewhere within the clouds, was the Ether Kingdom, where the Angels supposedly watched over humans. I've never seen an Angel before–no one has since the war–and I'm not sure I want to.

Niko took a turn in the opposite direction of our home and parked us on the side of a street. "Your bow's in the back."

I rolled my eyes, unfastened my seatbelt, and reached for my bow and arrows behind me, before following Niko to wait in the shadows until nightfall.

Usually smart people lock their doors and close their curtains during the night. The ones that don't pull stupid shit that get their name written on the contract after 'kill.' It was funny at first, but now it's just sad.

Being the best grows dull and people only feed me so much entertainment. I'm hungry, starving for a thrill. Craving a rush I never find.

Niko and I stood on a roof for hours, waiting for those we needed to eliminate to reveal themselves in the window of the building opposite us. Eventually, the light switched on and we pulled our bows back, aiming and waiting for the perfect moment. The string of my bow pressed against my lips as I took slow, deep breaths to steady my aim. Before either of us had a clear shot, the lights switched off.

Blood splattered against the windows, blocking our view, but we didn't need to see to know it was a slaughter. Slowly, we lowered our bows.

I hate being double-booked.

"Kokkino clan," Niko said, just as I spotted the red clothing. "There must have been multiple grievances with them."

Police cars surrounded the building as countless officers raided the inside.

"They're messy," I commented.

"But they get the job done. Even if they're caught, they won't be prosecuted."

"Why don't we become a part of a clan, again?" I sighed, even though I knew the answer.

It was meant to be rhetorical. We used to work with the Kokkino clan, before Silias took charge. We were never officially a part of it, but Niko was close friends with the previous leader.

"Because then we'd be restrained by rules and have to care for other people."

A figure opened the window and jumped out. Squinting my eyes, I recognised the twins, Leo and Sterling, having had a few encounters with them before.

"What–" Niko started.

The last figure wore the same outfit she had on earlier today, this time her hair tied up in a high ponytail.

What a busy girl.

The infamous twins with her confirmed it.

"I've only heard stories about her," I said in a low voice, as she hopped on the back of one of the motorbikes before they sped off. "They call her Reaper."

I lifted my bow once again, aiming it at the motorbikes.

"That's Reaper?" Niko laughed. Hardly anything shocks him these days. "She's so small."

I released my arrow, a warning shot not to take my job again, and it flew after them, piercing straight through the side mirror of the bike Reaper was on, causing the twin driving to wobble. He quickly swerved the bike to a stop, using one foot on the ground to steady himself. Then turned his head up towards where we were and stared at us for a long moment. Finally, he revved his bike and sped away.

Honestly, I'm not too interested in Reaper; if she doesn't stand in my way again, she'll live a long—well, longer life.

2

A FLEETING MOMENT, AN ETERNITY

July 70 A.D.

I took a walk around Soulesity's West side, popping a tiny illegal pill to make life a little more interesting, though it only distorted colours, making them more vibrant. It also relieved my constant headaches. When you get hit in the head a lot, the headaches don't really go away. *Probably why Niko forces me to take one day off a week.* I wasn't really paying attention to where I was going, looking down at the puddles underneath my feet, finding it unusually amusing at that moment.

Considering most in this city are criminals, witnessing someone get mugged or murdered isn't unusual. It'd be wise to be more careful with where I step. But I am the Vulture, trained by Niko, and surpassed him after just a few years. No one would dare to even think my name.

Two sets of feet stopped in front of me, forcing me to look up.

Oh, for blood's sake.

Even though the twins were identical, the same dark skin, same short dark hair, and the same dark eyes, it was easy to tell them apart by the way they carried themselves. Sterling walked with a straight back, giving him just a few added centimetres, and Leo's eyes were always alert, scanning rooms for exits and trouble.

I had grown a lot recently and for the moment we stood at the same height, but it never mattered. I have always looked down at them and everyone else for that matter.

"You're in my way," I said in a low voice, looking at them with disinterest.

"Rare to see you without any bloodstains." Sterling smirked.

"Well." I pulled out a cigarette from my pocket and lit it. If I was going to be forced to have a conversation with someone, I needed something to keep me from getting too bored. "You did steal my job the other week."

"Yeah, we got your warning," Leo muttered.

"Maybe you shouldn't have waited so long to do it," Sterling mocked. "You know, clients get impatient."

I narrowed my eyes at him. I never talked to clients. They all go through Niko and he selects which jobs I take on.

Leo nudged his brother. "I think Silias has a job for you, Vulture."

I scoffed. "Isn't Reaper competent?"

Ever since Reaper came about, Niko and I have noticeably received fewer contracts. Everyone wanted to test the new meat, see if she really was as good as they say. So beautiful, apparently, people paid Silias just to see her. And rumour said she didn't disappoint, even exceeded expectations, but I hadn't properly seen what she could do, so I had no opinion on her. Surely we would meet soon. We're in the same field after all.

"She's still learning, and it's a one-person job," Leo said.

I waved them off, inhaling smoke. "You know where to find me." I walked around them, tired of the conversation. From the corner of my eye, I caught sight of a girl concealed behind them, and my breath hitched as I abruptly halted, nearly choking on the smoke swirling around me.

Bloody hell.

I'm not one to be attracted to anyone. Honestly, I find everyone utterly forgettable, but never in my entire existence had I ever encountered someone so impossibly ethereal, so profoundly otherworldly. My legs trembled, desperate to crumble to my knees in reverence. No words could capture the essence of her being, any attempt wouldn't do her justice.

Poiesis, you really took your time on this one.

Though I'm tall, she was tiny, just reaching my chest. Her long, painted nails glimmered with embedded diamonds, casting tiny rainbows with each delicate gesture as she tucked a strand of long dark hair behind her ear, revealing multiple silver piercings sparkling against her porcelain skin. A black turtleneck paired with a short red skirt and black thigh-highs adorned her body again.

Did she have one outfit, or was this just her signature look?

With a slushie in hand, she took a sip, the icy drink staining her dark red lips with purple. Finally, she lifted her gaze to mine, and I was instantly trapped. Her eyes were a crystal, icy blue, a colour I had once believed didn't exist in this world.

There was something haunting in her gaze. Her eyes held an emptiness, void of any and all emotion. We were the same. Born incomplete, broken by society and stitched together by survival—two souls in a world that had failed to embrace us, both searching and waiting for something, but unsure of what. I had faced countless killers in my life, but none like me.

None like us.

Her lips parted slightly, and I held my breath, carefully leaning in closer, eager and anxious to hear the voice such a beautiful girl could possess.

The rumours were true.

Before she could utter a sound, Leo stepped in front of her, blocking my view and snapping me out of my trance.

I met Leo's eyes. "Reaper?"

His lack of response confirmed it.

Leo furrowed his brows, a squint of caution in his eyes. He had one hand in his pocket like Sterling, ready to take out their weapons to defend her.

"Chill—"I blew a cloud of smoke into the sky. "What do you think I'm going to do? Kill her?"

There was a slight pause before Leo cocked his head. "She is your competition, isn't she?"

Competition? Please. No one could compare to me. People may think I'm cocky, but cocky would mean I can't do what I say. "I don't kill little girls." I took a deep inhale of my cigarette and blew it out.

"She may be small, but don't underestimate her," Leo warned.

"She's the same age as you." Sterling smirked.

"Seventeen?" I almost laughed, but they weren't joking.

I took one last look at her, desperately wanting to hear her voice. Reaper, on the other hand, didn't seem too curious about me. She just turned her focus to her slushie, occupied with getting the last bit on the bottom. So, I left, disappearing into the crowd.

Our first meeting was just a fleeting moment, but it would last an eternity in my mind.

3
STRANGERS

July 70 A.D.

I entered Stygian clan territory behind Niko, meeting in the early hours of the morning at the Underworld Bar, much too early for me. He wasn't originally going to bring me, and I don't know why he changed his mind. I just wanted to crawl back in the comforts of my bed, but unfortunately I had school after this.

The Underworld Bar was located in the West side of the city, owned by the Mov clan. The entire place was drenched in their colour; purple. Though meant to be a neutral ground for all clansmen and those involved in criminal activity, the perfect place to negotiate and make deals with just two rules:

No fights. No weapons.

Kokkino clansmen guarded the outside perimeters of the place, with Mov clansmen inside cleaning up from the aftermath of the night before and preparing for the night to come. A few passed out women were strewn about on purple leather sofa and the stage, leaning on one another with money poking out from under their revealing purple dresses, their skin stained with glitter. A bartender, using a cloth to shine the glass in his hand, stared at us and gave us a polite nod when we made eye contact. Another man walked around with a mop, scrubbing the glitter and grime off the dark purple marbled floors.

The amount of purple in this room was sickening.

We walked past a few empty booths and one with a girl laid on her back on the sofa, her head hanging off the edge as she read a book. She was wearing an oversized hoodie and

14

loose pants, as though she had just rolled out of bed. She didn't acknowledge us coming in like the others in the room did.

"Reaper," I muttered to Niko as we passed her. *So, she does have more than one outfit.*

He nodded, not really caring for her at that moment, too occupied in his own thoughts. "Stay out here."

What was the point of me coming?

I sat in a booth in the corner, still able to see Reaper from where I sat, on the other side, three booths down. She flipped a page. *Does she know I am here, or does she just not care?* I squinted my eyes to get a look at the title, but couldn't make it out. She let out a small breath and closed her eyes.

In Soulesity, adulthood is marked at the age of twenty, coinciding with the maturation of immortals. At this age, their powers and physical features begin to emerge, resembling a sort of puberty. Development continues until they reach twenty-five, at which point they stop ageing altogether. For Reaper, who is just seventeen, this means she can navigate the world with relative freedom and minimal consequences, as few would dare to harm someone who has not yet crossed into adulthood.

The bartender approached Reaper with a glass of ice and either alcohol or apple juice, and a straw. He set it down on her table, before tapping her head to let her know, and left.

Turning her head, Reaper locked eyes with me, no doubt feeling my stare. Her lips curved up into a slight smile, and I couldn't catch my breath until she finally pulled her gaze away.

She reached for her book, searching and flipping the pages before ripping a certain part of it. Taking a knife from her thigh strap, she stabbed her blade through the paper and flung it towards me.

I didn't flinch when it hit the wall, just barely grazing my neck, leaving a tiny scratch with a sliver of blood. Reaper seemed entertained with my lack of a reaction, sipping on her drink, unfazed that she just drew blood from the Vulture.

Pulling the knife from the wall, I looked at the paper.

Hello.

My brain fumbled for a way to respond that was just as memorable. But luckily, Niko came out of the meeting room, cautiously looking around, giving me the signal that he was ready to leave. I stood up, letting Niko go ahead of me as I slipped the bit of paper into my pocket.

Stopping in front of Reaper's table, I set her knife on top of her book and took her glass, taking a tiny sip of it. *Apple juice.* As I put the glass down, she lifted her knife and licked the tiny bit of my blood off it, meeting my eyes with something playful. A cold feeling coursed through my veins at her audacity, and my eyes narrowed.

Are you sure, Reaper?

Maybe she doesn't know what she did. Drawing blood from someone ranked superior to you in the Underworld is challenge and she further mocked me by licking my blood, as if she owned me. But just because she was named doesn't mean she's been ranked, only that she's growing quickly with a unique style of her own indicating her work.

I shook my head, rolling my eyes and shoving my hands in my pockets. My butterfly knife rubbed between my fingers, tempting me to put her in her place, to stop this before it's even begun. *It's too early to deal with this.* Unluckily for Reaper, I too am seventeen. So if it is a game she wants, I'll bring the war.

I caught up with Niko outside the bar and didn't ask what he had discussed with Silias. He was angry, but it didn't quite mask his fear, and I wasn't sure I wanted to know.

***

Most of us grew up together, had parents that were friends, grandparents that were friends, and so on and so forth. We could get away with anything just because of the number of digits in our bank accounts. Old money. Of all the schools in Soulesity, this one held most of the wealthier clan children, mostly from Hriso and Prassino. Mov clan children weren't usually wealthy and liked to stick together, so the majority resided in the West side of the city. The Kokkino clan were too violent and didn't live long enough to have children. As for the non-Stygian clan children, there were only a few in this school, as other clans were normally Etherian and this wasn't an Etherian school.

So it was extremely rare for new students to enrol.

The new transfer student was in her final year of high school with me. And she brought a lot of talk. Reported missing for almost four years, she suddenly shows up, three weeks into the start of the school year, out of nowhere. I didn't really keep up with the news, unless it had to do with the Underworld, but her face was plastered all over the city when she first disappeared. I was put into a coma two days after it was announced, so I was too busy healing to care.

Though, she was all anyone could talk about today.

The Underworld has a strict rule that nearly everyone follows; no harm comes to children. So, we were all disgusted to hear that this twelve-year-old girl was killed by a sixteen-year-old boy who relentlessly claimed they were 'just friends', but it was obvious she was groomed by him. She was the city's golden Senator's daughter, so of course it was a big scandal. But honestly, who cares? People go missing all the time in this city. And yet, when everyone was proven wrong about her being dead, no one had come forward to apologize to the boy who had served time for it.

We had an assembly the day before she came, warning us not to ask her about her disappearance because it would be a sensitive topic. As if anyone would actually listen. Everyone was curious, even had their own theories.

"Oi, oi. Did you see the new girl?" Jamiel asked at our table during lunch. We sat outside behind the school so we could smoke.

"No, is she cute?" Galinthias asked. He was the only one of us who didn't smoke.

"Very." Jamiel's eyes sparked.

"It's the Vicary daughter, right? The one who went missing?" Lin clarified. He luckily missed the assembly.

Completely disinterested in the topic, I looked at my chipped nail polish, always black, accessorised with multiple silver rings. *Maybe I should invest in better quality nail polish.* Redoing them nearly every day was becoming annoying. Though the chips matched the heavy calluses on my palms and cuts and bruising on my knuckles. Until I stop fighting, they would permanently be there.

Iri nodded. "She's super popular already."

"Unsurprising. You saw her, didn't you?" Jamiel sighed. "Never thought someone like that existed."

"She looks so different from her photos." Iri smiled.

"Obviously. Those photos are nearly a decade old," Jamiel replied.

They used a photo from when she was nine years old on her missing posters. Apparently, the Vicarys didn't have a more recent photo that clearly showed her face.

I blew out a cloud of smoke. "Big deal," I muttered. "She's just another annoying teenage girl."

"Hey!" Iri shot me a glare, but I didn't take my words back.

Iri and Jamiel exchanged looks.

"Finish your cig," Jamiel demanded.

I rolled my eyes and just as my cigarette burnt into a stump, they grabbed me, pulling me with them. "Let go, I can walk."

Hands in my pockets, I smirked at Jamiel in Iri's skirt. They liked to switch bottoms, a small change to the uniforms we had to wear. Red trousers or skirts and black button-up shirts with a red tie or ribbon, and optional black jacket. I always wore my tie loose and jackets were too warm for me; I prefer the cold.

"Bet she'll shock you," Iri gambled.

"Bet she won't," I mumbled.

Lin and I followed Iri and Jamiel around the cafeteria, but I guess they didn't spot the new girl, so we went to the twelfth-grade hallway where they shoved each other to get to the girl. I couldn't see her with the three crowding around her, but her locker was right next to Jamiel's at the opposite end of the hall from mine.

Lin couldn't even speak, so taken by her, apparently.

"Hey, I'm Jamiel, the fun one."

"Angels above, Jamiel." Iri shook her head before turning back to the girl. "Hi, my name's Iri."

"And I'm Lin," Galinthias quickly blurted out in almost a shout.

"Give her some space," I said in a low voice. Not only was she probably overwhelmed by the sudden gang up, but I kind of wanted to see her too. They took a step back, and I could barely contain the look of shock on my face when we locked eyes.

Reaper.

I never made the connection that she was the girl from the missing posters. I wasn't interested in it back then, so I never kept the face in my memory.

She smirked, waiting for me to speak.

"You're Datura, right?" Lin asked.

How cruel for her parents to name her after such a poisonous flower. As if they wanted to give her a misfortunate life.

She pulled her gaze away from me to meet Jamiel's.

"I only go by my second name now." Her voice was so soft and pure, like snow gently falling from the sky. A sound you'd listen to with your eyes closed and feel serene enough to fall asleep but wouldn't be able to because you just couldn't get enough of it. "It's Celestine."

"Why'd you run away from home?" Lin asked.

"Yeah, isn't Senator Vicary super rich?" Jamiel questioned.

Publicly, the Vicarys are the second richest family in the city, after the Prime Minister. Though, there are those far wealthier than them who are able to keep their names secret.

"Where do you live now?" Jamiel and Lin continued bombarding her with questions, but didn't wait for answers.

"Guys, come on." Iri glared at the boys. "That's personal." She turned back to Reaper. "You don't have to answer these stupid people." Iri smiled, shocking all of us. She never smiles like that, especially not for us. The last time we'd seen that smile of hers was with her last partner. "You probably don't remember me, but I was friends with your brother." Iri knew everyone in this city.

Reaper lowered her eyes, not responding. *Sensitive topic, noted.*

"Have you already eaten lunch?"

Reaper nodded.

"How are you liking the school, Celestine?" Jamiel was being so polite and kind, it almost made me laugh.

"It's... It's nice, everyone's been really... Nice." Bloody hell, even her stuttering was cute.

Did I just—No! Stop it.

I quickly turned and walked away.

"Oi, where you going, Cinth?" Jamiel called.

"I'm bored and class is starting soon." I waved them off. I'd rather fall on my knife like an idiot than let them see my heated face.

"We still have ten minutes!" Jamiel shouted.

But I turned the corner and was gone. Popping a pill into my mouth, I sat against the wall.

After a few minutes, my friends found me, and I reached into my pocket and handed Iri a gold coin.

"Hah! I knew she would shock you." Iri laughed.

"Yeah, yeah." I wasn't going to tell them it wasn't her beauty that shocked me.

Jamiel gasped. "I can't believe it. You've never had a crush on anyone."

"I thought Cinth was an ace like me." Lin raised a brow.

I don't do labels because then I'd be confined to it. I don't know what I was or wasn't, nor did I care. I just hated everyone.

I never could understand the obsession with labels, everyone labelling themselves and each other. What's the point? To create the useless feeling of being different? Special? Important? Why can't people just be? Everyone is fundamentally the same anyway, with the same selfish goals, whether it be power, money, or love.

People are so bloody pathetic.

"I don't like anyone, and I don't like her," I growled. Just because she was insanely attractive didn't mean I like her.

Iri sat next to me with a smirk. "But you admit she's pretty."

"I'm not blind." Though even a blind person would know she was beautiful just based on her voice.

"You know you two met before, right?" Iri said.

I turned to her.

"Seven months before your accident."

Four years ago, I suffered a blow to the head and the majority of the year before the hit was wiped from my memories. If I tried to think of that time, my head would feel like it was about to explode, like right now. So, I don't try anymore.

"Do you think she remembers me?" I asked, fiddling with one of my rings.

None of the memories I lost were likely important. Just my normal life of school, assignments, sleeping, and parties I hardly ever participated in. But sometimes, late at night when I can't sleep, I think the God of fate caused it to happen on purpose, as if there was something Moira wanted me to forget. Not that I'm religious. If the Gods really cared, the world wouldn't be messed up to this extent.

"No idea." Iri let out a dramatic sigh. "More importantly, do you think she likes girls?"

This dog.

"She's out of your league, Iri." Lin and Jamiel snickered.

Iri kicked Lin in the shin, who was unfortunately closest to her. "If she doesn't, I'd still have more of a chance than you two combined."

I let out a laugh. "How old is she anyways?" She was in our grade level, but she looked far younger—small, slight, almost as if she hadn't grown into her age yet.

"She'll be eighteen in May, right up there with Lin."

The bell rang and a sea of students came back from the cafeteria.

There aren't many students at the school, my grade being the largest with forty. Our grade was split into two classes and thankfully Reaper was in the other class.

Though history was in the largest classroom to accommodate both classes and was one of the only ones that required assigned seating. It was the only class Reaper, and I shared.

The teachers knew Lin, Jamiel, Iri, and I caused less trouble when we're together and made sure to put us in the same classes and our seats near one another. So, we took our seats in the back corner, Lin and Jamiel directly in front of Iri and me. Reaper sat in the middle row, closer to the wall, the only seat available.

Pausing in the middle of her lecture with a sigh, the teacher walked over to Reaper, causing me to look up from texting Jerome and Symeon, separately of course, they couldn't stand one another.

She spoke in a low voice, but we could all hear it. "You seem to be distracting your classmates."

Reaper gave her a confused look. "I'm not doing anything."

The teacher gave her a tight smile. "I need you to move seats." She turned to one of the girls sitting next to Iri. "Willow, please swap seats."

Willow did as she was told, but Reaper took her time before she was now just one desk over from me.

But if the teacher thought she was distracting the class before, it was even worse sitting her in the back. People were constantly turning in their seats, pretending to stretch or look at the time, just to get a glance at Reaper. Their eyes lingered before turning back to the front. Reaper didn't seem bothered by it or even notice as her eyes glazed over, dissociating from the world.

"Hyacinth."

I snapped my head back towards the teacher.

"Please, focus. This will be on the exam."

The class snickered and giggled.

Why was I the only one being called out?

***

Classes were over before I realised they had begun, and I walked out of school with Iri and Jamiel. Lin ran tutoring sessions after school, so we never walked home with him.

"No detention for you today?" Iri laughed. I also hardly walked home with them.

"That's a first," Jamiel commented, taking out a smoke.

"I'm full of surprises," I muttered, taking a lit cigarette from Jamiel. Honestly, I might have had detention today, but no one reminded me.

"What's going on over there?" Jamiel nodded towards the gates, filled with flashes of light and camera shutters. There were even a few students talking to the cameras, excitedly answering their questions.

Iri turned and rushed over towards a tree.

"Oi, where are you going?" Jamiel asked, but she ignored us, so we followed her. I didn't even notice Reaper sitting under the tree, her body hidden from the cameras.

"Are you okay?" Iri asked, crouching down to her level.

"Yeah, I'm... Waiting for them to leave," Reaper said in a low voice, running her fingers through the grass.

"It must be so annoying to have the media follow you all the time." Iri laughed.

"I didn't know they cared so much."

"Your court case was a huge deal, of course they're curious." Jamiel snorted.

"Court case?" Reaper asked, as if she didn't know... Maybe she didn't.

The world thought she was murdered by a sixteen-year-old boy. The trial was blasted live on every news station the entire year it went on for. I think that guy went to prison. How embarrassing that everyone was wrong about him, or at least about how he murdered her.

Iri spoke before Jamiel could tell her. "It's fine now, you're alive and well and that's all that matters. Do you have anyone to call to pick you up?"

"Not really." Reaper took a peak behind the tree to see the crowd still there. "You don't have to wait with me. I'm fine."

Iri made herself comfortable across from Reaper, setting her bag down. "There's no way I'm getting my photo taken today, I don't have my lashes on."

Iri loved make-up. Able to create art on her face just as well as she was able to decorate a cake, which comes in handy since her family owns one of the most successful, high-class restaurants in the city.

Reaper cracked a small smile.

Jamiel followed suit. "I have nothing to do anyway." He offered Reaper a cigarette, but she politely declined.

Yeah, I don't have time for this. I have an assignment that I wanted to get over with and I needed to repaint my nails. I turned and walked to the gates.

A few teachers were trying to disperse the crowd, but they kept getting sucked into the questions.

"How is Miss Vicary?"

"Is she doing well in school?"

"What's she like?"

"What happened to her when she disappeared?"

"Is she in contact with Mr Gautier?"

How incredibly annoying.

One of them stopped me, her amber eyes wide with curiosity. "Could you give us a comment about Miss Vicary?"

I tried to go around her, but they would hardly let me pass, they definitely wouldn't let Reaper breathe. I couldn't do anything either, not with all these cameras.

Bloody hell.

I turned back to the tree, finishing my cigarette on my way. Taking Reaper's arm, I pulled her up, not caring that Jamiel was in the middle of his story. No one said anything as I brought her to the back side of the school.

What am I doing?

I lifted her up; she was so easy and light. She reached up, taking a hold of the stone wall, hoisting herself up on top of it, giving me a glimpse of the knives on her thigh strap. Thank the Neverworld she was wearing shorts underneath. I forgot to ask. I took a step back before jumping and climbing the wall with her.

"Oi, Cinth!" Jamiel called from below, irritation evident on his face for stealing her away.

"You guys have more tolerance for those people," I muttered, landing in the soft grass on the other side, Reaper following before I could help her.

The crowd must have spotted us up on the wall, because a group of them turned the corner, racing towards us. For a moment, all I could see were zombies, hungrily reaching their arms out for us. Yeah, honestly, it was slightly terrifying.

I cursed under my breath, took Reaper's hand, and bolted from the area. We sprinted through the streets, turning corner after corner, trying to lose them, but they were relentless. I'm just glad she could keep up.

The July heat was not ideal for running and when I turned back to check on Reaper, she looked like she was about to pass out and I could feel the change from leading to dragging her with me. It wasn't actually that hot, more warm, but Souics were more used to the snow.

I pulled Reaper into an alley and behind a wall so we could take a break. She leaned her back against my chest as we tried to catch our breaths. My heart was pounding from the run and the feeling of her—

Shit.

"Don't touch me." I pushed her away, and she didn't argue, moving her weight onto the wall instead.

The sound of the media shouting and wondering where we went closed in, and I cursed, hoping they wouldn't find us. *Maybe I should've just let her wait it out.* But they didn't look like they would leave without at least one statement from her and she's just a teenager. Don't they realise that? Whatever she went through in those four years must have been traumatic.

Not that I care.

"It's so..." She breathed. "Hot."

I caught her before she crumbled to the ground, her body completely overheated. I set her down, propping her against the wall and used my free hand to go through my bag for the water bottle I always kept in it. I opened the cap and poured a bit of the water onto her neck, watching as it slithered down her skin, over her collarbone and under her shirt.

Reaper's eyes were barely open as she took in shallow breaths. I felt a pulse against her neck, but it was weak. Resting the bottle to her lips, I waited for her to tilt her head and drink it.

When she had downed half the bottle, looking slightly more alive, she pushed it away from her. "You take the rest."

"I'm fine, you're the one who passed out."

"How embarrassing." She sighed, sitting up.

"Only a bit," I teased, especially knowing she was the infamous Reaper. Who knew the heat would be her biggest weakness?

She attempted to stand, but fell with a curse. "Why of all days is today so hot?" It was only twenty degrees, but the sun was for once beaming down on us as the Ether Kingdom had drifted to the West side of the city, so it felt just a bit warmer.

I pulled her down to sit between my legs this time. "Calm down, you just passed out."

"I have to get home," Reaper said, holding onto her head.

I pressed the water bottle against her forehead. "Is that better?"

Gross. Why am I being so nice? I'm going to throw up.

She nodded.

"Drink more." I handed the bottle to her. I quickly hunched over her when two people with cameras ran past. Absolutely relentless. "We'll wait five minutes and then go."

She nodded, sipping on the water, and leaned her head back on me, closing her eyes. "Thanks for helping me."

My heart skipped a few beats.

Excuse me? Help her?

"They wouldn't let me pass," I muttered. "And I don't think they were leaving anytime soon." Though I have no idea why I took her with me.

She let out a small, short laugh, before the water bottle fell onto her lap. I couldn't quite see her face, but her chest rose and fell at a steady and even pace, asleep. I checked her pulse again, just in case, it was slow, but she was fine.

You'd think being Reaper, a wanted assassin with a line of grievances, would be more careful. *She is so naïve.* I could easily take my knife out from my pocket and slit her throat if I wanted to. Carefully I moved her hair from her neck and lightly grazed my finger across it.

Right there.

I wrapped my hand around her neck, but didn't apply any pressure, just rested it there, teasing myself. Tilting my head back against the wall, I closed my eyes. Her neck was so slender and soft. The muscles in my hand tightened and twitched, aching, begging to grasp her just a little harder. Craving to feel the steady pulse against her neck weaken to nothing.

I shouldn't.

***

Beneath me a thin layer of still, clear water mirrored the above so perfectly, the line where the sky met the land was near invisible, merged into one. As though I were floating in this place. The Stygia mountains lay off in the distance. The sun just about to rise, painting the world in crimson reds and indigo blues. It was so peacefully silent. Only the sound of my steady heart beating and the blood rushing in my ears greeted me. I took in deep breaths, the salty, crisp air tingled the insides of my nose, I could taste it.

The salt flats. That would mean Soulesity would be behind me. Though, when I turned, there was nothing but the endlessness of the salt flats and a little wooden one-story house standing just fifty metres away. Elevated off the ground by half a metre, a couple steps led to the front entryway, a single small window next to the door.

I stepped closer to the house, the water rippling with each step. The lights inside were off and dust collected on the steps. The old, white paint was chipped, peeling off the wood...

***

I released a deep breath, blinking, reorienting myself back to reality. I released Reaper's neck from my grip, my back aching from the hard brick wall I had been leaning against. Without moving too much, I checked the time on my phone. I must have fallen asleep, we'd been sitting here almost an hour. The media was surely gone by now, but how could I be so careless?

Taking the water bottle from her lap, I poured the last bit of it on her collarbone and she winced awake.

"I need to go." If I was around her a moment longer, I was going to kill her, but for once, something stopped me.

She got off me, standing up, and I followed. "Why didn't you wake me?"

"I just did."

Reaper rolled her eyes, but she wouldn't have done that if she knew who I was. I couldn't wait for her to find out, the way she won't be able to meet my eyes. The way she'll do anything I say. She'll be just like everyone else.

Pathetic.

She wouldn't stop staring at me, her icy gaze intense, making me feel self-conscious. Almost.

Maybe that was what she wanted.

"Can you get home from here?" Part of the inner circle of the Kokkino clan, she lived in the estate near the docks. It wasn't too far from where we were.

Her eyes darkened before she nodded. "Thanks."

I didn't know what to make of that expression of hers and decided not to dwell on it.

***

Stalking my victims from above, I hid behind pillars. It was an easy assignment, I just needed to kill the people below. Deciding it was time, I dropped down just as another figure dropped from their hiding spot at the opposite side of the room.

I was shocked and confused to see Reaper who had the same expression.

You must be joking.

The men quickly pulled out their weapons. "It's an ambush!"

I rolled my eyes, there's only two of us.

The men split up and charged at us. I took the ones coming at me down faster than her and began running towards her. I got to her just as she pulled her knife from one of their eyes. She quickly turned towards me, holding out her hand. My knife rested against her throat as she rested hers on mine.

Reaper's chest heaved, her eyes squinting to a cold glare. "Why'd you stop?" Her voice was slightly muffled by the red bandana covering the bottom half of her face, but she sounded confident, still soft-spoken but more confident than she had been earlier today.

"I could ask you the same thing." My lips curled up into a smirk. "They call you Reaper, don't they?"

"And what do they call you?"

She should have recognised me by my hoodie, burnt orange and green, split directly down the middle, complimenting my eye colours. A black face mask covering the bottom half of my face. Black track pants, better for movement, and shoes the same colour as my hoodie that didn't slip on ice. I'm not one for stealth, if anyone sees me, it's best they run.

"Vulture."

She laughed, putting down her knife, and I followed suit. "No offence, but Vulture sounds kind of lame." She clearly had no idea who I was, no one would dare talk to me like that. But I thought she would have at least heard the name.

"I didn't choose it."

My street name wasn't that bad, right?

Reaper reached her hand towards me, her cold fingers gently brushing against my neck, sending a chill through my bones. Searching for a tattoo behind my ear, but she wouldn't find one.

"Don't touch me." I said, grabbing her wrist to stop her.

I glanced at her fingertips, long coffin nails encrusted with jewels, painted a deep shade of red.

How does she fight with these?

Those in the Underworld burn our fingertips long enough for our prints to melt, or wear gloves. Reaper did neither, exposed. Though, I guess, the Kokkino clan didn't really have to worry, having officers in their back pockets wanting to prove their worth.

"What clan are you?"

"I work alone... Kind of."

Police sirens bled through the walls, lights painting us in red and blue. But I couldn't move, completely imprisoned in her gaze. Her dead eyes morphed into amusement, as if she knew the power she held.

"Cel." Leo jumped down from where he was hiding. "We need to go."

"And why were you just watching?" I asked, releasing my hold on Reaper and shoving my hands in my pockets.

"I'm only here in case something goes wrong."

The Kokkino clan cares enough for their clansman's safety?

He put his hand against Reaper's back and pushed her a safe distance away from me. "Sorry if she's said something wrong, she's not good with people."

I tilted my head back with a smirk. "She's still alive, isn't she?"

I was mostly serious. He gave me a polite nod, before turning back down to look at her. "Let's go."

4

SPILLED COFFEE

July 70 A.D.

Lately, Niko had been forcing me to wake up at four in the morning to train on top of my assignments and normal evening training. He usually gets upset with me for training too much, but maybe he thinks this will get me to calm down a bit. It certainly drains my energy.

I got out of the shower and my body ached, still adjusting to this new training schedule. The sweet scent of pancakes caused my stomach to growl.

"Good morning, Cinth," Renee said with a smile too large for this early hour when I came for breakfast.

She was a rather plain woman, keeping her hair in a bun, wearing modest clothing, and always had a book with her. Her and Niko have been partners for a few years now and the passion they have for each other has been the same since the day they met. I was very surprised someone like her could be excited and unintimidated by someone like Niko. They were an unlikely and opposite pair, but they matched.

I politely bowed to Renee, she and Niko the only ones I ever bowed to. "Good morning," I muttered. "Late start today?"

"Didn't I tell you? I hired someone recently to help me out at the shop."

"Oh, right. How is that going?" I asked.

Her flower shop was located in the heart of the East Side. Even in the winter, the air was thick with the sweet fragrance of blooms, as pots of plants and flowers spilled out onto the sidewalk. Lush greenery climbed the walls in the summer, decorated with vibrant flowers. Inside, the shop was a labyrinth of carefully arranged bouquets, delicate petals brushing against one another in the small space.

"Atlas is such a sweetheart." She flipped a pancake before setting plates down for the three of us. "Though, sometimes he knocks pots over by accident."

The incredibly large man in his mid-twenties certainly had Angel blood in him. He looked like one, with dark skin and dreads tied into a low ponytail. I met him a couple times, but never bothered to strike a conversation with him. Atlas didn't seem like a threat, and if he gave a hint of it, Niko would take care of it.

Niko came out from his room with damp hair, his eyes lighting up at the sight of the love of his life, and he tenderly kissed her cheek.

Renee's laugh bathed the room in warm colours that didn't exist in our apartment. "Niko, Cinth is here." She blushed.

"I can't help it, Renee." Niko sighed, hugging her from behind and not releasing her as she continued to pour another bit of batter into the pan.

I rolled my eyes, avoiding looking in their direction as Niko continued to shower Renee with all his love. I hate witnessing such public affection, it's disgusting. Though, Niko and Renee's healthy and loving relationship made it feel as though they were my parents.

Stupid.

"You ready for school, Cinth?" Niko asked, finally letting go of Renee.

I nodded, sleepily taking a pancake onto my plate and setting blueberry jam on top of it.

"You have a test coming up, right? Have you studied?"

My eyes turned to meet his, licking the front of my teeth in agitation.

Renee nudged Niko. "Cinth's smart, he'll be fine."

"I just don't want his grades slipping, especially in his final year."

"You're training him too much. How is he to study if he's tired?" Renee argued.

The two continued to bicker, but were smiling and would, like always, end their disagreements with a kiss no matter what. Otherwise, Niko would grovel, as Renee is never wrong.

I finished my breakfast and cleaned up our plates before grabbing my bag and slipping on my shoes.

"Oh, and isn't there a new transfer student in your grade?" Niko asked.

"So?"

There was a pause as I waited for him to continue. Instead, Niko pursed his lips and gave me a nod. "Try not to get detention today so you can join Renee and I at the cinema this afternoon."

I would absolutely not be promising anything and left.

***

"Cinth." I turned to see Reaper approaching me in the hallway.

"Don't call me Cinth," I muttered. I wasn't in the mood to be nice, not that I am ever nice.

Her brows furrowed. "I thought that was your name."

That's right, we've never properly introduced ourselves to each other.

"It's Hyacinth, only my friends call me Cinth," I told her, maybe a bit too harshly. "What do you want, Reaper?"

Her eyes looked around in panic for wandering ears, but everyone was having lunch, so the hallway was empty. "Are you going to tell people?"

"That you're Reaper?" I smirked.

"Yeah." She bit her thumbnail.

Oh, the power.

"Where's the fun in that? But I feel like you should do something to keep me from telling anyone." I wasn't actually planning on telling anyone, there was no gain in it. Blackmail is something I only dabbled in, but any chance for it I'll take.

"Well, do they know who you are?" she asked.

I blinked.

Clan children were the only ones who really knew who I was, and they didn't mess with me, but my friends weren't involved in the clans. Would I even still be allowed to call them my friends if they knew what I did every night...

Reaper removed her acrylic nail from her teeth and her lips twisted up into a mischievous smile. "Then maybe you should be doing things for me."

Yeah, that's kind of attractive.

I gave her a hard glare, which usually sent people running. "I'll tell everyone."

"Oh, but." Reaper laughed. "Unlike you, I don't actually care."

I licked the front of my teeth, tilted my head back with a smirk, and cursed. Without any warning, I grabbed her by the shoulder, slammed her into a locker, and leaned down close to her face. "Listen here, you little blood sucking mosquito."

"No." She smirked. "You listen." She tilted her head back, resting it against the locker. "All I have to do is scream and cry." Her eyes began to well up. "And someone will come and when they ask me what happened, I'll tell them you tried to hurt me."

"You wouldn't dare," I growled. With the reputation I carry, they would believe her in a heartbeat.

"You don't think so?" She smiled, false tears streaming down her face. Reaper took in a deep breath, but before she could make a sound, I blocked her mouth with my hand.

"I will gut you like a fish and I swear to you I will laugh doing it."

Despite the tears, her eyes were playful, excited. Amused. I'm good at reading people, but with her it was as if the only thing she sought for was the entertainment in chaos, it was something I hadn't encountered before. This was going to be either really fun or really bloody annoying.

"Hey! What's going on over there?" a teacher shouted across the hallway, rushing towards us.

I quickly released Reaper, and she burst into tears, running towards the teacher.

"What happened, my dear?" He leaned down to her, putting a comforting hand on her shoulder.

"I got lost and when I asked him to help me, he..."

She even cried pretty. How is that fair?

"Are you hurt anywhere?" The teacher's face was red with anger, but he spoke to her in a gentle voice.

She shook her head. "I don't think so."

I was completely dumbfounded.

"I'll take you to the nurse's office so you can get examined just in case."

I barely touched her.

This is what they meant by pretty privilege, isn't it?

Then the teacher turned to me with a glare. "Hyacinth, I will see you at the principal's office."

As the teacher led Reaper away, she turned and flipped me off with a mocking smile. She won. I shoved my hands in my pocket, kicked a locker, denting it, and muttered a few curses.

***

I plopped down on the chair across from the principal, folding my arms in front of me. "So, I've been told you harassed another student."

"It's true. I saw him holding her against a locker with a hand over her mouth." The teacher shook his head.

There was no use arguing. I did push her into a locker. "She asked for it."

"She asked for it?" The principal raised her brows. "Would you like to reword your sentence?"

It did sound bad when they didn't know the whole context. "No."

"Would you like to tell me why you think she *asked* for it?"

"No." I'm not a snitch, nor would they understand what we were talking about.

She glared at me. "As much as I hate injustice, Celestine asked us not to punish you."

My brow twitched, knitting together.

"But your comment and your attitude deserve a detention."

This wasn't my first detention, I've been suspended multiple times and even hold a record at this school. But all those times were because of something I did, not because of someone else.

I left the room and my friends were waiting for me outside of the office.

"Cinth, we heard what happened!" Lin came towards me.

"You're the most unliked person in the school now," Jamiel stated.

Was I ever liked?

"Why did you hurt her?" Iri furrowed her brows.

"None of your bloody business," I muttered, storming away. I wouldn't hesitate to take any contract for Reaper's head, even if she was just a stupid girl.

***

After I finished serving detention and completing my assignment, I met up with a couple of my friends from the Underworld. We always met at the same club, Neon Nights, located in the West side. I wasn't necessarily allowed to go in being only seventeen, but because I'm Vulture, I could go anywhere I pleased.

Symeon and Kahlik were hitmen just like me, but obviously not as good, ranking just under Niko and me and in their late-twenties.

"Have either of you met Reaper?" I asked.

They shook their heads. "No, she keeps a low profile," Symeon said. "Trapped in that estate I heard."

"Like some monster," Kahlik joked. "Only coming out to kill."

"Has anyone actually met her?" Symeon asked.

Unfortunately. "She's so protected," I said. "What would happen if we killed her?"

Their eyes went wide. We'd done a few assignments together, but this was a different level.

"Usually your ideas are good, but this is not one of them," Kahlik said.

Symeon squinted his eyes. "Do you want to die?"

"I'm just wondering, is there a gain?"

"I think there'd be more loss to it," Symeon replied.

"She's in the inner circle of the Kokkino clan," Kahlik warned. "They'd come after you."

I sipped my drink. I could take them, but Niko would kill me.

"What did she do to you?" Kahlik snorted.

"We go to the same bloody school," I muttered. "She pisses me off."

"School?" Kahlik eye's widened. "How old is she?"

"Seventeen," I said. "Can you believe that?"

Kahlik choked on his drink.

"No way she's seventeen!" Symeon nearly shouted, slamming his glass on the table. "I still haven't been named and I've been doing this for a decade!"

Maybe you're just not that good.

Very few people in the Underworld received names and the group of us who have were called Apex. Which should have meant that we had no predators, but that wasn't necessarily true. So far, there were only six of us.

I was the youngest to get a name at just fifteen. Vulture, because if you're my victim, you're already dead. Mainly using my butterfly knife as a weapon or my bow if I'm lazy, but I could turn anything into a weapon.

Reaper, or the Grim Reaper, who never fails to leave death in her wake. There are never witnesses, the only reason people knew it was her was because she always finished her victims off with a stab in the eye. Honestly, eyesore is a better name for her...

Siren, a woman in the Mov clan who knows everything about everyone, and no one would dare cross her. Not only could she reveal secrets, but she was incredibly well liked, she could easily alienate someone. I've seen her many times, but I haven't properly met her, nor do I want to. No matter how useful she could be, she could turn on me at any moment.

Mercury, a mad scientist who worked with the Etherian clans, his signature poison. Whether it be in food, injected, or gassed. He knew chemicals like he was reciting the alphabet. His first victim was his daughter, who was only twenty-one at the time. I've done my best to avoid him, because I'm good at pissing people off.

Silver Lining, a vigilante and Mov clan's worst nightmare. I appreciated her morals. She only took jobs that involved misjustice, specifically on behalf of women and children. She and Niko often crossed paths, becoming good friends the last couple years.

Lastly, Jack Spades, a serial killer whose face and body was marred with scars, left his victims looking just like him. Jerome didn't care who he was killing, as long as it provided him with some sort of release. I think that's why he and I got along, put two psychos in the same room and it cancels out... Somewhat.

"Is she actually as good as they say?" Kahlik asked.

I inhaled my cigarette, shaking my head. "I haven't really seen her do anything."

I shifted the topic, not wanting to reveal too much of what I knew of her, not that I knew much, but clearly they knew nothing. I still didn't know if Reaper could be of use to me, if I wanted to engrave my name into her skin or shove her ashes in an urn.

My phone vibrated with a notification from Niko that I ignored. Then skimmed a few Underworld news articles. An article from the Underworld caught my attention: Man found dead in his apartment after brutally murdering his pregnant partner.

It wasn't that it was shocking, murder, mugging, an arrest. These things happen all the time in Soulesity. The local papers just don't report it, wanting the general public to be shielded from the nightmares that really go on. Some like to argue it's all lies, and those some were the ones who had the money and power to do something about it. But how do you convince people who live like kings to give up that luxury and privilege for equality?

If the local papers ever did decide to cover them, the articles usually stated that he was a kind man and how out of character it was for him to do something like that, but the fact is, everyone has an evil in them. Some are just lucky enough to live their lives without anything pulling it out of them.

The article from the Underworld database skipped the sugared words, focusing on the little details, in what order the man committed his crime, how many times, how hard, what tools, and which injury was fatal. I scrolled through the article quickly, wondering why it was popular. He wasn't well known, just an average citizen. *Oh.* His cause of death was a type of new, unknown drug and they blamed his actions on it.

"Have you two seen this?" I turned my phone to show Symeon and Kahlik.

Kahlik let out a snort. "Yeah, stupid. Someone in the Underworld is creating and testing their latest batch and clearly, it isn't going well."

"Who do you think is making it?"

"The Mov clan most likely." Symeon leaned closer to me. "From what I heard, the Etherian clans sell cheaper. This new drug is probably a way to draw clients back to them."

"But everyone knows the Etherian clan's quality is shit," I argued.

"Doesn't matter as long as it gives them some sort of high right?" Symeon said, coldly.

***

I was waiting for my friends to finish paying for their meals while I boredly looked around the cafeteria. Reaper was surrounded by a group of girls, all attempting to gain her attention.

She just looked disinterested, contributing to the conversation with nothing but a nod or a slight smile. Reaper tucked her hair behind her ear, revealing her many silver piercings, five on her left and six on her right. *Wondered if she had any more on her.* Her eyes shifted to meet mine, and she gave me a smile, not a teasing or mocking one, a real smile.

I dropped my drink, spilled it all over the floor and tripped over nothing but the air I caught in my throat.

Bloody hell. Is this a heart attack?

"Oi, Cinth, you good?" Jamiel asked as I gripped onto his shoulder for support.

A few witnesses laughed at me.

"I think I'm having a heart attack." I looked to Lin, the future trauma surgeon. "My heart just stopped for like, three seconds."

Lin chuckled as he paid for his meal. "I think if that were the case, you'd be on the floor."

The nearby janitor immediately cleaned up the mess. The janitor never really talked, probably tired of cleaning up after our mess all these years.

My heart was still racing and skipping beats, so I grabbed Lin's hand and put it on my chest. "Does this feel normal?"

Jamiel also felt my irregular heartbeat, laughing. "Sheesh, are you okay?"

"It's really beating." Lin snickered.

I shoved both of them away from me, even though I asked, and spat a curse at them for not taking me seriously.

I could drop dead any second now. Won't be laughing then.

I looked back to Reaper, but the seat was empty. Something warm pressed on my hand and I snapped my head down to see the same drink I had dropped, but new. I followed the hand up to Reaper, standing next to me.

"I can buy my own coffee," I snapped, moving my hand away.

"You dropped it because of me, right?"

"Yeah."

Wait, what?

"No, no, I did not drop it because of you. I just had a heart attack."

She bit her lip, trying to keep herself from laughing. "Just take it, I don't drink this." She pushed the cup towards me, and I caught it just as she released it.

I eyed her suspiciously.

Why is she being nice to me? Just a few days ago, she was threatening me.

"How do I know you didn't spit in this?"

She leaned closer to me and whispered, "Don't you want to taste me?"

Bloody. Hell.

My entire body heated up, and I felt so weak.

What is she doing to me?

"I don't think you know who you're talking to," I told her in a low voice.

She laughed. "The candy shop is my favourite story." Still laughing, she made her way back to her table.

Two years ago, back when I was a more reckless and angry teenager, I drove a stolen truck into a candy store. Not because of a hit, not because of clan orders—because they were out of my favourite sweet treat.

No warning. No self-restraint. Just blind sugar-fueled rage.

The crash didn't kill the owners, unfortunately. I had to crawl out of the crumpled truck and finish the job myself. Left their corpses stuffed with candy for the cops to find.

Niko was furious. He had to clean up the entire mess—bribe, threaten, erase. Prime Minister Malik personally banned me from ever getting a license, but honestly? No regrets. Totally worth it. They had it coming.

"So that's why you had a heart attack?" Jamiel mocked.

"Just the sight of her, hey?" Lin snickered.

"Because she's a scary little urchin," I bit back.

"Right." Lin and Jamiel exchanged looks.

I cursed at them and made my way to our table outside. Jamiel and Lin were quick to tell Iri what happened, and neither of them failed to tease me about it.

I don't know why I'm friends with these people anymore.

"Hey, we're just joking, Cinth." Iri laughed, playfully nudging me.

"She pisses me off so much." I put a cigarette between my teeth and lit it up.

"She bought you a new drink. Come on, she's so nice," Jamiel reminded me.

I rolled my eyes. "You should've heard the things that came out of her bloody mouth right after she gave it to me."

"What did she say?"

My face heated at the thought. "She just knows how to piss me off."

***

When I got home, I decided to finally do my research.

Datura Celestine Vicary.

Born in Soulesity Hospital on the nineteenth of May 54 A.D. (After Demons). *Exactly six months after me.* There was a long, long list of nannies hired to take care of her when she was an infant, up until she was four years old. She wasn't seen by the public until an interview on the Yarra Show, Soulesity's beloved talk show host, when she was six years old, though Reaper didn't speak throughout the entire segment.

She started competing in figure skating at seven and won countless silver and gold medals, well on her way to becoming Soulesity's best female skater. Her grades in school were below average, nearly failing, and she had received detention almost as much as I did.

The exact date of when she ran away was unclear. Soulesity Etherian School expelled her for fighting and she was officially reported missing the next day, on the twentieth of May. Octavius Gautier was tried and found guilty for her murder and grooming, but was now released.

Vasos Aspen Vicary, her older half sibling, moved to another city to work for the government as an ambassador for Soulesity shortly after her disappearance. She also now had a three-year-old half-sister, Marigold Cassia Vicary.

The Underworld database only showed her work as the Grim Reaper and nothing else. Her known kills only dated back to last year.

For someone who had such a high-profile family and was a part of the inner circle of the Kokkino clan, there was barely a thing about her and even less photos of her.

Reaper. Reaper. Reaper.

***

They split our science class into two and swapped half of us with the other class, forcing us to pair up.

"Today, we will be dissecting frogs." The teacher lifted a sheet of paper. "And don't forget to fill out the question sheet I've put on each table."

"You haven't taught us anything about the organs," one of my classmates retorted.

"Yeah, we don't know anything," another panicked.

"You'll be fine." The teacher waved the students off just as the other class entered.

My lucky day. Partnered up with Reaper...

"Could I get a new partner?" Reaper asked.

"Yeah, we don't work well together." For once, we agreed on something.

The teacher's amber eyes met ours for a moment before turning back to his phone. "Well, now's your chance to bond."

Some of our classmates gave Reaper a worried look, but they were worrying about the wrong person.

I'm the victim here.

I gave Lin a pleading look to switch partners, but he pretended not to notice.

Dog.

Slipping on some gloves, I stared at the animal in front of me. This frog did nothing to anyone.

Why couldn't we use real people instead?

After quickly convincing myself the frog was already dead and anything done to it now didn't matter, I stabbed the frog in the centre.

From the corner of my eyes, I saw Reaper put on a pair of glasses. "Since when did you start wearing glasses?" Not that I actually knew her.

"Recently," she said, leaning in towards the frog.

"You look like an absolute dork," I snarked, but she didn't really. She actually looked pretty cute.

Gross, what am I thinking?

Reaper gave me an annoyed look, then blinked. "Oh." She squinted her eyes at me, leaning close to my face.

I leaned away from her, my brows knitting together. "What?" Suddenly becoming self-conscious, but I had a really strict skin care routine and if she was going to point out that my eyeliner was smudged, I liked it like that.

Her blue eyes dilated. "You have a lot of piercings." Her eyes grazed down to my lips. I had several piercings in my ear, one on the arch of my brow, and ring snake bites cuffing the corners of my bottom lip. That's where her eyes lingered and I avoided her gaze.

"How blind are you?"

"Without my glasses? Everything's a blur." She pulled back and put her chin in her hands, watching me go back to stabbing the frog.

"You have a lot of piercings too," I said, causing her to look at me again. "Do you have more than just your ears?"

Reaper didn't try to hold back a smile. "Why?" she asked. "You want to see them?"

I stabbed the frog a bit too hard. "No." I was just trying to make conversation.

It was silent again between us for a while. "Aren't you going to explain what you're doing?"

"No," I replied, continuing to mutilate the frog.

"You don't know what you're doing, do you?"

"Of course I do," I snapped.

"Then tell me about it."

I rolled my eyes and pointed to "the heart," and then what I thought was, "the pancreas."

"That's the gallbladder," she corrected.

Lin snickered next to me, and I shot him a glare.

"If you're so smart, you do it." I gave her the knife, even though I probably shouldn't have.

She adjusted her glasses, slipped on some gloves and took it, pointing at each organ, identifying and giving me the function of each. I turned to Lin, he was the smart one–the book smart one of our group. He nodded, confirming what she had said was correct.

I snatched the knife from her. "Alright, little miss show off. So you're good at biology."

"I'm very good at biology," she whispered and looked up at me through her thick lashes. "I could come tutor you some time and we could study the human body together."

My face heated, and I broke the metal scalpel in my hand. She laughed as the two halves clattered onto the floor.

What is she bloody doing to me?

"What just broke?" the teacher called in our direction.

"I broke the knife," I admitted.

He gave me a weird look. "How did you manage that?"

I didn't answer, and he shook his head, continuing to text on his phone.

"Are you okay?" Lin nudged me.

"Yeah," I grunted, picking up the pieces off the floor.

Reaper leaned closer to me with a sinister smile and asked in a low voice for only me to hear, "Am I the only one who makes you lose control?"

I abruptly stood up from my stool, knocking it over and causing everyone to turn their heads in our direction.

How did she know?

I hurriedly made my way to the door before I killed her in front of everyone.

"Where are you going?" the teacher asked.

I tugged off my gloves and threw them in the bin. "Bathroom."

I slammed the door shut behind me. I was so warm. My palms felt wet. *I'm having another heart attack.* I barely recovered from the last one. I yanked my tie from its knot and released another few buttons of my uniform. The water fountain was just in front of me and I bent down, sipping water to calm myself.

I needed her gone. I needed her to stay away from me. *Why is she even here?* After four years of not going to school, who would go back? What was the point?

By the time I got back to the lab, Reaper was resting her head in her arms on the table, no longer wearing her glasses. She had also finished filling out the question sheet for the both of us. "Alright, Reaper, what game are you playing?"

She peaked her eyes at me and sat up with a sigh. "I'm just bored," she started. "But you're fun to play with."

"I'm not a toy," I spat.

"You're *my* toy, Hyacinth." She smiled.

The way she said my name did something to me. Bloody hell, her voice was like molten silver. *Don't say it again, for both of our sakes.*

I leaned close to her face and whispered, "With the right contract, I can kill you."

My words only made the mockingness in her eyes grow. "I don't need a contract to kill you." Her laugh was so innocent and graceful it even made the teacher look up from his phone.

"Stop flirting in class, Hyacinth," the teacher snapped at me.

The classroom filled with laughter, but quickly silenced when I took the frog and emptied its insides on top of Reaper's head. "You talk a lot of shit, Reaper. I mistook you for a bin."

She didn't look upset or angry or like she was about to cry, which was the reaction I thought I would get. Instead, she looked more amused.

"Hyacinth!" the teacher shouted, but I was already walking out the door.

5
NOT A SNITCH

It was one of our longer breaks between classes. We had the option to stay in class or go to the cafeteria for a snack. Jamiel followed me to the other classroom, where some students were sitting around studying or talking to each other. I found Reaper sitting in the back, studying her notes for our upcoming test with her glasses on.

She wants to play, so I'll bloody play.

I sat on the desk in front of hers, putting one of my feet on the chair and the other on the floor. Jamiel leaned against the wall near us. Her classmates whispered to each other, afraid for Reaper.

She didn't even acknowledge me, and it pissed me off. I took out my container and swallowed a pill. Reaper's eyes moved from one side of the page to the other, rereading the same sentence over and over. She was either nervous by my stare or didn't understand the content. She pretended to write, not knowing I could see she was rewriting the same thing again. Maybe that's just how she remembers things.

"I'm bored," I said. "Entertain me."

"Maybe later." She didn't even look up from her notes.

I kicked her papers off her desk, turning everyone's heads towards us. "Now." Finally, her eyes met mine, and I smirked. I pulled out my butterfly knife from my pocket, playing with it, and a few people gasped.

"Or what? You're going to stab me in front of everyone?"

Jamiel tossed me an apple.

"You would like that, wouldn't you?" I began peeling the skin off the apple.

She put her chin in her hand and gave me a smile that made me pause. "Only if it's by you." And she meant it.

I let out a light chuckle. "Good girl." I continued to peel the skin, letting it fall onto the unlucky chair. "If I call on you, you're going to come to me."

"And why would I do that?"

"Because I said so." I cut a slice of the apple and stabbed the centre of it with my knife, offering it to her. "I'm going to make you my dog."

Reaper didn't hesitate to lean forward and take the apple off the blade with her teeth. She stood up and put one knee on her desk, holding onto the top of the seat between us, and leaned close to me. She tilted her head up, waiting for me to take the other half. I moved towards her and bit the exposed half, our bottom lips nearly brushing against each other, but didn't touch.

A mistake.

She won.

Again.

"Sheesh," Jamiel sighed.

"You're already mine," she laughed. "So I don't know how this is going to work."

"Don't piss me off," I growled, tossing the rest of the apple back to Jamiel and he caught it, taking a bite of it. I licked the juice off the knife and for a moment, I thought I saw Reaper's eyes gleam a soft red. Must have been the light or the drug I took earlier.

"Hey, Cel, is Hyacinth bothering you?" one of the boys asked with his arms folded in front of him. A few of his friends came around as well, and one of them helped pick up her things off the floor.

"No." She smiled, sitting back down in her seat, her eyes never leaving mine. "He's leaving."

I narrowed my eyes at her.

"Excuse me, boys."

I rolled my eyes.

"This isn't your classroom," the teacher said.

Putting my hands in my pocket, I hid my knife from the teacher. Jamiel left first, but I wasn't done. I got up and put a gentle hand on top of Reaper's head, causing her to lift her head up towards me. "You're playing a dangerous game," I warned in a low voice. "You should stop before it goes too far." If she stopped messing with me, if she would just submit to me, I would leave her alone.

The spark in her eyes only grew with her smile.

The teacher raised her voice once again. "Hyacinth, I will not be asking you again. If you do not leave right now, I will be sending you to the principal's office with a pink slip."

But even as she scolded me, I never left Reaper's eyes. I pulled my bottom lip into my teeth, keeping myself from smiling along with Reaper, before standing up again and leaving the room.

***

"She wouldn't come when we told her to," Jamiel said as I smoked my cigarette during our lunch break.

"And why not?"

"She told us you had to come to her instead," Lin explained in a low voice.

They waited, afraid of my reaction, and I let out a smoky laugh. "Stubborn." I tossed the last of my cigarette away and sauntered inside the school in search of Reaper.

I've only seen her in the cafeteria a couple times before, so I was a bit surprised to see her sitting with a group of people, with only a cup of water.

I glared at the person next to her. "Move." They didn't need to be told twice, and I sat down, facing her.

The table shifted uncomfortably in my presence, my friends standing behind me, ready to be entertained. "Why didn't you come?"

"I'm not a dog," she replied, sipping her water.

I titled her glass up and it spilled all over her. Her friends gasped, quickly offering her tissues, while my friends snickered.

"Childish," she muttered, dabbing her chin with the back of her hand.

She didn't take the tissues, instead reached for one of her friend's pencil cases, searching for a marker.

Reaper turned to me. "You want my number, right?" She pulled me towards her by my tie and began writing on my neck and I let her. The marker tickled, but I didn't react to it. I stared at her face, eyes squinted in concentration. "There," she said, releasing me.

The people around giggled and my friends could barely contain their laughter.

"What did she write?" I touched my neck as if I could feel the ink.

"She drew a picture." Iri laughed.

I swear I'm being tested.

"I'm sure it's life sized, but maybe I was a bit generous and made it too big," Reaper taunted.

I gave her a bored look. "Unimaginative, aren't you?"

"Don't worry." She stood up. Even then I felt like I was looking down on her and leaned towards me. "It's not permanent." The last thing I expected was for her to run her tongue up my neck.

Bloody hell. It sent chills down my spine.

"It's gone." She smirked.

I caught some people staring and a lot more glaring at the interaction. *Very bold of you, Reaper.*

"Oh, sheesh." Lin and Jamiel groaned.

I pulled her down to sit on my lap, snatching the marker from her. She was calm, too calm, as I pulled one of her sleeves up to her elbow. There was a bruise on her wrist, so I took her other arm and slightly lifted the sleeve up. Same mark.

These were old bruises, healed but left a mark. How long and tight was she tied up for?

I gently grazed my finger over the mark. "Who did this?"

"No idea."

I met her eyes. "I don't like liars." People only lie when they're afraid.

"Why would I care what you like?"

I couldn't help but smirk. "I think you will." Then I turned back down and began writing on her arm, wondering if she was going to explain the source, but she didn't.

Reaper took a peek at the letters I wrote. "For someone who can do decent eyeliner and paint their nails, your handwriting sucks."

"Yours isn't any better," I muttered, dotting the 'i.' "Now everyone will know you belong to me."

"Hyacinth." The tiny hairs behind my neck stood. How does she make it sound so sultry? "I drew art on your skin and you just wrote your name? How boring," Reaper sighed.

I wouldn't call her work 'art.'

"Read it again." I needed to hear my name from her voice.

"Did I say it wrong?" She squinted at the ink.

"Say it."

"Hyacinth," she whispered.

"One more time," I muttered.

She turned to look me in the eye, a slight, knowing curve at the edge of her lips as she said slowly, "Hyacinth."

Oh, fu—

"Hyacinth, Celestine." A teacher stood at the front of the table, folding his arms across his chest. "PDA is not tolerated at the school, get off each other or I will be giving you both detention."

I was surprised the teacher warned us. They usually just skip right to it, but I assume it might be because Reaper was still the new girl, having only been here for a month now.

Reaper wrapped her arms around my neck and held me closer to her. "Not tolerated?" Her lips were just centimetres from mine and I don't know why I wasn't pulling back from it. She stared straight at the teacher as she did so. "At all?"

A part of me hoped she'd come closer, but our lips never touched. She smelt really good. Too good. Sweet almost like honeysuckles but... Better.

I felt my body heat up, my heart pulsing in my ear, and I couldn't help the smirk on my face. The teacher, however, wasn't amused and took out the pink slips from his pocket, writing both our names on it and handing it to us.

Reaper took the slips with her teeth and the teacher's face flushed before quickly rushing away.

She's really asking for it.

Reaper got up off me and put my detention slip inside my shirt as if she just paid a stripper. "See you in detention."

I was left completely and utterly stunned. And they say I was the troublemaker of the school. Once she was out of the cafeteria, everyone continued their chatter and it was only then that I realised everyone had silenced to watch us.

Lin clapped a hand on my back, bringing me back to reality, and laughed. "She really left you speechless."

I looked at the people at the table, her friends–or at least the people she sat with today, whispering and giggling about me to each other. I stood up and my friends followed me out of the cafeteria.

"She's insane," Jamiel commented with a laugh.

I reached into my shirt, taking out the pink slip to look at it. Her dark red lipstick and sparkly gloss stained the paper along with four holes pierced into it.

She has some sharp teeth.

***

I made it into the detention room a bit late and Reaper wasn't there yet. I handed the slip to the supervisor, and she brushed me off, reading her book as I took a seat. Half an hour passed and Reaper still hadn't shown up. Was she actually skipping? Was her plan just to get me in detention?

The door opened, startling the supervisor awake, and she looked up at the time. "Why are you late?"

Reaper set the slip down on the teacher's desk. "At least I'm here." Of all the empty seats, she took the one directly in front of me. There was no room to breathe.

The supervisor squinted her eyes at Reaper before reading her book again, her eyelids heavy with each page she turned. Reaper waited for the supervisor to drift off into her nap again before turning around in her seat.

"What do you want?" I snapped in a low voice.

"I'm bored," she whined, tilting her head.

I leaned over my desk, closer to her. "You're annoying."

She reached her hand towards my hair and played with it, curling it in her fingers. "It's soft."

I looked down to her lips, probably softer, then back up to her eyes, teasing me. "Don't touch me."

"I already am." She let out a light laugh.

"You know," I whispered. "As much as I like playing with you, all you have to do is ask."

"Would you say yes?" she whispered.

"Hm..." I leaned back in my seat with a smirk. "Maybe." *Absolutely not.* I took out my container, popping a pill in my mouth.

"What's that for?" she asked me.

"Helps me tolerate you," I replied coldly.

"You two!" the supervisor snapped at us. "One of you move to the other side of the classroom."

Reaper didn't hesitate to stand up to move to the desk the supervisor pointed at. She took out a small compact mirror and her lipstick, reapplying it. I couldn't help my stare as she ran it across her lips, staining it a dark red again. The colour of blood. I locked eyes with her through the mirror and a light laugh escaped her before she put it away.

Shit, she caught me.

We weren't allowed to do anything in detention unless it was schoolwork. I was doing maths first, the easiest subject for me. I didn't have to use my brain as much–they were just numbers.

"Miss Vicary," the supervisor called.

I turned towards Reaper, who had her head down in her arms, asleep.

The supervisor called her name again and when she didn't move or answer, the teacher stood up, frustrated. "Sleeping is not allowed in detention, Miss Vicary." She tapped her shoulder, but Reaper barely stirred. "Miss Vicary."

Reaper lifted her head up, her brows furrowed and eyes squinted. "What?"

"You are not to sleep in detention."

Reaper rubbed at her eyes and muttered. "Gods."

I felt a shift in the air and the supervisor stood frozen when she met her eyes. "Didn't you need to use the bathroom?" Reaper asked her in a low voice.

The supervisor slowly nodded, her eyes wide and glazed over. "Yeah... Actually... I do..." She turned, robotically, and left the room, closing the door behind her. Reaper set her head back down and fell right back to sleep.

I wasn't sure how to process that whole thing.

The supervisor didn't come back until the end of detention, allowing us to leave. I followed behind Reaper to get out of the school.

"Stop stalking me."

"Don't flatter yourself. There's only one working exit at this hour," I muttered.

Even though this school had the smallest number of students, the school wasted no expense on the building. It took about fifteen minutes to walk from one side of the building to the other and that wasn't counting the large space outside that was fenced off with large stone walls.

I never noticed it before, but Reaper had a slight limp when she walked. Was it recent or permanent? Finally, we exited the school, Leo and Sterling waiting for Reaper on their motorbikes.

After her first day being bombarded by the media, the twins started picking her up after school. A few Kokkino clansmen stood guard throughout the street to prevent any of the media from even seeing the entrance. This, of course, started rumours around school that she was involved with the clans, but no one knew she was the Grim Reaper. They just assumed she had a relative in it. Who would ever believe a young, small girl that looks like her would be involved in such violent acts?

"Silias isn't happy you got detention," Leo said in a low voice.

"He better get used to it," she replied.

"Come on, Cel..." Then Leo muttered something to her I couldn't hear.

"Vulture." Sterling stopped me from getting past them. "I can't imagine you're in the debate club, so I assume you also got detention."

I didn't respond.

"Was it Cel's fault?" The way he said it made me uncomfortable, as if he expected it to be her. She must get into trouble often. I looked at Reaper, but she didn't meet my eyes.

"Unrelated." I put my hands in my pockets. As much as I hated lying, I hated snitches more.

He nodded. "Let's go. Cel, ride with Leo."

She glanced at me before putting on a helmet and hopping on the back of Leo's bike. They started up their bikes and rode away.

***

Hidden above Stygian clan territory, I crouched in the corner on a beam behind a pillar, listening to the conversation below. The four leaders sat around the circular table, while their seconds and inner circle stood behind them, against the wall. This wasn't the first time I'd infiltrated one of their meetings, but it was the first time I'd seen Reaper join.

There were four Stygian clans, five really, but the fifth one didn't have a proper structure. Kokkino, Hriso, Mov, Prassino, and Galazio.

Galazio were, simply put, corrupt officers of the law who pledged their loyalty to Stygians. They had a tattoo of the Stygian symbol inked in blue, hidden somewhere on their body so no one could see it. Only the leaders of the Stygian clans knew who was a part of the clan as Galazio didn't have a leader and were only called upon when needed.

The meeting had already begun when I got inside. They were always spoken in Stygian and thankfully, I knew the language, having learnt it from Ender.

"...It must be time for Stygians to take back what's theirs."

"Let me remind you, Silias." Paxon's eyes glowed a bright red. "You are not a true Stygian. You do not get to make these large and dramatic decisions for us."

One of the four original surviving Demons from the Reckoning, Paxon was the leader of the Prassino clan. They worked with computers and oversaw the monitoring of Stygians for threats and distributing messages between clans. The Stygian symbol was tattooed behind their ear on their neck in green and all wore the same green leather bracelet.

"It is a bit soon," Ignatius said, his head resting on the table, boredly playing with the straw in his drink.

The leader of the Hriso clan and was another surviving Demon from the Reckoning. The politician puppet masters were the smallest Stygian clan. They worked in politics, attempting to change the laws and the way people saw Stygians. And they were the only clan without a tattoo signifying their clan, instead they used a simple gold ring on their middle finger.

"Soon?" Silias raised a brow. "Seventy years is soon?"

Silias led the Kokkino clan, in charge of the protection and security of Stygians. The tattoo behind their ear on their neck was red ink and were always seen wearing red on their heads, like hats, headbands, or hair ties.

Florica shook her head. "When will you two ever decide to finally fight back? The young ones are on edge. They want to fight."

Currently led by Florica, Mov clan was the largest of the Stygian clans. The previous leader, Zuriel, was a Demon, and she was his 'lover' or at least the person he trusted most to be loyal to his legacy. Originally, they were to supply Stygians with items they needed, whether it be food or weapons. Though, now they involve themselves in trafficking of weapons, humans, and drugs, simply for the money rather than the survival. They had their tattoo inked in purple and wore purple shoes or coats.

"Perhaps your children want to fight, but Ignatius and I have seen firsthand what war does," Paxon said. "It's nothing but blood, and our numbers are still small."

"No," Silias argued. "Our numbers are fine, we are currently in control of the city—"

"With undisciplined clansmen that do what they want," Paxon said. "And we are just barely in control. The Etherian clans are powerful too, and if we were to do anything, we would only add Angels into this fight."

"Angels," Silias spat. "They don't care about Soulesity anymore. If they did, do you think they would allow murders and suicides to happen every five minutes?" The statistics were rough estimates, but that was anyone's best guess. In all honesty, the numbers were probably higher.

Ignatius sat up, shaking his head. "You may have fought a number of people in your time, Silias, but Angels are a different breed. They are fast giants that can fly and if you tell them you're Stygian, they won't hesitate to slice your head off."

"Then what? You want to stay in hiding forever?" Silias snarled.

"The young ones are strong," Florica assured.

"The Angels are stronger," Paxon argued. "Ever since they killed every female Demon we have had to force ourselves to mix our blood with humans and our powers water down every generation and with every child. The ones who absolutely do not stand a chance against them are Zuriel's children and humans who claim to be Stygian."

"What is it then? What are you waiting for?" Silias urged.

Paxon exchanged a look with Ignatius. "Ignatius and I..." he started in a low voice. "We've been looking for Phobus."

"Phobus?" Silias let out a loud laugh. "The God who did nothing but watch as your friends and family were slaughtered during the Reckoning?"

"That is not true!"

"You cannot laugh at what you did not experience, Silias." Ignatius said in a calm tone. "Phobus may not have stood by us the entire time, but if he had, we could have won."

"And why didn't he?" Florica's eyes narrowed. "Because he doesn't care about any of you."

The room became silent, the shifting of clothes rubbing against each other being the only sound.

"The Gods care for no soul. Am I wrong?" Florica said.

Paxon shook his head, his jaw tight. "He cared too much. That was the issue. It hurt him a lot to see his Demons slaughtered like pigs."

"So? You haven't been successful at contacting Phobus. What then?" Silias asked.

"It's odd, is all," Paxon admitted. "Phobus usually gives some sort of sign at the very least when we contact him, but he's been silent for twelve years."

"More like seventy," Ignatius said.

"No," Paxon said. "Do you remember what the Book of Ice said?" The original religious text belonging to Stygians was located in the Ice Kingdom, deep in Stygia territory, but there were several copies in Soulesity. I also had one, given to me by Niko, who got it as a gift from his best friend Ender.

Ignatius waved his hand in the air. "Yes, yes, we all know. Phobus has a child."

My brows furrowed from the sure and casual statement. *Phobus has a child? I don't remember reading that.* I checked the reactions of the others in the room, but none were phased, not even Reaper—I locked eyes with her.

Shit. Shit. Shit.

My heart raced against my chest, knowing I'd have to run as fast as I could and reap the consequences later or fight them all now. I felt for my butterfly knife in my pocket, checking it was there, even though I never go anywhere without it.

She turned her focus back to the table in front of her, giving no indication to anyone that there was someone unwelcome in the room. She didn't snitch on me, at least not yet.

"And this child is what is needed to win this next war." Paxon glanced around the room. "Because he's the only person that can control her."

Silias opened his mouth to speak, but Florica beat him to it. "Just say Bernadette." Florica stuck up her nose and Bernadette straightened her back. "We already know it's her."

"We can't rule out other possibilities, Florica," Paxon said, Ignatius nodding in agreement.

Silias let out a gruff, looking towards Paxon and Ignatius. "And what is your progress with finding Phobus's child?"

"It could be anyone," Ignatius sighed. "We're not even sure what signs to look for or if the child even knows who they are."

"Someone who acts like a Demon, but isn't?" Silias took a sip of his drink to ponder.

"I've been attempting to narrow down children without fathers, but this child could have even been born long before the Reckoning," Paxon said.

"Then someone who has stayed twenty-five for generations?" Florica tapped her finger on the table.

"Or he may not even be born yet." Ignatius expelled another tired breath. "It's an impossible search."

"Not impossible," Paxon said. "We already have one half of the equation. All we need to do is wait. The child will eventually reveal himself."

Florica turned her head back to look at Bernadette. "Arlo is quite attracted to you, perhaps—"

"No," Bernadette said. "Arlo does not control me." She let out a small laugh. "If anything it's the other way around."

"Is there anyone else that you suspect could be them?" Florica asked her.

Bernadette shook her head. "No."

Ignatius leaned towards Paxon and asked in a low voice, "And what about—"

"I've been watching him closely," Paxon replied, quickly. "No signs of any powers, but definitely a powerful human. Silias is dealing with it from now on."

Silias nodded. "We'll see soon enough."

The clans chatted a bit more, nothing important or revealing, before concluding the meeting.

Honestly, I only ever understood half of what they said. They hardly ever go into depth with names and places or times, as if they've already had meetings between these. It's irritating to have to try to put the pieces of the conversation together. The only thing I want them to talk about, they never do, or maybe they do, but not in these meetings.

I have to figure out a way to get closer...

Eventually, the leaders stood up from their seats, giving each other polite nods as they made their way out.

Silias stayed in his seat, all but his inner circle now gone. "You can all go." He waved his hand. "Cel, stay."

The others closed the door behind them, leaving just the two of them. Reaper made her way towards the table, taking a seat on top of it across Silias.

"You've been watching Bernadette," he started, switching languages back to Souic.

Reaper nodded. "Every night after she finishes her shift at the Underworld Bar."

"Has there been any signs of Angels lurking nearby?"

She shook her head, boredly playing with her nails.

Silias leaned forward on the table, his hands intertwined together as he pressed his lips to his thumb. "After ten years, you'd think it would be fine."

Ten years ago, Bernadette lost control of her emotions and revealed herself as a Demon in front of several witnesses. Luckily, the footage was easy to erase as Paxon was notified immediately, but because Bernadette doesn't have it in her to kill a soul, the witnesses ran and rumours spread of her existence. They were soon hunted down by the Kokkino clan, but the damage was already done. Ever since, Bernadette has lived in constant fear that Angels would come for her at any moment.

Though Bernadette has her fifty brothers and the entire Mov clan protecting her. Not to mention the Grim Reaper was also assigned to personally protect her.

"Why haven't they come for her?" Reaper asked. "Surely they must know."

Silias shook his head. "I believe they're waiting for Phobus's son to reveal themselves."

Reaper lifted her eyes to his. "And then what? Gods can't be killed."

"No, but Angels will do anything in their power to stop Demons from thriving again. They might imprison him for all eternity."

Reaper laid her back on the table, staring up at me with a slight smile. "That sounds a bit dramatic."

Silias stared at her for a long moment. "You need to take this more seriously. They could kill you too if you're not careful." Silias cupped her cheek in his hand, making her face him again. The sudden shift in his personality to something more gentle was quick. "I will not lose you, Celestine, do you understand?"

She didn't respond.

"And your progress at school?" he asked, taking his hand back, "is Vulture becoming a problem?"

"No," she said. "I've not talked to him yet."

He raised a brow. "Is that so?"

She nodded.

Silias knew she was lying; it wouldn't be hard for him to get intel on the situation at school from the few other students who were a part of the Stygian clans. Though, it seemed Silias was giving her a pass this time. "Let's go home, Cel."

***

When I got home, I immediately pulled out the Book of Ice. Flipping through the pages, I stepped around the room while Niko sat on the sofa, finishing the last sudoku puzzle in today's newspaper.

"Have they changed this?" I asked.

Niko glanced up at me above his reading glasses. "Obviously."

I whipped my head towards him. "Why?"

"Before releasing their sacred text to the public, they removed crucial details." He waved his hand in the air, staring back at his puzzle. "You know, female Demons, weaknesses and such."

I felt so stupid. I hadn't even noticed there was absolutely no mention of female Demons at all and I had read it several times. What else have they removed from the original? "Does the original exist in Soulesity?"

He nodded, not as interested as I was. "It's with Mica." Paxon's only living son.

6
MUST BE A WITCH

AUGUST 70 A.D.

Recently, I've begun dreaming in my sleep. Odd because I never used to dream. Ever. It was always the same. I'd end up in the middle of the salt flats and sometimes I would see Reaper, but only for a moment before I'd wake up. She haunts me in my sleep too.

"Where's Lin?" I asked. Lunch was half over, but he still hadn't shown up to the table.

Jamiel shrugged. "Said something about tutoring someone."

"During lunch?"

Lin usually only tutors after school and on weekends, and when he wasn't tutoring, he was studying or interning at the hospital. The only time he ever relaxed was during lunch or when there was a party and I would say when he slept, but it's more like he passes out. Lin doesn't really show it and he never complained, but I knew the pressure got to him.

"Guess so."

I inhaled smoke, it wasn't the same when one of us was missing. I took out my container, but there were no more pills left. *Wonderful!* Thankfully I had a second container in my locker. "I'll see you guys in class." I tossed my cigarette on the ground and headed up to the twelfth-grade hallway.

Lin's voice, calm and gentle, was explaining some concepts to someone. As I passed the room, I got a glimpse of who he was with and halted dead in my tracks. There's only one girl in this entire school who had long, straight hair.

Dog.

I stepped back and stared from the open doorway, my hands shoved in my pockets. "Yeah, you got it." He smiled at her and a jolt surged in my stomach. "Now, for this next question—" Lin paused as he met my eyes, fearful. Reaper turned back to look at me as well.

"What are you doing with her?" I spat.

"She missed four years of school, so the principal asked me to help her with some subjects."

Traitor.

"I had to do it," he explained. "They specifically asked me."

"You really couldn't have said no?"

"It's only twice a week," Lin said.

"Afraid he's going to steal me from you?" Reaper's eyes sparked with amusement as she leaned closer to Lin, tauntingly.

"I'd be happy if you could mess with someone else's head, but my friends are off limits."

"Yeah?" She reached her hand up to play with Lin's hair, just like she did with me the other day, looking at me the entire time, slowly pulling him closer to her. "Doing something I'm not supposed to just makes it more fun, don't you agree?"

Lin was too stupidly mesmerised to stop it.

I was in front of her in a flash, grabbing her wrist and pushing Lin back in his seat. "Stop."

Lin's face was flushed as he cleared his throat.

Reaper smiled, looking up at me through her thick lashes. "Hyacinth."

My grip on her faltered. "Shut up." My gaze lowered to the thin silver chain around her neck. I've noticed it for a while, but I never knew what was at the end of it. Curiosity got the best of me and I reached for the necklace.

She smacked my hand away, a glimpse of fear on her face, though she covered it with a laugh, adjusting her glasses back up the bridge of her nose. "Could you leave now? I need to learn."

And I need a bloody smoke. I glared at her, then turned to Lin. "Don't fall for her witchcraft."

"I mean, I'm not gonna stop her." He shrugged.

I let out a breath and went around their table, pulling out a chair. "Don't mind me, I just want to make sure you don't get Lin to sign some contract, Rumpelstiltskin."

She rolled her eyes at my joke, but I could see she wanted to laugh, before turning back to Lin, waiting for him to speak.

He cleared his throat again. "Right, so..."

I couldn't help but wonder if Reaper dreamt about me too or if she was some sort of witch who casted a spell on me to have her on my mind every bloody second of the day. Though, I don't think witches existed. Then again, Demons, Angels, and Selkies were a thing, so how far off would it be to assume she was a witch?

She could be a Demon.

Though female Demons haven't existed in centuries, thanks to Angels hunting them down due to how powerful they were. A female Demon was rumoured to be lurking in Soulesity. But that was over a decade ago and Reaper wouldn't have shown any signs of being a Demon back then, and it was probably just Bernadette.

An Angel?

Angels weren't known to be attractive, only kind, and Angels only kill Demons. She's also much too tiny to be an Angel, they were giants, at least two metres tall.

Selkie?

She was as mischievous as one and had a beautiful voice. Though, Selkies didn't have nails and Reaper liked to paint hers. Their eyes were also more commonly green with wavy hair and iridescent skin.

But she couldn't possibly be human, there was a certain aura Reaper radiated that just wasn't. So, she must be a witch.

The muscles in my body became more and more tense as she continued to avoid looking in my direction.

"Cinth, you're distracting her."

"Good."

Lin shot me a glare, and I had to hide my laugh. I always found it funny when people tried me. "Come on, Cinth, I know you hate her, but this is her education. Don't mess with that." Knowledge was a line Lin never crossed. No matter how much he didn't like someone, he'd never want to see them fail.

I met Reaper's eyes and gave her a smirk. "Who said I hated her?"

With that I got up and left to my locker to pull out what I was originally getting. I desperately needed a pill or two.

***

Late Saturday night, I had just completed my assignment and wasn't too far from home, a half-hour walk. The weather wasn't bad either, just a bit of a cool breeze. The East side is much quieter than the West, with shops closing earlier and everyone on this side having normal nine to four jobs, so there weren't many people walking or cars driving.

Yet here were the Kokkino clan twins sprinting away from something or someone. I had been seeing them so much lately. Too much. I exhaled my cigarette, watching them disappear behind a building.

Then Reaper showed up, looking frantically around for them as a group of people shouted behind her. She locked eyes with me, and I thought she was going to ask for help.

Instead, she raced into an alley and seven people followed just behind her carrying bats and knives.

It's never a bore here, is it?

Dropping my cigarette, I pressed my foot onto it before heading in the direction of the alley, pretty sure it was a dead end and not sure how fast Reaper could scale the building. Not that I should care.

I was just going to pass it, see if she got away, but she was cornered and surrounded by the group. One of them noticed me standing at the end, watching.

"Vulture," one of them warned the group and all of their heads snapped towards me.

"Why are you cornering Reaper?" I asked, stalking closer.

"She and the twins stole something of ours." He glared down at her. "And we'd like it back."

With me as a distraction, Reaper took the opportunity to move. They attempted to grab her, but she managed to just barely dodge their grasps and slip through them, sprinting towards me and gripping onto my hoodie. It wasn't until she was close that I saw how tired she was. But why would she come to me? I could kill her right now and all the blame would go to these people.

How convenient.

I took out my knife, turned Reaper, and held her against me. Her arms trapped under one of mine while I rested my knife against her throat. She sucked in a breath.

"Leave."

They didn't need to be told twice as they scurried past us out of the alley.

"I haven't seen you all day," she said. "Did you miss me?"

"It was a good day until now." I leaned closer to her. "Are you afraid of dying, Reaper?"

"Are you?"

"I can't be killed."

"You sound so certain."

"I can't imagine my death." I pressed the blade further into her neck. "Do you want to die?"

"Not so much recently," she admitted in a whisper. "Are you going to kill me?"

I chuckled. "I can't do anything to you at school, but shit, it's hard not to," I said. "You trusted me to save you like some stupid, naïve little girl."

She didn't respond, but I could feel the ripple of her pounding pulse against the blade on her neck.

"You don't even know me, Reaper," I spat.

"Why can't you say my name?" Her voice was barely audible.

I ignored her question. "You know that night, when you caught me watching your clan. Why didn't you tell them I was there?"

She took a moment. "Well, what were you doing spying?"

"I was bored."

"Bored? The meetings are boring. They never talk about anything interesting."

There were several things mentioned I was curious about. "Phobus has a child," I started. "Is that true?"

I could hear the smile in her voice. "Can you guess who it is?"

"You know?" I asked.

"I know a lot of things, too much, actually."

"Why haven't you said anything?"

"Don't you think it'd be more fun to keep the mystery?"

How would she even know? As I pondered whether she was bluffing or not, the silver necklace around her neck caught the light with a quick flash. I pulled at the chain, slowly pulling it out from under her top. Her body tensed against me and my jaw fell at the sight of the silver ring with the skull of a vulture hanging at the end of the chain.

No.

There's no bloody way.

"Where did you get this?" I growled.

"You… Gave it to me."

I furrowed my brows. "When?"

"A long time ago," she whispered.

I thought I had accidentally dropped it and some girl found it. Using it and bragging about it as the rumours got far enough into the Stygian clans. I knew the Kokkino clan found her when they asked me about it after my accident. But because I didn't actually believe I would have ever claimed anyone, I denied it and never looked more into it. I didn't want to be threatened or blackmailed for someone I didn't even remember or told Niko and my friends about.

"Why do you wear my ring around your neck?"

"I'm not quite sure." *Liar.* "Did you want it back?"

I must have given it to her for a reason. "Why do you keep it on you?" I asked again. Someone must have told her it would protect her and it should've, but because I denied giving it to her, it might have put her in danger instead.

She shook her head.

"Why?" I pressed, tightening my hold on her.

There was a slight pause before she finally said, "You gave it to me a couple days before I… Ran away. As if you knew I was going to need it."

A couple days? Reaper was reported missing the same time I went into a coma. I lost that ring months before that. "If you wear this, it means I've claimed you," I said. "And I'll let you keep it." My gaze hardened. "If you stop disrespecting me."

She stayed quiet.

"You can do whatever you want," I told her. "But wearing this means that no one can touch you."

"No one?" she questioned.

"Everyone knows the consequences of pissing me off."

"I don't, so why don't you show me?" she teased.

Am I not holding a knife to her throat? "I thought you knew the stories."

"They're just stories."

Just stories? It took years of hard work for me to create my reputation, but it would all mean nothing if people didn't believe the things I'd done.

At the rate Reaper's going, she's about to be the most powerful person in the Kokkino clan. And the Kokkino clan is debatably the most powerful Stygian clan, and currently the Stygian clans are the most powerful clans of them all. So, Reaper was on her way to becoming the most dangerous and powerful person in Soulesity, next to Niko and I, and I'd need her if not by my side, then at least under me when the time comes. Otherwise, I'd have to kill her.

"So are yours," I said. "I guess, if we're speaking like this, Reaper must just be an incompetent, naïve little girl who can't walk anywhere by herself."

She stiffened. "You don't know anything."

"Yeah? Because all those stories had me believing Reaper would be this strong, confident woman who didn't take any bullshit." I leaned closer to her ear. "But all I see is some shy, insecure girl who constantly needs attention, even if that means making herself easy. So yeah, maybe you're right, maybe mine are lies because yours certainly are."

"I'm not easy," she spat.

"You've literally been begging me to sleep with you while hooking up with half the school." There were lots of rumours that went around and that was just one of them, not that I actually believed it. The timeline for some of the people claiming to have done something with her didn't add up.

"Vulture." Leo's voice sounded behind us.

I let out an annoyed sigh, releasing the necklace and securing Reaper to me again.

"Let her go."

"And why would I do that?"

Leo and Sterling went around so they could face us.

"If you kill her," Leo started, "not only will you be angering the Kokkino clan, but all the Stygian clans."

"You think I care?" Niko would kill me for causing that much trouble.

"I think you don't like putting in so much effort."

I let out a cackle. "You're right, I hate work, but I love blood." I turned down to look at her. "And Reaper's…" I moved the blade slightly across her neck, drawing a bit of blood. "Is just so tempting."

Leo extended his staff, and Sterling took out his dagger.

"But," I continued. "I want to take my time with her." I shoved my knife back into my pocket. "And the two of you being here is ruining it for me."

I grabbed Celestine by the back of her neck, turning her to face me. There were no tears, no fear, no emotion on her face. Just an empty, cold expression.

"Hyacinth." Her voice was barely a whisper.

I leaned down closer and spoke in the same quiet volume. "Yes, Reaper?"

"You cut me."

I let out a short laugh. "You drew blood from me once." I leaned down and licked the bit of blood coming out of the shallow cut on her neck and she let out a small whimper. "It's only fair," I muttered into her neck.

Sterling and Leo hesitated, nervous to approach.

I shoved her away from me, towards the twins. She stumbled back and Leo caught her before she fell, bending down to check on the tiny scratch on her neck.

"Silias will hear about this," Sterling threatened.

"I'm counting on it." I smirked. "Make my life a little less boring."

***

I waited on the sofa for Niko to get home from his assignment, knowing I was going to get in trouble.

He barged into the house, slamming the door behind him. "What did you do?" He grabbed the collar of my hoodie and repeated in a shout. "What did you do?"

"I threatened Reaper," I said in a bored tone.

And I'm not sorry.

Niko's face stiffened, and he bit the inside of his cheeks, his jaw twitching. "I don't know what conflict you have with Reaper, nor do I care! You're just lucky Silias isn't going to do anything!"

My eyes narrowed. "Why not?"

He ignored my question, maybe he didn't know. "For once in your life, show some remorse for what you do."

"It's not something I can feel," I muttered.

My words only angered him more.

"Cinth." He grabbed the back of my hair, forcing me to look up at him. "I still can't tell if you were born like this, or if I made you." He leaned down close to my face. "But either way you're a nuisance."

I was always like this.

"Don't act so bloody careless all the time," he growled. "You forget you're only human." With that he went into his room, slamming his door shut and locking it.

After a moment, I got up from the sofa and headed into my room, popping a pill into my mouth. Then I blinked, a sudden thought rushing through me. I quickly pulled out my phone and scrolled through my messages, going back four years.

When I had woken up from my coma, I had scrolled through my photos and past messages to try to regain my memory, but it didn't work.

I pressed one of them.

UNKNOWN NUMBER: she needs you

ME: who?

UNKNOWN NUMBER: the girl you gave your ring to

ME: where is she?

The texts stopped there.

I went into a coma three days after the messages were sent. I did look for her. I must have. I wouldn't have texted back if I wasn't going to.

But what did I see in her back then to have claimed her after only one encounter.

7

BLAME IT ON THE ALCOHOL

SEPTEMBER 70 A.D.

Why do I let my friends convince me to go to parties with them? I hardly talk to anyone and all I do is smoke outside or stand in a corner, making sure my friends don't do anything stupid.

Iri and Jamiel were off playing some drinking games and Lin was trying to, in his words, 'woo' Eloise. Someone he's liked since the ninth grade. Even though he didn't want anything physical, it was an emotional relationship he wanted with her.

It's actually my fault Eloise doesn't like Lin. He, Jamiel, and I were menaces our first two years and she was the 'perfect' student. Naturally, we butted heads. It was only when Iri became a part of our group at the end of tenth grade when we started growing up... Kind of.

I was leaning against a wall watching every interaction, disinterested in it all until Reaper's presence overtook the room. She wore a white long-sleeved top and a short pink skirt, covering her legs with thigh high socks, contrasting me in all black, with silver chains and a beanie. She's so feminine, you would never expect her to be one of Soulesity's deadliest killers.

She had come alone, but it didn't take long for someone to approach her with a drink, another hugging her in a greeting. My gaze followed her as she disappeared to another room with a few others. A moment later, even more people followed her. It almost looked like she was trying to get away from them. Her eyes met mine and held them until she was right in front of me. A move that successfully got rid of her fans or at least forced them to keep a distance, waiting for her to be finished with me.

Reaper lightly grazed her long coffin nails across my cheek, painted silver with red hearts tonight. An icy chill rippled through me from her gentle touch.

"Did you get in trouble because of me?" she whispered.

"Why would you say that?" I asked in the same volume.

"I'm sorry."

I quite literally threatened to kill her last night, and she's the one apologising? I grabbed her wrist, pushing her hand away from me. "I don't think I ever want to hear you apologise to me again," I muttered, releasing my grip on her. My gaze went down to the small cut on her neck, just a scab now.

"You don't drink?" she asked, sipping on hers.

"No." I've never tasted a drop of alcohol. I know what it does to people, and I wasn't about to lose control over my mind or body.

"The taste?"

"I don't like what it does to people." I attempted to end the conversation, not letting her use me to have some sort of solitude. If she doesn't like talking to people, she shouldn't have come. I could say the same for myself.

Her eyes shifted to amusement. "Try some."

I shook my head. "Don't force me."

"A sip isn't going to do anything."

"Then why would I try?"

"So you can say you did."

She wouldn't leave me alone until I did, so I took her cup and drank a bit. *Shit. Was there no mixer in it?* I coughed at the burn. "Gross, I can't believe you like this."

"Cinth! Are you drinking?" Jamiel shouted from the other end of the room.

I handed Reaper her liquid of death back, ignoring Jamiel.

"I like the burn," she said.

"Why?" I popped a second pill into my mouth. I probably shouldn't mix the two, but I only had one mouthful.

"I just do." She walked away, satisfied with getting me to do what she wanted. I think she won again.

"What are you doing talking to goth boys?" Eloise scrunched up her nose, throwing a dirty look in my direction.

Reaper didn't reply.

Eloise wrapped her arm around Reaper, leading her further away from me. "Let me introduce you to boys who are more... suitable."

I couldn't help the roll of my eyes.

There's a cosy shed with heaters inside, specifically designed for smoking, so I headed out to the garden and inside the shed. Reaper was there, inhaling whatever drug they were offering her, laughing with them. I was about to step out when one of them called me over. "Hyacinth, take a hit."

As long as I don't have to sit next to her, I'll be fine.

I took a seat in the corner of a sofa and took in a deep breath, my head already beginning to haze. "That's bloody strong," I muttered, glancing at Reaper, seeing if she could actually handle this, but she seemed fine, just tired. But she always looked tired with her half-lidded eyes, probably because she had to carry those long thick lashes of hers.

"Yeah, it better be for the price I paid." One of them laughed a bit too hard, intoxicated. "I swear they overcharged me."

"Nah, everything's getting expensive these days. D'you see the price of apples these days?" another exasperated.

A girl giggled, chiming in. "Yeah, my mum was off on another rant about the rise in cost of eggs just last night!"

"They've been putting tiny jars of honey inside these locked plastic cases. You'd think it's bloody jewellery, hey?" someone grouched.

I took one more hit before handing it back, then tilted my head back on the sofa, looking up at the ceiling and listening to the conversation, but not necessarily contributing to it. The topic constantly shifted with the drug giving them the attention span of a squirrel, I didn't bother to keep up.

The girl, who acted as a barrier between Reaper and I, got up and swapped spots with her.

"Why?" I groaned.

"Because I wanted to sit next to you." Reaper lightly smiled, taking another hit of the drug.

"Have you ever heard of personal space?"

She leaned closer, her shoulder touching mine. "No, what's that?" After passing the blunt, Reaper took my hand in hers and began playing with my rings, spinning one around my finger. The origin of this familiar feeling flashed in my mind for a brief second.

***

A younger version of Celestine had her head on my chest, playing with the rings on my hand while I used my other hand to play with her hair.

***

She stopped spinning the rings around my finger and placed her necklace with my ring in the palm of my hand, closing my fingers over it.

"After all this time, now you don't want it anymore?" I asked.

"No, that's okay."

"I told you, you could keep it."

"You don't remember giving it to me, it feels wrong to have it now." Her voice sounded distant as she took her time releasing my hand.

I waited for her to change her mind, but she didn't, so I slipped it into my pocket. A thought itched at the edge of my tongue. I saw her drink at least four cups of alcohol and take a few hits of that strong drug, so why does she look so sober? "Do you have a high tolerance to alcohol and drugs?".

"Yes, unfortunately."

Her body is so small, I assumed she'd be a lightweight. "How?"

She shifted her eyes to mine. "You ask a lot of questions."

I'm a curious boy and she's a curious girl.

"I've been doing it since I was twelve," she finally answered in a bored tone.

"Why would you do that to yourself at such a young age?" Octavius probably gave her alcohol and drugs so it was easier for him to take advantage of her. *That sick bastard.*

She shrugged.

I took out a cigarette, beginning to light the end of it. Just as I lit the flame, Reaper grabbed the cigarette out of my mouth and snapped it between her fingers.

"Cel," someone gasped. Everyone in the room turned and stared with wide eyes.

It took a moment for me to realise what happened. "What the bloody hell is your problem?" I glared at her.

"Don't smoke cigarettes." Her voice nearly pleaded with me.

"Don't tell me what to do," I snapped back, pulling out another one, but she grabbed it just the same. "Are you bloody serious?" I pushed her to the side, not taking into account her small size, and her body fell onto the sofa, knocking into the girl at the other end of it, who let out a small yelp. I cursed at her.

She's so bloody sensitive about cigarettes, but not drugs? Where is the logic?

Reaper kicked my hand, and the pack fell out of my grip. *Oh, you've bloody done it now.* I turned to her with dark eyes, but before I could do anything, someone quickly pulled her off the sofa and away from my wrath. They took her outside of the shed and I don't know what happened out there, but it was smart to get her away from me.

"Woah, what is her problem?" one of them asked.

I don't know and I don't care. I picked my pack off the floor, taking another cigarette, having lost two already. These are expensive in this city. I lit it up and enjoyed my smoke, not feeling any shame at all after manhandling a girl.

After a bit, I grew bored of the shed and decided to find one of my friends.

Lin was sitting on one of the many sofas, laughing with a few people and I didn't want to be in the conversation, but I needed to sit down.

"You and Cel got into a fight," one of them said.

"And it got physical," another said, joining in, taking a seat next to me.

"Yeah, whatever." I rolled my eyes.

"What's she got against smoking?" one asked.

"Probably nothing." Lin had a teasing smirk on his face. "Just doesn't like Cinth doing it."

The others snickered and made mocking noises.

"Shut up," I grouched. "If you think she cares about my health, you're so wrong." I'm sure if Silias told her to, she wouldn't hesitate to kill me and make it as slow as possible.

"It might be her way of showing it." Lin took a long sip of his drink.

"You disgust me," I spat at him.

"Oh, look, there she is." One of them pointed.

I turned to look, but I didn't see her.

The group burst into laughter. "You look like a puppy finding their owner."

Oh, bloody hell.

I stood up, glaring down at all of them, and cursed a few words their way, but it only made them laugh harder.

I hate this. I hate Reaper. I hate her so much.

I headed over to Iri and Jamiel in the kitchen, needing to find some sort of solitude. "What are you guys playing?"

"Spin the bottle," Iri said. "Someone get Cel in here!"

Two people rushed away to find her, shortly dragging her with them and forcing her in the circle.

Animals.

Is she actually going to play?

"Spin it." One of them nudged her.

"What happens?" she asked.

They waited for her to twirl the bottle before answering. "You kiss the person it lands on."

She attempted to stop the bottle from moving, but someone grabbed her arms. "You have to play."

Reaper squinted her eyes at the bottle, like she was trying to control it with her mind. I couldn't help my chuckle, but stopped when the bottle landed on me.

Moira really hates me.

I locked eyes with Reaper. "Uh, I'm not playing."

"You're standing here, that means you are," Jamiel laughed.

"I am not kissing her."

"Rules are rules, Cinth, and you have to follow them," Jamiel said.

My face heated. I've never kissed anyone before. "No," I said, sternly.

Someone let out an annoyed breath. "Fine, then the person to your right has to."

I glanced at the person next to me, a big smirk on his face. "My lucky day."

Yeah, nah.

I pulled him back to me. "She doesn't even want to do this, you guys tricked her."

Reaper laughed. "I'm not a drag."

I glared at her. "I'm not a drag either."

"Seems like you are."

"Prove her wrong, Cinth!" Iri's smile was a bit too wide as she pushed me towards Reaper.

"Iri," I hissed.

"Cel, kiss him!" Iri said.

"How long does it have to be?" Reaper asked, as if she were asking how long a cake needed to be in the oven.

"One minute," Iri replied.

"You just made that up, didn't you?" I growled at her.

"No." She waved her hand in the air, pushing me closer towards Reaper. "I would never!"

I let out a deep breath. "You're so bloody small," I muttered, picking her up and setting her on the high counter, now at more equal heights. I looked at her, but quickly turned away.

My heart raced against my chest. Are we actually going to do this? Everyone was watching us. I didn't know what I imagined my first kiss to be like, I've never really bothered with it, but this was probably at the bottom of the list.

"Do it, Cinth!" Jamiel urged.

I hesitated. I didn't know what to do or how to start this. *Do I tilt my head so our noses don't clash? Where do my hands go?* I cursed, my face heating. *I'm not doing this sober.* Grabbing Jamiel's drink, I downed it.

"Oh my gods." Reaper rolled her eyes. "You are so dramatic, you're just making this into a bigger deal than it actually is."

"Cel," one of them said. "He's never kissed someone before."

I heard a few snickers.

It wasn't a secret, but he didn't have to say it like that.

I met Reaper's eyes, wondering what mocking comment she'd make, but she didn't.

"Who would want to kiss that?" someone commented and more people laughed, making more cruel jokes about my inexperience and my spooky appearance.

I've never made relationships or intimacy a priority and besides, I'm only seventeen...

Her eyes shifted behind me towards those who spoke, but I couldn't read the expression on her face. The crowd quickly grew, eager for the show.

"Look, Cel, if you really don't want to kiss him, you can pick someone else instead," someone told her.

Celestine responded by cupping my cheeks and pulling me towards her. "Don't think," she whispered before her lips met mine.

Holy shit.

I knew they would be soft, but I wasn't prepared for the way she took it slow, allowing me to adjust to the sensation of our lips connecting before gradually deepening the kiss. Her hands found their way to my hair, fingers tangling in it as she gently removed my beanie, letting it fall to the floor.

Why does that feel good? Shit.

I pulled away from her for a moment, trying to regain my composure. "This means nothing."

She nodded, but I couldn't ignore the way my hands instinctively settled on her hips, dragging her closer. Reaper wrapped her legs around my waist, parting her lips just enough for me to slip my tongue into her mouth.

I don't even know who I am anymore.

Totally the alcohol and drugs. I would never do this sober, especially not with her—Or maybe only with her, if anyone. She pulled me down closer and had the audacity to let out a soft moan.

Bloody hell, Reaper.

I wanted to hear that again, I wanted to hear how loud she could be, to be the one who made her scream.

"One minute," Iri said, but we didn't stop.

No.

We couldn't.

Reaper took one of my hands, guiding it under her top. My fingers lightly grazed the side of her stomach, then travelled to her back. Her skin was soft, smooth, and toned, and I couldn't help but marvel at the lines of scars that traced her body, each one a testament to a story I could only guess at.

"They're really going at it," someone cursed behind us.

The music blasting in the house couldn't drown the hot blood thumping against my ears. Reaper lightly bit my lip and I breathed a curse, attempting to pull her closer to me, though it wasn't possible. How could I get closer? Why does this feel so good? Why does it feel so wrong but so right? Was it just with her, or was it like this with anyone? The very thought of doing this with anyone else disgusted me.

Her hand slithered up over my hoodie, her nails lightly scratching my neck as she made her way down past my collarbone to my chest, tugging at the collar of my hoodie. Electricity surged through her touch and goosebumps prickled my skin.

I've completely lost control.

Before I felt like we were even getting started, Reaper pushed me away. "This meant nothing," she mimicked, a playful curve at the edge of her lips, as she hopped off the counter and fixed her top.

"Absolutely nothing," I replied, shoving my hands in my pocket, but my body ached for more.

She picked up my beanie, handing it to me before turning to Iri. "I don't want to play this game anymore." Then she picked up a random drink and walked away.

Jamiel's face was flushed. "I have never seen two people kiss like that and turn everyone on before."

I have never been turned on before.

They all stared at me.

"I don't even think we need to ask if that was good," one of them said.

Yeah, it was bloody good, and I craved more. *What's wrong with me?* I am never drinking ever again, look at what it's doing to my mind, and I only had a bit. I hate Reaper. I thought about killing her. So why did I want her to come back and finish what we started?

I licked my lips, the last bit of her on it.

"You're welcome." Iri patted my chest.

"How does it feel to have your first kiss be Celestine bloody Vicary?" Jamiel smirked.

Like kissing will never be like that again, not unless it was with her. "Where the bloody hell did she learn that?" I muttered, slipping my beanie back over my head.

Jamiel shrugged, chuckling into his cup as he took a big chug of it.

I grabbed a random bottle off the counter and took a swing of it, wanting to forget what I'd just done. *Who knew I had such high tolerance to alcohol?* It still hadn't taken effect on me yet and I'd drunk quite a bit already.

"Oi, Cinth." Jamiel wiped his mouth with the back of his hand. "Maybe you should calm down a bit."

I slammed the now near empty bottle back on the counter. "Don't tell me what to do," I snapped at him, and he pursed his lips. I needed to go to the bathroom and cool off. I headed in the direction of it but was stopped by Lin.

"You dog! I can't believe you!"

"What?" I asked, boredly.

"You made out with Celestine!"

"It didn't mean shit," I told him.

He rubbed his face with his hands. "You actually need to get your head checked. She's the most beautiful girl in the entire city, I cannot believe you did that with her and didn't fall in love."

I'll get back to him on that.

I took the drink in his hand and poured it down my throat. It tasted horrible, but I wanted to forget this night, maybe I'd be okay to let loose for once.

"Oh, gods, Cinth," Lin gasped.

"I have control," I muttered more to myself than him, but honestly, I didn't know anymore. I brushed past him to get to the bathroom. I opened the door, but there was no lock.

Why?

When I turned around, Reaper was there, reapplying her gloss, with a slight smile. At least she wasn't doing anything.

"There's no lock," I said.

"I know," she replied, putting away her lip gloss. It was glittery, tasted like vanilla. I stepped to the side to let her leave, but she grabbed me by the collar and slammed my back into the door.

I cursed and reached into my pocket for my knife, but she pulled me down by the back of the head and stopped. Our lips just a breath apart. Reaper was waiting for me, to see what I would do, if I wanted this just as much as her, and I'd be lying if I said I didn't.

I think I craved it more.

I leaned in, closing the gap between us.

We hated each other, so why are we doing this? What is wrong with us? The mirror fogged up and all the contents that were once on the sink were scattered to the floor.

"Hyacinth."

I loved when she said my name, just like that, and I simply couldn't fathom just how beautiful she was, even when I was doing this to her. As I gripped onto the sink, the thought of choosing to do this over spilling blood was easy. There was nothing that I wanted more than to do this with her every day. All day.

I don't know how, but I stumbled back with her wrapped around me, quickly pulling her head into my chest, holding her tight as I fell into the tub next to us with her on top of me. *Shit.*

"Are you alright?" I asked, her face blurry now.

She nodded with a laugh. "Are you?"

If I'm being honest, I barely felt it. I guess they were right, alcohol makes you numb. "Gods." I laughed with her.

The door burst open, and we turned to it.

"Angels above!" Iri gasped.

"Cinth!" Jamiel laughed.

"Oh my gods." Lin's eyes were wide.

Instead of shying away or squirming at the sudden expedition we were giving, like I thought she would, Reaper pulled me up to meet her lips again and I deepened it.

I chuckled between our kisses, she didn't even care and that's where my memory of the night ended.

***

I woke up alone in my bed with my head throbbing. *No. No. This is all some sick joke. No way last night happened.* I fumbled around in my bed, grabbing my phone and group dialling my friends. The screen was too bright to read their texts.

"Hello?" Lin picked up first, his voice groggy.

"Hey!" Iri sang.

"Oi, it's too early for this," Jamiel groaned, hungover like me.

"What happened last night? What the bloody hell did I do?" I asked, my voice hoarse and parched.

"If you're wondering if it really did happen, yes, you did kiss Cel." Iri giggled through the crowds of chatter in the background. She must be at work.

I cursed. "And the... Bathroom?"

The phone screeched at their overlapping and loud laughter. "Yeah, you were so drunk!"

You've got to be bloody messing with me.

"Her and I—"

"Cel? She wasn't there."

No. I'd rather it have been her right now. "Then... Who did I...?"

"Who did you what, Cinth?" I could hear Iri's smile through the phone.

"Uh..." I couldn't think straight. "You guys didn't walk in on us?"

"Did you two do something in the bathroom?" Jamiel shouted into the phone, making me pull it away from my ear.

"No, they didn't," Lin piped up. "I followed you to the bathroom, Cinth, after you took my drink, and I went in when I heard a thud."

"He called us over," Iri chimed in.

I felt my phone vibrate at a notification and took a glance at it.

Bloody hell.

"You passed out in the bathtub in the middle of washing your hands and took the curtain with you." Lin laughed.

I can see that.

I put a hand over my face. "Delete the photo," I begged. "Please." If anyone saw this, my reputation...

"Okay, but we're keeping the video," Jamiel said, and I felt the vibration again.

I cursed at the sight of it, I wasn't even going to click play on the video of Reaper and me. Prassino would have seen this by now and soon enough Silias and the entire Underworld would know.

"Oi, you're such a lightweight," Jamiel mocked. "You only had one drink."

I think I had more than one and in my defence, I'd never drank before. No one warned me alcohol didn't take effect immediately.

"Shut up, Jamiel." My head felt like it was about to explode and my body heated at the thought of our kiss. I reached for my pills and popped one in, praying the headache would go away soon. "Bloody hell, I can't believe we—" I couldn't say it out loud. "What do I do?"

None of them answered for a long while.

"Just don't make it awkward," Iri replied. "It's fine, she wanted it too."

We were both intoxicated. "Who said I wanted it?" I snapped.

"Cinth." Iri laughed. "Please stop lying to yourself."

I cursed at them, but I didn't understand. "What does not making it awkward mean?"

"Act normal," Jamiel said.

Act normal? I just lost my first kiss at a party to the most beautiful girl this world has ever seen, clearly drunk out of my mind, because I would never do that sober. How could I act normal? That incredibly vivid, intoxicated dream too... *Shit. Don't think about that.*

"Anyways, I have to get back to work," Iri announced. "You'll be fine, Cinth."

"Yeah, I'm off too," Jamiel said. "I need sleep."

"Are you okay, Cinth?" Lin asked.

I didn't know how to answer that. "I don't know," I admitted. "I shouldn't have drank anything."

There was a long pause before he asked, "Do you regret the alcohol or the kiss?"

"I'm not sure," I said, slowly. "When we were doing it, I was thinking that this is probably why we mess with each other so much, because we wanted to do this, but we were both so drunk, I don't think it was okay for us to do that."

Lin was the first person I was able to call a friend. He wouldn't tell anyone the things I confided in him, and he was always honest with me.

"She took care of you while you were half conscious."

I furrowed my brows. "What? Why would she do that?"

"She felt bad because she made you drink."

She didn't make me do anything. "Right," I muttered. "How did I even get home?"

"By yourself," he sighed. "She managed to sober you up enough to walk. Anyways, if you really feel weird about it, you should talk to her and clear the air."

I felt my pocket for the necklace with my ring and took it out, analysing its engravings again. It didn't seem she ever took it off in those four years of having it. Tarnished, the tip of the vulture's beak was chipped off.

"Yeah," I said. "Maybe."

"Are you going to be okay?" he asked. "We can meet up after my tutoring session if you want?"

"I think I just need to think. Thanks, Lin."

"You'll be right, it was just a kiss," Lin said before hanging up.

I put my arm over my face and shouted a curse.

Just a kiss. It didn't mean anything.

"Cinth." My door opened, Niko behind it. "I've let you sleep in long enough. Get up, you need to train."

I groaned. "Can I just—"

"No, it's your fault for stupidly drinking last night."

"What time did I get home?" I asked.

"You don't remember?"

"Not really," I muttered.

"Five in the morning." His voice was sharper than usual.

Shit. I glanced at the time on my phone, that was just a few hours ago.

"You cannot act this reckless," he said. "Someone could have killed you in that state."

"I know," I said, dragging myself out of the bed.

"You're lucky no one did. If you bumped into the wrong person on your way home or someone followed you…" He continued his lecture about how irresponsible I was, and I tuned out of it, already knowing I made a mistake. "How did you even get home? You barely made it through the door."

I shook my head. "Honestly, I have no idea."

***

Lin rented a room in the public library for those from other schools. And I ended up finding him with still another half an hour of tutoring.

"So, the derivative—" he paused his markings on the whiteboard. "Cinth, what are you doing here?"

"Can I talk to you?"

He looked at his watch. "I guess so." Lin turned to the students in the class. "You guys can either continue studying until I come back or leave." Then he followed me out the door and kept his voice at a whisper as to not to disturb those in the library. "What is it? You look awful."

I felt so drained if I'm being honest. My heart had been through a lot in the last twenty-four hours. I had a beanie to cover my awful hair and a hood up over my head to block out as much light as I could. "I think I'm sick, Lin."

"It's called a hangover."

"No," I said. "Not that. My heart keeps beating weirdly, sometimes I find it hard to breathe and concentrate. And I've been so warm, I sweat. Also, I keep having these vivid dreams and it's making it hard to sleep, but I've also been falling asleep in random places. I don't know, it's weird." Lin stared at me, waiting for me to finish my list of things wrong with me. "Do you think I'm dying?"

"Wow. You really do need help."

"Gods, I knew I should've just gone straight to the hospital."

Lin chuckled. "No, Cinth. But most of these symptoms occur when you're around Celestine, right? Or when you're thinking about her?"

"Yeah. She makes it worse and won't get out of my head. I'm certain she's a witch."

He could barely contain himself.

"Lin, she's messing with my head. Take this seriously," I demanded.

"What do you mean?"

I shook my head, this was so weird to talk about. "She makes me so angry and we... You know, did that thing last night."

"Kissed." He couldn't help his smile at my fluster.

"I really don't think she likes me. She's just doing all of it to mess with me, but I don't know why." I don't understand girls, but maybe talking about it with him would help me figure it all out more clearly.

"You think she's flirting with you to mess with your emotions?"

"Yeah," I said, taking a step back to lean against the wall. "But that's so cruel, isn't it?" Even I wouldn't do something like that.

He mulled it over for a moment. "I don't know what's going on in her head, honestly I don't think anyone does. Maybe ask Iri. She talks to her a lot."

I shook my head. "We all know Iri only feels obliged to try and be friends with her because she was once good friends with her brother."

"No, Iri's friends with her because she *wants* to be."

I guess that came out a bit wrong. "Okay, whatever, but Iri's biassed and sees what she wants." And what she sees is Reaper as some sort of Angel who can do no wrong.

"Well, from what I've seen, Cel seems to really like you and I think maybe she just doesn't know how to show it properly."

"What is proper?"

Lin shrugged. "And no offence, Cinth, but you don't make it easy for her either. She's doing what she probably thinks is the way to be near you and get you to talk to her."

"She enjoys it a bit too much."

"No, I think what she enjoys is your presence."

"So, you think I should be nicer to her and then she'll be nicer to me?"

"Exactly that." He nodded. "Might be a bit hard for you, but try it."

"And what if this backfires? What if it really was her plan to get me to like her and then she breaks my mind and—"

"Gods, Cinth, you're so dramatic."

But everyone wants to take down Vulture and anyone would take the opportunity. Reaper is probably just like that. I cursed. "I don't understand her."

"Try to get to know her." Lin smiled. "Maybe then you'll figure out if *you* even like her and if not, then none of this really matters."

He was right. If I don't let her in, then she can't break me. "So, I'm not dying, right?"

"No, Cinth. You are fine."

I nodded. "Thanks, I'll let you get back to tutoring."

***

I didn't bother warning Albion and Mica I was coming. The only two Demons I still kept contact with were usually together anyway.

"Oh," Albion answered Mica's door. "I wasn't aware Mica was expecting you." The son of Ignatius wasn't too fond of me after what I did to his half-brother, Grey, but he also couldn't disagree that Grey deserved it, not that I'd seen him in years.

Albion might be fifty-three years old, but he still looked twenty-five, as all immortals did. His unnaturally dyed brown hair matched his dark grey eyes. He worked closely with his father in politics; assisting in Stygian culture becoming more accepted and trying to turn the city toward clean energy. Just thirty years ago, people were being hanged just for saying the word Stygian, at least today people just frown upon it. Currently, Albion and Ignatius were trying to convince the senators of the advantages of building a dam.

"He's not," I said, brushing past Albion to get inside. I knew my way around Mica's home. It was a modest apartment, and the only thing he kept under lock and key was his computer room. I headed straight to his living room bookshelf and Albion followed.

"What are you doing here?" Mica emerged from the bathroom. The son of Paxon was forty-seven years old with light grey hair like his father, and black eyes. Though, he was a bit more bold, dying his hair a bright neon green, because who would suspect a Demon that stands out. Mica was Paxon's second, assisting with monitoring and notifying Stygians of threats.

"I need to look at your Book of Ice," I muttered, finally finding it and pulling it out from between his cramped bookshelf.

"Why? Don't you have your own copy?"

I have the tampered copy that's been censored and edited. Though the book was thick and old, only around fifty pages of it were filled with vague descriptions and hand drawings. It was written during the creation of Demons, Angels, Selkies, and Humans and held future tellings. No one knows who wrote it. Theories lead to the Goddess of archives, Archaeia, but it's never been confirmed. So far, though, everything in it has come true.

I attempted to open it but it wouldn't budge, glued shut.

"You need Stygian blood to open it," Mica said, biting the tip of his finger with one of his fangs and smearing his blood on the cover. He licked his fangs, two on the top and two on the bottom, like all Demons. The blood slowly seeped into the cover and the pages loosened, allowing me to open the book. *Interesting lock.*

I flipped through the pages, noting there were quite a few pages missing from my own copy, but I didn't find them necessary to read at the moment. Stygians write from the right corner going downwards, the symbols at times difficult to decipher, as many words look similar to one another with just a single stroke being the difference between nightmare and sea. Their sentence structure was also much more simple than Souic.

I finally arrived at the end. The last page talked about the Reckoning and the near extinction of Demons where the book ended in all the copies the people in this city held, but here there was one more paragraph.

A Demon born after the Reckoning, her power remains a riddle. Only the heir of the Nether can bind her will, for without him, the living shall succumb to silence. The gaze of Moira lingers, and where fate's hand pulls, she falters, until the sky is split by light.

Beneath the sea, where ripples stir the deep, lie answers to questions unasked. And when the stars fall, the War of Wars shall begin.

"How many female Demons are living right now?" I asked.

They shook their heads. "Only one. Zuriel's daughter, Bernadette."

The Siren.

"Are you sure?" I asked.

"Why do you ask?" Mica exchanged a look with Albion.

I shook my head. If Reaper was a Demon, who was her father? If she was who the Book of Ice spoke of, what power were they talking about?

"Is this really about Siren?" I pointed at the last paragraph.

Albion shook his head with a bit of a laugh. "Doubtful."

"Bernie may have convinced everyone she's more powerful than she is," Mica started. "But I've been in charge of watching her, her entire life and I can confidently tell you it's not her."

"Do you think the female isn't born yet?" I questioned.

They shrugged. "Possibly."

I turned back to the words, memorising them in my head. "I didn't know Phobus could even have children." Demons were created in his image and they were incredibly infertile, which is why Demons were so rare, so it was also assumed Phobus was the same.

"Neither did any of us," Mica said.

Albion snarled at Mica. "You're not supposed to know any of this, Hyacinth." He threatened me with the red glow of his eyes.

"I've kept my mouth shut about a lot. This isn't something anyone else needs to know either," I said.

He gave me a nod and Mica turned to me. "Why the sudden interest?"

"Just a rumour I overheard." I couldn't tell them I had been spying on their clan meetings.

"Well, what do you make of it?" Mica asked.

"The odds of finding these two shouldn't be too difficult. I feel they'd stick out."

"You'd think that," Albion said. "But it's been nearly seventy years since the Reckoning and we've found nothing."

"Phobus's child and the female Demon are said to be incredibly attracted to one another," Mica said. "If we know one, the other will reveal themselves eventually."

I slipped the book back in its spot. "And what are the clans planning on doing with them once they're found?"

Mica shook his head. "It would depend on–"

"It's not any of your concern." Albion interrupted, shooting Mica a glare. "This is Stygian matters, and you already know too much."

"Right," Mica said, turning away from me. "You should get going, Hyacinth."

I nodded, it was enough information for now. I'd figure out more later.

I gave them a polite nod and headed out.

8

STATEMENTS AND INTERVIEWS

September 70 A.D.

Sunday morning, I laid in bed watching Ren and Delilah Vicary make a public statement about their daughter on my phone. The pressure of Soulesity finally got to them.

The camera shutters went wild as Ren and Delilah stepped towards the platform. Delilah, solemn in a modest white fitted dress, held their three-year-old daughter Marigold in her arms, Ren serious in a dark blue suit.

He looked towards his wife, giving her a reassuring nod. "Good morning." He spoke into the microphone, staring straight ahead, at what I'm sure was a crowd of media. "We thank you all for giving my family and I the space we needed to process all of what has happened in the last couple of months," he began. "After all these years of endless searching, Datura is alive." He paused as the clicking of cameras went feral again.

Marigold blinked rapidly and Delilah shielded her eyes from it.

"Though, as painful as it is, she has chosen not to live with us. We wish her all the best and if she ever does decide to come home..." His voice broke, and he fixed his tie, taking a moment to breathe. "We will wait for her to come home."

"Senator Vicary! Senator Vicary!"

Ren shifted his gaze to the press, patiently waiting for the questions to come.

"Is it true she's now affiliated with clans?"

101

"Yes, that's correct," he confirmed. "We do not condone this careless and violent lifestyle, but there is only so much we, as parents, can do. Though, as Senator of Soulesity, we are of course always continuing our work to make this city a safer place from these barbaric thugs."

"Do you know how she became a part of it?"

"After the manipulation and influence of Octavius Gautier." Ren sighed. "He and his friends pressured her into their circle. It only went downhill from there."

"We heard the clan is associated with Stygians, is that something you're concerned about?"

Ren's face didn't falter, composed and seemingly expectant of the question. "Of course, we are extremely worried for her. She has become one who abuses substances like alcohol and illegal drugs, selling her body to get what she wants. Stygians only encourage that type of antisocial behaviour."

"Has she attempted to contact you since her disappearance?"

"No, she has not."

"What are Vasos's thoughts on the matter?"

Ren paused for a long moment. "Due to the heartbreak of what we all assumed happened to Datura, he could not bear to be in Soulesity. This news has hurt him far worse than before, knowing she did not want to be with us and instead choosing to become this degenerate delinquent over her family."

"Do you still love her?"

"Delilah and I have had a difficult and long discussion." Ren exchanged a comforting look with his wife before turning back to the crowd. "Datura is not the same innocent, good little girl we raised her to be before she was manipulated by the likes of Octavius Gautier. There is nothing we can do except wait for her to come back to us and until Datura returns home safe with us, we will not be associating our name with hers and she is no longer considered a Vicary. Delilah and I will be putting our attention and focus on our daughter, Marigold, and will no longer be addressing anything to do with Datura."

The crowd roared into more questions and rumours they wanted clarified, but Ren steadied himself. "No further questions will be answered."

Resting a hand on the curve of Delilah's back, he gently guided her and Marigold off the stage and the video ended there.

I wondered if Reaper watched the announcement. It was streamed live before playing on repeat on every screen the rest of the day. I'd be surprised if she hadn't seen it... I guess I was more curious on what her thoughts about it were, if she'd go back to her old life as a Vicary.

And I wasn't the only one. Every media and talk show host, every person in Soulesity wanted to know what was going to happen now. People were dissecting the statement, replaying it over and over, discussing and laughing about it. I had assumed there would be an update that she was back with the Vicarys that evening. Instead, another interview had been released.

Eugene Vicary, father of Ren Vicary and now a retired Senator, had given a short interview. It was only ten minutes long and filmed inside Eugene's home. He sat on his deep brown leather lounge chair, next to a fireplace, wearing a simple button-up shirt and trousers.

"Was there a time when you realised there was something wrong with Datura?" the interviewer asked out of frame.

Eugene cleared his throat, adjusting the collar on his shirt. "Datura has always been a bad egg. It must have been something she caught from her biological father." He waved a hand in the air dismissively. "She never had any friends in school and people didn't like her because she was rather odd." His eyes narrowed. "I always told Ren and Delilah to take her to see a psychologist. There was something... Not right with her, you know? She was very quiet, didn't like to play with her dolls and never looked people in the eyes. She was always getting into trouble, both at home and school. Always causing problems for my poor son." He let out a frustrated breath, shaking his head. "She's not my biological granddaughter, but I still cared for her."

"And so when she met Octavius? Did you see any changes in her?"

"No, because I hardly saw her during that time at all. She was always off with that boy and his friends, doing who knows what!" His face grew red with anger. "If I had known how bad it had gotten, I'd have done something myself!"

"So you haven't seen her at all since she met Octavius Gautier?"

He propped one of his elbows onto the armrest, leaning his weight towards it. "She came to me once." He rubbed his lips and shook his head. "And I knew something was terribly off." His brows scrunched up, the wrinkles on his face more prominent as his head lowered. "She wasn't herself, on drugs I could only assume."

"Do you know which drugs?"

"How would I know? Whatever it was made her very emotional. She was sobbing, begging me on her knees to give her money." He nodded a gesture behind the camera. "My staff had to physically remove her off my leg."

"Did you give her money?"

"I knew it was going to be used on alcohol and drugs."

"So, you didn't help her?"

"Of course I offered help!" he snapped back. "I told her she could stay with me, that I would take her to the hospital, and she blew up at me, screaming like she was in pain... She left my house—"

"And you didn't stop her?"

"I *couldn't* stop her. She left so quickly and was scaring myself and my staff. I had to let her go for the safety of all of us."

"Do you know what happened to her during the time she was missing?"

Eugene shook his head. "As far as I know, she was hiding from everyone who was looking for her. She didn't want to be found."

"There's talk that she sold her body for alcohol and drugs. Do you believe these rumours?"

"I wouldn't be surprised. The desperation on her face when she had come to me that day... She told me I was killing her if I didn't help her."

"And... What of Octavius Gautier. What do you think about his sentence?"

"I think that boy got what he deserved." Eugene's voice was cold and uncaring. "Though we were all wrong that he murdered her, it doesn't mean he didn't do all those other things to her. Datura had her faults, but she wouldn't have fallen so low if it weren't for him." He shook his head and released a sigh. "Though, we can't completely blame the boy, she knew what she looked like and always liked to tempt the people around her. She always found herself in the attention of grown men and enjoyed it."

"So, are you saying she wasn't innocent before meeting Octavius Gautier?"

"I'm saying that, that boy fell for her little trap and now she's out manipulating clans. Datura has no idea what she's dealing with anymore, the type of danger she's in."

"How do you feel, knowing that your grand– Apologies, adoptive granddaughter has lost herself like this?"

"Disappointment," he replied, "in myself for not trying harder."

"What would you say to Datura now?"

Eugene looked straight at the camera, his glassy eyes soft and sorrowful. "Datura, I do hope you realise what you are doing and get help. It's never too late and there is no shame in it. Your parents and I only want what's best for you. I love you and I miss you every day."

The interview ended there.

***

The Yarra Show hinted to the world that she had a special guest involving the Vicary's, a response to their statements. So, that same Sunday night, everyone, including myself, tuned in to watch who would be interviewed next.

"Hello, how is everyone doing tonight?" Yarra began with a beaming smile and the crowd cheered. Yarra nodded and waved, waiting for them to settle before continuing. "Now, unless you've been living under a rock, you've seen the Vicary family and their interviews on their missing daughter, Datura Vicary." The crowd murmured in anticipation. "Well, tonight we've got the exclusive, hearing the side of the story I'm sure we're all dying to hear. Please, join me in welcoming Octavius Gautier and Thessaly Zorlu!" She clapped, and the camera panned to Octavius and Thessaly walking towards her, greeting her with a respectful bow of their head.

Thessaly smiled, no doubt here to try to convince everyone of Octavius's innocence again, not that it worked in his trial. But Octavius didn't, nor did he look at the crowd who were now murmuring. The two sat on the white velvet sofa, across from Yarra who sat in her own white velvet chair.

For some reason, in my head Octavius was some creepy old man, even though I knew he was a young twenty-one-year-old man. An incredibly average-looking Souic; short dark brown hair, olive skin, dark eyes. The only defining part was a nose far too big for his face and dark circles under his eyes.

Thessaly was a bit taller than Octavius. Her hair had been recently cut and styled, dyed a honey blonde and curled down a bit past her shoulders, with medium tanned skin and brown eyes. Her large chest, made her look bigger than she was.

"Are you nervous?" Yarra asked Octavius.

He shook his head. "No, I..." He paused for a moment. "I just want everyone to know the truth."

"And what is the truth?"

"That I'm innocent."

Thessaly took Octavius's hand in hers and gave it a squeeze.

Yarra nodded. "You spent three years in prison for a murder that never happened. What was it like being in there?"

"Well, the food was terrible." He got a bit of a laugh from the audience. "But no, in all seriousness, it was awful. I was just a kid when I was put in."

"Sixteen when you were suspected and seventeen when you were imprisoned, correct?"

"Yes, and they put me with all the other adults."

"Was it scary?"

"I was terrified, among those who actually had done awful things, but there were also many in there who were like me and hadn't committed crimes but were also wrongfully accused."

Yarra furrowed her brows. "Why do you think that's happened?"

"We all had one thing in common. We weren't wealthy, we were nobody."

"You think wealth plays a part in the justice system?"

"I know it does," Octavius stated in a sure voice. "No matter what I said or what evidence I had to prove my innocence, I was going to be used as a scapegoat to save the Vicary family's face."

Yarra raised her brows. "But she did run away to be with you, correct?"

Octavius scoffed, with a shake of his head. "No. She didn't. I only allowed her to stay at my place for two weeks after finding out she had been homeless."

"Why only two weeks?"

Octavius's eyes shifted from Yarra to something off camera, distracted. Thessaly glanced at what he was looking at. Octavius nodded before finally turning back to Yarra and answering her question. "She didn't think anything we gave her was enough for her and eventually left."

"His family are very generous people," Thessaly piped in. "Datura grew up a spoiled child, so she couldn't see that they were giving her everything they could."

Yarra turned to the audience. "Now, if you didn't know, the Gautier family are the lighthouse keepers. They have been for generations and the government pays them to tend to it. They live quite modestly." She then turned back to Octavius. "Do you still live with them now?"

Octavius shifted in his seat. "I had a difficult time being back home, so I'm currently living with my partner, Thessaly." He gave Thessaly a small smile.

"You two have been friends since high school?" Yarra asked.

"Yes, she visited me nearly every day when I was locked up and we officially became partners when I got out." His gaze stayed with Thessaly. "She's what kept me going."

Thessaly mouthed an "I love you" to him.

The audience awed, gushing over their little interaction.

Yarra pursed her lips in sympathy. "Were there times in prison where you lost hope?"

"So many times. I..." Octavius's voice shook. "When the others inside found out what I was in there for, they thought being in prison wasn't enough."

"There were a few times when I visited him and he had bruises and broken bones." Thessaly's eyes turned glassy. "It was so hard to see him like that, so broken and hurt, especially knowing that he didn't deserve it."

"I'm sorry that happened," Yarra said. "It's an awful crime to be committed for." There was a moment of silence before she asked. "Do you feel anger towards the Vicary family?"

Octavius took a deep breath, his eyes quickly flashing to whatever or whoever was behind Yarra, off camera. "I understand they wanted justice for their daughter, and I think they were blinded by what they believed to be true."

"Now, I'm sure everyone is curious, but why did you become friends with her in the first place? She was, after all, four years younger than you."

Octavius shook his head. "Look, if I could turn back time, I'd never have talked to her after we were paired up for that activity at school. I guess I just felt pity for her."

"Her grandfather mentioned in his interview that she had no friends. Was that true?"

"Yeah, the other kids in her class didn't like her."

Thessaly piped in. "Datura took advantage of Tav's kindness and misinterpreted it, inappropriately falling in love with him."

"How do you know she was in love with him?"

"She was so clingy with him, and she knew Tav and I were a bit more than friends at the time." Thessaly's face distorted to one of loathing, blinking rapidly. "Datura slithered her way between us every chance she got, always jealous when I was near him and called me horrible names. She even went so far as to throw tantrums whenever Tav would hang out with me instead of her."

Octavius glanced at Thessaly before turning his focus back to Yarra.

"What are your thoughts on how Datura is now? She's alive, and she's a part of a clan now."

He shook his head as Thessaly answered. "I don't believe either of us are surprised with how she's turned out. She made choices Octavius tried to warn her about, but she never listened."

"Choices like what?" Yarra asked, leaning forward in her seat.

Octavius shifted in his seat. "Well, after she left my place, she met this older man, a Stygian clansman." He sighed. "That's when she started drinking and taking drugs."

"There were even times where she was intoxicated at school." Thessaly scrunched her nose. "She smelt so bad too, like she never showered."

The crowd made sounds of disgust, gasping.

"Tess," Octavius said, trying to make her stop before she said something she'd most likely regret. "Look, we're not here to bad mouth Datura. There were many people around her who were trying to help her, but she *chose* her path and continued down it."

"There was nothing you could have done to help her," Yarra said in a solemn voice.

"Exactly."

"Do you think Datura will ever come forward to speak about the situation? I have invited her multiple times to come on the show, but I never get a response." She laughed.

Thessaly rubbed her other hand over Octavius's in a comforting manner.

"Honestly, I don't think she will. For three years I was in prison, and she said and did nothing."

"And what are your plans now for your future?" Yarra asked. "Do you think you will ever reach out to Datura?"

"No, I don't want anything to do with her anymore." Octavius's back straightened. "Datura brought nothing but bad things into the lives of those around her, and I don't wish for anyone to be met with the same fate. She has ruined my life, my family's, my friend's, and the Vicary family's lives. We all just want to move forward from this. I'm working on myself and repairing my relationship with my family and friends. It's been rough, but we're getting there."

Yarra gave them a smile. "I'm glad to hear that, and I do hope everything works out for you. Thank you very much for coming on to the show."

"Thank you." He and Thessaly rose, giving Yarra a polite nod before walking off the stage.

***

On Monday, Reaper wasn't at school and everyone's minds drifted to her return. They'd probably make a movie about this or at the very least a documentary, a happy ending, as it looks like it's become.

Was I relieved she was finally gone? Good riddance. I can finally have my sanity–

Reaper entered history and everyone stopped, turning and watching her walk to the back of the room, whispering.

"What are you doing here?" I asked.

She didn't look at me as she passed my desk.

So I made Iri swap seats with me so I could sit next to Reaper.

"What are you doing here?" I asked again.

Reaper turned her head up towards me and gave me a weird look, rolling her eyes. "I go here." But that big, playful smile couldn't fool me. The red irritated skin at the corner of her eyes from having rubbed at it too much and the bit of make-up missing on the tip of her nose said she wasn't ok.

Why aren't you with your family? It's what I wanted to ask, but the words died as the teacher entered. "Alright, I hope everyone completed their assignments. I'll be coming around to pick them up." She went around the room, doing a quick glance at each person's paper before taking it.

"I thought she went back home," Jamiel said in a low voice.

Iri nudged Jamiel. "There's obviously a good reason that she chose to run away," she snapped. "She wouldn't go back after all these years. Why would she?"

If Iri couldn't see through the mask Reaper was wearing, no one else could. Though, maybe Iri was right. Reaper did make the choice to run away and she must have had a good reason, especially to go so far as joining the Kokkino clan and allow the entire city to think she was dead. She didn't want to be found. *So what brought her back?*

"Wonder what happened between Celestine and Octavius," Lin said.

Everyone had seen the video of the physical fight the two had the day she disappeared, but no one knew why that fight happened. And when asked in court, Octavius's response was 'no comment.'

Iri leaned over her desk, closer to the three of us as she spoke. "I heard it's because Cel found out Octavius was in love with someone else and she flipped." Probably the most explainable answer.

"Is that what she told you?" I asked.

"No," Iri replied. "Just what I heard. She dodges questions like the plague."

"I wonder what she thinks about Marigold," Jamiel said with a mouth full of food, having snuck in a snack as he often did. "Has she met her yet?"

Iri shook her head. "Don't think so."

"I can't believe she's in a clan though. That's scary." Lin shook his head.

Jamiel laughed. "What? Who did you think all those men who pick her up from school were?"

Lin had never seen them since he always stayed back after school for tutoring. It was always suspected amongst the students that she was involved with the clans, but the interviews released over the weekend confirmed it.

"Jamiel, no talking in class. Are you eating?" the teacher scolded him.

I glanced at Reaper, but she was staring down at her desk and probably heard us talking about her. She hadn't opened her notebook yet, barely gripping onto her pen in her hand.

The teacher arrived in front of her desk and waited for her to hand in the assignment. "Where is your assignment?"

Reaper didn't answer.

The teacher leaned down and spoke in a low voice. "Look, I know your weekend was probably difficult, so I'll give you to the end of the week to hand it in. How does that sound?"

"I don't need your pity or favours," Reaper mumbled.

The teacher stiffened, slowly standing upright. "Go see the counsellor."

"I'm fine."

"It's not a suggestion, Miss Vicary—"

"It's just Celestine," she snapped.

"Datura Celestine Vicary." The teacher's voice was sharp. "Either you go to the counsellor or you're getting detention for your behaviour, which one would you prefer?"

The temperature in the room dropped as Reaper lifted her eyes to finally meet the teacher, daring her to do something. After a long, tense moment, the teacher pulled out the pink slips from her pocket, wrote on it and placed it on Reaper's desk.

About half an hour later, the counsellor came into the room. He smiled at the teacher, apologising for the interruption, who gave him a nod and continued her explanation on the history of food scarcity in Soulesity. The counsellor walked to the back of the classroom, nodding and smiling at some of the students, urging them to not mind him. He stopped next to Reaper's desk and put a hand on her shoulder, giving it a squeeze.

Crouching down to her level, he whispered, "I heard you're going through a bit of a rough patch."

Reaper didn't answer nor look at him.

"Those interviews must have been really hard to watch," he said. "Come, Celestine, we can have a cup of tea together."

Reaper released a breath, knowing there was no getting rid of the counsellor, and stood up with him. He took her things for her and rested his hand on her back, guiding her out of the classroom.

Throughout the rest of the week, hardly anyone saw Reaper except in class, but apparently she had skipped most of them.

***

By Friday we thought all the interviews about the situation had finished and the talks had died down until the Soulesity news channel decided to chime in.

"Good afternoon. I'm sure we've all seen the recent interviews regarding the Vicary family and the scandal surrounding it. Today we have an exclusive interview with someone who worked for the Vicary's at their manor."

The screen split to reveal the silhouette of a woman. "Good afternoon." Her voice was modified to something robotic.

"Do you mind telling us why you chose not to reveal your identity to the public?" the broadcaster asked.

"The Vicary family is one of the most powerful families in Soulesity. I'm risking my life being here today talking about this."

"Do you really believe you'll receive negative consequences for this interview?"

"Everyone who works for the Vicary family signs an NDA."

The broadcaster nodded. "Why don't you begin by explaining what you did at the Vicary manor."

"I was just one of the many housekeepers in the manor. It's a rather large place, you see, so there were a lot of us."

"So, you've seen many things, then?"

"Yes. I worked there for twenty years, and I watched both Vasos and Datura grow up. I feel that it is my duty to be the one to remind everyone that Datura was just a little girl, a child, when all of this happened. She is a victim."

"How was she when she was younger?"

"I hardly saw her as a child. As we know, she is not Ren Vicary's child but another man's. Delilah tried to keep her distance from Datura, hiring countless nannies to take care of her."

"Why so many?"

"Delilah is a narcissistic mother and when the nannies would get a little too close to Datura, Delilah would get jealous and fire them."

"Did she do that with Marigold and Vasos?"

The woman shook her head. "She was a present mother for Vasos and Marigold. Once, I had to go into Datura's room to clean it because the one who usually did was sick that day. Datura woke up when I came in, even though it was well into the afternoon." She took a moment to pause. "She jumped out of her bed and grabbed one of her picture books off the shelf, urging me to read it to her." The woman's shadow crossed her arms in front of her chest, rubbing at her upper arms in a way to comfort herself. "I sat down on the floor with her and while I read, she snuggled up against me. When I finished, I knew I had been in there too long and I was worried that someone would get suspicious, so I told Datura that I had to leave and her face–I'll never forget her face–It was like I was betraying her."

"Was she alone often?"

"Her door was constantly locked; they wouldn't allow her to leave her room. I heard from others that she had tried to escape multiple times, but the furthest she got was a couple steps into the hallway."

"Do you think this sort of solitude contributed to why she decided to run away?"

The woman sniffed, as if she were crying. "I was there the night she left." Her voice cracked. "She was having an argument with Vasos, because Vasos was worried Octavius was taking advantage of her."

"Do you believe he was?"

"Oh." The woman let out a short, cold laugh. "That boy was much older than her. I believe we can all draw our own conclusions from that." The woman shook her head. "No. Datura didn't leave because of Octavius, she left because the Vicarys forced her to. In the middle of the argument, Datura broke Vasos's arm. Now, it was an accident, you see, but they'd been waiting for an excuse to kick her out."

"How can you be so sure they wanted her to leave?"

"I've overheard Ren and Delilah arguing many times about Datura. Her existence was a reminder to Ren that there was a time Delilah didn't love him and that put a strain on their relationship and the Vicary reputation. But it wasn't Datura's fault, you see, she's just the product of a mistake Delilah made." The woman took a deep breath. "I once heard Eugene tell Ren to get rid of Datura by any means necessary, and Eugene often referred to her as a bastard."

"You are one of the few people who believe that all of this has been a plot against Datura. Do you know why they hated her so much, to the point where they wanted to get rid of her?"

"It's obvious isn't it? They needed to save face and blaming her for running away sounded better than her getting kicked out. Why do you think they were so convinced Octavius killed her? Why they spent so much money on sentencing Octavius and putting him somewhere he couldn't talk? Why Vasos left the city days before he was meant to stand trial? Then there's Marigold. They used her as someone to distract from their previous daughter, because if you look up 'Vicary's daughter,' the only thing that pops up now is Marigold, not Datura. They wanted to erase her. Don't you find it convenient that just a month after Datura was reported missing, Delilah fell pregnant? How convenient it was that Marigold was born in the beginning of the trial against Octavius?" She took a moment to breathe before continuing. "Marigold was a distraction from the negative focus on the Vicary name, you see. It obviously worked. What heartless person wouldn't melt at the sight of Marigold's big eyes and innocent laugh. The media nicknamed her Soulesity's sweetheart, but who really thinks that—"

9

SLUSHIES AND APOLOGIES

SEPTEMBER 70 A.D.

I made my way to the bathroom to wash blood off my hands–someone had pissed me off on the train to school that morning–when Reaper came out of the girl's bathroom and paused in front of me. It had been a week since the Vicary's statements came out and to my dismay, it looked like Reaper wouldn't be going back. She glanced down at my hands, then back up at me. "Are you alright?"

"I could ask you the same question."

Her eyes lowered as she laughed.

Before she could get past me, I asked her. "Are you?"

She avoided my eyes and whispered, "always."

I took her hand and pulled her into the restroom, forcing her to face the mirror. "How do you see yourself?"

She met my eyes through the mirror. "Why are you doing this?"

"I'm curious to know what's going on in your mind." *I want to know you.*

Her eyes shifted down to meet her own, but she quickly looked away. "I think you may have mistaken me for someone else," she muttered. "I'm just wasting your time."

"Okay, then, waste it," I said. "Tell me something no one else knows about you."

She hesitated before she finally answered. "I—um, I really like slushies, I guess."

"Why?"

"I like that it's cold."

"Not the taste?"

"I don't quite care for taste."

Turning on the tap, I washed my hands. "Does no one know that about you?"

"I mean, some people know."

"I said something no one knows." I applied more soap.

She washed her hands as well, as when I touched her, I smeared the blood onto her. "There's really nothing to know about me."

"Honestly, anything."

She let out a small breath, drying her hands with some paper towels. "Why don't you tell me something that no one else knows about you first?"

"Okay." I thought a bit. "I get detention every day because when I leave school I'm reminded of what I do and what I've done." Deep, but I want her to tell me something more personal.

"You don't like what you do?"

"I do, but I want to feel normal sometimes." I dried my hands. "Your turn."

She looked at the stalls, but they were all empty. I checked when we went inside. "I have a really bad memory."

"Yeah?"

"Sometimes I find myself in a different place and time has passed."

"Is that scary?"

She shook her head. "It usually happens when something bad is happening." Then she met my eyes with genuine curiosity. "So maybe it's a good thing?"

"Your mind is protecting you?"

"Yeah." She nodded. "I guess it is."

What is so bad her mind has to protect her from it? I'm not sure she would tell me if I asked.

"Did you watch the interviews?"

Reaper let out another breath, expectant of my question.

"How are you feeling about it?"

"Doesn't matter how I feel. They said what they said." She didn't look at me as she spoke, not wanting to discuss it further, especially not with me. Reaper looked to the door. "I should probably go to class."

I nodded. "Yeah, same." And we walked out together. "Thanks for taking care of me while I was drunk."

She laughed at the memory.

"I'm surprised you didn't draw on me."

"No one had a marker." She gave me a teasing smile. "But I think you embarrassed yourself enough with all your rambling."

Oh, no. "What did I say?" I don't think I want to know.

"We were sitting on the sofa." She started in a low voice, taking my hand. "You put your hand here." She adjusted it so it was around her neck, her back pressed into my chest, reenacting the memory. "And you muttered into my ear, 'louder. I want everyone to hear you. I want them to know you're mine.'"

"I didn't..." I paused. I had absolutely no explanation for my words, nor could I come up with an excuse.

She removed my hand and stepped away to face me. "It wasn't meant for me, was it?"

"No," I lied. "I was thinking about someone else."

Yeah? Who bloody else, Hyacinth? Idiot...

Reaper nodded, avoiding my eyes again.

"And what we did," I started. "We shouldn't have done that. We were both intoxicated."

"It meant nothing," she said. "I know."

Before she left, I had to know. "Did you follow me home?"

"Of course I did. You could barely open your eyes." She paused, smirking. "But don't worry. I won't tell anyone where the great Vulture lives."

***

During lunch, I left school grounds for the nearest convenience store. It was our longer break, so I had a bit of time. I bought a slushie and walked back, joining my classmates in history, finding Reaper already sitting at her desk, her head down in her arms.

I set the slushie down next to her water and she opened her eyes to look at it. My hands rested on the table on either side of her, and I leaned down close to her ear. Our classmates turned to stare, but I ignored them.

"I'm sorry for the things I said before. I actually kind of like talking to you," I whispered for only her to hear. "You're interesting."

She's not boring, she's just closed off. She spent four years hiding, of course she's forgotten how to have normal conversations with people her own age.

"Did you poison this?" she asked in a tired voice.

I took a sip to prove it. "No." Poison was a boring way to kill people, and she deserved a more memorable and exciting death.

Reaper turned the cup in her hands, sitting up, and I followed her movements. "What do you want from me?"

"Nothing," I replied, moving her hair to one side of her shoulder, revealing her slender neck, her red inked tattoo behind her ear, and I was tempted to bite that very spot.

"Then why are you being so nice to me?"

"I'm not nice. I just don't want people touching my things." Especially if they don't appreciate and value her.

She shook her head. "I'm not yours."

I smirked, glancing at the silver chain I had just placed back around her neck after moving her hair. *She still hasn't realised it.* "I wrote my name on you once. Do I need to make it permanent?"

"You know I have a bad memory."

Bloody hell.

I couldn't stop myself from biting her neck, exactly where her tattoo was. She sucked in a breath, quickly putting her hand over her eyes, and I felt the glares of those witnessing it.

I wondered if she knew what this meant. How intimate biting another's neck was in Stygian culture. Among Demons, it was a way of claiming a significant other–not that, that was what I was meaning by this–they drew blood to secure the bond.

"Hyacinth," she sighed, and my heart stopped.

My smile grew as I muttered into her neck. "You drive me bloody insane, Celestine." I pulled away, acknowledging the small mark I left on her soft skin.

I finally won.

Before I could get far, she grabbed the sleeve of my shirt, stopping me. Her eyes stared at the floor, but I noticed a soft red glow in them. "You said my name."

Did I? Shit. Now she'll be more difficult to kill if I ever decide to. Niko used to say it was best I didn't know the names of the people I killed, otherwise it would give them a history and life that I decided to end. "What of it?"

She smiled and released me.

I stood upright and was faced with the teacher, who stood ready to give me a detention slip. I'm pretty sure the teachers already had my name pre-written on them. I took the slip and took my seat next to Iri's while our classmates murmured, whispering about us.

"What was that?" Iri asked.

I shrugged.

"You're getting a bit bold, Cinth," Lin teased.

Jamiel turned in his seat. "Did she taste good?"

Yeah, she bloody did. "Shut up," I muttered. "I just said some mean things to her yesterday."

"You felt guilty?" Jamiel raised a brow. "You? Hyacinth Kolden? No way."

I rolled my eyes and cursed at him. I didn't feel guilty, that's not something I'm able to feel, but I didn't want her feeling bad over stupid things I said to her.

My friends exchanged looks with each other, and I glanced over at Reaper, her eyes were turned down, but she finally took the first sip of the slushie.

***

As I walked up the stairs, my friends behind me, I spotted Reaper at the top walking towards us. She hadn't noticed me yet, occupied with whatever conversation she was having.

Then her eyes met mine, and I gave her a smirk.

Her mouth parted as if to say something, but then she missed a step, her friends screaming on her behalf. I was quick to grab her before her body could impact with the steps. I don't know why I caught her, usually I would have just watched and laughed.

I had one arm around her waist, while her hand gripped onto my other hand. She breathed a curse in my ear, sending a shiver down my spine. *I want to make her say that again.* Exactly how she said it.

"Smooth." Iri laughed.

"How the bloody hell did you get up there so fast?" Lin asked from below.

I ignored them, muttering in a low voice. "Reaper is surprisingly clumsy."

"You distracted me," she admitted in the same volume, holding onto my hand for dear life as she found her footing. Her friends helped her pick up the things she had dropped.

"You need to concentrate walking down the stairs?" I mocked.

She shot me a glare.

"Are you okay, Cel?" one of them asked, handing her books back to her.

Reaper was quick to change her expression back to neutral and nodded at her friend with a slight smile. She took her things, holding onto my hand, and I waited until she felt ready to let go of me. I should have just taken it back, but I didn't.

Another one of her friends piped up. "We should get to class."

"Yeah, we don't want to be late again," another said.

Celestine locked eyes with me, waiting for something, but I wasn't sure what. Then her gaze shifted down to our hands, tangling them together, as if testing something. My heart raced against my chest, but before I could pull back, she released me, leaving with her friends.

"You're bloody welcome," I called after her.

"I didn't ask you to save me. I don't owe you anything." She flipped me off.

I smirked.

"Sheesh," Jamiel said. "It's like watching a movie."

My friends laughed, and I rolled my eyes. "Shut up." Then we headed up to our last class of the day.

The teacher left the room to do something, I wasn't paying attention, and the room broke into chatter. I had taken out my butterfly knife and was absently carving the edge of the wood on the desk. The girl sitting in front of me turned around in her seat to face me, eyes widening at the knife in my hands. "Hey, uh, Cinth."

"Don't call me Cinth." I squinted at her.

"Sorry," she squeaked. "Hyacinth. Do you know if Cel is–"

"Why would I know a thing about Celestine?" I turned my focus back to the desk, peeling the wood.

"Aren't you two close? I see her talk more to you than her own friends–"

"No," I muttered. "We're not close." We hardly talk, I don't know what she's saying.

"Hyacinth," another guy in the class called my name from across the room. Why does everyone think they can talk to me? "Is it true you and Cel are secretly dating?"

"Bloody hell," I cursed under my breath. "No."

"What a lie!" Someone else laughed.

"He wants her, obviously," another piped up, sparking more conversation. Possessive is a better word for what I felt. She doesn't mean anything to me.

"He doesn't even like her. He messes with her all the time." The classmate in front of me turned back to me. "Right?"

"Stop talking to me," I said in a low voice, my lungs burning. I deepened the knife into the desk, taking a large chunk of it out. I really have a low tolerance when it comes to Reaper.

"She doesn't like you back. Is that why you two aren't dating?"

Gods. "Celestine and I hate each other. That's why we're not together." Why did I have to explain myself? "Now stop asking me about her. You're pissing me off."

Though they ignored me. "Didn't you see them kiss at that party?"

"Bet they already did it."

"Was she good, Hyacinth?"

"Guys, stop," Lin intervened.

"Shut up," Jamiel snapped at them.

When I was a kid, before Niko found me, I moved between multiple foster homes and youth houses. I never understood why there are so many selfish people who have children, only to abandon them or why people who despise children become foster parents. Every one of us who had been in there either became like me, where the very thought of ever being intimate with someone made them want to throw up, or came to crave the feeling, wanting to erase the memory or hoping to recreate the scenario but this time with control.

But then when I think of doing any of it with Reaper... It just gives me heart attacks.

I handed my knife to Iri, sitting closest to me, before I stabbed someone. My friends were trying to quiet everyone, but they were drowned out.

Was the fear they had for me really less than their curiosity of Reaper?

I'm not sure if I still wanted to kill her, but I might if this is what it's like to be around her. Before it got to the point of me jumping out the window, the teacher came back, quieting the room and I'd never been more relieved to see a teacher in my life.

***

Niko was on the sofa with Renee, their tongues shoved down each other's throats when I walked in the door. "Bloody hell," I muttered. "Can't you do that in your room at least?" I kicked off my shoes, setting them to the side.

Renee pushed Niko away, flustered. "Oh, hi, Cinth."

"Hi, Renee." I gave her a polite bow.

"Do you want your assignment before or after dinner?" Niko asked.

I'd like to get out of the house, so I don't have to listen to them going at each other. "I'll do it now."

He pulled out his phone and texted me the details. I nodded, going into my room to set my bag down and change, then looked at the message Niko sent me. *How fun.*

Avoiding looking in the direction of the sofa, I made my way out, trying to slip on my shoes as quickly as I could. They really didn't care that I was there.

I took the train to the edge of West Soulesity and walked the rest of the way to the warehouse. This area was quite comical. Most clans had their own warehouse for their lower-ranking clansmen or for storing or producing whatever it is they do. All right next door or across from each other. Walk into the wrong door and you'll face consequences of trespassing on another's territory which could lead to a clan war.

This assignment had me slaughtering the leader of a small gang. Calling them a clan would mean they were influential, but they were currently only a small group. So, I'm not sure exactly why I was here, most likely it was due to their potential and threat of shifting power dynamics. But I trusted Niko's choice in assignments, he would never accept them if it wouldn't let us sleep peacefully at night.

Wanting to have a bit of fun with it, I walked straight in, turning the heads of at least thirty people. Some wearing red hats, among them were Leo, Sterling, and Reaper.

Reaper sat on top of a box, her legs crossed over her, meeting my eyes with amusement. Right under her stood Sterling and Leo, their arms folded across their chest.

Wait, what? Why is the Kokkino clan here? If there's one rule Niko stressed to me ever since Ender's death, it was to avoid the Stygian clans. He'd never accept jobs that involved them anymore, even though theirs were always much more fun.

"You're the one sent to kill him?" Leo cursed under his breath.

My phone vibrated in my pocket, and I pulled it out and answered.

"Your assignment is compromised," Niko warned.

"Amazing timing as always, Niko," I muttered. "Kokkino clan's here."

"Why are they there?"

I pulled the phone down and nodded to the twins. "What are you guys doing here?"

"They paid us for protection," Leo replied, extending his staff, ready for me.

"Hear that?" I asked Niko.

"Can you get out of there without a fight?"

I glanced at the door, a couple Kokkino clansmen now blocking it. "Unlikely."

"Don't kill them," he warned.

"Obviously." I hung up the phone, slipping it back into my pocket.

"Who sent you?" Sterling asked.

I shrugged. "No idea." I never cared to ask, nor was I a snitch. "But I'm leaving now." I headed towards the door, but they didn't move. "You're in my way."

They looked towards the twins for instructions.

I let out a deep breath, annoyed, turning to face the twins. "Why don't you save their energy and let me go?"

Sterling smiled. "I've always wanted to see the untouchable Vulture fight."

Leo chuckled, twirling his staff. "Same."

"If he wants to leave, we should just let him," Reaper said.

Sterling's head snapped up to her. "Since when have we ever done that?"

How troublesome. Kokkino really enjoyed pointless killings. My eyes scanned for an alternative exit. There was a window at the far end that I could reach with those crates stacked conveniently below it. I pulled out my container, popped a pill in my mouth, then shoved it back in my pocket.

I slowly walked towards the twins, trying to get as close to the escape route without alerting them. "Let me leave," I said, stopping just in front of them. "I don't want any trouble with you."

"You don't want to fight us?" Sterling mocked. "Are you scared, Vulture?"

"I'd rather not have to finish what the Angels started."

Reaper looked the most offended out of everyone, narrowing her eyes at me. She hopped off the box and got up close to me. "That's a little racist, don't you think?"

I rolled my eyes. "I couldn't care less what you are, but if you Stygians come after me, I won't make the mistake of leaving any survivors."

She grabbed the collar of my hoodie, pulling me down to her level. "You Stygians?"

I pried her fingers off me. "You're so bloody sensitive."

She cursed at me and threw a punch, but I grabbed it before it could contact me.

"Are you sure you want to continue that?" I asked.

"I want you to apologise," she spat, snatching her hand back and shoving me, but I barely budged.

I shook my head. "They're just words. I hate everyone equally." Although I hated the way she was looking at me more, it wasn't amused or playful like usual. She was genuinely insulted and angry. I took a deep breath. "I'm sorry, Reaper." I'm only apologising to her, no one else.

She blinked, as if not expecting that I was ever going to apologise for my words, but they were insensitive, I'll admit. Reaper took a step back and nodded.

"Cel, why aren't you fighting him?" Sterling asked.

She turned to him. "He apologised."

Sterling took out his daggers. "Who cares?"

I stepped to the side to avoid Sterling's slash and caught Leo's staff, shoving him to the side. Then bolted for the boxes, the others hesitating to approach me.

"What are you guys doing?" Sterling shouted. "Get him!"

They came at me from the side, but I blocked their strikes, pushing them away from me. I couldn't hurt them, no matter how much they asked for it. Just before I reached the crates, someone tackled me and I quickly rolled us over, swiftly striking their temple and knocking them out before beginning my climb up the crates.

Reaper was waiting for me on the very top of it, a playful smile on her face. *Is she going to kick me down to the wolves?* She opened the window for me and stepped to the side. Surprising everyone, including myself.

"I didn't need your help," I sneered.

"I know." She smiled.

"Cel!" Sterling barked, but she ignored his anger. No one dared to climb where Reaper and Vulture stood.

"Do you have no loyalty?" I asked her, stepping closer to the window. *Nothing below, perfect.*

"No one's quite earned mine." *Interesting.* Even I have some loyalty to Niko, Renee, and my friends. "But I am yours now, aren't I?"

I turned to look at her and gently patted her head. "Don't put yourself in danger for me again, yeah?"

She closed her eyes at my touch and nodded.

"Good girl." Pulling away from her, I slipped out through the window, landing in the grass below. I sprinted to the station, not looking back to see if they were following me. They weren't, they wouldn't.

Niko and Renee were cooking in the kitchen when I made it home, looking extremely worried. "What happened?" he asked.

"It was fine." I mumbled.

"They wouldn't let you leave?"

I shook my head. "No, but Reaper helped me escape."

He gave me a weird look. "Why would she do that?"

I shrugged.

10

SMALL WORLD

OCTOBER 70 A.D.

"**Y**ou seem distracted, Cinth." Niko commented, his bow aimed at our target.

"I'm not," I lied.

My classmates were becoming less afraid of me, coming up to ask me questions about Reaper as if I would know. *Irritating*. The reputation that took me years to build was crumbling because of her.

He released his arrow, finishing our job. "I've known you since you were just a boy, I know when something's bothering you." He quickly packed up his things, and we bolted from the area.

"I can handle it."

We stopped running when we got down to a crowd of people, blending into it.

"Come on." He nodded towards a nice restaurant; the streetlight caught his eyes, turning them amber. "Let's eat here."

I followed him in and we ordered. "Now, tell me, what's going on?"

Reaper and I had been messing with each other for three months now, and it was clearly affecting me enough for Niko to notice. I sighed. "It's this girl from school."

"Huh." He was surprised. "Thought you were immune to these things."

"It's not like that. She's so weird. She messes with my head. It's like..." I didn't know how to explain it. "One moment, she's mocking me and the next she's licking my neck."

He raised a brow and repeated my words slowly. "Licking your neck?"

I waved my hand in the air, a bit embarrassed I just told him that. "She's just trying to get a reaction out of me and she's actually managing."

"Sounds like she has a thing for you." He chuckled.

"No," I said sternly. "Definitely not. I don't know what it is about her, but she's making me lose control."

Niko squinted his eyes at me. "That's... Odd. I've never met anyone with more control over their mind and body than you." He scoffed. "You even have better control than I do."

"I want to kill her," I muttered. She's messing with my plans and if it extends outside of school, I don't know what I would do. I need to contain the situation. Quickly.

"Probably not a good idea to kill a classmate." Niko sipped his wine.

There was loud laughter at a nearby table, and I turned to look at who was causing a ruckus at such a restaurant. *How?*

I locked eyes with Reaper, and she gave me a smile, melting the world around us. The red-headed man next to her followed her gaze, spotting us, before making his way over to our table.

"Nikodemus," Silias greeted.

"Silias." Niko nodded.

Silias smiled at me. "It's been a long time, Vulture."

Not long enough.

After getting my name, he hated my guts more than he did before, but that was most people.

His face lit up. "You two should be eating with the Kokkino clan."

No, no, no. Absolutely not.

"Bring the tables together." Silias snapped his fingers and a few waitresses moved tables, sending a couple from their table to make room for us.

"That's very kind of you, Silias." Niko nodded at him as we took our new seats next to them. I don't know why Niko was being so nice to Silias. He's never failed to curse his name after he killed Ender.

I also want Silias dead, for my own reasons, but I'm not ready to face him yet. There were still things I needed to do before I could take control of the Underworld. I also knew people wouldn't take a teenager seriously, even if I was the Vulture.

"Allow me to introduce everyone," Silias began, more for my sake than Niko's. Silias gestured to an old man. "This is Oremus."

I already knew Oremus, from when I was a lot younger, I hadn't seen him since Silias took over. He still looked the same, just a little more wrinkles on him. He shot me a smile, recognising me even after all these years, and I nodded back at him.

Silias motioned towards a woman in braids, his second in command. "Rayne." Then the twins, his loyal stooges. "Leo, Sterling."

Rayne's gaze was analytical, and the twins were scowling, probably still pissed about the warehouse a few weeks ago.

Finally, Silias put a hand on Reaper's back. "And Celestine. Though, you may know her as the Grim Reaper." Silias stuck up his chin, proud of what he had created.

Niko's eyes widened at Reaper's youth, beauty, and street name. "Reaper?"

Reaper gave him a slight smile and nodded. I was indifferent but also cautious of Reaper being a bit too close to my bubble. Normally she taunted me as much as she could, but now, sitting so close to each other, she hadn't even looked at me.

"Demons below." Niko rushed to Reaper's side, kneeling before her. My eyes widened and brows furrowed. *What is happening?* He took her hand in his, a soft expression on his face. "I had no idea you were Reaper," Niko started with a laugh. "You probably don't remember me, Datura. The last time I saw you, you were this small." He measured just over a metre in height.

Excuse me, what?

"She goes by Celestine," Silias corrected him. "I'm surprised you still remember her after all this time."

"Of course, she's his daughter."

Whose daughter?

Then Niko nodded at me. "And the only person who could get this one to be nice back then, even if it was only to her." He turned back to Reaper, staring at her intently. "I'm sorry, Celestine, you just look so much like your father." He released her hand and went over to the other side of the table to sit across from me.

Silias shifted his gaze to me. "Do you remember her?"

Niko shook his head and responded for me. "I think they were both a bit too young to remember. They were only nine."

We met nearly a decade ago? How many times have our paths crossed? I've met thousands of people since I was nine and taken countless blows to the head, so my memory wasn't the best, but how could I forget those icy blue eyes of hers?

"They'd be sharing a chair if they did." Niko chuckled, and I saw Oremus laugh, but I didn't understand the joke.

Silias cut into his food. "She keeps his ring around her neck, refuses to take it off."

Reaper didn't respond to any of what was said, sipping on her water. I don't think I've ever seen her eat.

"This is the girl you gave your ring to?" Niko was surprised.

"Apparently," I muttered.

"You didn't claim her, did you, Vulture?" Silias asked me.

I locked eyes with Reaper, I claimed her before, even if I can't remember why, and I'm contemplating publicly claiming her again now. "What if I did?"

"Cinth." Niko warned, but in this case they pissed me off. Stealing what was once mine.

Silias laughed. "Then that would be a problem."

For him. "Yeah, it would be." *Try me, I dare you.*

He shook his head with a dark smile and asked again. "Is Celestine yours?"

Yes.

No.

Shit!

"He doesn't remember me, Silias," Celestine replied in a low voice, not looking up from her drink. "It was a long time ago, and he lost his memory."

"Right, of course," Silias said. The news of my coma and memory loss was an advantage to those who sought revenge on me. I was lucky to have Niko there to protect me in my vulnerable state.

I met Niko's eyes, melancholic and heartened.

"What?" I spat at him in a low voice only he could hear, pissed off that my memory was so bad I couldn't remember a thing about Reaper before meeting her months ago.

Niko slowly shook his head. "It's just so tragic." He matched my volume. "You two have always had such a strong bond, but for reasons we don't know, Moira keeps tearing you and Celestine apart."

I blinked at his words. Did we really used to be that close as kids? Then that meeting we had again four years ago... I wanted to protect her, so I gave her my ring. I turned to Reaper, but she was staring at her water. Eventually she turned up to meet my eyes. Then her eyes shifted to Rayne, watching the both of us, before quickly looking back down at her glass.

The table changed the topic and continued talking. I tuned everything out, trying to recall my memories, but I couldn't quite grasp them. It all just looked like a haze. A sharp pain in my head stirred, as if an attempt to even try to visualise it would get me killed. I gripped onto my head, closing my eyes, praying the pain would subside.

"You're right, Silias, Hyacinth should train Celestine."

I snapped my head up. "I should what?"

Niko shot me a disapproving look at my rudeness, but I've never been known for being polite. "We were just discussing that you and Celestine are very young but talented, and I'm sure you both have a lot of things to learn from each other."

Silias nodded. "Exactly, she's currently learning to be more independent and who better to teach her that than Vulture."

Everyone turned to me, waiting for my answer. *I couldn't look like an asshole.*

"No." *I mean, I could.*

I noticed the slight curve on Reaper's lips, hidden by her glass, but Silias's smile fell as he asked me. "Why not?"

"I don't like Reaper," I admitted, bluntly. As if I would train her to my level and be forced to spend more time with her. Seeing her at school was enough, and she was already ruining my reputation there. I couldn't imagine what the streets would begin to whisper about me if I started training her.

Silias shot his head to look at Reaper. "What exactly is your relationship with Vulture?"

"He attempted to kill her a couple months ago, remember?" Leo reminded him.

"We actually don't get along," she said. "We're a bit competitive at school."

"Competitive," I repeated in a mutter, rolling my eyes.

"Oh, sorry," she taunted. "I guess it's not really competing when it's with you."

What is she doing? I laughed. "Yeah, you know what? You're right, it's just you who literally gives me no room to breathe with all your bullsh–"

"Um, excuse me." She leaned forward in her seat, a sudden spark of enjoyment in her eyes and a small smile. "You dumped a frog on me."

"That's because you started it."

She laughed. "No, I did not start anything."

"Yes, yes, you did," I retorted. "I think I would remember you threatening me."

"You threatened me first."

"You know what you are?" I smiled. "A piece of hair stuck to my tongue that I can't get bloody rid of."

"And you know what you are? A little cockroach. No matter what, you keep crawling back to me for more."

"Little? Have you seen the size of you?"

Leo burst into laughter and had to excuse himself from the table, but I barely noticed it. I was too focused on her and she was too.

She gasped. "I'm still growing and one day I'll be taller than you."

"Fat chance," I mocked. "You know what makes a good comeback?"

"What?"

"Something realistic."

"God below." She shook her head. "I swear, Cinth–"

"Don't call me Cinth."

She spat a curse at me.

I squinted at her, licking my front teeth. "Say that again." When she didn't, I grabbed the knife on the table, gripping onto it. "Say that to my face again, Reaper."

Niko was quick to snatch the knife out of my hand. "Alright, I think it may be time we go."

Silias glared at Reaper. "I didn't raise you to have such a foul mouth." His sudden change of attitude was unnerving as he turned back to Niko and me with a large, charming smile. "I am so sorry that Celestine has been such a troublemaker to Hyacinth. I promise I will have her punished accordingly."

I was the only one who saw Reaper roll her eyes, the others shifted uncomfortably. *This whole thing… did she plan for us to bicker in front of all of them? Why?*

"There's really no need," Niko reassured. "I'm sure it was actually Hyacinth who pissed her off to start with." He gave me a warning look. "He can really get under people's skin."

Did he just not see that Reaper started it?

"No, if Celestine's behaviour isn't fixed, where will it end? She should not be starting or continuing fights, of course unless I tell her to." He erupted into laughter and the table joined him, but it almost felt forced.

Niko immediately stood up with trembling hands. I've only ever seen him scared of one person before, but Ender's dead. "Hyacinth will train Celestine." He looked at his watch. "But I'm afraid we must leave, we have some things to take care of." I didn't even care that I didn't finish my food, wanting to get out of here as soon as possible.

Silias put his hand up. "Of course, Nikodemus, and don't worry, I got the bill."

Niko smiled and bowed. *He doesn't bow to anyone.* "Thank you, Silias. We'll talk soon."

I followed Niko out of the restaurant.

"Don't speak yet," he told me as we passed a few men in red hats standing around and outside the restaurant.

When we walked a safe distance away he looked at me.

"Cinth," he began, sharply. "You know Silias as the leader of the Kokkino clan, the most powerful clan in this city."

I waited for him to continue.

"There's a reason I never wanted you to see Silias anymore or allowed you to take jobs from him. You know why he's the most feared person in the city?"

"Because he's rich and has a lot of people under him," I guessed in a bored manner.

"Because he has no limits."

"I know," I muttered. It's one of the reasons why I never could find any respect for him.

"Then can you imagine what he's doing to Celestine?"

I didn't really want to think about it. She was a bit off, but I didn't realise it was because of Silias. Though it seemed like she wanted to start a fight with me in front of him and get in trouble for it. *Why would she want that?*

"You need to be careful around Silias. If there is one person you should fear, it is him." Niko sighed. "Do you understand?"

I nodded.

"He betrayed his entire clan and killed Ender, Cinth." His eyes lowered, still grieving over it after all these years. "Ender."

I didn't respond.

Rumour said guilt of being one of the last four Demons to survive the Reckoning consumed Ender and he broke into a rage of madness, killing the majority of his inner circle and the staff that resided in the estate. Silias and Oremus were forced to kill him, or he'd have continued his rampage on the entire city.

I've heard all the theories and Niko was convinced Silias purposefully murdered Ender for power. In the years I had known Silias, we only trained. I never took the time to actually get to know him, so I couldn't make a proper judgement of him. I knew Ender quite well, and I knew he didn't go insane. He couldn't have. Ender was one of the few people who was able to earn my respect, the one I looked up to. One of the only people in the world I had genuinely feared at times.

Demons have incredible strength, especially adults, able to shift into their true form. So, I have no idea how Oremus and Silias were able to kill Ender.

"So, Celestine's the girl you were talking about earlier, isn't it?"

I nodded.

"Next time you see her at school, please be nicer to her, not out of pity, but because I know you are a good person." I don't know why he believes that, I know what I am and I'm not ashamed of it.

I let out a deep breath.

"Cinth."

"Fine," I finally said, not wanting to argue any more.

We began walking again, Niko breaking the silence. "Do you know who her parents are?"

"Why does that matter?" I muttered.

"Answer the question, Cinth," he snapped.

I groaned. "She's a Vicary."

Daughter of Delilah Vicary, one of the most famous and iconic supermodels to walk this city, who easily married into wealth because of her looks. She received a lot of scrutiny from her affair and was forced to retire, still barely able to leave her home without getting spat at. Infidelity was not uncommon in Soulesity, but when you're the city's beloved and most watched couple, it hurts the people too.

"And her father?"

Celestine looked nothing like Ren Vicary. People would have asked questions and speculated, regardless if they had come clean or not.

I shrugged, shoving my hands in my pockets. "How should I know?" I rubbed my fingers against my lighter, needing a bloody smoke, but Reaper kept pick-pocketing my cigarettes and throwing them away.

"I thought you were perceptive." We finally found Niko's car, and he unlocked it.

"What are you on about?" I asked, when we climbed inside.

He shook his head. "Gods, why did you have to lose your memory?"

I licked the front of my teeth. "I didn't ask for it."

He started the car and our journey home, releasing a breath. "I know, Cinth." His voice soft now.

PART 2
RULES, RISKS AND PUNISHMENTS

II

TOO STYGIAN TO TRAIN

October 70 A.D.

"Don't be stupid in there," Niko warned me before getting out of the car.

The twins opened the door and escorted us to the living room.

The Kokkino Estate had three stories, if you count the basement. The top floor was where all the many bedrooms were. The ground floor held the living rooms, dining, kitchen, and a ballroom, and the basement had a training facility, medical room, freezer, and soundproof rooms for 'interrogations.'

We found Reaper sitting with her feet on the sofa, knees bent, leaning her back on Silias's shoulder, sharpening one of her knives in her assignment outfit. The only light came from the fireplace, bringing a soft, warm glow into the room.

This isn't the first time I've been inside. When Ender led, we were often invited to dinners and gatherings. I even trained with them and had my own room at one point.

It's different now.

But it wasn't just the Kokkino clan that changed. After Ender's death, the whole Underworld had and not for the better.

Now we were all waiting for the next move.

Reaper's eyes shifted to mine. Despite the smile on her face from just laughing at whatever Silias had said before we came in, her eyes were completely empty. Sterling and Leo took seats on either side of them, Rayne stood behind the sofa, and Oremus was in the seat on the side. The sound of a blade running across the stone was satisfying. One of my favourite sounds.

"So, you finally agreed to train Reaper," Silias started, gesturing for us to take the seats across from him.

Why else would we be here?

Reaper shifted her gaze back to her knife, continuing to sharpen it.

"Yes, Vulture can start training her tonight," Niko said

"And how will these training sessions go?" Silias asked.

I actually didn't have a plan, I was just going to play it by ear. But I needed to think of something quick. "I'm taking her on assignments with me."

"How many times a week?"

"Every day," Niko answered for me. "There's a lot she needs to learn."

Every day? I refused to spend that much time with her, though I couldn't say anything.

Silias nodded in agreement, then turned to Reaper. "You won't give Vulture a hard time, will you?"

"Maybe," she said in a low voice.

Dog.

He chuckled. "That's right," he said. "You only listen to me."

She nodded, boredly analysing the blade.

"They can do her assignments as well," Niko said.

Silias looked at us, squinting.

"Oremus will work out the finances," Rayne said.

Niko shook his head. "No, you keep the profits from the assignments."

Silias smiled, relaxing. He liked money. "Then what benefits you to train her?"

"Her father would have wanted it," Niko said, and though his voice held steady, there was a hint of spite. Reaper turned locking eyes with Niko, no emotion on her face, before continuing her motions against the rock.

Silias took a deep breath. "It's a sensitive topic for her, so don't speak of it."

Niko nodded.

"And if anything happens to Cel, I'll have you both killed."

I must have heard that wrong. Did he just threaten me?

"She'll be back alive, but we can't promise she won't be injured," Niko replied, before I could say anything.

"You can be as rough as you want with her, as long as she's functional," Silias warned.

Niko looked at me. "Cinth will take care of her."

Gross.

Silias met my eyes. "Will you, Vulture? You won't try to kill her again?"

I took my time to answer, and it took a lot for me to get the word out. "Sure."

"Good." Silias tilted his chin up. "You don't secretly like Celestine, do you?"

Not this again.

Reaper paused mid-stroke. "Why would you ask him that?"

"I'm simply shocked, Cel," he said. "It's rare to meet someone who doesn't." Silias turned back to me. "So?"

"I would rather cut my fingers off than be around her." I caught the slight curve at the edge of Reaper's lips, but Niko glared at me and I rolled my eyes, muttering, "but I won't harm her."

"That wasn't the question."

Was I not clear? "No, Silias, I don't like Reaper."

He nodded. "Keep it that way."

Stop telling me what to do.

Silias snapped his head towards Reaper, but before any words came out of his mouth, she said, "I already told you, no."

"Does he know that?"

She lifted her eyes, completely annoyed, then shifted her gaze towards me. Out of absolutely nowhere, that little snapping turtle flung her knife at me.

Niko cursed.

I grabbed the knife right before it punctured me. "Are you actually bloody asking for it?"

"Now he does," she said.

Niko quickly grabbed the knife out of my hand before I did anything everyone would regret.

I looked at Niko, exchanging silent glances with him. *The absolute audacity.* I wanted to leave, I really did not want to train her now, but Niko urged me to stay.

"Your reflexes are insane." Leo sighed in awe.

They all seemed to be laughing at what had just happened, as if Reaper almost didn't just try to kill me. I looked at her, but she was turned away from me.

I blinked slowly, licking the front of my teeth. I really didn't understand what she was doing. Replaying the moment in my head, I watched her give me a warning, aiming towards my hand, knowing I would catch it more easily. She also looked relieved when I actually stopped it.

Silias put an arm around her. "Good."

Good?

And she had the nerve to smile up at him.

Silias handed her a small black note. "You can go now."

She gave the stone to Leo and waited for Niko and I at the arch.

I stood up with Niko, but I didn't bother with goodbyes as I brushed past Reaper to get to the door.

Reaper hurriedly put her shoes on and caught up to me to slip the small black paper with an address and a name written in red ink into my hands. Niko took it from me and drove us there. I couldn't even look at her.

"Um," she broke the silence with whispers. "I'm sorry I threw my knife at you."

I glanced at her reflection through the rearview mirror. I couldn't tell if she was crying or if it was just the light.

"Could I have my knife back, please?"

Niko pulled it out of his pocket and handed it to her. She thanked him, but I didn't reply to her apology. "It's okay, Celestine, I know Silias is scary," Niko said.

"I'm not scared."

I jumped at how sharp her voice was. That was probably the least convincing sentence I've ever heard coming out of her mouth. One thing Reaper was known for was being a liar.

"What is he doing to you?" Niko asked her, his voice angry, but it wasn't directed at her.

"Nothing," she mumbled. "He doesn't do anything to me."

Niko restrained his voice to a softer tone. "You can tell us, Celestine. We won't judge you for any of it."

"Silias wouldn't do anything to me," she snapped. "Stop talking about him like he's a bad person."

Niko and I exchanged looks, neither of us liked Silias. He had never done anything unless he had something to gain from it, the last thing anyone expected him to do was take in a child. *So, why did he take in Reaper?*

"If he's so great, then why did you throw that knife at me to convince him you don't like me?" I spat.

That shut her up and hopefully opened her eyes to the manipulative grip Silias had on her. We rode the rest of the way in complete silence.

Niko dropped us off near our location and we headed out.

Reaper's hair was up in a high ponytail, a strand wrapped around the hair tie, revealing her slender neck and the small, red Stygian tattoo behind her ear. I looked at her outfit, very feminine. A black long-sleeved, turtleneck, a red skirt, and black thigh high socks.

"Isn't a skirt impractical?"

She gave me a sideways glance, lifting the side of her skirt to reveal her black shorts underneath and her thigh straps, packed with six throwing knives and a pocket for whatever weapon it contained. "Easier access, easily hidden."

"I guess."

"And if I'm the last person someone sees before they die, I should look my best," she added with a laugh. Her make-up was a darker look compared to what she usually wore at school and the black made her icy eyes look piercing.

I let out a slight chuckle at her thought process. "How considerate of you."

"I know you don't actually want to train me," she sighed. "So I can go by myself and you can leave."

She can't go on assignments by herself.

Reaper played with her long hair, deciding to add. "As if you actually have anything new to teach me anyway."

"I have plenty to teach you."

She rolled her eyes, adjusting her hair.

Just a little closer, so I can strangle that pretty little neck of yours. "You've been in this field for, what, four years? I've been in it for nine. I think I'll surprise you with my wisdom."

"Oh, yeah, so wise," she said, sarcastically, folding her arms across her chest. "You don't even know the human body."

Just because I didn't know the names and functions on a frog... "I don't need to know the human body to know where to kill it."

Reaper walked to me and condescendingly leaned towards me. "Yeah? Well, did you know just a tiny slice here." She grazed her pointer finger across my neck. "Keeps them alive and silent?"

Who doesn't know that?

"Don't touch me." I growled.

She pulled her hand back with a gentle laugh. "You're a hypocrite."

"So are you," I snapped back. "Drinking and doing drugs, but not allowing me to do the same."

"I don't smoke cigarettes," she clarified. "They're bad for you."

I furrowed my brows. "So are alcohol and drugs."

"It's different."

I shook my head, letting out an annoyed breath. "My career will sooner kill me than the consequences of smoke in my lungs."

She turned away from me. "I can't stand the smell of it."

"And that's my problem?" I snapped. "Half the city smokes, yet I seem to be the only one you put a stop to."

Reaper rolled her eyes, beginning to walk away, towards where we needed to be. "Whatever," she said, "do what you want."

I muttered curses under my breath, contemplating taking her earlier offer to leave and let her do this on her own. We hadn't even started the assignment, and I was already vexed by her.

I scaled the building up to the roof, and she followed behind me. I didn't need to wait too long and continued walking on top of the roofs of the townhouses.

"You're in my way." I pushed her away from me and, because I didn't consider her size, she stumbled a bit too far off the edge of the roof. *Oh, shit.* I caught her hand, and she dangled there.

"Cute," she mocked. "You saved me."

"I'll drop you."

"Then, do it." Reaper challenged.

If I did, I would win, if I didn't, she would. She released her grip on my arm and waited for me to decide.

"You really want to die so bad?"

"Only if you do it," she teased. "Afraid to let go?"

I wondered if she'd make the five-story drop, but her hand was slipping, so I didn't have much time to think. I quickly pulled her back up. "You're an idiot."

She stepped back up to safety. "And you're a coward."

"Silias would kill me if anything happened to you."

"Scared?"

"Why would I be scared of a silly, old man?" I asked. I don't doubt any of the stories about him, but aside from his limitless brutality, he was only human.

The expression on her face softened. "You're right," she said, "he is just a silly, old man." She lifted her hand up to show me my rings she had somehow taken off me while I was saving her life. "Can I have these?" She slipped them over her fingers, but they were much too big for her.

"They don't even fit you." I snatched them out of her hands and put them back on, continuing our walk. She already had one of my rings, I wasn't about to give her another.

"Why do you wear rings?" she asked.

"Because I like them," I told her, annoyed.

"Why do you wear eyeliner?"

"Because I want to."

"Why do you wear nail polish?"

"Because I can."

"Do you always colour them black?"

"Yeah," I muttered.

"How come?"

I whirled to face her. "Will you shut up?" I snapped. "Why are you asking me all these questions?" Then I blinked and let out a breath. "Black is my favourite colour." *Though I am starting to like blue.*

She stayed quiet the rest of the walk.

We crouched on the roof, looking at the building opposite us. "Don't you need to put your glasses on so you can see our target?"

"I don't have much pigment in my eyes, so they're sensitive to light," she said, wrapping her bandana over her face. "I can see in the dark perfectly fine."

She stood up about to just go for it, but I quickly pulled her back down. "What are you doing?"

"I'm going to kill him," she said casually, as if she were saying she was just going to the bathroom.

"We're doing this together, so let's talk it through about what each of us are going to do."

She rolled her eyes and looked at me, tapping her fingers, impatiently.

"I'll shoot the power box, causing a black out on this block, then–"

"Okay, cool." She stood up again. "I'll meet you inside." She jumped down and scaled the building. *Stygians.* Can't work as a team, but I guess I'm not good at that either.

Taking out my bow, I shot an arrow at the power box causing sparks and the entire street to go dark. I quickly got to the other building and when I arrived inside, most were already dead. Messy, but I'd be lying if I said I wasn't impressed she did it so quickly.

I groaned. "We were only supposed to kill one person."

"No witnesses," she explained, slicing one of their necks and finishing them off by stabbing them in the eye. She didn't even blink as she did it.

I sucked in a breath. *Can she get any more attractive?*

I turned, scanning the corpses for our target, kicking one man to roll over onto his back so I could see his face. I snapped my head around the room, but our target wasn't in here at all. "Where is he?" I asked.

She shrugged, uncaring. "Who knows," she said, slaughtering the last person, ignoring his cries and pleas.

"What do you mean? You let him get away?" I growled in a low voice.

"Maybe if you came quicker, instead of wasting time with the power box, you could have blocked the exit."

I cursed. "Now he knows we're after him."

She walked towards the window looking out. "He's not far."

I ran towards it and saw a man sprinting down the streets, frantically looking at his surroundings, shoving people out of his way. She's made this simple job so much harder.

Jumping out the window, I landed two stories down without a sound, the people walking on the streets startled by my sudden appearance. I didn't bother to check if Reaper was following me as I raced after him.

The man was running on adrenaline so he wouldn't get too far and would tire out quickly, especially considering his heavier stature. Stupidly, he turned a corner to an alley, making it easier for me to finish him off without so many people watching. The man put a hand against the wall, leaning his weight into it as he struggled to run any further.

"As much as I love the chase, it's hard to watch you try," I said, taking out my butterfly knife, lips twitching at the thrill.

He whirled towards me, with wide eyes, trembling. "Please." He dropped to his knees. "Spare me." His hands clasped together.

"It's nothing personal, really, I'm just doing what I'm told." I let out a cackle that made him flinch. I took one more step towards him into a light and his eyes widened at the sight of my heterochromia ones.

"Vulture, Vulture." He pressed his nose to the dirty ground, pleading with me.

Reaper jumped down, right behind him. She grabbed the back of his hair and pulled him back, up off the ground. "And Reaper." Then she placed the blade of her knife against his neck. "You should consider it an honourable death to have both of us tasked to you."

I snarled at Reaper. "He's mine."

She smiled at me. "I know we're the bad guys but you're so slow with all your mono-loguing." Slowly, she dragged her knife against his neck, drawing a bit of blood, teasing me, waiting to see what I would do.

The man whimpered, shutting his eyes.

I tightened my grip around my knife. In a quick move, I shoved Reaper away from the man, stabbed him in the stomach and pulled the knife up to his throat, letting his corpse collapse to the ground. I then pushed Reaper against the wall, pressing my bloodied blade to her cheek. "You've pissed me off."

She licked the blood off my knife. "You say that a lot, but you never really do anything about it." She met my eyes. "Do you like me, Cinth?"

"Don't call me Cinth," I spat. "Why do you seem to only continue to piss me off?"

She didn't answer, she just gave me this blank stare.

We didn't have time for this, I could hear the sirens getting closer. Cursing, I released her.

"Get home on your bloody own," I muttered.

I shoved my hands in my pocket and left the scene before the police could come.

***

I entered the apartment and slammed the door shut.

"How did it go?" Niko asked from the kitchen.

"No," I said, not even looking at him.

"No?"

"No, it was awful, I never want to train her again." I didn't even train her, she just went ahead and killed everyone she could see... Or maybe she actually couldn't see and lied saying she didn't need her glasses but actually just forgot to bring them and didn't want to admit it.

"What did you do?"

"Why is it always me?" I asked, offendedly.

He laughed. "Because I know you and you are a pain in the ass."

He should properly meet Reaper.

I shot him a glare, only making him laugh more.

"Try harder."

"She doesn't respect me," I explained. "She treats me like the shit she just stepped on."

Niko looked up in thought. "Really?"

"What?"

"Why not try to talk to her, get to know her and let her get to know you." That's what Lin suggested before too. "Your next training could focus on meditation and control, you know what I'm talking about." He didn't need to say any more. I had experienced Niko's training.

"Can I use the dojo?"

Niko owned a quaint dojo near the forest. He allowed anyone to use it whenever they wanted, but at night, it was closed for only Niko and I.

He nodded. "Might be good for her, I can only imagine that whatever Silias taught her was wrong and brutal."

"You want to trade places?" I almost begged.

He shook his head. "You know what you're doing and besides, she might be more comfortable around people her own age."

I sighed. "Why did you even agree to let me mentor her?"

"Because you need to learn responsibility and hopefully she can give you that emotion you lack." He tilted his head. "Empathy."

"Bloody hell, of all people it had to be her?"

"Cinth," he started. "You know when you two first met nearly a decade ago, you both ran off on your own together. She was the first and only person I've ever seen you willingly touch since I met you."

"Where did we go when we ran off?"

He had to dig deep into his memory. "We found you two on a roof."

"We?"

"Her father and I."

"Her real father?"

"Cinth, do you really not remember?"

"No... Why did we run off?"

He shook his head. "I have no idea, but you two were like magnets. You met her a few times the next few months at her father's house. We couldn't separate you two and we never heard what either of you were talking about because you were always only whispering in each other's ears."

We still talk to each other like we're telling secrets. A sharp pain sizzled deep in the core of my head, slowly engulfing my brain in a scorching fire as I tried to remember.

"Every time we would eat dinner, you both decided to share a chair to eat."

How embarrassing.

"You really wouldn't let her out of your sight, nor would you let anyone else touch her."

Bloody hell, I still act like that with her.

"You wouldn't even let her own father hold her and when he did have the audacity to in front of you, you would break something." He laughed.

Why was I so attached to her? Why am I still so attached to her? No matter how much I try to fight it, I find myself lingering around her.

"And we caught you two snuggled, sleeping together when the both of you slept at his house."

I rolled my eyes, even though the motion made my head hurt more. "Okay, now I know you're spitting lies." I could *never* be that close with someone.

He shook his head. "If I wasn't there, I wouldn't have believed it either. Her father was so angry at you, but you would just glare back at him. Demons below, you had a death wish."

I pulled my hood up over myself as I used my other hand to cover my mouth. *Holy shit. Why do I have no memory of it?*

He sighed. "Who knew she was the Grim Reaper." He met my eyes. "This is the life her father worked so hard to avoid for her."

He walked towards his room, but stopped and turned back to me. "Her father and I thought you two were going to be friends forever and maybe even more someday."

Yuck.

"I know you two lost contact and I know she's changed a lot, but why do you hate her so much?"

I don't think it was her that I hated, but the fact that I couldn't comprehend what I really did feel towards her. I shoved my hands in my pocket and leaned against the wall. "She messes with my head, I doubt she did that when we were younger."

"Demons below, Cinth." He shook his head. "Just let yourself feel and see where it goes."

I furrowed my brows. "Feel what?" I can't feel anything, except when I'm with her, but I don't know what the feeling is. Having these constant heart attacks around her could lead to my death, which means this is a bad feeling, therefore, I hate her.

"Gods." He sighed. "You're probably confused because you were kids before and didn't know you could get closer–"

"Niko." I stopped him. "That is definitely not it."

"Just... Let it happen."

"What if I lose control?"

"Then, you lose it." He shrugged, opening the door to his room. "You're not going to die."

I might. "She's the one who will," I muttered, instead.

He laughed. "I know for a fact you won't actually ever kill her."

I smirked at the challenge. "Now I really want to do it, just to prove you wrong."

"How many times have you tried to kill her?"

At least twice.

When I didn't answer, he asked. "And why didn't you go through with it?"

"That's exactly what I don't understand." I've never felt this before. Killing someone was like breathing for me, it was so natural and easy, so why was I struggling when it came to her?

"Cinth, you're an absolute idiot, confusing wanting to kill her and wanting to–"

"Niko," I warned.

He quickly closed his door shut and locked it for his own safety. Not that I would do anything to him, there was no gain in killing him. I'd already thought about it.

12

EVERYTHING MEANS NOTHING

October 70 A.D.

"What's gotten into you?" Lin asked.

I played with my lunch. "Celestine is so irritating." I had been meditating more frequently to calm my mind and gain control over my emotions, but it didn't seem to be working.

"What's she done now?"

I couldn't tell them I started training her, and she was making it so difficult for me. "I've just had enough of her." I muttered as I took out a cigarette and lit it up.

They exchanged looks and changed the topic.

"What are your plans for the formal, are we going?" Jamiel asked.

They already knew I wasn't showing up to that. And it was too early to even think about it.

"I got a new suit, guess who I'm asking?" Lin stuck up his nose.

"Eloise," we all said at the same time.

"Did I already tell you?"

"Only about a hundred times, but you still haven't asked her." Jamiel rolled his eyes.

It was ages away, he had plenty of time.

"I'm working on it!" he argued. "What if she says no?"

"She probably will, you're a creep." Iri laughed.

"Excuse you!"

"Nah, she won't reject him because he looks like a creep," Jamiel said.

"Thank you," Lin said.

"It'll be because he's an idiot."

Lin's mouth fell. "Coming from you? I'm sitting at number one of this school."

Jamiel rolled his eyes. "I mean you talk like an idiot."

"You're both the worst, at least Cinth likes me." Lin put an arm around my neck.

"Don't touch me," I growled, exhaling smoke. "You smell like shit."

He dramatically released me, as if he'd just gotten shot, quickly sniffing the inside of his shirt. "Why am I always the one being picked on?"

"You make it too easy," I muttered.

Lin shot me a glare then gasped. "But Iri, you've been getting quite close to Eloise recently, haven't you?" Lin leaned towards her. Iri was friends with everyone.

She squinted at him. "I'm not going to ask her for you."

"Can you just suss her out? Put in a good word for me?"

"You're so desperate, it'll turn her off."

"I *am* desperate, please." Lin clasped his hands together. "This is our last year, I may never see her again!"

Iri let out an exaggerated sigh. "Okay, fine, I'll talk to her."

Lin let out a small cheer. "Yes! Thank you!"

I cursed. "I just remembered I have to drop off some library books," I said, standing up before heading to the library before lunch was over.

I had borrowed a few books on dreams, since I had been having constant recurring ones. For the last decade or so, there had been some recent phenomenon about people experiencing being in an endless hallway, but I hadn't found anything on the meaning of the salt flats. Maybe I needed to look into the history and formation of the salt flats to gain some sort of insight into what my mind was trying to tell me. *Is it a warning?*

As I was returning my books, I spotted Reaper searching for a book. *So, this is where she goes to hide from everyone else.* She stood on her toes, too small to reach the top shelf. I walked towards her, before she started jumping for it and pointed at the book above.

"This one?"

She shook her head, adjusting her glasses back up the bridge of her nose. "Next to it."

I pulled out the book and handed it to her.

"Thanks," she mumbled. "Thought we weren't talking to each other anymore."

"What makes you say that?"

She gave me an annoyed look.

I rolled my eyes. "Just because we had a small argument last night doesn't mean I'm going to stop training you." I wanted to, but Niko convinced me to try and after some thinking, I could use her to get closer to Silias and figure out his weaknesses.

"But maybe I don't want you to train me anymore."

"Don't be so stubborn."

She ignored me, skimming over the first couple of pages of the book.

"You're really going to give up this opportunity to train with the best over one bad night?"

"Yeah." She flipped the page. "You can leave now like you did yesterday."

"I shouldn't have left you," I admitted, but I wasn't going to apologise. It wasn't my fault, she drove me to do it.

She began walking away.

Nope, I wasn't letting her get her way. I pulled her back to me. "Meet me after school."

"Busy."

"With?"

"Not you."

I rolled my eyes and left.

***

If she were going home or on an assignment, she would have just said so. So, who was she meeting and why was she carrying such a large bag?

She didn't say anything as I followed her. I'm not one for stealth nor did I have any shame in this. I don't think she quite cared honestly. I sat directly across from her on the train and stayed just two steps behind her. It was a bit of a walk from the station to the upper West side, but eventually I realised she was headed to the only ice-skating rink in Soulesity. It's not the most popular sport, no one wants to be cold in a city that's already cold.

"You still skate?" I asked as we entered the building, the temperature only slightly colder inside than it was outside.

"Just for fun now," she said sitting down on one of the benches before changing out of her shoes and into her skates. Her skates were worn, the laces fraying near the aglets, the off-white leather was tearing at the toes, and the sides were greyed with scratches and use. "Want to join me?"

I had never stepped on an ice rink before. "I think I'd break something."

She gave me a slight smile, stood up and headed towards the door to get to the ice. She transitioned from the ground to ice so smoothly, like it was natural.

Half the ice was blocked off for lessons that included a teacher and four young children, learning to spin. The other half was available to the public, but only Reaper, an old woman who looked like she shouldn't be on ice, and another girl around the same age as Reaper and I were there. Reaper warmed up with a few laps of forward strides, twisted and continued backwards.

The parents on the other end of the benches, yelled encouragement towards their children, causing me to take my attention off Reaper for a brief moment. I glanced at the kids who began pointing in awe, and followed their gaze back to Reaper who was currently spinning on one foot, slowly grabbing the blade of her skates up over her head.

Wow.

It was beautiful to watch.

In a graceful manner, she exited the spin, continuing off, and I had no idea how she wasn't dizzy from that many twirls. She circled the half of the arena and glided past me. Then turned, skating backwards and I could see the slight concentration on her face as she prepared herself. She lifted one of her legs behind her and with her toe, picked the ice, using her momentum to jump and twirl in the air.

"Triple!" the other girl skating near her shouted. "Where's your triple?"

Reaper shook her head. "I can barely do my double anymore."

"Come on, Cel. We all know you can do better than that!"

Reaper bit her bottom lip, glancing at me and turned once again, preparing herself to do a triple. When she jumped this time, she hesitated and though she made it around three times, she landed too much on the side of her blade and fell.

She quickly got up, dusting the ice off her. I stood up and went over to the barrier and as she skated past me, I stopped her. "You hesitated."

She shot me a glare. "You don't think I know that?"

"Why did you hesitate?"

Reaper just rolled her eyes, ignored me, and skated away.

I headed over to the only two staff members I could see working in this place. They were sitting behind a counter with a hundred skates behind them available for rental that looked like they were hardly touched. I told them my size and put them on, already regretting my decision.

How hard could it be? Reaper noticed me walking towards the entrance and rushed over, stopping smoothly just in front of me with a beaming smile.

I put one foot on the ice and felt absolute terror. "Now what?"

She laughed. "Now, your other foot."

I gripped onto the barrier, shifting my weight and standing on the ice with both my feet. *Oh shit, shit, shit.* "Okay, now what?"

She bent down and readjusted the straps for me. "Take your time, let go when you're comfortable."

I already wanted to get back on non-frozen ground, what in me thought I should do this? No one forced me. She wasn't pressuring me, she only asked me once and probably as a joke.

Reaper showed me how to glide forwards and I attempted to copy her, but it wasn't as easy as she made it seem.

"Oh, gods. He's going to break his ankles," someone said from behind me.

My ankles were bent inwards, and I didn't even realise it, so I quickly fixed them straight.

The girl who spoke skated around to face me, stopping me from continuing forwards. I stumbled a bit not knowing how to stop, but I also wasn't really going anywhere in the first place. She was quite pretty, with long wavy dark hair, dark eyes, and deep skin. Wearing a school uniform from one on the West side of Soulesity.

"Who is he?" she asked Reaper.

"Some creep from school, he followed me here."

The girl let out a laugh, revealing the gap between her front teeth. "I'm Osiria, but everyone calls me Ria."

"Hyacinth."

"Oh…" She turned to Reaper with a knowing smile. "Finally a face to the stories."

Stories?

Reaper grabbed Ria's hand and pulled her away from me. They held each other close as they skated away, whispering and giggling together. Then they parted and Reaper came back, offering her hands.

"What?" I asked.

"Trust me."

I hesitantly took her hands, and she began to skate backwards, guiding me away from the sanctuary of the barrier towards the middle of the arena. She was doing all the work for me. "You can't see where you're going."

"I assumed you would tell me if I was headed towards someone," she joked, glancing back to check.

I felt a bit embarrassed when I caught the group of kids staring at us and my lack of talent on the ice. Then Reaper let go of my hand. *Oh, no.* My arms flailed around aimlessly, and I made the mistake of leaning my weight forwards, slipping and attempting to keep my balance for about ten seconds. Finally and animatedly, I fell flat on my stomach and slid a couple metres across the ice like a starfish.

Kill me.

The loudest laughter was coming from Reaper who knelt down next to me. "Are you alright?" She gasped, covering her mouth to keep from laughing, but failing miserably.

Pushing myself up, I sat up but couldn't help my own laughter, joining her at how absolutely ridiculous and dramatic that fall was. It was hard to breathe between the fall and the laughter. She kept her hand over her mouth as she laughed and there were little creases at the edge of her squinted eyes. She glowed so bright and warm at that moment, the ice could have melted around us.

This must be the version of her old self that remained, before her life of violence.

Ria quickly slid on the ice on her knees towards us, catching Reaper's head as she suddenly collapsed.

"It's okay. You're okay." Ria was out of breath.

My laughing quickly subsided. "What's happening?"

"When Cel feels strong emotions, it triggers cataplexy," Ria explained.

Reaper was still laughing, though it was lessening, but her body was completely limp in Ria's arms.

"It's why she can't do her triple anymore. She had an episode in the middle of doing it and injured her knee quite badly."

"So, what is this cataplexy thing?" I asked, still a bit confused.

Ria gave me a weird look. "She has narcolepsy. Didn't you know?"

No. But it explained why she falls asleep so randomly and constantly looks tired.

"It's not a big deal," Reaper said, though it seemed like it was in fact a big deal as she was quite literally completely immobile. It wasn't long before she regained her strength and sat back up herself. "Gods," she groaned, putting her face in her hands.

"You good?" I asked.

She nodded. "Just annoyed."

Ria laughed, helping Reaper stand again and then both girls helped me as I had no idea how to get up from the ice without slipping back down. Then Ria skated away back to practising her own skills.

After about half an hour, I was able to skate forwards without any assistance and only fell two more times. Reaper did her own practice with jumps, spins and whatever she felt like. She was truly captivating when she skated. Ria was just as good as Reaper and left earlier along with the children and the teacher.

As I returned my skates, Reaper went to the bathroom. The old woman was the last to get off the ice and sat down near me on the bench, taking off her skates. "I haven't seen her look so lively in years, it's almost like she's back to her old self."

I glanced at the old woman, her greying hair tied up into a tight bun.

"I used to coach Datura when she was younger," she explained with a grin.

Curiosity got the best of me. "What was she like before?"

Her coach sighed. "Well, she was quite shy, a lot more shy than she is now, and she used to... smile and..." she paused again. "Laugh. I'm not sure what happened when she disappeared and I'm afraid to know, but she's not really *here* anymore."

I knew exactly what she meant. Sometimes, when I caught Reaper before she noticed me, it looked like she was lost in another world.

"So... Thank you for bringing her back."

"I'm not really doing anything," I admitted.

"You showed up," she said. "Her family never came, not even to any of her competitions because, well, you must know the Vicary family, they're quite busy. So, I'm sure she's grateful that you came with her."

I nodded, unsure of what else to say.

"Actually," she started, "I wanted to ask, there's a man who comes to watch her sometimes." Her face was etched with concern. "He has red hair and Datura doesn't say it, but I can see that he makes her uncomfortable. When I asked her about him, she told me he was her guardian. Do you know anything about that?"

"Uncomfortable in what way?" I asked.

The woman shook her head. "I'm not one to jump to conclusions and perhaps I read into it too much, but Datura completely avoids interacting with anyone, even Ria, when he's around and keeps her eyes down."

So, just like at the restaurant.

"I think if she doesn't want to talk about it then it's not my place to say either," I said. The amount of things this woman had revealed to me about Reaper's life with me barely asking and we don't even know each other's names.

She pursed her lips. "Well, whatever your relationship is with her, whatever you're doing, thank you." And with that she left.

Reaper came soon after. "What did she say to you?"

I shrugged. "Nothing, really."

She eyed the old woman as she left the stadium. "So, where are we going?"

"East side."

***

We took the train and got off as close as we could to the edge of the forest, the dojo stood just outside of it.

"What is this place?" she asked.

I gestured for her to put her bag down and take off her shoes as we entered. "It's Niko's dojo," I said in a low voice, in case there were still others inside.

"It's pretty." She matched my volume, not that hard for her as her voice was naturally soft. There were two rooms, the first had floors of mats and large windows for walls that faced the forest. The second was a small kitchen and a bathroom at the end. No one was in the first room, and I slid the door to take a peek at the second to find it also empty.

"It's just us, that's good," I muttered, taking off my tie and tossing it on top of my bag. I sat in the centre of the room, crossing my legs. "Come."

She sat directly across from me.

"We're going to train the mind."

"The mind?" she asked.

I nodded. "Meditation."

She stood back up and headed for the door.

"Where are you going?"

"This is a waste of time."

I sighed, that's exactly how I acted when Niko took me here the first time. "If you can't control your mind, you can't control your body."

"I can control my body just fine."

I shook my head. "No," I started, "I noticed you don't like to use your left leg." I concluded that the limp she had was permanent.

"Past injury."

"And you hesitated before you did your triple jump spin."

She turned to face me. "It's called an lutz and I'm just thinking about what I'm about to do."

"Thinking gets you killed."

"I don't do it when I'm out there obviously."

"But there's a chance you might," I said, "so let me teach you how to avoid it."

She folded her arms in front of her chest. "I don't need you to pick apart every little thing I do."

"I'm training you, that's what I'm supposed to do."

"Well, stop, I'm doing fine."

Does she know what being trained means? I shook my head, frustrated. "You really can't handle criticism, can you?"

"I just don't like being analysed."

"Alright." I stood up. "If you can get one hit on me, I will let you walk out of here and admit that I was wrong." I stepped closer to her. "But if you lose, you will stay, let me properly train you, and start listening to me."

Reaper stared hard into my eyes. "Lights off."

I went towards the switch and turned them off. The only source of light came from the window, but it was still quite dark as the Ether Kingdom was drifting directly above us that night.

My eyes adjusted to the lack of light. "Remove all your weapons."

She did, as I took out my knife, putting it off to the side. We stood in the middle, taking our own stance. "Whenever you're ready. One hit and you win."

She attacked. I stepped to the side to avoid her first strike and every strike after. She was good, she knew what she was doing, and there was precision in her blows.

"I admit, you have near perfect technique." Just as she threw a kick, I grabbed her ankle. "But you lack in power, confidence, and I would say speed, but let's be real, no one is faster than me." I used my foot to drag her other leg out from under her and she fell onto her back with a grunt. I got on top of her and held her wrist down. "Done?"

She attempted to kick me off her, but I didn't budge, instead flipping her over so she was on her stomach and twisted her arm behind her.

She winced at the pressure, but I didn't care. I waited for her to admit defeat. There was no way out, but she kept her mouth clenched, holding her breath. Stubborn like a Kokkino clansman. "You're done, Reaper."

She didn't respond. I waited a beat before finally releasing and getting off her. She sat up from her spot, out of breath. "How?"

"Because my body is not blocked by my mind. You hesitate, even if it's for a fraction of a second. If you're going against an experienced fighter, they'll pick up on it," I said. "Since you lost, you have to listen to me now."

She rolled her eyes but reluctantly did as I told her.

I took a candle from a kitchen cabinet and lit it up between us, four thin pieces of tissues next to me. She sat across from me, mimicking my cross-legged position. I started with the first question. "What are you afraid of, Reaper?"

She squinted at me, suspicious. "What are *you* afraid of?"

I already expected her to get defensive, I would be too. "Alright, let's try this a different way," I started. "I will ask a question, I'll answer it first so that you can understand what I mean and then you answer it. Will that make you more comfortable?"

She let out an annoyed breath but nodded.

"What are you afraid of? I am afraid of losing everything," I admitted. "I've worked too hard to get here and I know that it just takes one wrong move, one misstep, and it could all taken away. Everything I built, all those sacrifices—it would mean nothing... Now, it's your turn."

Reaper turned towards the door. "Can I skip this question?"

"No."

She let out a small breath and barely whispered. "I'm afraid of being alone."

I didn't expect her to answer so honestly, I thought she would joke and say spiders or clowns. I waited for her to continue but she didn't so I urged her. "Why?"

"I don't want to say."

"I'm not going to judge you, Reaper. You need to say these things out loud, you cannot let fear control you."

She couldn't meet my eyes, ashamed. "I'm scared because," she paused, "everyone I've ever known has kicked me out of their homes and their lives. My family, my best friend, strangers even. Silias is the only person in the city who wants me, at least, for now."

Kicked out? Everyone said she ran away. *They lied.* Though, it was best I didn't pry, she might open up more later.

"I guess we both have that in common," I told her. She finally looked at me. "I was dumped at a youth home when I was really young and I jumped from foster home to foster home, because none of them could stand me." Her eyes softened at my words, "I don't know how many foster families I went through before Niko took me in and I'm really lucky to have him, but there are still times where I think he might kick me out because of all the trouble I cause him."

We stared at each other for a moment, understanding each other's pain. How terrifying it was to not feel secure and safe. How hurtful and humiliating it was to not be wanted, to be rejected.

How lonely it was to have no one.

I cleared my throat, not meaning to reveal so much about myself. "That feeling," I said, "it's in your stomach, a sick feeling that makes you want to throw up. Some fears you will never overcome, forever forced to carry them with you throughout your life. Allow yourself to feel it, but don't let it consume you." I handed her one tissue. "This represents your fear, burn it up into nothing. Fear means nothing."

She took the tissue from my hand, and it burnt so quickly it didn't have time to turn into ash.

"Regret," I started. "Four years ago, someone managed to sneak up on me and hit me in the head. My head split open, and I was in a coma for a week."

She nodded, listening intently.

"I was on some stupid assignment and I hadn't slept but I had Niko with me. It's just so stupid that it happened and it's messed me up ever since. If I had just slept that night or admitted to Niko that I was tired..."

"What part of you is messed up?" she asked.

"I lost a lot of my memories from the year leading up to it and I still have these bloody headaches. It also ruined my reputation at the time. People had already been whispering the name Vulture around me before the incident, but afterward, they saw me as weak and vulnerable — still just a kid — and questioned if I ever really deserved to become an Apex. So I had to work even harder. I had to become even colder. Until it finally stuck."

"I heard people tried to kill you at the time."

I scoffed. "Yeah, they did, but Niko stayed at the hospital with me the entire time."

"He must not have slept."

"I remember waking up and seeing his eyes red and these awful bags under them." The relief on his face when I woke was something I would never forget.

She cracked a small smile. "He really cares for you."

I still wonder how long I'd need to be in a coma before Niko abandons me. "What do you regret?"

"I had a fight with my brother," she mumbled. "I was just being stupid because I thought–" she paused, embarrassed about the argument. "I overreacted and the next thing I knew I was on the streets."

"Do you blame him for it?"

She shook her head. "No, it was my fault... I hurt him pretty badly. So... While he went to the hospital with–with Ren, Delilah packed my bag."

The staff member that was interviewed mentioned she had broken his arm. *Was everything she said true?* None of it was in the articles I read nor was it ever mentioned in court, so people brushed the woman off as having a psychotic break.

"Your mum didn't stop you from leaving?"

"It was either I left or Ren was going to have me killed for hurting his son."

"Killed? Isn't that a bit extreme?"

"Maybe he didn't really mean it, but at the time, I believed it."

My heart clenched. "You were twelve," I breathed. "That must have been really scary."

She didn't respond.

"Didn't you have other relatives to stay with?" I asked her, curiously.

"They–I don't really know them."

"Your grandfather? Eugene Vicary?"

Her eyes narrowed. "He's not my blood," she replied, coldly.

I knew I should stop prying but I couldn't help myself. "How long were you on the streets for?"

"Um." She thought about it for a bit, but I had a feeling she knew exactly how long. "Around seven months before Silias found me."

Seven months. A twelve-year-old girl was on the streets for seven months and not just any of the months, but the coldest ones of the year. How did she survive that? Where did she sleep? How did she find food? I had so many questions, but I didn't want to ask, afraid she would leave if I did. She seemed extremely uncomfortable, no longer meeting my eyes.

I waited to see if she would say more, but she didn't. "Regret rests in the mind. It is something people try to run away from, but the only way to get rid of the feeling is to reflect on it and forgive yourself even if others affected by it won't." I gave her the tissue. "Forgive yourself and allow your regret to burn into nothing."

She hesitated to burn this one, but eventually she did.

This next question was a bit lighter. "Who do you love?" I didn't actually love anyone, It's not an emotion someone like me could feel, but if I had to choose... "I love Niko. He took me in when no one else wanted me. He saw the potential in me and he treats me like a son."

I waited for her to speak, curious of her answer. "I..." She hesitated, her brows furrowed. "I love my clan."

"Your whole clan?" I asked. "I'm talking about someone you feel deep love for. Someone you want to be with all the time. Someone you would protect with your life," I said, urging for a more specific answer.

She stared at me, a slight subtle shift of energy in her eyes, then she looked away. "Silias."

"Silias? Really?" I didn't believe that at all. Silias isn't a man who could be loved, the ugliness inside him was so strong it was on his outsides too. "Everything said to me is confidential, in this dojo and outside," I reassured her.

She shifted her gaze back to me and nodded.

"So, you can be honest." Still she said nothing. "Why do you think you love Silias, Reaper?"

"I don't know," she muttered, "he took me in."

So she used my logic to get to her conclusion. I almost rolled my eyes. "Do you feel love, Reaper?"

"Yeah."

"Yeah? Describe it. What exactly is your relationship with Silias?"

"He gives me a place to stay, food to eat, he would protect me, and he always wants me near him."

"And what does he force you to do?"

"He doesn't force me," she said. "I'd do anything for him because I want to."

"And if you refuse?" I narrowed my eyes, analysing her body language. The subtle shift in her posture, her nails digging into her palms to calm the shaking, the daze in her eyes.

"Then, he would ignore me, along with everyone else in the house, until I do it and I will. I always do."

I bit the insides of my cheeks. "Do you know what conditional love is?"

"I know what that is," she said in a low voice, "but I don't believe in unconditional love."

"Why?"

"Everyone wants something." Reaper met my eyes. "And people are only nice if they get something in return."

"What about your old family? Your brother, mother, father?"

She shook her head, but didn't answer.

"Don't you love them?"

"I love my brother," she admitted, "but I don't think he loves me anymore."

"Because you hurt him?"

"He raised me to be a good person and as long as I was kind, he was proud of me," she started, "but I'm no longer kind and I've done a lot of bad things. He would be really disappointed to see who I am now."

"You can still love someone even if they don't reciprocate those feelings."

"It's not the same."

I didn't know her well enough to argue her case, but... "From what I know, you're still kind, sure you kill people, but you're the type of person to buy a new coffee for someone who dropped theirs. Not everyone would do that."

"You don't even know half the things I've done."

Reaper had a lot of self-hatred, that was evident. "You're just surviving in a cruel world."

"Surviving," she repeated with squinted eyes, "you make me sound like a victim."

I shook my head. "You're only a victim if you let them make you one."

"I'm not a victim," she said in a soft voice, "I did this to myself."

Bloody hell. "Do you need... Like, a hug... Or something?" It came out more awkward than I thought it would and it was hard to string the sentence together.

She eyed me suspiciously. "I don't need your pity and I have a feeling you don't give good hugs."

I chuckled. "I'm not pitying you and yeah, I probably don't." I can't remember ever hugging anyone in my entire existence.

Reaper came over to me, put her arms around my neck, and dropped her weight onto me. Why didn't she warn me? We fell back onto the mat. "You're supposed to hug me back," she muttered into my chest.

"Right," I muttered, knowing she could feel my heart pounding. I wrapped my arms over her and lightly patted her back. *Is this what it feels like?*

"You really are bad at this," she laughed.

"I don't do this stuff."

"That's sad," she said, tightening her hold around me, "you need this more than I do."

I'm not sure that's right. "I've been fine without this," I said, "you can get off me now." But she didn't move. "Reaper," I muttered, "this is weird."

"You don't like it?" she asked, and when she shifted her body, I felt mine heat up.

"Uh, I'm not sure," I admitted. *I don't think I'd ever do this with anyone else nor would I ever tell anyone I did this.* "Don't tell a soul we did this."

"No one would believe me if I did," she sighed with a smile.

A small laugh escaped me. "Yeah, they wouldn't." I sat back up, but she didn't let go of me like I thought she would when I moved. I let out a small breath of defeat, allowing it for now. *She needs this.* "Love is located in the heart, it pumps through your veins, giving people motive to live, but it's a distraction. There is no control when it comes to love. Though it feels good, and it makes us feel safe, it can be taken from us at any moment."

I handed her the third tissue. "This tissue represents love. Burn the love you feel. Love means nothing." She reached behind her towards the candle and burnt it, then went back to me.

"Who do you hate?" I asked. *I couldn't answer this entirely truthfully.* "I hate everyone. They're all the same. I can't even choose a single person I hate more than anyone else, not one that's alive at least."

"I hate…" she paused. "I don't hate anyone," she admitted, "I think it's pointless to do so."

That surprised me. After all she's been through, after all the cruel people she's met, she didn't hate the world. "You really don't feel hatred?"

"I feel angry sometimes for people's behaviour, but I don't think it's quite possible to fully hate someone."

Oh, you'd be surprised.

"Everyone has something good in them," she said. "Even if they don't show it. I don't believe there are completely awful souls. We never really know people, we only get the chance to see a glimpse of what they show in the moment we're with them and if it's a bad moment, then it's just unfortunate that we see them in that state."

What a mature response, but she sounds like an Angel. They don't feel hatred for anyone aside from Demons. *Maybe she is an Angel.* "Who taught you this?"

"My brother and Leo," she said, "they're always able to see the good in the world."

I didn't think I needed to tell her what I was going to say.

"What were you going to say about hatred?" she asked me.

I had to take a moment to speak. "Hatred is associated with the lungs, being unable to breathe properly and having to take deep breaths to calm yourself when you're in a state of hatred. It's a strong emotion that often derives from hurt. You are unable to control other people and their words or actions, but you can control your response. Understanding that gives you power over them and yourself."

I gave her another tissue. "This tissue represents hatred. Burn it into nothing. Hatred means nothing."

She burnt it, and turned back to me, meeting my eyes. In that moment, we were mirror images—two empty reflections unable to show anything but emptiness. I wondered if she felt that too.

"Celestine," I breathed, "you should get off me." I didn't understand the things I was feeling and I might have to get rid of her to make it stop.

"You offered." She smiled.

"I didn't think you were going to take it."

She unwrapped her arms around my neck, resting them in front of her, but she was still in my lap, facing me. "Why do you hate me?"

"I don't hate you." That much I knew.

"But... You're always so mean to me, and you stay away from me."

"I just—" I hesitated, I didn't know what I felt towards her, it was so complicated and I was still trying to figure it out. "I think it's safer for you if you stay away from me."

"Why?"

"I might kill you." *At least, I think that's what I want.*

"Is that all you'll do?"

"I think so." Maybe take my time with it.

Celestine reached up and lightly grazed her long, painted nails across my cheeks. "You're not scary, you know?"

My eyes darkened, "I don't scare you, at all?"

She laughed. "Are you trying?"

Bloody hell. I allowed my eyes to get colder, but not too much. I don't think I actually wanted to see her afraid of me anymore.

"I like when you do that." A certain tease lit her eyes.

I think I stopped breathing. "Celestine, I'm going to kill you if you don't get off me soon."

She rested her head on my chest. "How long do I have?"

She let out a small wince when I pushed her off me before leaning over to blow out the candle, cleaning up our area. I couldn't let her see my face and needed to distract my mind as quickly as possible after being so close to her for so long.

How am I going to survive training her?

13
THE HALLWAYS

This was not my first visit to the nurse's office, nor would it be my last. "Ah, Hyacinth." The nurse nodded at me. "I assume your latest victim will be coming in shortly?"

I rolled my eyes. "Not a fight this time." I cut my palm during art, yeah, no idea how. I headed over towards the cabinet, knowing exactly where everything was, the nurse knew not to touch me.

As I was grabbing the disinfectant and some wrapping for my hand, the door opened.

"Why, hello, my dear." The nurse's voice turned soft. "It's a bit early for your visit."

I turned to see Celestine, but she avoided my eyes. "My stomach is also hurting," she whispered.

He stood up, leading her to one of the beds for her to lie down. "Did you eat something bad?"

"No," she replied, gripping onto her abdomen. "It just hurts."

I shuffled through the cabinet for the medications.

"Are you on your cycle?"

"I haven't gotten that yet."

Should probably get that checked. Pretty sure that's dangerous for women.

"Do you know what could have caused it?" He squinted his amber eyes, trying to figure out what the root of the problem was.

She curled up onto her side, holding her breath. "I just need a painkiller, please."

I stepped towards her and held out my hand with one. "Or do you need two?"

"I can suck it up with one," she mumbled, taking it. "What happened to your hand?"

I didn't want to tell her, but maybe it'd distract her from the pain. "I was in art and a paintbrush assaulted me." I dabbed the cut with the disinfectant.

She took the painkiller and chewed on it like a psycho. *My gods.* Celestine cracked a small smile. "Who knew a paintbrush could take you down? That's embarrassing."

"Don't tell anyone." I smirked, wrapping a bandage over it.

"What were you painting?"

"You," I said, but my tone came out more serious than I intended.

Celestine covered her face with her hands. "Ew."

"I'm joking," I reassured, "we're doing landscape."

"Hyacinth." The nurse got my attention. "I'm going to grab my lunch before the other students. Would you mind keeping Celestine company?"

"Yeah, I would mind." I can't be near her.

Celestine called me a curse under her breath.

The nurse chuckled, thinking I was joking. "Will you be alright, Celestine?"

She nodded and with that he left. *Oh no.* One of us is going to end up dead and I have a feeling it was going to be me.

"Are you here often?"

She gave me a look. "Is that your pick up line?"

"No. The nurse just made it seem like you're always here."

"I usually come here during lunch to take naps." She took my hand in hers. "It's warm."

"And you're cold." Her skin was like ice.

Celestine tugged her top out from under her skirt and forced my hand to rest on her bare stomach. *Holy bloody shit.* I felt my face heat. "What are you doing?" I asked, but I didn't pull away.

"My stomach hurts." She closed her eyes. "But this feels better."

I think I just passed away.

"Celestine." My breath caught in my throat as she pushed my hand to add more pressure. I quickly pulled away from her, turning towards the cabinet once again. Finding the heat pack, I cracked it so it would begin to heat up and handed it to her. "This–Use this–Just–Not my hand."

She put it on her stomach. "It's not the same."

"Bloody hell," I muttered, pushing at her shoulder to turn her on her other side. "You should lie on your left, it helps with stomach pain."

"You know a lot," she commented, letting out a sigh. "Lie with me."

"I would rather you pluck my eyeballs out."

"Please."

It was the way she said it, desperate, pleading, melancholic, causing my heart to sink.

"Bloody move over then." Her back was against my shoulder, and she reached behind her, searching for my hand. I gave it to her, I don't know why, but I did, and I let her pull me towards her. As I shifted to a more comfortable position, her back moved against my chest, our bodies slowly melting together. I could feel her steady breathing and she could feel my heart racing.

This felt familiar, but not like I've done this before, but as if *we* had done this before.

I instinctively dragged her closer to me, closing my eyes, burying my nose into her hair. She smelt so good. If I loosened my hold around her, even just a little, she was going to disappear.

Just like when we were kids.

I opened my eyes. When we were kids, we did this back then. Niko even said so. A heavy feeling set in my chest, making it difficult to move. The memory was just a picture in my head now, her hair was shorter, but it was her. The same scent, the same cold skin, the same feeling of calm and... Something.

***

I stood in the centre of the salt flats again, the sky just as brilliant and vivid as it looked the last time I was here, the sun on the verge of rising. The Stygia mountains were North of me and behind was the same little wooden house.

I still hadn't made it inside and I was determined this time. As I took a step towards it, something in the water's reflection caught my eye and I paused.

Two figures stood near me, but when I looked up, they weren't on the surface. I turned back down towards the water. It seemed as though they were on the other side. Stepping closer revealed a younger version of Niko with another man, his face blurred by rippling water from an unknown source. They stood next to an open door, but there were no walls.

"Niko," the blurred man called him over in a deathly low voice. It sounded as though he were behind a thin glass wall.

Niko approached him and froze. "What on all the stars?" He breathed.

In the water, appeared a nine-year-old version of myself and Celestine sound asleep on a bed, close and facing one another, holding each other's hands.

"If you don't–"

Niko pulled the man away, quietly closing the door, and the two kids disappeared. "Hyacinth won't let anyone touch him, ever."

"That's my daughter, Niko," the blurred man said through clenched teeth.

I crouched down and touched the water, thinking I would be able to get to the other side and see everything more clearly. But I was stopped by the wet sand.

Niko shook his head, speaking in a low voice. "He went through something horrible last year. His foster family... they hurt him. Badly." He hesitated, unable to say more. "He had his reasons for killing them." Glancing at the closed door, he sighed. "I'm honestly shocked he wants to be around Datura at all. He barely wants to be around me." A pause followed before he added, "Hyacinth doesn't have friends—at school or anywhere. He barely speaks, always picking fights. Whatever comfort he finds in Datura... please, just let him have that."

"I forbid them sleeping on the same bed together."

"They're only kids, what do they know?"

***

Blinking my eyes, I woke up in the nurse's office. I couldn't believe I fell asleep with her. Again. How does she make me feel relaxed enough to do so? It's careless, someone could have killed us or worse, seen us. I glanced at the window, dark and gloomy, hail crackling against the window.

Reaper had shifted in her sleep to face me, her arms and legs tangled with mine.

Bloody hell.

How long have we been here? Carefully getting off the bed, I noticed the curtain had been closed around us. *Strange.* I pulled open the curtains, but no one was in the room and the clock said it was way past school hours.

"Celestine," I called.

"What?" she asked, her voice tired.

"It's six." We slept for seven hours, but it felt like only minutes had passed.

"How?" Celestine sat up from the bed, rubbing her eyes. "Did the nurse not wake us?"

I pulled out my phone to multiple texts from Niko asking about my whereabouts. "You need to go home."

"We're not training today?" She hopped off the bed, fixing her clothes and setting the heat pack, no longer warm, on the nurse's desk. Even with all that sleep, she still looked exhausted.

"It's Tuesday, you have the day off." I walked out with her into the hallways.

"You don't want to hang out with me?" she teased.

"Go home," I muttered, pushing the door to get outside of the school. "I'm meeting some people tonight."

"Can I come?"

"No." I'm not sure if I trust the Underworld people around her, and these two had a misogynistic view on women.

She sighed. "I'm not allowed to do anything, am I?"

So dramatic, oh my gods. "Go home, relax or do your bloody homework." I pushed her in the direction of the station. "Pester someone else for blood's sake."

"Rude," she muttered, leaving.

I went home before heading out to the West side. Walking into Neon Nights, I made my way to the reserved circular booth in our usual corner.

"You got here earlier than we thought you would." Symeon looked at his watch, snapping his fingers. The night ladies scooted out of the booth and left so I could sit across from Symeon and next to Kahlik.

They raised their drinks, and I nodded in acknowledgement, remembering Cassius. We lost him about a year ago, and since then, Jerome had stopped coming around, and I cut back on my visits too.

I took out a cigarette for myself and lit it. Then popped a pill, the noise giving me a headache, especially with all the flashing lights.

After catching up a bit, them telling me about their lives and recent jobs, Symeon turned serious. "There's an assignment." He looked to Kahlik, nodding before turning back to me. "That we want you to join us for."

"Who is it?"

"Silias, leader of the Kokkino clan," Kahlik whispers.

Finally.

"The pay is extremely high, our grandchildren wouldn't even need to work," Kahlik said with a sigh.

We all knew we wouldn't live long enough to have children or get married or any of that normal life bullshit. It'd be selfish to do so, putting those you love in danger. And we didn't quite care for the money–at least I didn't. But there's a sort of high that I get in knowing how much someone would pay to see another dead, what they were worth. How difficult a job was deemed and the satisfaction of being able to prove that I could do it.

"Will you be asking Niko as well?" I asked.

Symeon shook his head. "No, we already know he wouldn't do it."

He's not wrong. Niko hardly works anymore, distancing himself from the Underworld.

"Interested?" Symeon asked, leaning forward in his seat.

This is exactly what I've been training for.

"We really need you," Kahlik admitted. "I'm not sure we could do it without you."

They couldn't, but I couldn't do it alone either.

"There's no rush for it, the longer we wait, the larger the sum," Kahlik stated.

Celestine would be so upset–Wait. Why do I care about that?

"But we don't want to wait too long." Symeon scrunched up his face.

Am I attached?

"That bastard doesn't deserve to breathe any longer," Symeon sneered.

"Vulture."

I snapped my head towards Leo standing next to me. He pulled Celestine in front of him and forced her to sit next to me. "I'm so glad you're here, I lost Sterling, but there's this girl."

You must be joking.

"And we're hitting it off. Anyway, if Sterling doesn't come to get Cel, then just drop her off at home."

Leo spoke quickly and left just as fast, I didn't have time to argue. I blinked slowly, licking the front of my teeth.

"What are you doing here?" She can't—or at least shouldn't even be able to get inside, the only reason I could is because I'm the bloody Vulture.

"The twins wanted to go, and I had nothing else to do," she sighed. "But I'll go home now."

She started getting up.

"You're going to let *her* go home by herself?" Khalik asked, his and Symeon's eyes wide. Seemingly sobering up as fast as they could so they could properly see how beautiful she was.

Celestine had her hair half up and half down, with glitter all over her face and skin. Her lashes curled up to touch her brows, little black jewelled hearts decorated under her eyes. Her black dress was cut short, with sheer tights underneath and black thigh-highs over it.

Bloody hell, Celestine.

Reaching out, I grabbed her wrist before she could get far and pulled her back down to sit right next to me. Her upper thigh bumped against mine and I felt the metal knife hidden underneath her dress.

You've ruined me.

I turned to Symeon and Kahlik and narrowed my eyes at their hungry gazes.

"Well, are you going to introduce her, Vulture, or what?" Symeon asked, impatiently.

I didn't want them to know who she was, but now I couldn't avoid it. "This is Reaper," I said, hoping that would help lay them off her. "This is Symeon and Kahlik. They're hitmen." I think that would be enough of a warning to her to be careful with what she tells them.

They cursed.

"You're Reaper?"

"You don't disappoint."

"You haven't seen me do anything," she said with furrowed brows.

Unfortunately, her skills weren't what they were talking about.

"Why don't you come sit between us so we can get to know you better?" Kahlik patted the space between him and Symeon.

Celestine moved her hand under the table, placing it on my leg, searching me for comfort.

"She stays by me," I growled.

They laughed. "How old are you, Reaper?"

"Seventeen."

"I'm training her," I said, nonchalantly.

"Those rumours were true?" Symeon raised a brow.

I took one last exhale of smoke up into the lights and killed the rest of it on the table before Celestine decided to make a show of taking it off me. "Yeah."

"So, Reaper," Symeon started. "What's Vulture's biggest weakness?"

She stared at them, unamused and bored before turning her head away from them, watching the dance floor.

I couldn't help my smirk and rested my hand over hers, encouragingly rubbing my thumb on the side of her hand. "Good girl," I said under my breath.

"Alright, fair enough. What's your real name then?" he asked.

Still, she didn't respond or look at him. Completely ignoring his existence.

"What's her deal?" Symeon spat, not used to girls rejecting him. Though, the girls he did get, he usually paid for.

"Her deal?" I snapped. "Just leave her alone."

"I'm just trying to make conversation, I'm not the one being a dog!" Symeon's nose flared.

"Shut up, Symeon."

Something in the air shifted, as if I was on some sort of drug. The noise muffled and all I could hear as clear as a crystal was Celestine's soft voice. "Do you want to play a game?"

In this place? "What game?" I dared her to try to entertain me.

"Hide and seek," she said. "You're the seeker."

This place isn't that large, it would just be hard to spot her in the crowd. "If I win, then what?"

She turned to meet my eyes with a slight smile, as if offering me everything I desired, things I didn't even know I wanted. "You'll find out."

I smirked, then gave her a minute head start, watching as she went behind the dark curtains behind the bar. The bartenders didn't notice her, too occupied with the customers in front of them.

"Are you leaving?" Kahlik asked.

I nodded, not looking at them as I got out of the booth. "I'll let you know about that assignment later."

I slipped behind the bar and drew the curtain aside, unveiling a long, narrow hallway that stretched endlessly into the shadows. As I stepped through, the heavy curtain fell back into place, and I was struck by a jarring transition—from the oppressive humidity to a biting chill that nipped at my skin.

The pulsating music faded to a distant murmur, leaving only the soft, disjointed ticking of clocks that seemed to have lost their rhythm. The air that was thick with the remnants of sweat and alcohol, quickly gave way to the musty scent of dust and melted candle wax.

I pressed on, my footsteps muffled by a long, luxurious rug woven with gold, silver, and deep scarlet. The walls and ceiling, made from rich grenadilla wood, were covered in endless carvings that spiraled like a living echo. Lanterns flickered every few meters, casting a warm yellow light across the arches and highlighting the ornate details of the hall.

With each corner I turned, an old grandfather clock loomed, its face frozen between 6:06 and 6:07. After what felt like an eternity wandering the corridor, I finally reached a door at the end, leading into another seemingly infinite passageway. I glanced back, only to find that the threshold I had just crossed had vanished into the shadows.

Where did it go?

With only one way to go, I continued forward. The hallway began to split and with no signs and being unable to see the end, I took it to chance and chose to go left. It split once again until I found another door that led me to the same structure of the hallway, but in the form of a maze, having multiple different routes.

Taking deep breaths, I calmed my mind and kept from panicking.

These rooms were all familiar. Something from a dream, but I hadn't fallen asleep. An eerie feeling crept up my bones as I began walking around, looking for an exit.

"You're so calm."

I snapped my head behind me, catching a glimpse of the end of Celestine's hair as she rounded a corner.

I followed after her but was met with more hallways that twisted and turned and split.

"When Sterling was here, he panicked."

I didn't know where her voice was coming from but continued my search for her. I certainly did not feel calm, but I guess I'm just good at hiding it.

"Where are we?" I asked.

"Where do you think?"

"The Hallways," I muttered under my breath. I'd read about them in books about dreams—a strange, recent phenomenon that many around the world reported encountering. This place felt eerily familiar, a realm where one could easily become trapped and disoriented. It was an endless maze of winding corridors and random doors, each one drawing you deeper into the labyrinthine complex, where unknown creatures roamed—some friendly, others not.

There was no certainty of an exit; the only way out was to wake up. But how does one awaken when everything felt so achingly real?

"Yes." She laughed. "That's right."

"How do we get out?" I asked, muffled music beginning to seep into the room, debris falling off the now cracked ceiling and onto my face.

When I turned my eyes back from above, Celestine stood just a few metres before me. She had silver hair and the blue in her eyes was gone, just a cold pale grey. She wore a plain white dress that was slightly dirtied and stained with bits of blood. White socks scrunched down to her lower calf and ankles, and she had no shoes on.

She had a dark, playful look on her face with a powerful smile, standing so composed and dominant. "No one leaves this place unless I say."

A large, slender, shadowy creature emerged from behind her, a wide, almost painful smile stretching across its elongated face. Its excessively long, bony fingers inched their way around Celestine's shoulder, while its grotesque face loomed closer, contorting in ways that defied the limits of normal anatomy. The creature's body twitched and trembled, and a long string of drool dripped from its many sharp teeth, pooling ominously on the carpet below.

"Cel..." My words barely came out of my mouth. I had never seen anything like it.

"This is Paralysis."

So she knows it's there.

"He's a bit shy."

Its eyes were wide, bulging out of its skull. A white iris that seemed to glow against its pure black sclera, deep red veins gripping the edges into place. It was staring straight at me.

"Cel." I couldn't seem to form any other words.

"He's kept me company since I was a baby," she continued. "Along with a few others."

My body wanted to run, but I was frozen in place, my blood pulsing louder against my ear. *This is just a dream.* A figment of my imagination. How she was here too, I didn't care to know.

A strange sound of whispers and whining came from the monster, but his mouth didn't move. Celestine tilted her head, shifting her gaze to Paralysis for a moment before coming back to me, as if the creature had said something to her.

The thumping of muffled music grew louder, as the debris continued to fall, a bit of it getting into my eyes. I shut my eyes, rubbing against it.

The music was clear now and when I opened my eyes, I was in the centre of the dance floor, back in the club. Bodies of sweaty people dancing bumped against me. My head turned side to side, unsure of how I got here and then my eyes locked with Celestine's pale ones across the room.

"You lost," she mouthed to me.

I blinked then stared at the ceiling of the club. My neck ached as it had been stretched back to rest against the top of the booth. I lifted my head, suddenly sitting back in the spot I once was with Celestine leaning against my arm. Symeon was on my other side and Kahlik across from me, both pale and staring at nothing but what was in front of them in a daze.

The memory of the Hallways, like waking from a dream, slowly became further and further from my grasp, until I could barely recall them anymore.

Celestine moved off my shoulder, and the others snapped out of their trance. "So what," Kahlik started. "Have you claimed Reaper, then?"

"What?" I asked, my mind hazy and jumbled. *What were we talking about again?*

Oh, right. They called her a dog for ignoring them.

"I've been claimed by Silias," Celestine said.

They laughed at the fact.

She turned to me. "Why are they laughing?"

People usually reserve claim over their loved ones to protect them, being able to prioritise them, like Niko had claimed only Renee and I. Silias's claims were far stretched. He had claimed countless people and areas in exchange for money that it was now worth nothing. The claimed areas were now in need of protection from the Kokkino clan if they didn't keep up with the payments.

"You really think he can protect you?" Symeon asked.

"What do you mean?" Her brows furrowed.

Let's not scare her. "We should go."

"You're not going to tell her? Does she even know?" Kahlik asked.

"Tell me what?" I could hear the frustration in her voice.

"Do you know what's going to happen to you when you turn twenty, Reaper?" Symeon had a cruel grin on his face.

"Stop," I said. This isn't the time nor the place for this.

She shook her head. "No."

"I always wondered why all those people have only been saying what they want to do to you. I didn't realise the reason they hadn't gone through with it yet was because of your age." He laughed with wide eyes.

"People want to kill me?" she clarified, but Celestine wasn't shocked by it. It's obvious there'll be people who want revenge for those you've murdered.

"That and..." Symeon glanced at me for my reaction, but I wouldn't give him the satisfaction. "They're going to make it slow, Reaper." He began describing exactly what they were going to do in as much detail as he could recall.

"Enough," I snapped at him. "You're done."

"Woah, you're getting upset over nothing." He smiled. "I'm just warning her. Something *you* should have done."

"No, you bloody sadistic dog." I growled. "Not like this." I would have told her eventually, but she wasn't ready for it yet.

"You think I'm afraid of threats from people I don't know?" Celestine asked him. "You don't know me."

"I don't need to know you," Symeon said. "You're small and you will never be stronger than anyone who's just a bit larger than you."

Celestine's mouth parted slightly.

"Hey, man," Kahlik muttered to Symeon. "She's just a teenager, calm down."

All this because she decided Symeon wasn't worth her time and his personality flipped. Celestine didn't owe it to anyone to be nice to them, but if she isn't, if I wasn't here, what would people like Symeon have done to her? The thought made my stomach churn.

Celestine bit her lip, turning away from the group. "I want to go home," she mumbled to me.

I nodded for her to get out first, hating Symeon more than I already did at that moment.

"Oh, come on, I'm giving you the truth of the world!" Symeon shouted as we made our way out of the club. "You should be thanking me!"

We took the exit leading to an alleyway. The fog had set in the city, neon purple lights illuminating the narrow way. The crisp air swept through our skin and as the door closed shut behind us, the music dulled.

Celestine asked me in a low voice. "Is Symeon one of them?"

One of those who've threatened her safety? Not that I'm aware of, but after his behaviour tonight, I'm not so sure. He wouldn't cross me, I know that, and he now knows I'm training her—But he wasn't afraid to say all those things to her in front of me. If I could just claim her—Properly and publicly claim her...

"I don't know," I finally answered.

"How many people do I need to worry about?"

You can't trust anyone. "You just need to focus on your training–"

"Training? Isn't Symeon right? No matter how much I train I will never be strong enough to take care of myself."

"You're going to be fine, Celestine. You're agile and you're talented in wielding a knife. You can go up against anyone if you wanted to."

She snapped her head towards me, her eyes flickering a red hue. "And when were you planning on telling me any of this?"

I shook my head. "Honestly, it's not my responsibility to tell you. Silias and your clan should have– Actually..." I let out a short laugh. "If they really cared about you at all, they would have never let you make a name for yourself or kept your capabilities a secret. They shouldn't have even asked me to train you, because that only puts your name more out there."

"Well, what about you? Niko let you do this."

"That's different," I said, "I *chose* to do this, and I *wanted* my name out there. I don't believe you did, did you?"

Her eyes lowered. "What are they waiting for?"

I shook my head. "You're seventeen, Celestine. Your age is the only thing protecting you from people who are worse than I am, worse than anyone you've ever encountered." I never wanted to be the one to tell her this, but clearly no one warned her. "Everyone in the Underworld knows who you are and has heard about you. There are people waiting for you to turn twenty, so that they don't lose respect for doing unspeakable things to a child, but they'll have no shame when you're legal. Some of these people may go after you before you're twenty, but it's unlikely."

"Who exactly are these people waiting for me?" she asked.

"I'm not quite sure." I admitted. "There are those who are so twisted in the head, who do things completely unspeakable. They go by the name Kynigos. It's a group of four families who used to be Demon Hunters. I haven't been able to track them down." *I'm no detective.* But Silver Lining goes after them... maybe I should introduce Celestine to her.

She squinted her eyes at me, not having heard of them.

"You may think that the clans are in control of the Underworld, Celestine, but it's actually the Kynigos. Everyone knows about them, but the reason no one talks about them is because no one knows who they are."

"I thought the Stygian clans controlled the city."

Yeah, that's what it looked like. "Power shifts between Stygian clans and Etherian clans, but neither are really in control."

In reality and only if you were deep in the Underworld, would you understand that the real puppet masters were the Kynigos.

Which is where my plans falter.

I could take down the clans, but I still wouldn't have complete control over the Underworld. Not fully. I've got two years to find them before they take me and then Celestine for a test that would completely traumatise and destroy us if we didn't die from it first.

"So, there's nothing I can do but wait for them to find me?"

I nodded. "They'll be the first ones, then the rest will follow. It's the rules of the Underworld."

"Like an initiation?" she clarified. "But why do they do it?"

I shrugged. "Why does anyone do anything? Power, money, control. At the end of the day, it really doesn't matter why. They just want to scare us and remind us that we don't own the city and that we aren't invincible like our names mean."

There was a long silence as she let those words sink in.

All of us had or will go through it, all of us, except Siren. I don't know how, but she had managed to avoid the Kynigos.

"And why do you care so much about what happens to me?" Celestine asked.

Because I realised that I may have accidentally become attached to you.

"Cel, there you are!" Sterling approached us.

Celestine shook her head and muttered something to him as she passed him.

Sterling turned to me. "Thanks for taking care of her. Do you need a lift to the East?"

"Sure," I said. The trains weren't running at this hour.

He nodded, and I followed him to the car, parked illegally, but when you're in the inner circle of the Kokkino clan, you can do whatever you please. He let out a sigh. "Leo's sleeping at some girl's house."

I didn't ask. I got in the passenger seat, watching Celestine from the rearview mirror.

"The guy I was with apparently had a partner already," Sterling ranted. "Can you believe that? He didn't even say anything, and I only found out when his partner showed up!"

"That's rough," I commented.

Sterling started the car and reversed into the streets, completely disregarding the people standing behind the car.

"What were you doing in there? I saw you with Symeon."

"Just catching up," I said. "Nothing interesting."

Sterling never talks this much, at least not to me. I'm pretty sure he hated me and the feeling was mutual. *Is he...* I turned to look at him, his head bobbing back and forth.

Oh, gods, he's drunk, and he's driving.

"How much did you drink tonight?" I asked when Sterling swerved the car left and right, attempting to merge into another lane without indicating and receiving a few honks from angry drivers.

We're going to bloody crash, aren't we?

Sterling waved his hand in the air, and I almost screamed at him to keep both hands on the wheel. "Don't worry," he said. "I can see just fine."

This is not how I wanted to go, it's such a boring, preventable death.

I glanced back at Celestine and we exchanged looks. She rolled her eyes like he does this all the time, but that was more alarming than reassuring.

Sterling's eyes squinted at the sign ahead of us. "What's that sign say?"

"Oh, bloody hell," I muttered, gripping onto the handle above, as if it would do anything for my safety.

Sterling burst into a laugh. "I'm only joking! I'm a great driver. Right, Cel?"

"Debatable," she mumbled.

"Just drop me here." I pointed at the centre of the East side of the city.

I couldn't get out of the car fast enough and Celestine immediately hopped into the passenger seat. "Thanks." I nodded at Sterling. "See you, Reaper."

She gave me a small smile in reply and I closed the door before they sped off towards the South side.

My phone buzzed in my pocket with a text from Symeon and my breathing ceased.

SYMEON: Didn't think you'd let a girl of all things be your downfall. But I guess she's got her uses. Best to keep her close, it'd be a shame if something happened while you weren't looking.

14

ICE COLD WATER

November 70 A.D.

Celestine and I had been training together after school nearly every day for over a month now, switching from the dojo, training, and assignments. I'd also go with her to the ice-skating rink, but I didn't always skate with her. Her stamina and strength were what I mainly focused on when we were in training, and they had improved quite a bit since we first started. She was also opening up more in the dojo, slowly, very slowly, but I was starting to pick up and understand the subtle, micro expressions on her face.

Assignments were the most difficult for us to adjust to. I figured since I'm training her to become independent, I'd just go with her and step in if she needed me. In theory it would have worked, but for some reason, the very thought of anyone touching her pissed me off and realising this made me want to stick needles through my fingernails for being so... protective of her.

Gross.

Lin bumped me and I came back to chemistry class, lab coat and goggles on, paired with Lin, Iri and Jamiel across us. We stood at the very back corner of the room near the door, trying to put chemicals together to create some sort of reaction, I'm not sure, Lin knew though. I squinted my eyes at the instructions, why are there so many unnecessary words? It's like they are purposefully trying to confuse us.

"What are you doing here, shouldn't you be in your lab?" Lin asked.

I snapped my attention to Celestine standing between us. She ignored his question and pointed at the main flask with the mixture of chemicals we were concocting. "What's in here?"

As if I know.

Lin replied and as much as I tried to listen to what he said, his words went through me like a ghost. The teacher didn't notice Celestine, she's so small, even if the teacher looked over, our bodies hid her well.

She picked up one of the bottles and since she didn't have her glasses on, pulled it close to her face and squinted to read the label. She twisted open the cap and didn't hesitate to pour the whole thing in our mixture.

"Woah, woah, woah." Lin put his hands out, his eyes wide with fear, but it was already too late. She quickly slipped out of the room right before the chemicals exploded in a mushroom of blue foam, splattering my friends and me. None of it was toxic... I think.

It's decided. "I'm going to kill her," I muttered, wiping the foam off my face, taking off my goggles. We might somewhat get along during training, but she's still a menace to me at school.

"Galinthias, Hyacinth, what did you do?" the teacher barked from across the room.

"These instructions are hard to read," I said.

"Detention, both of you."

"Lin didn't do anything. It was my fault, miss, I read it wrong." Lin couldn't afford going to detention and I'm not a snitch.

"Fine, Hyacinth, you'll be getting a double detention then, for not discussing with your partner or at least me. All of you, clean yourselves up."

"Thanks, Cinth." Lin gave me a thankful pat on my shoulder.

I shrugged. "Don't worry about it." We took off our coats and goggles and headed towards the bathroom, Jamiel and Iri shooting glares at me.

"What?" I snapped at them.

"This is your fault, if you just stopped messing with Cel–"

I held up a hand, to hush them, spotting Celestine at the end of the hall, still skipping her class. "Let's get our revenge first, yeah? Then you can lecture me."

They nodded in agreement.

I picked up my pace and grabbed Celestine's shoulder, pulling her back and pushing her between all of us. "And where do you think you're going?"

"I almost got in trouble because of you," Lin snarled at her.

"Yikes, you three were collateral." She attempted to push through us, but we kept her in the centre.

"I told you before," I said, sternly. "My friends are off limits."

Celestine met my eyes and for a moment I thought she would listen and apologise. "You know I have a bad memory." She gave me this smile that made my face warm and I suddenly forgot why I was mad at her.

Jamiel nudged me, snickering.

"Angels above." Iri shook her head with a laugh.

"Need to sit down, Cinth?" Lin mocked. "Think you may be having another one of your heart attacks."

"Excuse me!" A teacher patrolling the hallways barked from the other end. "Are you four meant to be out of class?"

There's five of us? But when I looked down, Celestine had disappeared along with the pack of smokes from my pocket. My friends and I looked like lost ducks as we turned our heads side to side to look for her.

"What are you all looking for?" the teacher snapped. "And what is all this blue dye on you?" She continued to babble about whatever, and I disregarded it, allowing my friends to step in and explain the situation.

We eventually made it to the bathroom to wash all the blue foam off us, thankful it didn't stain our skins, only our lab coats, and didn't splatter onto our uniforms. I ran my black eyeliner under my eyes, smudging it to my liking and double checked that all my piercings on my face were clear of the blue dye, before joining my friends back in the classroom.

***

I groaned spotting Celestine at my locker after school. "Stop talking to me during school hours."

She rolled her eyes, leaning against the locker next to mine. "We're going to the same place."

"And when did I say we could be seen leaving school together?"

"Just hurry up, you're so slow."

Now I was going to take my time.

"Why is she talking to him?" A few of our classmates whispered as they passed us.

"Do we need to save her?"

"Hey, Cel." Eloise stepped towards her but I didn't bother turning to look at her. "Some of us are going to the cafe across the street, do you want to come?"

Celestine shook her head. "I'm busy."

I could feel the girls staring at me and I wanted to squeeze my body into my locker. "With Hyacinth?"

"Maybe," she replied.

They exchanged a few more words before taking their leave.

I let out an annoyed breath, popping a pill into my mouth. "Get away from me, Celestine."

She leaned her weight on me. "No."

A few teachers looked our way, muttering to each other, and I quickly pushed her away. What will it take to get her away from me? She drew so much attention.

"Hyacinth, you have a detention today," one of the teachers reminded me, undeniably curious about Celestine's closeness with me.

I glanced back at her. "I'm serving it tomorrow." Niko wanted to meet Celestine and I after school, so I texted him about my detention and he talked to the principal for me.

"Yes, that's correct," the principal said, approaching us. It really is crowded now. "I see you and Celestine have sorted out your differences."

I let out a scoff, shutting my locker. I didn't look at anyone as I walked out of school, Celestine following behind me. We rode the train to the West side and after a bit of a walk from the station, I turned the corner into a dark alley. At the end of it were stairs that led underground, where it was too dark to see the door at the bottom of it.

I was surprised when Celestine fearlessly walked down the steps, she didn't even know what we were doing or what this place was. I quickly grabbed her arm. "Do you just carelessly walk into a place all the time?"

"Is there a reason I should be afraid?" she asked with cold eyes.

I released her. "No." *Not if I'm here.* I took a pill before knocking on the door. A large brute woman opened it, recognising me. She wouldn't dare question who I brought with me and stepped to the side, allowing us to enter.

This place was a small underground bar—Not the infamous Underworld Bar, but similar vibes and similar people. Less classy, more chaotic. Skol was open all day and all night, no time for any cleaning and because there were no rules on weapons or fighting, it was normal to see people on the blood-stained floor unconscious among vomit and spilled beer. The cops avoid this place, the whole West side really, and if they did decide to come in here, I doubt they'd be allowed to leave without some sort of blackmail hanging on them.

When we entered, nearly all heads turned towards us, normally they would quickly look away, but they seemed to be more captivated by Celestine than scared of me. *She might actually be more powerful than me.*

I spotted Niko arm wrestling another man, much larger than he was. People around them were shouting and placing bets on who would win, but Niko looked incredibly bored while the other man was struggling. It was obvious what the outcome would be.

As Niko picked up his drink to take a sip, his eyes met mine. "Ah." Without much effort, he quickly finished the man off. "Better luck next time." He patted the man's back and downed the rest of his drink before turning to us.

Celestine gave him a bow and Niko laughed at how polite she was.

"You never bow to me," I grouched.

"You're only supposed to bow to those who are superior to you," she mocked me and I squinted my eyes at her.

Niko rolled his eyes at our childish banter. "Silias specifically asked us to teach you something." Then he nodded for us to follow him to the back.

In the back of the bar was a room, and due to the roaring noise outside, it was basically soundproof. Inside a man was tied to the armrest and feet of a wooden chair. He sat in the centre, stripped down to his underwear, his back turned to us. On one side of the room was a table, a bunch of different tools displayed, and two men stood on the opposite side.

"What are we getting out of him?" I asked, already knowing what this was, but was it really necessary for Celestine to know how to do this?

"Undercover cop. He and his little buddies are planning an assassination on one of the clan leaders, but he refuses to tell us the names of his friends," Niko explained.

I could have shown Celestine how to do this without him, he didn't need to be here.

As if he read my mind, Niko added. "I'm just watching to see how you train her."

I nodded. A test. *Celestine better behave.*

Celestine looked at the tools on the table, before carelessly shoving some of it to the side, a couple tools falling off the edge and clattering to the floor, making space for her to sit on it. She crossed her legs in front of her, amusement in her eyes.

Bloody hell.

"You've done this before?" I asked her.

"Maybe." She smiled. "But I do find it quite hard to keep them alive."

I rolled my eyes. "Of course you do." *You lack patience.* I walked in front of the table, trying to decide which tool to use. "Which one?" I asked her.

She leaned over the tools, biting her lip, then pointed at a pen. As if she thought I couldn't turn anything into a weapon. *Cute.*

I picked it up and stalked towards my victim. He had a cloth in his mouth, glaring up at me. I love undercover cops because they're trained for situations like this. *I'm going to have fun with this one.*

I pulled out the cloth from his mouth. "Well, go on then."

"I'm not telling you–"

I stabbed the pen into his hand, and he let out a groan, stifling a scream. I smirked. "What was that?" I pushed it in more when he didn't reply, as he clenched his teeth together. "I don't think I heard that right."

"You can hurt me all you want, Vulture," he growled. "But I'm not telling you a thing."

I smirked, not intimidated that he knew who I was, which was probably what he expected. "Your pain tolerance seems to be quite low." I yanked out the pen, and he winced. "And this is just a pen."

I looked to Celestine, for her to pick out her own tool and come to me. She understood without any words, hopping off the table and picking up a giant hammer.

"You are not using that."

She let out a small breath but put it down, before pulling out a knife from her thigh strap, and whined. "You never let me explore my creativity."

"That hammer is too big, we're not trying to kill him."

She rolled her eyes. "Then why is it there?"

Good question.

The man's eyes softened at the sight of her, as if she were an Angel sent to save him. "You're a child." He breathed.

"Yeah?" Her eyes sparkled with delight.

"Shouldn't you be playing with dolls or something?"

Celestine laughed so innocently it caused my heart to stop for a single moment. I grabbed hold of the wall nearby and gripped onto my chest, preparing for this attack to be the one that would take me to the Netherworld.

She cupped his cheeks with her hands. "You're my doll," she whispered. "And guess what?"

He was so taken by her, forgetting about the pain in his hand. "What?" He leaned forward, closer to her, eager to hear her next words.

I didn't have time to stop her as I was preoccupied with my frail heart and ailing health.

She slashed her knife across his face, his nose falling into his lap. "I got your nose."

The man shrieked, mortified.

Niko cursed, impressed with her brutality.

I stepped back to Celestine and groaned, but I couldn't help laughing at the joke she made.

"Oh." She picked up the nose and pushed it back into his face, the squelching noise causing one of the men at the side to cringe. It stayed for a moment before dropping back down onto his lap. "I didn't do that."

"I'm going to put you in this chair after this." I smirked.

She smiled, a bit too excitedly. "Really?"

I pushed her away. "Go sit back on the table, you're in a timeout."

Niko coughed to cover his laughter and the other two men next to him were biting their lips to hide their amusement.

She pouted. "I want to play too."

I gave her a hard look. "Then, wait for me to tell you what to do."

Celestine stepped closer to me and waited.

"If you cut here." I pointed with the pen. "It causes barely any damage, but it'll be painful." I met her eyes. "Do it."

She rested her knife on the spot. "Here?"

I nodded. "Half a centimetre deep."

She did as I said and the man's screams were halted by Celestine shoving the cloth into his mouth. "Does it actually hurt that much?" she asked him.

The man nodded, whimpering and trembling.

Her eyes moved to me, a certain fascination evident on her face. "Can I feel it?"

"No," I snapped.

"Cinth," Niko piped in. "She should know what her victims feel."

Celestine's smile widened.

I contemplated for a moment, then nodded for another chair for her to sit on. One of the men pulled it over. I pushed Celestine down onto it and crouched to her level. She lifted her top up a bit while I pulled out my butterfly knife and my lighter, running the flame over the blade to kill any bacteria before it touched her skin. I couldn't hesitate. Not in front of Niko or those other two men. So, I did it quickly, watching her reaction. She winced at the slice, and I grabbed her wrists before she could touch the wound. "Don't touch it."

"Please." She let out a shaky breath. "Do it again."

Bloody hell.

I almost did, before I remembered the others in the room. I let go of her wrists and turned to Niko whose brows were raised. "Do you see what I have to deal with?"

He didn't have a response to what he was witnessing.

I locked eyes with Celestine. I almost lost control, and she knew it. Then she turned to the man on the chair next to her with a mocking smile. "You must be so embarrassed that you screamed so loud."

"Pathetic." I laughed with her. My smile dropped when one of the men came over, about to clean her wound, and I roughly pushed him away. "Don't touch her," I hissed, snatching the disinfectant out of his hands and he quickly went back to his post. I gently cleaned and covered the cut. "I hope you don't ask everyone to do this to you," I said in a low voice, pulling her top back down.

She stood up with me and grabbed my collar to pull me down and whisper in my ear. "I only like it when you do it."

I cursed with a smirk, pulling away and kicking the chair she was just sitting on to slide to the other end of the wall. "Now, shut up and listen."

She nodded.

We continued our mutilation. I taught her how to make it as agonising as possible without killing and showed her a few more spots that usually had them singing.

"I thought you didn't know the human body," she commented.

"I only know pain." It came out sounding darker than intended but whatever. This was surprisingly a hard one to crack, and I was getting bored.

"I'm not..." The man could barely breathe, sweat pouring down his face. "Telling you..." His body twitched and trembled. "Anything."

Very stupidly and pointlessly noble of him. Doesn't he know they must have posted a job opening for his position by now and would have it filled soon enough? He's dispensable, everyone is.

I looked at Niko and when he nodded his approval, I pushed Celestine towards the table and lifted her to sit on it. Then, I tugged on her bandana she kept wrapped around her wrist.

"What are you doing?" she asked me.

She let me cover her eyes with her bandana, tying it behind her head. "Don't look," I said in a soft voice.

"Why?"

"Because I'm pissed off," I muttered, taking out my phone and earphones.

"At me?"

I gently rested my hand on her head. "No." I placed the earphones into her ears and put on a song for her to listen to. Then I turned to the man with eyes so dark even Niko shifted, uncomfortably. I tossed the bloodied pen back onto the table and took out my butterfly knife from my pocket.

Picking up the cloth from the floor, I stuffed it back into his mouth to drown out his screams. She didn't need to hear them. One of the men who stood next to Niko threw up into a bucket and rushed out of the room, but I ignored them. When I felt he was ready to talk, I took out the muffler.

I swear if he says—

"I'm not—"

I shoved the cloth back in his mouth, breaking his front teeth as I did and continued. The other man standing next to Niko swayed, on the verge of passing out.

The man finally spilled all the names and more, things we didn't even ask for nor wanted to know. His disclosure quickly turned to pleading for his death, as they always do.

Pathetic.

"Good." Niko put a hand on my shoulder. "Finish him."

I didn't need to be told twice.

The man standing at the side offered me a towel to clean myself, his hands shaking, not meeting my eyes. I took it and handed it back before making my way over to Celestine. I took my phone and earphones back, placing them in my pocket. Not wanting her to see the aftermath of the man or what was left of him, I led her out of the room before taking off the bandana.

"Why didn't you want me to watch you?" she whispered.

"Trust me." Niko laughed. "You wouldn't have wanted to see what he did."

She looked a bit annoyed and offended.

Celestine and I split off into the bathroom to clean up. Niko stood next to me washing his hands in the sink, giving me this sly look through the mirror.

"What?" I asked.

"You don't want her to be afraid of you."

I shrugged, cleaning my knife of blood. "She's young, Niko, she doesn't need to see that."

He raised a brow with a teasing smile. "You're the same age."

"She's my responsibility, not my concern," I snapped.

He patted my back. "Sure, Cinth."

I needed a smoke, but I didn't smoke in front of Niko.

He squinted his eyes at something on the back of my neck. "What is this blue stuff in your hair?"

"You can ask Reaper about that," I muttered.

He chuckled, using a paper towel to wipe it off for me. "I see why you've been coming home frustrated now."

"Yeah, she's stubborn and annoying, isn't she?" I sighed, glad he finally understood, as I added more soap to my hands.

"A different type of frustrated, Cinth," he teased.

Bloody hell. I snapped my head to face him, abruptly turning off the faucet. "You're reading into it."

We headed out, and he stopped me. "Then, you don't mind someone else chatting her up?"

I furrowed my brows. "What?"

He pointed, and I followed it to the other end of the bar, seeing Celestine talking to a group of men with large white beards and leather jackets. A biker gang.

"She can handle herself," I muttered, shoving my hands in my pockets.

"You're not going to do anything?" he taunted with a smile.

I watched her laugh as one of them pulled her into a hug.

I don't even remember walking there, but I shoved the guy away from Celestine, putting her behind me. "Vulture?" he gasped, the others around him taking a step back.

"Don't touch her," I scowled.

"I'm– I'm just a big fan of her work." He stumbled over his words. "And yours too, of course."

Biker gangs may look scary, but they usually have the biggest hearts and are quite soft in nature.

"And you *had* to touch her?" My eyes darkened.

It didn't mean I trusted them or anyone in this room or anyone for that matter, but especially the people in here. These people fed off the vulnerable and she's too new and young to be taken seriously.

"I asked." His eyes lowered to his feet. "I didn't know…"

"Don't make that mistake again." I picked up Celestine and held her close to me, walking back to Niko. I needed to touch her, and I think I liked it when she wrapped herself around me, it was calming. Like an ice pack on a headache. I pulled out her necklace, so that my ring was in clear display, while subtly trying to see if she was hurt in the few minutes she was gone from my sight.

"You smell like him," I growled in her ear. "I hate it."

"It's cute when you're jealous." She played with my hair.

"Shut up." I dropped her knowing she could catch herself and she did.

Niko laughed, but didn't say anything about it.

"Hyacinth," a voice said from behind me.

Son of a bi–

Niko cursed under his breath with a chuckle. "Today is not your day, Cinth."

Not at all.

"I'm going to get another drink," Niko said, leaving me alone to deal with this.

I took in a deep breath before turning to the ugliest face this Angel-forsaken world had to offer. *I really can't do this today.* "Grey," I spat.

He was the only person I couldn't touch. I always prayed someone would give me a contract with his name on it, nothing would satisfy me more, but even so I wouldn't be allowed to accept it. The worst part was that he knew it.

"Funny seeing you here." He smiled, that repulsive, painfully perfect, pearly white, polished, politician's smile that makes you question your own sanity. All charm, no substance. "Shouldn't you be eating carcasses?"

"Shouldn't you be stirring a pot filled with children?" *You repugnant, revolting, reprehensible rat.*

"Fifty metres." He reminded me and gestured his hands to shoo me away.

"You came to me," I snapped.

He ignored me and set his gaze on Celestine, pausing for a moment. "Reaper." He took her hand in his, kissing the top of it. "You really are beautiful."

Celestine didn't respond to the compliment, she just looked jaded.

Grey glanced down at the necklace around her neck. "You're not actually Vulture's are you?" he asked, still holding her hand. "Someone like you should never be tied down, especially not to some psychopathic freak."

She blinked at the comment, glancing at me to see if I was going to do anything, but I couldn't. If I did, I'd go straight to prison, and I wasn't going to put Niko through that again.

"Do you speak?" He leaned close to her face, running a hand through his dark hair. "Or do you just want to come home with me?"

"I'm underage," she told him in a soft voice.

"We don't have to tell anyone. It'll be our little secret."

She looked at me, waiting for me to do something. "I think that may anger Vulture."

Grey's eyes glanced at me for a moment, a mocking smile on his face. "He can't touch me." She didn't understand, so he added. "I'm the son of the Prime Minister and I have a restraining order against him." He left out the most crucial detail, the only detail that really mattered.

I cursed at him.

She laughed. "Oh, you're friends with my brother."

His brows furrowed.

"Vicary."

His eyes widened at the realisation. "So, you're his famous little sister, Datura Celestine Vicary."

"It's just Celestine." She pulled her hand back.

Grey took her chin and tilted her head up to face him. "You know our parents talked about us getting married when you got older, but your brother was so against it and now I see why he was always so protective over you."

Bless her brother.

Celestine smacked his hand off her. "As he should, you're a decade older than me."

"Not quite. I'm only two years older than your brother. Just a young dashing twenty-four." He smiled, stepping closer to her, forcing her back into a wall. "And I heard you liked older guys, Datura."

She pushed him away. "It's Celestine."

He quickly grabbed her arm to stop her from getting far. "Don't you know we're the same?"

The atmosphere shifted into something cold, and this time it wasn't me doing it. Everyone snapped their heads towards us when Celestine flipped Grey over her and onto his back.

I taught her that.

The crowd laughed and cheered her on as she sat on top of him. "This is what you want, right?"

He smirked, holding onto her hips, moving under her. "And Vulture watching me take his girl."

I'm going to prison.

She laughed. "Yeah?" Before I could do anything, she pulled out her knife and aimed it at his eye. "I hate the way you're looking at me."

Niko came to my side, sipping on his drink, completely entertained by the whole scene in front of him. He hated Grey just as much as I did.

"Should we stop her?" I asked, but I didn't really want to.

"She doesn't have a restraining order." He smiled.

"Don't you know who I am?" Grey shouted through the noise of the bar. "I am the son of—"

"I really couldn't care less who you are." She brought the tip of the blade closer to his eye, "Should I..." An eerie smile crossed her face. "Take it out?"

The crowd urged her to do it, shouting and hollering words of encouragement.

"Come on, Datura, I was just joking."

"Call me Datura one more time," she dared him.

His eyes welled up, shaking under her. "Please, no."

"Do you stop when people say that to you?" she asked him, curiously.

He swallowed hard. "I'm sorry."

I crouched next to them and took her wrist before she could move any closer to his eye. "Silias would probably get mad at you." Not only was he the son of the Prime Minister, he was one of the last living Demons, but I wasn't going to tell her that. It's not my place.

She pouted. "But I could pretend I didn't know who he was."

I shrugged. "Maybe, but he'll always be pathetic whether you take his eye out or not." I released her, letting her decide.

"Pathetic," she repeated in a whisper. She turned back to Grey with a small sigh. "You should get a restraining order on me too." Then she slipped her knife back in her thigh strap and got up, kicking him between the thighs, laughing as she did it.

Grey curled up into a ball, wheezing.

The Demons are never going to repopulate.

Everyone in the bar laughed and resumed what they were doing, as if nothing had happened. Just another night at the bar.

Celestine took the sleeve of my hoodie in her hands, pulling me down to her level so she could whisper in my ear. "You lied to me."

"What?" I could hear another fight breaking out at the other end of the bar.

"You said no one could touch me if they knew I was yours." She sounded so angry and insulted. "What a joke."

Ice ran through my veins at her words. *A joke? I'm a joke?* I pried her hands off me. I wasn't going to respond to that, if I did it'd be hard to take back.

"Is a restraining order really all it takes for you to not kill someone?"

It was a lot more complicated than that. "You don't even know what you're talking about." I could kill him if I wanted to, it'd just be a lot of bloody work and I wasn't planning on angering the Demons. I have absolutely no idea how Silias got away with his crime.

"Then, why didn't you do anything?"

"Because you can clearly take care of yourself, Reaper, you are not helpless."

Her eyes narrowed into a cold glare. "I'm not helpless, but you didn't do anything after all the things he was saying to me."

"If he actually had the guts to do what he said, I'd skin him alive."

"How do you know he wouldn't?"

I rolled my eyes, watching Grey crawl away from us. "I've unfortunately known him for a long time, he's all talk." I met her eyes. "Now, are you done being mad at me for letting you handle your own shit?"

I didn't expect it, so Celestine had a clear opening to punch me square in the gut and the entire room silenced, even the ones who were fighting halted. Horrified that someone had struck the untouchable Vulture. She really liked punching people in the stomach, probably because she's so bloody short. I coughed. *Did she really just do that in front of everyone?* People are going to lose their respect for me if I don't do something.

"You're so mean to me," she told me.

I tilted my head back with a short laugh and cursed. "Oh, Reaper." I matched her glare, cupping her cheek with one of my hands. "You haven't seen me mean." I moved my hand down "–and I can be really–" I wrapped my hand around her neck "–really–" and pulled her towards me "–mean."

"Cinth," Niko warned, but I ignored him. He wouldn't physically get involved, not when I'm angry, he learnt that a long time ago.

I didn't hold her tight, only a bit of pressure, a warning, but despite feeling the pulse on her neck racing, she wasn't backing down. She was waiting for me to continue. She was enjoying this. *She'll be the death of me.*

"Tighter," she whispered.

I felt the tug at the edge of my lips and cursed. I released my grip on her neck, shoved glasses off the bar, letting it shatter to the floor, and pulled her up to sit on it so we were at a more similar height.

No one dared to say anything, they just kept watching, taking steps back and moving a safe distance away from my wrath, but I didn't care. I put my hands on either side of her, leaning close to her face. "Careful Reaper," I muttered, "I have less control of myself around you. I might do something you'll regret wanting."

"But will *you* regret it?" she asked, amused and excited.

"I don't feel remorse," I reminded her.

Her eyes went down to my lips and back up to my eyes, knowing exactly what she was doing. "Then, what are you waiting for? Do it."

I smirked at the challenge. "You think I won't?"

She leaned towards me and whispered, "prove me wrong." Her lips were so close to mine and I was tempted to close the gap between us, but I also wanted to stab her in the face for humiliating me like that.

"Hey, man." Someone came up behind me and put a hand on my shoulder. "I don't thin–"

I didn't hesitate to take my knife out and stab him in the stomach. He wouldn't die, but I was too heated and pissed off to give him a less painful warning. Celestine was the only person in the room who laughed, everyone else gasped or screamed. *She's as psychotic as I am.*

I turned back to Celestine and lifted the bloody knife between us. She grazed her tongue up one side of the blade and I did the other, like we were sharing a lollipop. Our tongue's never touched. If they did, it would be the end for me. I felt the room shift uncomfortably at our sick intimacy.

When we both reached the tip, I took the knife and stabbed it into the wood right between her thighs. She didn't even flinch. "If you piss me off anymore, I'm going to put it through you." I used my thumb to wipe off the bit of blood at the edge of her lips. "Yeah?"

She nodded, unable to help her smile. "Yeah."

"Good girl." I yanked the knife out of the bar and shoved it back into my pocket.

Niko took that as his opportunity to get in between us and I took a step back from her. The bar resumed their chatter and I'm certain they were talking about us. "It's late and I doubt Cinth has given you any food."

"She didn't want to bloody eat," I grouched, but was completely ignored.

"Would you like to join us at home for dinner?"

"No," I objected. "I need to cool off." And Celestine made me heated in too many ways, but I was once again ignored.

"I'm not sure," she muttered, hopping off the bar.

"I make a mean steak."

"Steak?" Her eyes lit up, completely changing demeanour.

He nodded with a smile, knowing he had reeled her in. "Come join us, it's the least I could do for you to have to put up with Cinth."

It is quite literally the other way around.

She covered her mouth as she laughed, gracefully. "That would be really nice. Thank you."

I cursed and Niko shot me a glare, so I let out a sigh of defeat.

Niko went out first and I noticed Celestine had stopped. I turned around, but her back was facing me. *Did she forget something?* The air shifted, but I couldn't exactly describe the feeling of it. Almost like we were slowly going into a dream, but I seemed to be the only one who knew it wasn't real. Everyone hushed and stared at her with wide eyes.

"I wasn't here," she whispered.

Celestine turned back to me, meeting my eyes, but she didn't say anything. I looked back at the crowd, they all looked like they were in a daze. Just as she disappeared out the door, the entire room went back to what they were doing, as if nothing had happened.

"You don't know do you?" Grey walked up to me.

I furrowed my brows. "What?"

"What she just did," he said. "I knew she was going to be powerful, but I didn't realise..." he paused and met my eyes. "Do you know?"

"Know what, Grey?" I growled, my patience thin.

He chuckled, shaking his head. "You're going to love it." And with that he walked towards the bar, ordering another drink. I didn't want to be forced to talk any more with grotesque, grinning, ghastly, gargoyle Grey so I didn't bother getting it out of him.

Of course I knew, though I had my doubts, there were a lot of signs that confirmed it. Celestine was a Demon. I just couldn't believe she was able to do things at her age. I was already shocked that her powers developed so early, they don't start until they turn twenty. *So why did hers come so soon?*

There's a reason why I stay away from Bernadette, I don't want her penetrating my mind and I'm a bit surprised Celestine hasn't used it on me—not to my knowledge at least. Though rumour says even Bernadette could hardly control others, let alone alter the memory of an entire bar and she's already past twenty-five, so she wouldn't get any stronger.

The last time a female Demon was this powerful was over a millennium ago. I wasn't sure who Celestine's father was. None of the living Demons could create someone so powerful, maybe Ender, but he's only ever had Finlay, and he died in the Reckoning. I would know if Ender had another. Was there another Demon who survived the Reckoning I didn't know about?

Finally, I went through the doors.

"I parked the car nearby," Niko announced when I finally caught up to them and we followed him to it.

I sat in the passenger seat of the car while Celestine was in the back.

"Did you learn a lot?" Niko glanced at her from the rearview mirror.

She sighed. "Cinth sucks at teaching."

I scoffed. "Maybe you're just a bad student."

"All you do is say 'you're in my way' and cackle."

Niko burst into laughter. "Yeah, that sounds like him."

We came to a stop light and Celestine leaned forward in her seat, meeting Niko's eyes as he turned to face her. "Would you mentor me?"

Niko froze for a good moment, completely struck by her.

Car horns sounded behind us. "Niko," I snapped him out of his trance, and he turned to face the front, stepping on the throttle. Celestine sat back in her seat again, waiting for his answer, but she already knew she had him wrapped around her finger.

I wondered if she uses her powers on Silias.

Niko cleared his throat. "Cinth is far better than I am," he admitted. "But you and I can train together if you want, only if that's okay with Cinth," he teased me.

"Do whatever you want, I need a break from her," I muttered, looking out the window.

"I'll train you, Celestine." And they set a day to do it without me.

I glanced back at Celestine from the corner of my eyes. I've never seen her look so genuinely relaxed before and among the two deadliest people in all of Soulesity. If someone decided to crash this car to kill us, Soulesity would be significantly safer.

"I need to stop for fuel," Niko announced, turning into a station. "Don't..." he paused, "don't kill each other." Then, he stepped out of the car.

Celestine crawled to the front and into my lap. What is she doing? "I'm stealing Niko from you, are you going to hate me?"

Bless these windows, fully tinted, so Niko couldn't see this.

"I already hate you." I avoided her gaze.

She took my hand in hers. "I hate you more."

"Don't touch me," I muttered, but I didn't pull my hand away.

Celestine ignored me and played with my rings, spinning them around my fingers. She really wasn't afraid of me. Is she afraid of anything other than bugs and being abandoned? "Did I do well today?" she asked me in a low voice.

I turned to her, but she kept her eyes focused on my hand. "Yeah."

"I'm sorry." She spun the rings faster. "For punching you and stuff."

I didn't reply.

"I'm sorry," she said again, pulling my hand closer to her chest and I could feel her heart pounding, "I'm really, really sorry." Although she pissed me off, I wasn't going to stop training her over it.

"Drop it," I told her. "I should've stopped him from even talking to you, but don't ever test me in front of other people again." If she must do so, she better do it in private.

Celestine nodded and played with my rings again. "Grey was kind of scary," she admitted in a whisper. "Because he wasn't scared of you."

"He's more annoying than anything," I muttered, hating myself for not stepping in earlier. "I will be really offended if you're actually scared of that guy and not me." Though, he was a Demon, so if she was afraid, it wouldn't be too insulting. *No, it would still be insulting because it's bloody Grey.*

She turned up to meet my eyes. "You don't do anything more than kill people, right?"

"If your asking about my limits, yeah, I keep to torture and murder of adults or people my age. I also don't hurt animals."

"Do I need to make limits too?"

Does she not have any?

"If you want, it keeps me human."

"Are you not human?"

I turned to look out the window and muttered. "I'm sure you have your own theory."

"I hope you're not."

That's the first time I've ever heard that. People either tell me I'm not to ease their own fear or reassure me that I am, and it makes me feel pitied, but they don't understand that I can't change, and I don't want to change. I like how I am.

I locked eyes with her. "Why?"

"Selfish reasons."

Bloody hell.

"Why do you try so hard to be the best?"

Her eyes bored into me as if she already knew the answer, but wondered if I knew and the thing is, I didn't know. I didn't know why I had this intense urge, this intense *need* to be the most powerful person in the Underworld, to control it.

"Power hungry," I finally replied. Though, if I'm honest, I feel as if there's a stronger reason, something I've been forced to forget, something that happened in the memories I lost.

Her lip twitched. An answer that was wrong to her. "Power hungry," she repeated with a bit of a laugh.

"You're probably the same, aren't you?"

"I only crave two things," she whispered, "and it's not power."

"What is it you want, then?"

"Chaos and calm."

"Those are two complete opposites."

Her eyes filled with amusement. "Depends on my mood." She moved her eyes down to my lips. "Sometimes I like to see the limits of a person's mind." Then back up to my eyes. "And other times I want the silence."

"So, messing with them to the point of insanity and when you're bored you take your little knife and stab them in the eye?"

The corner of her lips twisted up into a smile. "Exactly that."

Celestine will be the reason the Angels come back down. "Is that why you like to piss me off in front of everyone? Because you think that making me angry will bring you some sort of joy?"

She didn't respond for a good moment, her eyes squinting ever so slightly. "You've got it all wrong."

"Then, explain it to me," I demanded.

She turned her head away from me. "I don't care to."

I took in a deep breath, licking the front of my teeth, agitated by all her mysteries. With my free hand, I tugged the collar of her top down, pulled her close and caught her neck with my mouth, biting and sucking on it. She let out a small moan, and my body heated up. *Shit.*

"Lock the door." I let her go for a moment so she could reach for the lock.

"There's a thrill in getting caught," she said.

I chuckled, reaching for the lock myself. I wasn't planning on getting caught, locking the door would give us a warning that Niko was back.

"Coward."

I responded by taking her neck back between my teeth. My hands moved up her back, under her top. *Where did she get all these scars?*

She shifted in the seat to face me and I got a glimpse of her eyes glowing a soft red. It was her turn to mark my neck. The touch of her lips on my skin radiated a pleasurable tingly feeling that reached inside my bones.

"Celestine," I groaned, which only encouraged her, sucking and biting harder.

She pressed her body against me and scratched at the other side of my neck, hot blood rushing through me. How is she doing this? I should kill her before she ruins me, but the thought left as she slowly moved up to kiss my jaw, taking her time, making her way up to me. She paused right before she reached my lips, just a breath apart.

"We won't be able to go back from this," I told her. Neither of us were intoxicated, so we couldn't use that as an excuse. Not this time.

"I know," she whispered. *That's why she was hesitating.*

Niko attempted to open the door, but we didn't move. Neither of us could decide and were waiting on the other, but it was an almost impossible decision. I shouldn't have started this.

Niko knocked on the door, attempting to open it once more. His voice muted by the soundproof walls.

Celestine let out a small breath before pulling away and slipping to the back of the car.

His knocks grew louder.

I reached over and unlocked the door, facing the window before he could see my heated face.

"Celestine better not be dead in here," he grunted as he climbed into his seat. "Why was that locked?" he asked, suspiciously.

"No idea," I replied, taking in slow, controlled breaths to calm my racing heart.

Niko put his seatbelt on and glanced at Celestine through the rearview mirror. "Are you alright, Celestine?"

I glanced back at her, she was covering her eyes. "Hyacinth just gives me a headache." Okay, not a bad lie.

Niko chuckled, looking at me, then his eyes went down to my neck and I cursed. "What is that?"

I pulled my hoodie up, turning away again. "Mosquito bite." Not my best lie, but I really couldn't think of anything else.

He turned on the car and began the drive. "Was that mosquito a seventeen-year-old girl?"

I smirked. "A very annoying one."

"I'm going to kill you," Celestine sighed.

"I think Niko might beat you to it," I muttered.

"He didn't force you, did he?" Niko asked her.

"I think it might have been me who forced him," she admitted.

"You didn't," I told her.

"Please, both of you, be careful. If Silias finds out." He shook his head. "I don't know what he'd do. Especially that scene you two caused at the bar..."

We were reckless.

"They won't remember I was there," Celestine whispered.

Niko glanced at her from the rearview mirror. "Let's hope not."

***

We finally arrived at the apartment and Celestine's eyes widened. "It's so pretty," she complimented.

Everything was kept minimalistic, modern and dark. Niko and I liked it like that. Black furniture, dark grey walls, dark wooden floor, and dimly lit. I was a bit surprised she liked it because she's quite feminine and in my head, I imagine her room being just that.

"Cinth, why don't you show her around the apartment and both of you can clean up while I cook dinner."

"Uh, okay," I muttered. I gestured to what we walked into first, a large open area. "The kitchen, dining room and living room–" pointed at the door on the right "–Niko's room and he has his own bathroom in there–" the door next to it "–training room–" then, pointed to one of the doors on the left "–my room and I have my own bathroom–" and the last door "–guest bathroom." Not that we really ever have guests over except for Renee and Jerome.

"You're better as a tour guide than a trainer," she told me, monotoned.

"Yeah, yeah." She followed me to the guest bathroom. "You can clean up here." I pulled out a towel from a cupboard and handed it to her. She nodded a thanks, not meeting my eyes, and I left her to go to my own bathroom.

As I let the warm water drizzle onto me, I slammed my forehead onto the tiled wall. *What did we do in that car?* I let out a deep shaky breath, swearing to myself that I'd never do that to her again. I turned the faucet to the coldest setting.

I walked out of my room to hear Celestine and Niko laughing in the kitchen. She had taken her hair out of its ponytail and let it fall to her waist and was back in her school uniform.

"I can't believe you've never cooked before." Niko handed her an ingredient. "You can cut these now. How do you like your meat, Celestine?"

"Rare."

We stared at her.

"You don't want me to…"

"Medium… Medium-rare," she corrected herself.

I closed my eyes and bit my lip to stop myself from laughing. *Shit. Maybe I should just tell her I know, but this is too funny.* Niko couldn't help his chuckle as he sizzled our meat on the pan.

I took my seat across from Celestine and Niko set down our plates, sitting at the end of the table.

"So, how are you adjusting to your new school, Celestine? Have you made lots of friends?"

"It's okay." She smiled. "The school is really big and even after four months I still get a bit lost sometimes, but everyone's really nice."

They're obsessed with her.

"Yeah, the first time I had to visit for the parent-teacher conference I had no idea where I was going and ended up in the wrong classroom." Niko laughed at the memory. "Did you join any clubs?"

She shook her head. "I don't have time to do anything outside of school, but Silias lets me go ice-skating sometimes." She took a bite of her steak. "This is really good, Nikodemus, and it's cooked so perfectly." I glanced at her meat, barely cooked.

"Thank you, I used this new spice my partner, Renee, suggested to me."

"You have a partner?"

"Yes, we've been together for a few years now." The mention of Renee always gets him gushing with excitement. He pulled out his phone and showed Celestine a picture of them. "This was us last weekend on a date."

"She's pretty," Celestine commented.

He looked at the picture for a moment more before putting his phone away. "What about you, do you have a partner?"

Her eyes shifted to mine then back to Niko. *Subtle.* "I don't like anyone."

"Weren't you two kissing in the car?" he teased.

I felt my face heat up. "No, we weren't. Niko, please."

He laughed. "Sure." Then turned to Celestine. "But you sound just like Cinth when you said you didn't like anyone."

She bit her lip to suppress her smile.

"I swear it's like you want to be me," I muttered. *I'm flattered, but... I'm deranged.*

"I want to be better than you," she corrected.

I shook my head. "Why?"

"Because." She shifted in her seat, looked down at her food and mumbled, "you're like, kind of cool."

I clapped my hands together with a big grin. "Please, say that louder for Niko."

"I said kind of." She glared at me.

"Cinth, you know why you'll never be cool to me," Niko started.

I narrowed my eyes. *Don't you dare tell her any of my humiliating stories, I will throw this table out the window.*

He turned to Celestine with a light chuckle. "The first bone Cinth broke was his arm, and it looked like a noodle. He had these fat crocodile tears running down his face and couldn't stop cackling."

Celestine nodded, intrigued.

"Gods, Niko," I sighed.

"I was helping him out and wondering why there were quiet pauses between..." Niko couldn't stop laughing at this point. "And when I looked up..." he could barely finish his story. "I realised those quiet moments were him passing out."

Celestine used both her hands to cover her laugh. "God below."

"Yeah, alright, I was ten, give me a break." I rolled my eyes. I'm used to seeing people severely injured, but when it comes to my own body, it doesn't really process well.

Celestine mocked, "I guess you're not *that* cool to me anymore."

I hate these people.

When the laughing subsided, Niko asked Celestine, curious, "have you gotten injured a lot, Celestine?"

"When I'm on assignments?" she clarified.

Niko shrugged, trying to keep it as casual as he could. "In general, I suppose."

Celestine nodded. "Yeah, but I don't remember every time."

"What's your worst?" I asked her.

She thought about it for a moment. "My knee, I think, it's been years and I still have problems with it."

"Ah," Niko started, "that's a rough injury. I've known many people who have injured their knee, and it's never been the same since."

"Yeah, I didn't realise how much work it does until I couldn't use it." She laughed, turning her gaze down to her food and began to ramble. "Which sounds so dumb, every part of the body is important." *Is she nervous?* "It's just that it holds your whole weight and then when it's injured you can feel the strain and the... I don't know." She stopped talking, her breathing heavy and her hands trembling as she cut into her meat.

I turned to Niko, changing the topic. Asking him about his day and how Renee was doing, giving Celestine time to recollect herself. Though eventually, I ran out of things to say.

Niko turned to Celestine. "So, what are your plans after high school?"

"Actually." She cleared her throat shyly, looking down at her plate, but it seemed she decided not to say. "I don't know."

"Cinth here wanted to be a veterinarian when he was younger." I knew he only told her because he thought it would make her more comfortable to open up.

"Him?" She probably couldn't believe I wanted to do something that would help anything.

"Oh, yeah, he has a big soft spot for animals, he even turned vegetarian for a year when he was fifteen."

"That's why I treat you so nicely," I muttered.

Celestine responded by kicking my leg under the table and I let out a groan. Niko gave me a weird look. I kicked her shin back, obviously not hard, and it was her turn to let out a wince. She glared at me, and I matched it. Instead of aiming for my leg this time, she kicked my chair, and I fell back with it.

"Cinth!" Niko called my name, but it was angry at me rather than worried for me. Celestine couldn't help but laugh.

I got up from the ground, scowling. "You bloody–"

"Don't you dare finish that," Niko interrupted me, "apologise to Celestine."

I let out a breath of defeat, sitting back down. "Alright, s–" I stopped when she stuck her tongue out at me and pointed at her. "Do you see this?" I swear Niko is blind sometimes.

"Both of you apologise to each other!" Niko exclaimed. Celestine and I folded our arms in front of our chests, refusing to be the first to apologise. Niko put his face in his hands. "Demons below, you two are exactly the same, so stubborn."

I looked up and met Celestine's eyes, playful, and I couldn't help my smirk. We continued to eat and chat and even moved to the sofa. Niko seemed to take a liking to her. Of course he had, he wouldn't have brought her to the apartment if he didn't trust her. She was also unfortunately difficult not to like.

"I need to use the restroom, but I don't know what you two are going to do." Niko squinted his eyes at us.

"Gods," I muttered, "you're a pain."

He raised a brow. "Talking to yourself again, Cinth?"

Celestine laughed a bit too hard at his comment. This whole night the two have just been teaming up against me.

He let out a sigh. "I'll be quick."

Niko left to his room, and I turned to Celestine. "We're never doing what we did in the car again."

She nodded. "Sure."

"I'm serious–" she crawled closer to me "–we're not–" and sat on my lap facing me "–doing that..." and played with my hair, amusement in her eyes. "Again." My heart raced against me.

"Yeah?" she asked, leaning down towards my neck and gently sucking on it. *Not again.*

I cursed. "What are we doing?"

"Do you want me to stop?" she whispered against my neck.

No, I don't.

I didn't say anything, so she continued.

Shit, Niko, come back, I can't control myself.

"I can't do this to you."

"Stop fighting it," she breathed. "We're not supposed to follow the rules."

She's right, why should I care? I've committed nearly every crime in the book and if she's consenting, it should be fine. I brushed my lips on her neck. "You're killing me."

"Good." She laughed. "You bloody deserve it."

"I want to rip you apart so bad," I muttered in her neck.

"Hyacinth," she whispered, sending a chill down my spine.

I pulled away to lock eyes with her. "Yeah?"

She gently grazed her nails across my cheek. "Can you choke me while you do that?"

I groaned with a curse, resting my forehead on hers, and we closed our eyes. Her skin was so cold. "I have barely tasted your blood, Celestine."

She let out a sigh. "Just stab me already."

"Gods, you're so impatient," I said, "let me." I lightly kissed her jaw. "Take my time with you."

One of her hands went down to my sweatpants, and I let her, as she took out my butterfly knife. She pulled away from me, playing with it. "Can I do it?" she asked with an excited smile.

"Do what?"

Her eyes lowered to my chest.

"Oh," I said, "sure." I lifted my hoodie up a bit and pointed to where I wanted the next tally mark, on my lower stomach, just above the waistband of my pants.

Slowly, she grazed the blade across, a bit of fresh blood oozed out and she shifted off me and to her knees, between my legs. She leaned in and pressed her cool mouth over the wound, gently licking it. Heat crept up my cheeks, and I gently caressed the top of her hair.

"What..." Niko's voice sounded behind the sofa and I froze. "What are you two doing?"

I pushed Celestine away, adjusting my hoodie, and walked towards the window, opening it. "See you in the Netherworld." *Because I'm clearly not going to the Ether.* Then I jumped out, three stories down, and landed on the streets with barely a sound. If only I died doing that, though I did nearly slip on ice.

I walked to the corner of the street, leaned against the wall and took out a much needed smoke, cursing at myself and at the world.

Why can't I control myself?

After my cigarette, I went back up to the apartment to Celestine leaving. An ache in my muscles and a pit in my stomach.

"You're certain you don't want me to take you home?" Niko asked her.

She nodded and bowed. "Yes, I'll be fine, thank you so much for dinner."

Niko nodded. "If you're sure."

Before she could step through the threshold, I grabbed her arm and pulled her back inside.

Something's wrong.

"Cinth, what are you doing?" Niko asked.

I'm not really sure, but I had a strong feeling not to let her go. I shifted my eyes to lock with Celestine's and somehow, I think she knew what I was thinking. She shook her head, reassuring me that she really would be okay. I pursed my lips. After a moment, I released her and she left, closing the door behind her.

"Demons below," Niko shivered. "I haven't seen you two do that since you were kids and it's even creepier now." Then, he turned to me and smacked my head. "But you're an idiot."

I rubbed the back of my head, muttering, "as if I didn't already bloody know that." I considered following her, to make sure she got home safely, but I didn't.

As Niko and I were cleaning the kitchen, his phone rang, and he went to the living room to answer it.

"Yes, Celestine left a while ago." He glanced at the clock on the wall. "Around half an hour ago, she should be there soon." Niko nodded as he waited for the other end. "She's more than capable of taking care of herself–" he paused. "Right, from now on we'll drop her off every time." Another pause. "Good night."

He hung up the phone and turned to me. "Silias was upset because it's past her curfew."

It was fair, she's only seventeen, but she should be fine. *Right?*

15

CHAOS AND CALM

NOVEMBER 70 A.D.

My friends didn't hesitate to make fun of the marks on my neck, unfortunately one on either side.

"Who gave it to you, Cinth?" Lin smirked.

"Yeah, just tell us, we won't tell." Jamiel laughed.

"Shut up," I muttered.

"Did Cel give it to you?" Iri teased.

I felt my body heat up at the thought of Celestine's icy lips against my hot neck, on my stomach, the way she looked up at me... "Drop it," I said and they did for the moment, but pestered me about it again later.

I hadn't seen Celestine for a couple days, since she had dinner with Niko and me. It wasn't unusual for her to skip; I don't think she's actually ever attended a full week of school. Due to her narcolepsy, there are days where she isn't able to leave her bed at all.

She announced her arrival during lunch by throwing an apple at my head, while I was waiting for my friends to finish paying for their meals. I caught it and turned to her. "I forgot you exist." I tossed her apple back to her.

"Angels above, Cinth, how fast are your reflexes?" Iri asked me.

Very fast. "I was lucky," I replied.

Celestine looked drained. Her usual glow wasn't there, a bit of sweat coated her forehead and her half-lidded eyes more droopy than usual. "I know you dream about me." She stood close to me.

Was she guessing? Or did she actually know?

"Oh my gods, you actually do dream about me?" she laughed. "What am I doing in them?"

"Uh," I hesitated and felt my face heat up, I had to think of something quick. "I'm killing you in my dreams and you're killing me in my nightmares."

"Sure," she said, usually this is the part where she would leave, but she stayed and stared blankly at my hand holding my drink. I wasn't hungry today.

Jamiel put a hand on my shoulder and shook his head. "You should have just kept your mouth shut, Cinth."

"I'm getting severe second-hand embarrassment right now," Iri said.

"It's your birthday today," she whispered.

I blinked. "How did you know that?"

Not even my friends knew.

Celestine reached for my wrist and put her weight onto me as she swayed a bit, the apple slipped out of her hand and rolled away across the floor.

"Are you good?" I asked. She was growing pale–paler than usual and her eyes were fading.

Before she could answer, Iri handed Jamiel her food, putting her arm around Celestine to help hold her up. "Cel." She pulled her away from me. "Let's take you to the nurse."

Celestine didn't argue, leaning her weight on Iri as they walked out of the cafeteria. Her limp was much more prominent today.

"She looked like she was about to pass out," Jamiel said.

"Yeah," I said, watching as they turned the corner out of the room.

"Come on, Iri will tell us what's happened." Jamiel nodded towards the door leading outside, but I didn't move. "Or you can follow them."

I snapped my head towards him. "Why would I care enough to do that?" I muttered following Jamiel to our usual table, Lin already there.

"You guys took your time." Lin was stuffing his face with a sandwich. "Where's Iri?"

"Taking care of Cel, she looked sick," Jamiel replied.

"What? What happened?" Lin gasped.

Jamiel shrugged. "No idea."

Iri didn't get back from the nurse's office until our class started. "What happened with Cel?" Lin asked.

She shook her head. "She passed out right when we got to the nurse's office and I thought it was just her narcolepsy, but when the nurse and I were helping her get into the bed, we saw this bruise on her thigh, under her skirt. When we looked... There were so many bruises on her body."

When Celestine and I train, I never let anyone touch her. Ever. She's too young and small to be injured and one blow could be fatal on her or worse, ruin her entire career. She already had a permanent knee injury and didn't need another one on top of it.

"They were all over her body," Iri said. "And they were huge. The principal had to come in too."

"Who would have done that to her?" Lin gasped.

Iri shook her head.

It's highly unlikely Reaper would get randomly assaulted on the streets because of how young she looked, especially considering her height. On top of that, not many people knew what the Grim Reaper looked like, most people assumed she was in her late-twenties. *Silias.* Was this Silias's doing?

"Well, did you ask her?" Jamiel asked.

"She was still out, and the principal made me leave."

"Hyacinth." I turned to the teacher behind me. "Come with me."

"Why?"

"The principal wants to see you."

Oh, bloody hell.

I walked behind the teacher slowly, not ready for this interrogation, but I know I didn't do it. There were a few teachers inside already, along with two security guards.

"Hello, Hyacinth," the principal greeted.

I took the seat directly across from her, feeling all their stares.

The principal sat back in her seat. "I'd like you to tell me your relationship with Celestine."

"Complicated," I muttered.

"Complicated?" she repeated, "un-complicate it."

I shook my head. "If you're trying to figure out if I was the one who gave her all those bruises, it wasn't me."

"How do you know about her injuries?" She acted as if she got me.

"Because Iri, the girl who brought her to the nurse, is one of my closest friends," I snapped.

The principal squinted her eyes at me, unappreciative of my tone. "So, you wouldn't hurt Celestine at all?"

"No."

It didn't look like she believed me. "I know you and Celestine have a rather rocky relationship and recently you two have been getting close, but–"

"Why don't you ask her for the story before you go and accuse me?"

"I haven't accused you of anything, Hyacinth, but we will." She nodded. "You can go back to class now."

I stood up, shoving my hands in my pockets and left the room. I headed towards the nurse's office and found the nurse gone and Celestine laying on one of the beds. She turned to me but avoided my eyes, pulling the sheets over her face.

"Who hurt you?" I walked to the side of the bed.

"I'm fine," she mumbled under the sheet. "I'm just sleepy."

I yanked the sheet off and began tugging her top up. There was a slight grimace on her face at my touch.

"What are you doing?" she asked, pushing at my hand, but I was stronger and she was significantly weaker than normal to put up much of a fight.

I hesitated for a single moment. *What gave me the right?*

With my other hand, I took her wrists and held them in place. Finally, I could look at her stomach. The bruises were completely black and the size of my hand, I lifted her top a bit more to see the edge of another. I've seen worse injuries, but even on Niko I never had this sick feeling in my stomach.

"How many bruises?" I asked in a whisper. These were done by someone who knew what they were doing, inflicting enough damage to cause pain but not enough to break anything.

Celestine turned her head away from me, letting her hair cover her face. "Stop, Cinth."

I gently grazed my finger over the dark marks. "Did it happen the same night you had dinner with Niko and me?"

She nodded, biting her lower lip.

"Was it Silias?"

"No," she snapped. "It wasn't. They wore masks, I don't know who they were."

"Then?" I urged. "Why didn't you fight back?"

She's talented enough to take anyone down, I've seen it.

"They surprised me and... I froze." Her voice cracked, like she hated herself for even saying it.

I pulled her top back down and put the blanket back over her. "What did they do to you?"

She shook her head. "I don't remember it all." Her mind protected her.

"What do you remember?" I urged.

It took a moment for her to answer. "Nothing," she muttered.

I didn't understand. Why would anyone jump her? Why did she freeze? "Do you know why they did it?"

"No."

I cupped her cheek with my hand, and she leaned into it, closing her eyes. "Don't lie to me."

Celestine finally met my eyes and told me. Her memory was short and choppy. She was walking from the station, when two people in ski masks assaulted her. They pulled her into an alleyway and called her Stygian scum–*disgusting racial slur*–demanding she tell them everything she knew about Vulture. They left her bloodied and bruised, but didn't touch her face because it was 'too pretty to touch' and she 'wouldn't be worth anything without it.' The twins were the ones to find her, and she spent the last few days recovering.

My veins ran cold. She's being targeted because of me. It's supposed to be the opposite, she's supposed to be protected by being associated with me. *But why her?* I've never had this problem with Iri, Lin, and Jamiel. Was it because they knew she would know more?

She's not safe.

"So it was because of me that this happened?"

"No," she whispered, "it wasn't."

"But they only questioned you about me."

"I didn't tell them anything about you."

I trust she didn't. "I wouldn't have been upset if you did, they hurt you." I'd rather her tell them everything she knew, than go through something like that again.

"I would never do that to you." She let out a shaky breath. "I'm so tired of this."

I gently brushed her hair out of her face. "Tired of what?"

She had a completely emotionless expression, but her eyes welled with tears. "They gave me this name, the Grim Reaper, but it doesn't mean anything. No one respects me."

Even though she was almost as powerful as I am and–especially at the rate she's going–will one day be my equal, there was a big difference between how people treated me compared to her. I'm not really sure what it is, if it's because she's new or a girl or young or maybe because she doesn't look scary.

"I respect you."

"Do you?"

I nodded. "You're one of the few people I actually respect." Then, I added, "but you shouldn't use fear." That wouldn't work for her. "You should get people to adore you." Like what Siren does.

She muttered under her breath. "They only like looking at me." Her tone wasn't bitter. It was hallow, as if she'd accepted it long ago.

"Use it."

The tears began. "I'm sorry, I'm so weak."

"Why would you think that?" I asked in a soft voice.

"Because I'm crying."

"There's no shame in crying. It doesn't make you weak."

"Do you cry?" she whispered.

I wiped her cheek with my thumb. "Sometimes," I admitted. "If this ever happens again, you will tell me, yeah?"

She slowly nodded.

"Good girl." I smiled.

I don't know why I did it, but I brushed my lips against her hairline. She wrapped her arms over my neck, and pulled me back towards her, her grip desperate for me to ground her and keep her from breaking completely.

Our foreheads rested against each other, eyes closed. Our breathings synchronised, and I swore to myself to always listen to my gut feeling.

"Hyacinth." I turned to the nurse's voice behind me. "You shouldn't be in here. Please go back to class."

I nodded and left.

***

"Hyacinth." A teacher called my name as I was exiting the school with Celestine. "You have detention, where do you think you're going?"

"Detention starts half past, I'll be there in a bit," I told her, dismissing her disapproving stare.

"You don't have to walk me out," Celestine mumbled.

I ignored her comment knowing the twins were waiting for her just outside the school gates, but she was injured and vulnerable. Wearing their helmets, the twins turned towards us as we approached. Sterling took off his helmet and got off his bike, but Leo stayed on his.

"You were supposed to protect her!" Sterling shouted, getting up in my face.

"Sterling, there are people around us," Celestine warned.

"Let them hear! Let them hear how the notorious Vul–"

I clasped my hand over his mouth, shutting him up. "I need you to lower your volume."

Sterling smacked my hand away. "Why did you let her go home on her own?" he growled, lowering his voice.

I shook my head, not having an answer to it.

Sterling let out an irritated noise. "You have as much responsibility for what happened to her as the ones who hurt her."

"Sterling," Celestine started. "It's not his fault, don't make him feel guilty–"

"Guilty? He can't feel that." Sterling spat. "He can't feel anything."

I shoved my hands into my pocket, rubbing my thumb against my index finger. Without a reply, I turned and headed back into the school.

***

I came home to the smell of a fresh apple cake baking in the oven. I glanced over at the kitchen to see Renee and Niko, bits of flour on their faces, laughing with one another as Niko grabbed Renee from behind, lifting and twirling her around.

"Niko, Cinth! Cinth is here!" Renee giggled.

Niko carefully set Renee back on her feet before turning to me with a large smile. "You're just in time!" The small timer dinged.

I set my bag down in my room and went over to them. "What's the occasion?"

Renee opened the oven, releasing the sweet scent in a wave, pulling out her famous apple cake. It takes her hours to make, and the recipe has been passed down to her going back to her great-grandmother. "What do you mean, Cinth?" She beamed, setting it down on the counter.

Niko took out three plates and poured each of us a glass of milk. "It's your birthday, Cinth! Don't tell us ageing has already affected your memory."

It's not really my birthday, it's the anniversary of when I was dropped off at the orphanage. Though, I guess legally I am eighteen now.

"Right," I muttered.

Renee cut a large piece for me, before serving one for Niko and herself, then we sat around the table to eat. "Happy birthday, Cinth!" she exclaimed. "Do you have plans with your friends tonight?"

I shook my head. I couldn't think of celebrating when Celestine was injured because of me.

"Why not?" Renee asked. "You have the night off, don't you?"

Niko nodded in confirmation.

"I need to visit Silias, Niko," I told him. "I'm going to stop training Celestine."

He paused, his fork halfway to his mouth. "Why?"

I told him about her injuries, and he called Silias to let him know we would be visiting him later in the evening.

"You must really care for her to stop the training," Renee said, comfortably rubbing my back.

I didn't reply.

Renee pursed her lips. "Well, was there anything you wanted for your birthday?"

I want to know who the two behind the masks were. Instead, I met Renee's eyes and smiled.

"The cake was all I wanted. Thank you."

***

That night, Niko drove through the gates of the Kokkino Estate and parked in front of the door. He got out, meeting me at the steps. I didn't want to go inside without him, even if Celestine was in there.

"Best behaviour," Niko reminded me.

The twins opened the door, and it felt like déjà vu. Sterling's hard eyes glared at me, but Leo stared straight ahead.

Only candles illuminated the walls as the twins led us to the dining room.

Silias sat at the very end of the long table that seated a dozen people. Rayne sat on his right, Sterling on his left, Leo next to Sterling, and Oremus next to Rayne.

I glanced around but didn't see Celestine anywhere.

"Please, sit." Silas gestured.

Niko took the seat next to Oremus, and I sat across from him, next to Leo. Just as we sat down, chefs entered the room with dishes that were served in small portions.

This was certainly not going to fill me at all.

Silias was the one to start the conversation. "So." He lifted his glass for a server to fill with wine. "Cel tells me the training is going well, but she doesn't go much in depth with it." He met my eyes. "How do you think she's going?"

"It's fine," I muttered. What else do I say? "She works hard."

"Care to elaborate? I'd love to hear the stories of her training." Silias sipped his wine. "You know, Cel's so shy, but I'm sure there are some interesting things that happen."

"Stories?" I repeated. "Not really. Just typical training sessions. I teach her techniques and she mimics me."

"Hm," Silias said. "Surely there are some things that shock you?"

"She's quick," I stated "I don't usually need to show her how to do things more than once."

"And do you ever get frustrated with her?"

I shook my head.

"Hyacinth understands how young and novice she is," Niko said. "So he wouldn't get so easily angry at her."

That's a lie, I get angry at her in every training.

"Ever?" Silias questioned.

I replied. "I may be harsh, but that's just how I talk."

"You know, with your reputation as Vulture, I always thought you'd be colder to Cel, but ever since she's begun training and doing her assignments with you, she comes home without a scratch on her."

"Just because you don't see any injuries on her, doesn't mean she hasn't been working," I said. I let out a breath, knowing I needed to get this over with. "Speaking of training Reaper, I would like to stop."

There was a long silence of utensils against plates before Silias looked at me. "And why is that?"

"There's a reason why I don't allow people to get near me–"

"Because you're a dog?" Sterling muttered.

I shot him a glare. This was not the time nor the place to start something with me. I ignored him and continued, "she's become a target."

"Target?" Silias repeated.

"I'm sure Reaper told you, the reason she was attacked was because they were interrogating her about me."

Silias pursed his lips and exchanged a look with Rayne. "No," he said, slowly. "She conveniently left that part out."

I glanced at Niko, hoping I didn't just get Celestine into trouble. Though, he gave me a reassuring nod, letting me know soundlessly that they should know this.

"Wouldn't it be best that you train her so that she can take care of herself?" Leo asked.

I shook my head. "This is for her safety."

Rayne circled the tip of her finger on the top of her wine glass. "It sounds as though you've gone soft, Vulture."

Don't taunt me.

"Perhaps..." Niko intervened before I said something I wouldn't be able to take back. "A solution to this could be if you allow her to live with us, while we train her. It would accelerate her training and lower her risk of being attacked as there would be no travelling."

"You will be training her as well?" Sterling rose a brow. Celestine would be only the second person he'd train in his life.

Niko nodded. "I had a chat with Celestine a while back, but we haven't had the chance to start just yet."

"No," Silias immediately said. "She stays here."

"It wouldn't be permanent," Niko explained. "Simply… Until she's ready to be independent."

"And how long would that be?" Silias asked.

Niko turned to me for an answer, having not yet trained her.

"I would assume maybe a couple months," I said. "She has training already and improved a lot in such a short amount of time. With the holidays approaching she should be independent by the time it ends."

"What if you two move into the estate instead?" Rayne suggested.

Niko shook his head. "No, I've made myself very clear multiple times to Silias, I even told Ender no." Associating with a single clan or person would limit our work and put more targets on us. Niko would never budge on that.

Silias bit his cheek. "I'm surprised you care so much about her."

You and I both.

He pondered over the option for a moment more before answering, "you aren't doing this because you've fallen for her, correct?"

"She's a liability I can't afford to ignore," I said. I don't quite understand the relationship between her and Silias, but it would be best to keep whatever relationship we have a secret from everyone, especially him.

There was a long pause as he exchanged looks with Rayne. It wasn't until we had all finished eating when he finally spoke again with an answer. "Perhaps she can stay with you two during the holiday." There was a certain sadness in his eyes. "She knows her place is with me." Though it sounded like he was trying to convince himself. Silias shook his head, letting out a deep breath. "If you hadn't created Vulture, I would never allow this." Silias looked at Niko.

"Naturally." Niko nodded.

Silias led us out the door. Just before he closed it behind us, he said, "oh, and happy birthday, Vulture."

***

The next day, during our shared history class, Celestine and I were called into the principal's office. When we arrived, the receptionist nodded a greeting at us. "Everyone's waiting for you." He gestured towards the principal's door.

Everyone? We entered the room to see the principal sitting behind her desk, while Niko and Leo sat across from her, two empty seats between them.

"Celestine, Hyacinth," the principal greeted us as we took our seats.

Celestine and I exchanged looks. She seemed confused, but I could guess what this was about.

The principal took a deep breath. "I'm going to skip the formalities and cut to it. The teachers and I have reasons to believe Hyacinth may be abusing Celestine."

How troublesome.

"Now, we haven't informed the police just yet, but we will if it's necessary."

There was a long silence. None of us knew what to say and I knew I definitely couldn't defend myself, it'd only make it worse if I tried.

"Are you serious?" Celestine asked.

"I wouldn't have called both of your guardians if I wasn't," she replied.

Celestine looked at Leo, gripping onto the collar of her shirt.

"You didn't even ask me who did this," Celestine said, her voice shaking with disbelief.

"I don't believe we need to ask," the principal said.

"But Hyacinth has never hurt me before."

"Was he not harassing you when you first arrived at this school?"

"I started that," her voice was low. "And I was messing with him too." She was just better at not getting caught, while I didn't care enough to hide it.

"Celestine," the principal started, "it's okay, you can tell me the truth. I'm going to protect you."

Celestine's body trembled, but she managed to keep her voice steady. "The only people who have ever protected me are sitting next to me, not across."

"Honestly, I don't know what you're talking about," Leo said, "Cel's fine."

"Telling me she's fine is rather concerning, sir. The teachers and I have all witnessed scars and bruises on her legs and arms and most likely there are others on the rest of her body. Am I wrong, Celestine?"

Celestine's eyes welled up again. "It wasn't him."

Niko shook his head. "Hyacinth wouldn't hurt her, he wouldn't do that."

The principal raised a brow. "Hyacinth has a record for assaulting other students at this school. The only reason he hasn't been expelled is because you, Mr Kolden, pay us not to, but this may be the final straw."

Oh, this is the final straw? Even if I did do it, I've done much worse, and they just gave me a suspension. *Why is this case different?*

"I said he didn't do it," Celestine repeated.

"Celestine, if he didn't do it, who did?" the principal asked. "Is this going on at home?"

"No." Celestine released a small breath, embarrassed about it. "I was attacked on my way home."

"Just nod your head if Hyacinth has ever hurt you."

There was nothing I could say, but I don't know why she would have asked me to join this conversation. If I actually did do something, what was the likelihood that Celestine would be honest in front of me?

The door knocked and in came the same two school security guards from a couple days ago. After Celestine's first day of school, the Kokkino clan lingered to scare off any media, but it didn't make the school look good, so the school hired security. Though, they are primarily just for show.

"Is this really necessary?" Niko asked. "You're going to do it in front of the whole school?"

A small whimper escaped Celestine. "I just told you I was attacked." She squinted her eyes back at the principal. "Why are you so convinced he did it?"

"I've had a lot of students come in here worried about you because of Hyacinth and how he treats you."

"It's just a game we play," she argued.

"Celestine," the principal started, "I know you're quite young and frail, that's why you're more vulnerable and you may not understand but some victims fall for their abusers–"

"Stop," Celestine warned, closing her eyes.

But she continued, "and I'm afraid you may be feeling this way for Hyacinth since you're protecting him."

"You don't know anything."

The security guards came up behind me.

"I know Hyacinth can be very intimidating and that most people in this school have taken an interest in you because of your appearance. I, along with all the teachers, have heard many rumours that you and Hyacinth have slept together, and we can't help but think that he forced–"

Celestine jumped out of her seat and wrapped herself around me protectively shielding me. "Don't touch him, don't touch him." She begged, pulling my head into her chest.

I had never been more shocked in my life, I couldn't move a single muscle.

"Cel!" Leo stood up from his seat.

I felt tears on top of my head. "Don't take him away from me again." Her voice cracked as she sobbed. "Please."

It should have been me protecting her, not the other way around.

"Celestine, this is obviously an unhealthy relationship you have with Hyacinth. Normal people do not get attached to another person like this unless they have been brainwashed. I know you've slept around with *unworthy men*, starting with Octavius Gautier, and I am afraid that history is repeating itself."

"Stop it, you don't know anything," Celestine cried. "Hyacinth's the only one in this school that actually tries to get to know me," she spat. "He's the one who's been protecting me from all the people who only want to sleep with me and he's the only one in this bloody city who genuinely doesn't want anything from me."

Her body trembled against mine and I could feel her heart racing. "How could you assume such awful things about someone and as if he wasn't in the room with us?" Then, her body crumbled, collapsing onto me as the cataplexy took hold.

I took a deep breath and carefully adjusted her position to be more comfortable, cradling her. "They're not going to kill me," I reassured her. "I'm not going anywhere."

"On the contrary, Hyacinth–"

"You've got no proof that he did it," Niko started, "and Celestine has continuously denied that he had anything to do with what happened to her. So, will you drop it?"

I shifted my gaze between the two. The principal was not pleased to say the least. "If you see this dependency Celestine has with Hyacinth as normal, you are wrong. He is doing something to her, I know he is," she insisted. "Everyone saw the two leave the school together, then Celestine missed a few days of school and came back with severe injuries. Where did you two go?"

"She came to my place," I replied.

The principal raised her brow. "And what happened there?"

"We're not sleeping together," I groaned, frustrated. "We've never done anything."

"That's not what it looks like, Hyacinth," the principal said and Leo and Niko turned to me, also not believing my words.

The air shifted. Everyone in the room stopped breathing, their eyes dazed and fixed on Celestine. She shifted position, turning to face the principal but staying on me, the back of her head resting on my chest. "Hyacinth's never hurt me." Her voice was so calm and dream-like. "I was assaulted on the streets, and everything's been sorted."

The principal slowly nodded.

"Never threaten me with the police and don't ever disrespect Hyacinth like that again."

She nodded once again.

"Get back to your job," Celestine said. The two security guards turned on their heels and left the room, but the principal sat there, dazed and motionless. Then Celestine shifted her eyes to Leo. "The principal just wanted to follow you up on how I'm doing in school."

Leo nodded, in the same daze as the principal.

"Leave," Celestine told him and he did. She looked at me. I had no idea what was going on. "Hyacinth." She gently cupped my cheeks, regret in her eyes. "I'm so sorry I have to do this."

"Celestine." Niko stopped her. "You can trust him."

She shook her head, "I don't want him to remember the things that were said about him."

"Why?" I asked in a low voice. I wanted to remember how she felt about me, the things she said to defend me. I didn't care what the principal and everyone else assumed, I didn't care about anyone but her.

She didn't answer me. Her eyes glowed a bright red as she leaned close to me and gently placed her lips on my forehead, whispering, "forget being in here."

No. Not again.

"Cinth," Jamiel whispered from the desk next to mine. "Oi."

I turned my focus away from the board and to him.

"What did the principal want with you?"

I furrowed my brows. "What are you on about?"

"Jamiel, Hyacinth," the teacher snapped at us. "Is there something you'd like to share with the class?"

"No, miss," Jamiel and I muttered.

16

CORPSE KILLERS

November 70 A.D.

Celestine started coming back to school again more regularly. Her injuries were now fully healed and Niko stole her from me a few times throughout the next couple of weeks, taking her for the entire evening. Sometimes I would come home to find them having dinner together. I used the extra free time to meet up with my friends, the ones at school, in the Underworld, and even the living Demons.

Niko never told me what he and Celestine did and I had too much pride to follow them, but I was... I don't know. Though, she had improved even more after his training. Obviously. He created me.

"So, that's it," Symeon ended his explanation of his take down on the Kokkino clan waiting for me to comment on it all. Kahlik stood behind Symeon, pacing back and forth as his eyes flickered from the page up to my eyes then back on the ground.

I stared at the piece of paper with all the messy, ineligible scribbles, leaning back in my chair in Kahlik's apartment. "That is the shittiest plan I've ever heard," I said, exhaling smoke.

Kahlik's mouth fell open, insulted. He slammed his hands onto the table leaning over it. "What– what part?"

It had taken a month for them to come up with it and I shut it down with eight words. "The whole thing," I said. "Killing the entire inner circle–firstly, you are not to touch Reaper."

"Did you not hear us?" Symeon's face was red. My mind was distracted, but I was still half listening to this. "That's why we told you we would do it while she's at school."

I shook my head. "And when she finds out who killed her clan, she'll come for all of us." She would never forgive me for it.

"Then, we have to kill her," Symeon stated. "We can't have anyone in our way."

My eyes darkened, my voice low and calm. "Say that again."

Kahlik's eyes widened as he looked between Symeon and me.

Symeon's lips tightened as he swallowed, and he could barely get out the words. "What is the point of you saying yes to this, if all you're doing is shutting down every idea we come up with? It's like you don't actually want us to do it."

"Killing the leader of the Kokkino clan is not simple," I said. "If it were, then we wouldn't need to plan this much. We kill Silias and then what? The Underworld would be just as chaotic as it was when Ender was murdered. This job requires thinking years ahead."

"The Underworld will become better."

I inhaled my cigarette deeply, shaking my head. "No, someone else needs to step into his spot and who can you think of would suit it?" No one was more suited than Ender, even I could not compare myself to him.

"Us. We could lead the Kokkino clan," Symeon suggested.

This is a cycle that will only get worse with each new leader. It needs to be broken. There cannot be this many leaders with this many opposing views on how the city should and shouldn't be. It's chaotic. The entire structure of power doesn't have any sense to it and is constantly shifting between clans. Taking down the Kokkino clan would change nothing.

"You want to lead a clan? Do you know the work that goes with it? Do you know that people will fight you for that spot?" I said. "Silias killed hundreds of competitors to secure his place."

"And we will do the same. Kokkino clan has too much power, we would split it between all of us." Kahlik said.

"That's not going to work and you know it," I bit back.

Symeon let out a frustrated breath. "So what, Vulture?" His voice was rising with his anger. "What do you suggest we do?"

I released a smoky breath. "Give me some time to get some intel on the clan. I'm getting closer to Reaper and I'm trying to figure out her relationship with the clan."

They stared at me, waiting for me to continue, but I wasn't going to tell them what I assumed, because I could be wrong.

"If it turns out she doesn't like her clan, we could use her to kill him for us," I said. "Who would be better at doing the job than someone from the inside?"

Kahlik and Symeon exchanged looks.

"Fine," Symeon said. "But if you're only stalling us to protect her, we'll revert to the original plan. And if she gets hurt, then that's on you, Vulture. You could have aligned with us to keep her out of harm's way."

I let out a short laugh, holding my cigarette between my teeth. *You absolute idiot.* With a quick move, I stood up, grabbed Symeon by his neck, flipped him onto his back, and pinned him to the table. I moved one hand up to his face, squeezing his cheeks to force his mouth open. With my other hand, I inhaled one long breath of smoke into my lungs before taking it and dropping the burning stump into his mouth. "If you even look at Reaper, the next thing going in your mouth will be your own eyeballs. Yeah?"

Symeon's flushed cheeks wetted with his own tears and he struggled to nod through my hold.

I couldn't help my smile. "Now swallow."

He made the strangest sound as he did so. My phone vibrated in my pocket, and I took it out, still gripping onto Symeon. Niko's name filled my screen. I licked the front of my teeth, rolling my eyes. *It's as if he knows what I'm doing.* Without letting Symeon go, I answered the call.

"Come home now," Niko commanded.

"Why?"

"Did you forget you're training Celestine?"

Since she wasn't at school today, I had assumed we weren't training.

"She's waiting for you here."

I hung up and slipped my phone back into my pocket. I released Symeon, and he quickly sat back up, coughing.

"Come up with a better plan that includes what we do after, we'll meet again another day." In all honesty, I don't really think all this work is worth what they think will happen. There's surely a better, more promising plan... I just needed to think of it.

"But–"

I turned to Kahlik, and he quickly closed his mouth.

Yeah, that's what I thought. I shoved my hands back into my pockets, making my way out of their place.

Just as I opened the door, Symeon said, "your weakness for her is showing. The old Vulture wouldn't have wasted a thought on collateral."

I didn't respond, slamming the door shut behind me.

***

Celestine was in the bathroom getting changed when I arrived home.

"Cinth," Niko started, putting down today's paper with half the sudoku puzzle filled out. "Be careful with what you say to Celestine."

"Yeah, I know," I said, pouring water from the tap into my glass.

"No, I don't think you do," he said. "She doesn't know the difference between right and wrong. I don't want her going down the wrong path."

"Bit late for that, don't you think?" I muttered, leaning against the counter facing him as I drowned my dry throat with water.

He shook his head. "It's never too late, but she's quite confused and I know she looks up to you."

I scoffed. "Not sure why she would think I'd be a good role model."

"You have good morals."

I'm going to let him rethink that.

"You're just a little too violent sometimes."

There it is.

I laughed. "Yeah, but have you seen her? She's just as insane as I am."

He shook his head. "She wants to be like you. So, just... Calm down a bit, at least in front of her."

I've never shown her my dark side, I never wanted to because I knew she wanted to be like me. And because I didn't know how she'd react to it, if she could handle it. "She once told me she wants to be like Phobus," I said.

He shook his head and muttered, "of all the gods, that's the one she idolises?"

"He's not that bad, is he?"

"Phobus, Cinth?" He gave me a look. "He's the God of fear, pain, darkness, and death. He doesn't have any morals, infants die because of him."

No, we should blame Poiesis, Goddess of Creation, for not giving infants a fully functional immune system and making birth complicated and life-threatening. "Right," I muttered.

"The only good thing he's done was create Demons and even that's debatable." He shook his head. "But you were right about how stubborn Celestine is," he chuckled. "She's almost as bad as you were."

I let out a breath of relief, I thought she only acted like that with me. I'm so glad it was just her personality and not because of how I'm so soft around her.

"If she ever asks if what she's doing is right, think before you answer. There's already too many bad people in this city and we don't need another one," he scolded.

I rolled my eyes, putting my glass away.

Celestine came out a couple minutes later. Her eyes lit up for a moment before she quickly came back to her neutral expression. I went into my room and grabbed one of my black hoodies then tossed it to Celestine. "Put this over you."

"We're not training?" she asked. My hoodies are oversized on me, so they easily reached her knees.

"We are."

We weren't given an assignment tonight, so we headed to a place that might give her some more insight into the world she's a part of.

We were on the West side of Soulesity and headed in the direction of the warehouses.

"You should put your hair down, the place is run by Etherians," I warned her.

She paused in her steps, narrowing her eyes. "You're taking me to Etherian territory? They'll kill me if they find out who I am or worse."

"They won't," I said. "And even if they find out, you're under twenty and you're with me. Just cover your Stygian tattoo to avoid any attention."

She bit her bottom lip but eventually walked by my side again, trusting me. She released her hair and pulled the hood up over her.

There were about twenty warehouses in this area and I knew that one belonged to the Mov clan and another was an Etherian clan. There were a few Etherian clans, but the most dangerous was the Corpse Killers. They thought it was more intimidating to have a racial slur in their name—couldn't just leave it at Demon Killers. Their group was large, rumour says the leader had Angel blood which easily helped expand their clan. They were also the most violent Etherian group and directly clashed with the Kokkino clan.

Every week, the clan held a fight that anyone could participate in, and everyone bet on. The large man at the door gave me a nod to enter and barely looked at Celestine close behind me.

The inside was dark, only the elevated cage standing in the centre was lit, showcasing the fight. The two men wore nothing but shorts, their hands bloodied and bruised and their faces swollen. Around a hundred people were watching, some wearing masks to hide their faces, and some who didn't care. The air was stuffy, the smell of sweat and cigarette smoke lingering.

I pulled Celestine in front of me so I could see her and allowed her to lean back against my chest. "You see the guy in the black shorts?" I started in a low voice. "He's the Corpse Killers' most ruthless fighter, Elijah Voss. Watch how he finishes the others."

Whispers said he's a descendant of one of the four families in the Kynigos. He was only a year older than me, but with all the fighting, the tattoos and the muscle, he looked closer to mid-twenties. His hair was braided back and out of his face, displaying his cauliflower ears and the Etherian tattoo on his neck inked in white. All the Etherian clans had a white tattoo, the only way to distinguish them was that the Corpse Killers had the letters 'CKC' branded on their chest.

Elijah ducked before his opponent could strike him and using the momentum to stand up right, he threw a punch that struck his opponent's temple. The man flew back into the fence, blood shooting out of his nose, and he crumbled to his knees. Before the man could get up, Elijah whipped a kick at him and his body slammed down, completely knocked out. Elijah got on top, continuing to punch the unconscious man over and over. The crowd yelled, cheering Elijah on.

"Is no one going to stop him?" Celestine gasped.

The man was barely recognisable as a human being, when someone finally stepped into the ring, yanking Elijah off him, shouting at him to step back. Elijah spat blood onto the floor, turning his head sideways to crack it.

"He gets more and more unhinged as he ages," someone said next to me.

I turned to meet Jerome's eyes.

"Hey Psycho."

A wide grin spread across his face, one marred by scars he usually hid beneath a ski mask and hood. When he was Jack Spades, though, he let everyone see exactly who he was. Jerome was only a couple of years older than me. His shaved head accentuated the heavy brows and long lashes framing his hazel eyes. He was tall but wiry—too much caffeine, too little real food.

I smirked at him, clasping his hand. "Socio."

His eyes curiously looked down towards Celestine. "Who's that?"

Celestine turned up to meet his eyes and a deep blush crept up Jerome's cheeks and ears. His smirk faltered.

"Celestine," she said after a beat.

Jerome's hand lifted automatically to his face, as if suddenly aware of his scars. "Jack Spades," he muttered, avoiding her eyes.

While I looked back to the cage where Elijah was waiting for his next fight, Jerome's gaze lingered on Celestine a moment longer than it should have.

"So, you know Vulture how?" Jerome asked Celestine.

"We go to the same school."

"I'm training her," I said under my breath.

Jerome's eyes widened, connecting the dots. "Are you insane? Vulture, if they find out—"

"Shut your bloody mouth," I growled as a few people turned to look in our direction at Jerome's sudden outburst. "They won't."

Jerome pursed his lips, realising his mistake and quickly deflected their interest away from us. "So, the other day, yeah? I was waiting in line, like a good citizen, you know?" The thing about Jerome was that even if we hadn't spoken in months, he talked as if we had just seen each other an hour ago.

"In line for what?" I asked.

"For this new frozen yoghurt shop, we should go, it's actually really good—anywho, so I was waiting, and these two guys just cut me in line, not even subtle about it!"

"How rude."

Those around us grew bored of listening to our conversation and one by one they turned away. His shoulders eased slightly once no one was watching.

"So you know what I did?" He asked.

I waited for him to continue in his dramatic style. One time, he was skateboarding, and a pebble got caught in the wheel, causing him to fall and scrape a bit of his skin. So what did he do? Took the pebble and threw it off the Great Bridge, so that it would 'drown.'

"I found where they lived. You want to join me?"

"When?" I asked.

"Tomorrow night." He smiled. "Two people, one for each of us."

I nodded.

The next fighter entered the cage, a man twice the size of Elijah and Elijah wasn't that small. Reaper stiffened against me. "There's no way he could take him down, right?"

"Just watch," I said as the two circled each other. "See what Elijah is doing?" Elijah used his foot to kick at his opponent's legs. "He's trying to break his base. Without a solid stance, he'll lose balance and it'll give Elijah the advantage."

Just as I said it, the man wobbled and Elijah took that opportunity to lunge at him and throw punch after punch, not allowing the man any breaks, forcing him down to his knees. The giant grabbed onto Elijah's ankle and pulled, sending him to his back with a grunt. The crowd roared in shock and excitement. The man grabbed Elijah, lifting him up over his head, and threw him against the cage. While the man took a moment to celebrate his early victory, Elijah got back up to his feet, swaying a bit, fire in his eyes. He charged at the man and sent a flying kick to the back of his head, knocking the large man out instantly.

"The fight was so quick." Celestine breathed.

"That's how it usually is," I said. "Just because you're small, doesn't mean you can't fight those who are larger than you."

She turned back up to meet my eyes with a slight smile. "Thanks for showing me this."

The knocked-out man came back to consciousness after being slapped a few times in the cheeks and he was assisted out. Elijah left the cage to grab some water and take a break while another two fighters took the space.

Elijah spotted Jerome and I, and pushed away his clan's medic who was mending his injuries before making his way towards us. "What are you two troublemakers doing here?" Elijah said with a smile. He was missing his front tooth and had quite a few chipped teeth that he replaced and fixed with shiny gold ones. "Decided to finally fight against me?"

"Just here for the show," I replied.

"You were great in there, thought that giant had you for a moment!" Jerome said.

"He would have if he didn't take the time to celebrate." Elijah sighed.

It wasn't until Celestine turned her back on Elijah to face me that Elijah noticed her. His eyes dropped to her. "And who's that?"

I put my arm around Celestine, pressing her closer to me and Jerome took a step forward, ready to step between Elijah and Celestine.

Elijah lifted his eyes up to meet mine, then Jerome's, and back down to Celestine, a spark of interest in his eyes. "Let's see... Two Apex protecting a girl, hm... must be Vulture's little sister. Niko adopt another one?"

"Drop it," I said.

"Tell me, Vulture, why bring such a fragile-looking person here?"

I could see it, the calculation behind his eyes. Elijah had spent his life reading weakness, watching people bleed for less. He wasn't curious because of her, but because *Jerome and I cared.*

Jerome looped an arm around Elijah's neck, laughing it off. "Come off it, Elijah. What does it matter anyway?"

Elijah wasn't stupid, he knew there was something off about our reluctance in him knowing who she was. "You're training the Grim Reaper from the Kokkino clan, aren't you?" His eyes widened as the thought clicked. "But I don't think you're stupid enough to bring Stygian Scum in here."

I was staring so intently at him—watching him piece it together—that I didn't react fast enough to the two large men yanking me away from Celestine. Two others restrained Jerome before he could move. Celestine was left standing alone with Elijah just in front of her.

Elijah stepped closer, grabbed her hood and pulled it back. His breath hitched, shock flickering across his face. "Angels above..." he mumbled.

He caught the back of her neck before she could pull away, tilting her head as though to make sure what he was seeing was real. His fingers pushed her hair aside until the red Stygian tattoo on her neck came into view. He scoffed, a sharp, disbelieving sound.

I twisted out of the hold I was in, pulled my butterfly knife from my pocket and pressed it against Elijah's throat. At the same time, Jerome tore free, flicking out his deck of metal cards, the edges sharp enough to split a hair. He aimed them at anyone who moved. Around us, the crowd bristled, hands drifting to weapons, air growing still.

No one moved.

Elijah exhaled slowly, the corner of his mouth curving into something that wasn't quite a smile, more like something breaking. "So, just three years until I come and get you."

"Only if you find me." Reaper smirked.

He raised his brows, laughing softly. "Oh, I'll find you, don't worry about that."

My eyes darkened at the audacity he had to threaten her in front of me.

"Elijah, what are you doing?" The leader of the Corpse Killer's, Aaliyah, yelled.

Though, Elijah didn't take his eyes off Celestine and I didn't take my eyes off him.

The crowd parted for Aaliyah, a towering figure, her voice heavy with command. "Get your hands off that girl!"

"This *girl* is the Grim Reaper," Elijah snarled. "Stygian scum."

Gasps and murmurs rippled the room.

Aaliyah froze when she got close enough to see Celestine. "Release her, Elijah," she said quietly.

He obeyed with a sharp inhale. I moved Celestine behind Jerome and me, then pulled my knife from Elijah's throat. Aaliyah stepped closer, crouching to meet Celestine's eyes.

"You're the Grim Reaper?" She asked, disbelief softening her tone.

Celestine studied her. "You have Angel blood."

The woman nodded once.

Celestine frowned. "Why do you call yourselves *Corpse* Killers?"

"Because that's what we do. One day we will rid this world of all evils." She reached out, grazing a hand across Celestine's cheek. Her expression flickered, a shadow of pain crossing her features. "You still have such sad eyes," she murmured, almost as if speaking to herself. "You know, it's not too late to cleanse your heart, choose the good side. You'll be safer and happier with us."

Celestine moved away from her touch.

Aaliyah stood upright, the warmth leaving her tone. "It's best you leave. Stygians are not welcomed."

I didn't say anything as I guided Celestine towards the exit, Jerome following close behind.

"See you in three years, Reaper," Elijah called as we exited the building.

***

Jerome followed us back to the apartment, and I was a bit glad he did because I wasn't in the right headspace to watch my surroundings. None of us spoke the entire way.

"Hey, Daddy Vulture," Jerome said with a smirk when we entered.

Niko stood in the kitchen on the phone. He turned to us, nodding at Jerome in a greeting before his eyes shifted to me in a glare. "I really had no idea." He paused as the person on the other side of the phone spoke. "Yes. Right."

Jerome quickly made himself at home, getting a glass and pouring himself some juice before plopping down on the sofa. Celestine followed him to the sofa and took the other end. She pulled her legs to her chest and tucked her head into her knees.

"You alright, Reaper?" Jerome asked.

She didn't respond.

I cautiously went towards her and patted the top of her head. Her hands trembled as she reached up and took my hand in hers, holding onto it tightly.

"I felt her." Her words were muffled.

"What do you mean?" I asked. "Aaliyah?"

She nodded her head. "I felt her inside me."

I exchanged a look with Jerome who gave me one equally confused.

"I'll let him know," Niko said before ending the call. He let out a large breath, leaning against the counter.

"What's up, Daddy Vulture?" Jerome asked.

He was not in the mood for Jerome's jokes. "Celestine, the twins will be picking you up at city hall. Jerome, do you mind taking her there?"

"I can take her," I said, but when he looked at me with such rage and disappointment, I shut up.

Celestine lifted her head, letting go of my hand. "Why?"

"Silias heard about where you were tonight. He wants you home immediately."

She shook her head. "We didn't do anything wrong."

"Celestine. Not only were you in Etherian territory, you were in the Corpse Killers' territory." Niko's voice was sharp. "You know the rules." Any clansman who steps foot in another's territory is usually beaten or killed. The fact that they let us go without any consequences, knowing who she was, could start a clan war.

"It's fine, though, they didn't do anything to us," Jerome piped in.

Niko's eyes moved to Jerome. "Only because you two were there and because she is underage. Do you two understand the danger you've put her in?"

"She should know the other side and what she'll have to deal with in the future," I argued.

"Is that why you brought her there?" Niko ran a frustrated hand over his hair with a curse. "You are supposed to train her to become strong and independent enough to take care of herself. You are not meant to introduce them to her, that's dangling meat in front of a wolf!"

"They know about her anyway, you've heard the threats they've made." I glared back.

Niko took large steps towards me so we were face to face, but I wasn't intimidated by him and stood my ground. "You are just so bloody lucky she looks young, otherwise they'd have had no hesitation killing her! You clearly don't think about the risks before you do something, nor do you seem to grasp the responsibility you hold to protect her."

"I calculated the risks, and I knew they wouldn't—"

"Knowing what you were doing is even worse, Cinth. I cannot trust your judgement anymore, so I will be taking over training Celestine. You've been a bad influence on her and continue to disappoint me by constantly putting her life in danger."

He's right.

I've been conflicted by my feelings towards her. I didn't know if my intentions were because I wanted her dead or if it really was to help her. Training her was supposed to teach me responsibility, but I only hurt her. I had allowed Symeon and Grey to scare her, she was assaulted and tortured to reveal information about me, and now she had been threatened to her face by the Corpse Killers. And I allowed all of it to happen. If I really cared about her, I would have done something, right? The thought made me sick to my stomach.

"No," Celestine protested, standing up from the sofa. "You can't do that."

"I'm sorry, Celestine, but you are too naïve to understand."

Her eyes flickered red, and she grabbed onto me, but I pushed her off. "Hyacinth," she breathed, cautiously taking a step towards me. "You protected me, I'm safe with you."

If I really had been protecting her all this time, she wouldn't be so careful to come near me, she wouldn't look at me with that damaged expression.

"Shut up," I snapped. "Don't—Just—I like being the villain, I like killing people, I don't give a shit about anyone, and I like it like that. Stop trying to see me as some Angel, as if there's something good in me. There's nothing in my heart." It was like breathing through a straw, my lungs couldn't grasp a single particle of air. "You're seeing things that aren't there."

Her lips tightened.

"Why do you like me, Reaper?"

She hesitated. "Why do you find it impossible for someone to like you?"

"Because I'm not a Demon, but I'm much, much worse. You haven't even seen me at my normal, this." I gestured to all of me. "What you see right now, is not me."

She furrowed her brows. "I don't understand."

As I stared into Celestine's eyes, a flicker of something unrecognisable surged within me—an urge to let her in, to share these thoughts. For a brief moment, I imagined a world where I could be vulnerable, without fear of losing control. But that thought was a dangerous fantasy.

I swallowed hard, shaking off the warmth that spread through me.

No.

My eyes darkened. "I'll scare you. I'll make you suffer, and I'll enjoy every second of it."

Her eyes lowered at my words and she whispered. "You shouldn't talk out of anger."

"You need to understand that I will never see you as anything more than something that will one day die. You're nothing to me, Reaper. So, stop acting like you are something to me."

Her eyes flickered red as they welled up with tears. "One day, you're going to realise—"

"Enough," I growled. "I have had enough of you." My hand twitched, but I refrained from touching her. "Ever since you came into my life, everything started falling apart, my reputation that I spent years creating is ruined because of you." Training Celestine made it difficult to deny that I stand by Stygians when I want no association from any of the clans.

"Do you remember when we were kids, we—"

"Stop. Talking. Reaper." Every time someone mentions the past we shared, this throbbing ache begins in the core of my brain. "I don't know what you remember from when we were kids, but that's not me anymore. Get over the past." Being stuck in the past of how we used to be won't solve the issues of the present.

Niko's eyes travelled down to my white fists. "Hyacinth, get control over yourself."

"If I see you again. I'll kill you."

Before I could move, she grabbed the sleeve of my shirt, holding me firmly in place. "When we were kids, you and I made a blood bind." *What?* Blood binds couldn't be broken, if they were, the other could see as much blood from the breaker as they pleased. "You promised me. You *promised* me we would be together. Always. And that you would be the one who would take me for my Aldring."

Aldring was a highly important Stygian ritual. When Demons turned twenty, males would decide their clan and females would decide who they would bind with. "We were children, Reaper," I said coldly.

Celestine shook her head, her eyes filled with despair. "Don't say that."

My intense need to protect her and be around her all the time was only because I mistakenly became attached to her. All of it was because I didn't keep my emotions in check. "Grow up. You're a smart girl, but you're stupid for thinking I could ever feel the same."

She dug her nails into my sleeve. "Hyacinth," she started and my heart beat just a bit faster.

"Don't say my name," I warned her.

"The only way you'll ever get rid of me, is if you kill me," she whispered. "So if that's what you want." Her hands trembled as she released my arm. "Don't hesitate this time."

I didn't want to kill her, I just needed her to hate me, to leave me. I'm reckless, unpredictable and too many people were threatening her life because of me. "You aren't worth killing." A lump formed in my throat, disgusted with myself and my words. "Just get out of my life."

Tears streamed down her face, eyes glowing a bright red and she began to pant, finding it difficult to breathe. Niko caught her as she was overtaken by a cataplexy episode.

I didn't say anything as I walked towards the window, opened it, and jumped down to the pavement below. I walked a couple metres and leaned against the wall as my body ached and felt too heavy to hold. My heart was being crushed by thousands of rocks.

Is this what dying feels like?

With the open window, I could hear her sobs making my stomach churn. My legs wobbled, and I was forced to sit on the ground. I took out a cigarette and lit it, taking in a deep inhale.

Footsteps approached me, stopping directly in front. I turned my eyes up to see Jerome, as he crouched down, his face unreadable at that moment. "I know you love her," he whispered to me.

I shook my head. "No, I don't."

"Vulture," he started. "I've heard the rumours—"

I cursed. "So people have already been talking about me going soft?"

"No," he said. "They're talking about how Vulture has met his match and she's just as deadly as you. They're talking about how no one will be able to touch either of you. They're talking about how Vulture actually may be human."

"People have hurt her," I said. "Because she's around me."

"And?" Jerome said.

"I was so stupid to bring her there."

"Yeah, you were. Especially because you know what she is," he said, flatly. "But you were also right to take her, the best way to fight an enemy is to know them, that's what you've told me. She would have met them eventually, but at least now she knows a bit about what she's up against."

I shook my head.

"Denying your feelings for her and suddenly cutting her out of your life will make it a lot worse for her, you know? Remember what happened to Cassius? He broke up with his partner because he thought she would be safer and they killed her."

A few days later we found Cassius at home with an empty bottle of pills.

"Don't make the same mistake he did. It's already too late now, the entire city knows about you two at least being friends."

I didn't realise I was crying until I saw the tears dripping off my chin and onto the ground.

I hate this.

"You're really going to let Niko and Silias tell you what to do? You're *the Vulture*."

"I've hurt her so much, Jerome. I tried to kill her a couple of times."

"You've tried to kill everyone a few times, pretty sure you attempted murder on me three times." Four and a half times, but he doesn't need to know that. "But anyway, you obviously couldn't go through with it, because you love her."

"No, no, stop," I said. "Don't say that. No one would ever do that to someone they care about. How selfish could I be to even think that I could possibly..." I couldn't even say the word aloud.

"If you accepted your feelings for her, instead of fighting them, you wouldn't act like this."

I didn't even know what I was feeling. I met Jerome's eyes. "Have you ever been in love?"

He nodded his head. "Yeah, once."

"What happened?" I asked him.

"She saw my face." He let out a laugh, but it wasn't a happy one. "I'm too ugly to be loved, but you're not."

Jerome wasn't ugly. He just had a lot of scars on his face, people just needed to see past that. "My heart is ugly."

"But that's something you can change," he said, extending his hand for me to take. "Don't let this one get away."

I chewed on the piercings on my lip, before nodding. I took his hand and stood up with him. Jerome followed me up, Niko and Celestine gone. I went into my room with Jerome who invited himself to stay over, and I didn't bother arguing.

"You can't tell anyone about what you saw," I said, locking the door to my room.

Jerome raised a brow. "I think you forget you're my only friend." He fluffed one of the pillows before plopping his head down. "Also, her being a Demon just makes her so perfect for you."

Jerome fell asleep first, snoring loudly.

***

The storm coming in through the window woke me to a large pile of hail and a puddle of melted water underneath it. My curtains flapped around my room and lightning blinded my sight for a moment.

"Hyacinth." Her voice sent shivers down my spine.

I blinked a couple times to see Celestine on top of me, her weight on her hands and knees. "Cel," I breathed. Her hair was silver instead of dark brown, wearing that same white dress as in my dreams.

"You left me," she said, there was no light in her eyes.

"I..." I hesitated, turning to see if Jerome had awoken from her entrance, but he was gone. He must have left through the window and that's why it was opened. I turned back to her. "I wanted to tell you that I'm sorry."

"Sorry?" she asked.

"Sorry for everything I said, everything I've done to you, everything I've put you through." My brows furrowed as I tried to blink back tears. "I'm so sorry."

She didn't respond, and I didn't expect her to.

I reached up to cup her cheeks, and she leaned her head into it, closing her eyes. "I don't mean to push you away, I just don't understand what I feel for you."

She put her hand over mine. "Let me be around you," she whispered, kissing my palm. "Please."

I shook my head. "I hurt you so much, too many times."

She pulled away to look at me. "But you don't mean to."

No, but that's not the point. "I never want to hurt you, but I do, and I am so sorry for all the times I've done so."

She shook her head. "Stop saying you're sorry." She played with my hair. "I can handle a lot of things."

She can't handle me, even if she were a Demon, she wasn't a full Demon yet and if I showed her my true self, she'd be frightened. Just like all of them were. "I need to figure myself out and I can't be around you because I'm only going to keep hurting you."

"It's not you, it's me?" she spat, sitting up. "Are you really saying that right now?"

Yeah, but it really is. I sat up with her. "Celestine, I can't do this to you anymore and besides, Niko and Silias don't want me training you anymore."

"I don't care."

"But I do," I said, firmly. "I was born heartless, but meeting you... I've realised that maybe there is something inside me. It's a weird feeling and I can't process it." I let out a breath. "All I do is harm the people around me. How could you like someone who only brings you pain and enjoys it?"

"Maybe I'm a masochist," she said with a smile.

"This isn't a joke, Celestine."

"I wasn't joking," she said, pushing me back down on the bed, "I know you want to take control of the Underworld."

It's not too hard to guess that. I don't tell people, but if anyone wondered why I worked so hard, it was obvious. "Yeah."

"I want to be by your side when you do," she said. "I want to help you. I know deep down, you really do like me and would never want me on your bad side. That's why you want to stay away from me, so that you don't push me to hate you, but Hyacinth." She laughed. "I could never hate you." She gently grazed her lips on my jaw. "I can be useful," she whispered. "Right?"

Yeah, she is, and I already knew she would be.

"What is it?" she asked, kissing my jaw.

I shook my head. "Nothing."

She pressed her chest against mine.

"It's just... Why would you want to help me?" I asked, releasing a shuddering breath as she got closer to my lips again.

She curled my hair between her fingers. "Because I know you're going to be great."

I chuckled. "You have no intention of taking control too?"

"No," she said. "Control isn't something I crave."

Interesting. "What do you crave?"

She moved to nibble on my ear, circling my piercings with her tongue. "You."

"You don't have any goals?" I asked, trying to distract my mind from her light touches.

"I prefer to take it one day at a time."

One day at a time.

She doesn't have loyalty to her own clan, a clan who has given her a second chance at life, she doesn't have any family she is able to be loyal to because they don't want her a part of their lives. I'm not her blood, I'm not someone who's given her a home. I'm nothing to her.

So, how do I trust someone who has no loyalty?

She doesn't want control, she only wants me, but that doesn't make sense. What did she want before she met me? Everyone wants something, I just needed to figure out what her true intentions were, her motives, her drive.

As if she heard my thoughts, she pulled away from me to meet my eyes. "Why don't you trust me?"

"I..." I hesitated. "You have no loyalty. How *can* I trust you?"

Her brows knitted together. "What?"

"There are times where you purposely piss me off and get under my skin—"

"I'm trying to protect you, Hyacinth," she said, as if it had been obvious this entire time. "They can't know we're actually good together."

"What are you on about?" I asked. "Who are *they*?"

She shook her head. "You said it before, we can't trust anyone."

"Trust anyone to know what exactly? Are we not allowed to be just friends?" I don't even know if I would call our relationship that.

She let out a short laugh, a smile forming on her lips. "Hyacinth," she started. "We're not going to be *just* friends." My heart was about to suffer yet another heart attack at her words and my eyes widened. Then, her eyebrows furrowed again, her smile staying. "You really can't remember anything, can you?"

"Hyacinth," Niko called through the other side of the door and we snapped our heads to the banging. "Hyacinth!" He began knocking hard, I thought it might break down. I turned back to Celestine, but she had disappeared. "Hyacinth!"

I blinked and daylight had set into my room. The windows were closed and there was no hail storm outside. Jerome was somehow sleeping through Niko's yelling.

Was that all really just a dream?

"Hyacinth!" Niko continued to pound on my door.

It felt like I'd been asleep for a couple minutes, but it was ten in the morning, though I had already decided not to go to school today. I took my time reaching the door, not looking forward to what Niko had to say about what happened last night.

"What is it?" I asked him, opening the door.

"You've overslept!" he shouted. "And why did you lock your door, you know I don't like that!"

"I... I thought you wanted me to stay away from Reaper," I reminded him. "That's why I didn't wake up for school."

His eyes turned cold. "That doesn't mean you can become lazy and sleep all day."

I didn't respond to that.

"I had a chat with Silias last night and he wants to see you now."

"Now?" I asked. "Are you coming as well?"

"No. Just you alone."

That... Did not sound good at all, but I'm not afraid of Silias, just the conversation ahead.

He glanced behind me at my bed, seeing Jerome still snoring and taking up the majority of the bed. He really sleeps like he has no responsibilities. Niko shook his head at his lack of survival instincts. If someone wanted to kill Jerome in his sleep, he wouldn't even notice.

***

Silias was already waiting for me at the Underworld Bar. I was led to the back, Leo and Sterling personally guarding the door, scowling and muttering curses at me, but I didn't respond to them. They let me enter the room and closed the door shut behind me.

Silias sat behind the table, Celestine curled up in his lap. "Hyacinth," he greeted with a false smile, as I took my seat across from them. "It's not been long since I last saw you."

Celestine didn't look at me, her face buried in Silias's shoulder. I think she was asleep.

"You're not stupid, I know you aren't," he started. "You know Cel's a Demon."

It wasn't his place to tell me that. What if I hadn't figured it out?

He caressed Celestine's hair. "She's very precious to the clans. And you, well... you've always had a way of walking the line between loyalty and self-preservation."

I'm not loyal to Stygia, Niko is. Religion is stupid and only separates everyone more than is needed.

Silias moved his eyes from Celestine to mine, a certain coldness in them. "We're looking for someone who's able to control her, well." He tossed his head side to side. "Her or Bernadette. It could be either of them." He went on to continue to explain. "All you and Cel do is argue and last night you upset her so much she wouldn't even speak—Nikodemus filled me in on the things you said to her. You don't control Cel nor do you have a connection with her. Otherwise, you wouldn't have attempted to kill her, and I know the only thing that's stopped you from doing so is because you know she's a Demon."

I didn't respond.

"Cel is loyal to me and only me, but I'm not the one we're all looking for. Cel also hasn't yet developed her powers, she's still young, so they won't come in for a couple more years."

That's not true, none of that was true.

"Do you know what powers female Demons possess?"

"Mind control."

"Influence," he corrected me. "Males can transform twice their size and strength, but females can influence people to do things they wouldn't normally do. That's what makes them so incredibly dangerous."

It's why Angels killed female Demons when they're infants, because they're a threat. Celestine's head turned towards me, her eyes faded, pupils dilated to the point where there was no blue left. I only saw her face for a brief moment before Silias adjusted her back to him again.

Ice coursed through my veins, and I had to take slow, deep breaths. "Is that why you drugged her?" I asked, barely able to contain the disgust in my tone. "Because you're afraid of her?"

Silias let out a low, deadly chuckle. "She only needs to be sedated when she's acting out," he said. "You remember Grey when he was a teenager with all his hormones?"

Of course I did. He was a menace and drove me up the wall to the point where I beat him so bad he was hospitalised. That's why he has a restraining order against me.

"Hardly anyone could control him and females are much, much worse. Especially when her previous family had her on pills that suppressed her emotions."

"Pills to suppress her emotions?" I asked. "Wouldn't that have been dangerous?"

"Tell the Vicarys that," he grunted. "Now, I am the one who has to deal with her becoming overwhelmed and the only way to help her is to sedate her."

"And she lets you?"

"It's either this or putting her back on those pills that make her sick," he said. "She prefers to sleep. So to answer your question, yes."

I'm sure there were other ways that didn't require drugs.

"Now," Silias said. "Have you noticed anyone around Cel that she seems to be naturally drawn towards?"

I thought about it for a moment. "No."

He nodded. "Perhaps, the child has not been born yet, or it really is Bernadette." Then he let out a short laugh. "Some even thought it was you, once. You fit the criteria—except, of course, for the lack of powers. Shame."

He's right there. I can't see in the dark any better than the average human, I don't manipulate darkness, nor do I crave blood for food. "I'm only human, Silias," I confirmed.

There was a point in time where the entire city demanded I take a blood test to prove that I didn't have Demon blood. Their blood count was significantly lower if they hadn't eaten in a while and was also contaminated with multiple different blood types. That test came back negative for me.

His smile was eerie. "Just as I thought."

"How do you know it's either Reaper or Siren? What if the female isn't born just yet."

Silias took a sip of his whisky. "You know the story of the phoenix, don't you?"

"Yes."

The legend was woven into bedtime stories for generations. The phoenix with a lifespan of a hundred years, the only one of her kind, capable of transforming into a bird of flames. Indestructible, she moves across realms to establish peace and restore balance—a sign that something monumental was on the horizon.

"What of it?"

"The phoenix of this century already knows her mission and she'll step onto Soulesity soil within the next few years."

"How would you know that?" I questioned.

"I have connections everywhere, Vulture." Silias smirked proudly. "And according to a reliable source, she's been informed of her duties."

"Do you know who she is?"

"No, that, as you can imagine, is kept secret for obvious reasons."

I let out a breath. "Honestly, Silias. I don't know why you're telling me any of this."

"Nikodemus already knows of everything we've discussed thus far, but I want to ask you." He paused, checking on Celestine when she stirred. "To join the Kokkino clan and publicly confirm that you are Stygian."

"Why?" I asked. "I almost killed Reaper several times, I constantly and knowingly put her in dangerous situations. Why would you want me anywhere near her?"

"Though you're human, you're a very powerful and valuable asset. Having you on our side would further assist us in what's to come."

"And what is to come?"

"War," Silias said, his voice dropping. "When the phoenix arrives, it will confirm the beginning of the War of Wars. The last time she appeared in Soulesity, the world nearly burned and the Demons were brought to the edge of extinction."

I tried not to show it on my face. Everyone could feel the tension on the streets, something big was coming, and it was only a matter of time before the world turned to chaos once more.

"And when it begins, even those who've forgotten what side they're on will have to remember."

"And what has Niko said to this?" I questioned.

Silias's lip twitched. "You're eighteen now. I assumed the decision is up to you. Unless, Nikodemus really does control you."

"Nobody controls me," I muttered. "But I will think about your offer."

He nodded. "Of course."

17
JACK OF SPADES

November 70 A.D.

"Was it worth it?" Jerome growled. "Cutting me in line?"

The men shook their heads, their mouths gagged.

"Yeah, I didn't think so." He laughed.

It was a good release for the both of us.

We sat on the floor of the kitchen after Jerome found a bottle of gin in a cabinet and I took out a smoke. The two corpses sprawled across us like broken art.

"So, how are you feeling?" Jerome asked, pouring the drink straight into his mouth.

"Fine," I muttered. "You?"

"Way better." He ran his fingers over the many scars on his face. "Is it really bad?"

I glanced at him, they must have commented on his scars. "I don't think so." When people look at Jerome and me, they get scared, just another thing we have in common. "It gives you character."

"Character," he laughed.

"A conversation starter," I added.

He shook his head. "Why did they do this to me? I can't go anywhere without being stared at."

I didn't answer, there's nothing I could say that would make it better.

"I tried to go to an arcade a couple weeks ago with some people I knew." He sighed. "They wouldn't even let me in."

I furrowed my brows. "Just because of your scars?"

He nodded. "It was so humiliating, I pretended I got an urgent text and let them go without me."

"Want to go now?" I asked.

He turned to me. "I don't want to go back there for them to tell me again that I'm so ugly I scare children."

I chuckled. "Scars don't mean you're ugly."

He let out a small breath. "You don't have any on your face."

I do, but they're not as visible. I took out my knife and pointed it at my cheek, I grazed it down to my jaw, blood pouring out. It stung, but I've felt worse.

"Oi! What are you doing!" he shouted.

"Now we're matching," I said, putting my knife away.

"You didn't–Why did you do that?"

"Because you think you're so ugly with all your scars, but I think they tell stories." I turned to him with a smirk. "Now let's go scare the kids together."

He put his hands over his face. "Gods," he chuckled. "I think I'm in love with you."

"Why aren't we together?" I joked.

"Because unfortunately you're not a girl."

I knew a girl version of me, but she's mine.

I cleaned the wound so it wouldn't get infected and stopped the bleeding, before we went to the arcade to anger parents for daring to show our faces to children.

"They won't stop glaring at us," Jerome said in a low voice as we tossed balls into baskets, competing against each other with who could score higher.

"Who cares?" I said. "We're minding our own business and so should they. They don't know shit."

He glanced at me but continued with the game. Jerome, as confident as he seems, actually hardly leaves his house because of how he looked.

We decided to eat there too, and I could see the parents talking to the staff about us, but they seemed reluctant to approach us and eventually decided not to.

It made me wonder—why are scars on a face so offensive? How could visible stories etched into skin be so controversial? Why would they assume he's dangerous, when they don't know a thing about how he got them? He's the victim, yet they treated him like the threat, and so he became a threat.

"This is the best date I've ever been on," Jerome teased.

"Oh, honey," I mocked, "only the best for you."

We laughed.

"Cinth!" Lin called for me.

Shit.

"Hey, why didn't you tell us you—" Jamiel's words halted. "What happened to your face?"

"Are you okay?" Lin took my cheeks and analysed the wound.

I gently pushed him away from me. "Matching scars." I nodded towards Jerome. "These are my friends from school. Jamiel and Lin."

Jerome nodded. "I'm Jerome."

Jamiel slid into the spot next to Jerome. "So, how do you know Cinth?"

Lin took a seat next to me.

"Cinth," Jerome repeated my real name, but it sounded weird coming from him. He knew my real name, he just always called me Vulture. "We've known each other forever."

That's what it felt like. It'd only been two years, but we had one of those friendships that just seemed to click instantly.

"What are you two doing here?" I asked, taking a bite of my food.

"Just hanging out. Iri's with us too, but she ran into Cel."

"Where?" I asked them.

"I think they're still outside," Jamiel said, stealing one of Jerome's chips. Jerome looked so confused with how comfortable Jamiel was around him.

She's outside? She's so close.

"Gods, *Cinth*, just go see her," Jerome said, mocking my nickname.

I can't.

Lin and Jamiel snorted. "Why would Cinth want to see Cel?"

"They hate each other."

Jerome just became more lost in the conversation. "You really live a double life, don't you?" he asked.

You have no bloody idea.

Luckily, Jamiel and Lin didn't pick up on what he said, distracted by a birthday party near us.

"Jamiel," Iri came over to our table. "You have my scarf."

I didn't look at Iri, I knew Celestine would be right next to her.

"Hey, Cinth," Iri greeted me. "And who's this?"

Jamiel pulled off the scarf and handed it to her.

"Jerome," he introduced himself.

"I'm Iri," I could hear her smile. "It's nice to meet you."

He nodded towards where Celestine was. "Celestine."

"You two know each other?"

"We met last night." Her soft voice almost got me turning to her, but I kept my eyes locked on my glass. I'm not allowed to be near her.

"Move over, Jamiel," Iri told him, wrapping her scarf back over herself.

Why is everyone here tonight? If Symeon and Kahlik appeared, I wouldn't know what personality to use anymore.

Lin scooted closer to me to make room for Celestine and I was squashed against the wall.

Bloody hell. She doesn't need *that* much space.

"What happened to you?" Iri asked me, noticing the gash on my cheek. She reached over and pulled Jerome's plate of chips closer to her so she could nip a few.

"He wanted to match scars with me," Jerome answered for me, giving Iri and Jamiel an annoyed look for stealing his food. "Isn't he romantic?"

"So romantic," Jamiel mocked.

I couldn't help my chuckle.

Jerome got along with everyone at the table, I'm not surprised, he's refreshing to be around and no one commented on the scars on his face nor stared too long at them.

"Are we going to play some games or what?" Jamiel asked the table after they had finished the last of Jerome's chips with absolutely no remorse.

Jerome locked eyes with me, I think he felt weird because my friends were different from everyone else. They didn't judge, and they didn't care who you were as long as you knew how to have fun. That's why I liked being around them, they simply never cared.

"Let's go," Lin said, and they all got out of their seats.

"Are you not going?" I asked Jerome.

"Uh," he hesitated.

"Jerome, come on," Iri took his arm and pulled him out of the booth.

"What time is it?" Celestine asked.

"Half past ten." Lin showed her on his phone.

"I should probably get going," she said. "But I'll see you."

I finally turned to look at her, she was in her assignment outfit, probably just having been with Niko when she bumped into Iri.

"No," Jamiel whined. "You just got here."

She gave him a soft smile, "I have a curfew."

She'd need to leave within the next half hour to make it on time, but Jamiel managed to convince her to stay out a bit longer.

I followed everyone to the different machines. As Jerome, Iri, Lin, and Jamiel competed in a racing game, Celestine stood next to me, watching. "Niko told me you weren't training me anymore," she said in a low voice.

"I'm not allowed to see you," I said, avoiding her eyes.

"I know," she said. "We have to keep it this way." Celestine gently grazed her hand over my cheek, avoiding my scar, but I still didn't look at her. "You almost look as cool as Jerome."

Her light touch sent electricity through my veins, causing me to lose my train of thought. I smirked. "Tell that to him."

"No, that's weird." She took her hand back.

"Jerome," I called, "Celestine thinks you look cool."

"Why would you tell him that?"

"Cel," Jerome groaned, tilting his head back with a big smile.

Lin laughed. "Do you really have a thing for bad boys, Cel?"

"Oh, she definitely does." Iri giggled.

"I think she's making it quite clear now," Jamiel teased.

She wasn't confirming it, but she wasn't denying it either.

"Bloody hell, Celestine," I muttered.

Jamiel shouted a curse as Iri passed him in the race, causing a few parents to shoot us disapproving looks, ushering their children away from our group.

"Do you trust me now?" Celestine asked me in a whisper.

"What?"

"You met with Silias this morning," she said. "You've put it all together now, haven't you?"

I shook my head, "I'm not the child of Phobus. You've got it all wrong." I'm not even sure how to feel about the clans and Celestine suspecting that I was. Flattered? Debatable. Offended? Possibly.

"I never said you were," she laughed.

"But you're what everyone is looking for." I didn't want to say exactly what out loud in case someone overheard us, even if we were speaking in whispers. "Aren't you?"

We locked eyes for the first time that night. She gave me a small smile, brushing past me and taking her leave without telling anyone.

My friends groaned, "Why are you so good at these games, Iri?"

"Honestly, it's no fun playing with you guys." She laughed, getting out of her seat. "There's no competition." She turned her head side to side. "Hey, where's Cel?"

"She left," I said.

"I should get going as well," Jerome announced. "But it was really nice to meet you all." His words were genuine.

"I'll come with you," I said.

He nodded, and we said our goodbyes.

"They're really nice," he said in a low voice.

"You should hang out with us more," I said, taking out a cigarette.

He chuckled. "Well, bloody invite me then."

I try not to mix my normal life with my Underworld one, but this went better than I expected. We were passing an alley and Jerome noticed Celestine first. He grabbed my arm and pulled me back, nodding towards the alley.

An orange cat, completely dazed and wide eyed, stared straight up at her. She crouched down towards it, and it jumped into her arms. She rested her forehead on the cats, closing her eyes and the cat did the same.

Even animals loved her.

"She's like a princess," Jerome commented.

Celestine heard him, turning to us and began walking towards us with the cat. "Do you want to pet her?"

Jerome reached his hand towards her, the purrs loud. "She's cute."

Celestine nodded. "And pregnant." The cat shifted and stretched in Celestine's arms, showing off her large belly.

"Are you going to take her home?" he asked.

"Silias doesn't allow animals," she said. Just as Celestine crouched back down to release the cat, it sprinted and disappeared into the alley.

"You need to get home before curfew, Celestine," I said.

She nodded.

"Why didn't Niko take you home?" I asked.

"We bumped into Iri before he could," she explained. "But I'm a bit upset with Silias, I'm not sure I want to go home tonight."

"You can come with us," Jerome said. "Vulture is sleeping at mine tonight."

I don't recall agreeing or being asked to do that.

She nodded, following us. Where was she going to go if not with us?

Jerome didn't live too far, just a few blocks away. It was a small apartment building, only four stories with about five small flats on each level. As we took steps up, I noticed Celestine falling behind.

"Are you alright?" I asked.

She flickered her eyes back to me, giving me a nod, and I didn't pester her more on it.

As Jerome fumbled with his keys, she stared at the door across from his. "Who lives across from you?" she asked Jerome.

Jerome turned to look at the door, shrugging. "Some lady and her kid." He finally managed to unlock the door and pushed with his shoulder, jamming it open. We entered his small, quaint flat. Celestine took a shower and Jerome gave her a shirt to borrow.

"Let's go to that frozen yoghurt shop I told you about tomorrow," Jerome said, rummaging through his fridge for some food. I don't know how he's still hungry, we literally just ate.

"Sure," I said, slumped on the sofa. "It must be bloody amazing if you killed two people for it." We had a movie playing, but we weren't really paying attention to it.

He snorted. "It was about the disrespect, Vulture!"

Celestine emerged from the bathroom, Jerome's shirt going down to her knees, the back of it damp from her hair. It revealed some of the scars and bruises on her body that were recent and Jerome sympathised with it. Her arm was bandaged, and I still hadn't asked her about it.

"Are you hungry, Reaper?" Jerome asked.

"No, I'm okay," she replied, making her way towards him and hopping up the counter. They chatted a bit, while Jerome made himself a simple sandwich. "You make money playing video games?" Celestine asked him.

"Yeah, for some reason people like to watch me play." He shrugged, spreading peanut butter onto his bread. "But I also enter competitions as well and they often have big prizes."

"You've cut yourself," she said.

Jerome looked at her confused. "Did I?" He hissed, lifting his finger to see the tip of it bleeding.

"With a butter-knife?" I chuckled.

"It's still a knife!" he snapped at me.

Celestine took his finger and licked the tiny bit of blood off. Jerome's face flushed from the touch and his eyes widened, quickly looking at me.

"How did you two meet?" She wondered, releasing his hand, distracting the both of us from what she had just done.

"Gods." He chuckled at the memory, going back to his sandwich, unable to contain himself enough to tell the story.

"We've known about each other for years," I said from the sofa. "But we didn't meet until two years ago."

"I found Vulture buried alive in the woods," Jerome said with a wide smile.

"What?" She glanced at me. "How?"

"Some people tried to kill me." They captured and tortured me for days and when I finally made it home, Niko scolded me, thinking I had just gone off on my own like the teenager I was. Even though I was dirtied, battered, and bruised, he assumed I had just gotten into another bad fight. I never bothered correcting him.

"And then?" she urged.

I shrugged. "I got my revenge."

She and Jerome later joined me on the sofa. The two weren't focused much on the movie as they continued to talk.

Celestine rested her head on my arm and was the first to fall asleep. "You can put her on my bed and sleep with her," Jerome said. "I'll take the sofa."

"No, it's your place," I said.

He laughed. "Are you two going to squish on the sofa?"

"You don't want to sleep with me tonight?" I teased. Celestine's clearly been rubbing off on me.

"Wow," he said. "Calm down, we've only been on one date."

Turning off the television, we left Reaper on the sofa and went over to his room, changed into new clothes, he let me borrow some as well.

Jerome let out a sigh. "This was a good day. Thanks."

I nodded. "Yeah, it was."

His bed was quite large, enough space for the both of us to lay comfortably without touching each other. The bed moved as Celestine crawled in between Jerome and me. "You left me," she whined in a sleepy voice.

Jerome laughed. "Sorry."

She made herself comfortable between us and forced both of our arms around her, facing Jerome, her back pressed against my chest. I exchanged an awkward look with him. *Maybe, I should move to the sofa.* I carefully removed my arm off of Celestine but she gripped onto me, keeping me there.

"This is so weird," Jerome said into the silence, afraid to move.

"Only if you make it weird," she muttered.

My eyes slowly became heavy, and I buried my nose into her hair.

"Is this actually okay, Reaper?" Jerome asked, even though she's the one who made him do it.

She nodded. "Yeah. I just want to try something."

"Try... What?" But the words barely left my mouth as I fell deep into slumber.

***

I was back in the middle of the salt flats again. The house behind me was in the same distance it always was. Though, I wasn't alone this time. Jerome stood a few metres away, his mouth agape, eyes wide, looking around us.

"Where are we?" he asked, his voice echoing.

"The salt flats," I said, but that was as far as I knew.

He turned to meet my eyes. "How did we get here?"

Underneath me, on the other side of the water, a younger version of Jerome dragged the corpse of his latest victim behind him by the ankle, a shovel in his other hand. Leaves, rocks and branches caught on the person's hair, creating a trail behind him. Jerome's breaths were heavy, sweat dripping off his face, the summer night warm.

"That's me!" Jerome said, crouching down towards the water, squinting his eyes. He touched the water as his younger self passed him. I followed the image from the surface and Jerome quickly followed with me.

The younger Jerome released the person's ankle, letting it fall to the grass, and stared at the space before him. He wiped his damp forehead before aiming the tip of the shovel at the ground and started digging. He was about halfway through when he heard the ground just a few metres away moving, but he dismissed it, most likely an animal digging.

Younger Jerome glanced at the noise and let out a shout when he saw the hand, it pushed the ground out and away until a head finally stuck out. "Bloody hell." A younger version of myself groaned, gripping onto his head.

"This is how we met." Jerome breathed.

"Are you a zombie?" The younger Jerome asked younger me. "Is this the start to the apocalypse?" He looked up at the sky, cursing Poiesis.

Younger me gave him a weird look. "What? No."

"Then, what are you doing coming out of the ground like that?"

"How else was I supposed to get out?" Younger me grouched, pulling the rest of his body out of the ground. "I was just buried alive."

Younger Jerome chuckled. "Not your night, hey?"

"Not my week." younger me corrected, patting the dirt off him. Younger me noticed the corpse sprawled on the side and younger Jerome tightened his grip on his shovel. "Need any help with that?"

Younger Jerome glanced at the body, relaxing. "Sure."

I felt another presence nearby and turned to see Celestine staring at us. She had her silver hair and that white dress. "Celestine?" I called for her. Jerome looked up.

***

I woke up to Celestine gone and Jerome snoring in front of me. Getting out of the bed, I looked to see if she was even still here, but she wasn't. I'm not sure how she snuck out without either of us waking. I changed back into my own clothes and told a sleepy Jerome I was leaving and he groaned, waving his hand in the air. "Yeah, alright, see you, Psycho."

"Socio," I said back.

Jerome and I ended up meeting later that evening for frozen yoghurt and somehow, we ended up making our way to Niko's favourite bar.

Jerome pushed me as we entered Skol and I instantly retaliated, grabbing him, shoving his back onto the bar, before stealing one of the liquor bottles aiming it above him. "Drink up, Jerome." A sinister smile on my face.

Jerome opened his mouth, sticking his tongue out allowing the alcohol to be poured into his mouth. He coughed and spurted the liquid out. "Shit, Vulture." He pushed me away. "Not tequila!"

"You shouldn't have pushed me," I spat back, but stopped, putting the alcohol back on the bar.

"Oh, but if you pushed me—"

"Shut your bloody mouth," I growled.

Jerome rolled his eyes and spotted something in the distance. I followed his line of sight and found Celestine and Niko sitting in a lonesome booth, opposite one another. "Oh, hey, Daddy Vulture." Jerome shouted.

Niko lifted his glass in a greeting.

Jerome took that as an invitation and made a beeline for the table. "Reaper." He cupped her cheeks in his hands. "Why were you crying?"

"What?" Her eyes wide. "I'm not crying."

"Were." He emphasised.

"Um…" she hesitated, shifting her gaze to Niko.

"She's just had a rough day," Niko said.

"Who made you cry?" I asked from behind Jerome, my hands in my pockets.

She shook her head. "No one, I'm just tired."

We all knew that wasn't the truth, but none of us argued.

Niko couldn't help his chuckle.

"What?" I said.

"It's just quite funny," he laughed. "You two are so rough with each other and everyone around you, but when it comes to Celestine, you're both so gentle."

I snarled at him.

Jerome slid in the seat next to Celestine, forcing her to scoot over, and stole a handful of the chips that sat in the centre of the table.

I roughly pulled Jerome out of the seat and took his spot.

He rolled his eyes, sitting next to Niko. "What are you two doing here anyway?" Jerome asked, stuffing his mouth with the chips.

"I just finished training Celestine for the night, we stopped to eat before I take her home." He then looked at me, a bit of a wary warning. "Speaking of, we should get going. Move Cinth, so she can get out." Jerome also got out of his seat and she and Niko left.

"You're still not allowed near Reaper?"

"No," I replied, sitting back down and taking a chip from the bowl that was left unfinished.

Jerome sat back across from me. "Well, maybe one day you'll get to claim her."

"I did claim her," I muttered, "Silias stole her from me."

"Excuse me, what?" Jerome asked. I told him the story, everything that had happened between Celestine and I, leaving out the part about Phobus and the prophecy of course.

"Damn," he said. "That's... A lot."

I didn't respond, allowing him to take the last chip.

"What are you going to do?"

I shrugged. "What I do to everyone who pisses me off."

He smirked, knowingly. "Nobody messes with Vulture."

18

SOMETHING WE SHOULDN'T HAVE DONE

NOVEMBER 70 A.D.

I opened my locker to grab my water bottle when a glitter bomb went off, splattering me and all my contents with pink glitter. "What the actual–"

"Demons below," Jamiel said. "What happened?"

There was a little note inside, a heart signed with her name.

"Celestine." I shoved the paper into my pocket, not bothering with cleaning up anything as I stormed towards the other end of the hall, a trail of glitter following me. I felt like some fairy princess. "I'm going to slaughter you," I said in a deathly low voice.

"Good morning to you too," she muttered, closing her locker, and when she finally looked at me she burst into laughter, covering her mouth as she did. "You finally opened your locker, hey?" Students around me giggled as they walked to their own class, the hallways quickly emptying.

"I thought we were on somewhat good terms." Neither of us had pulled anything on each other for a long time.

"Cute that you thought–"

"Clean it up," I demanded.

"Not my mess."

"You *made* this mess."

She turned away. "I'm going to class."

I pulled her back to me. "Clean it up, Reaper."

She sighed. "Can't I do it later?"

"No," I said, dragging her towards the janitor's closet. I shoved her in and closed the door, so teachers wouldn't ask us why we were skipping class.

She intentionally smacked her book on my arm as she put them down on a shelf. I shot her a glare while she picked up some tissues, attempting to wipe it off the sleeves of my uniform. "You know it's edible."

I didn't trust her enough to try. Celestine was struggling to get the glitter off, only managing to spread it with the tissues and push it more into my clothes. "Lick it off me then."

She looked back up at me. "You're weird."

"You said it was edible, so eat it. Unless it's actually poison and getting me to eat it was your plan all along."

She rolled her eyes at my dramatics and licked the glitter candy off my hand first, her cold tongue tickling the tips of my finger.

"Good girl," I teased.

She met my eyes with a smile as she sucked on my finger. *Shit.* "You're missing out." She smiled, continuing to clean me off. "It tastes good."

You're a Demon, Celestine, you can't taste, but thanks for the excuse.

There was glitter at the edge of her lips, and I took her head in my hands, pulled her closer and licked the corner of her lips. "Tastes like shit," I lied. It was sweet, like candy. I released my hold on her. "Or maybe it's you."

She grabbed my tie, pulling me down again, dragging her tongue across my jaw in one long glide. "Try again." She stuck her pink glittery tongue out, revealing her sharp Demon canines.

I licked the glitter off her tongue, and she put her hands behind my neck, pulling me closer so our lips would finally meet but only for a moment before she pulled away. It was so innocent, timid and as if she was slightly unsure I wanted it, but I'd be lying if I said I didn't.

Bloody hell.

I stared into her eyes; cold, dead, like mine, but at that moment, there was also a soft gleam. "Did you taste it?" she whispered.

I leaned towards her. "No." And gently placed my lips to hers again.

We can't go back from this.

I picked her up, so I didn't have to lean down anymore, and she wrapped her arms and legs around me, not removing our lips from each other. Our hesitance quickly turned into need. She played with my hair, pulling me closer and I pushed her against the shelves, the items falling and clattering to the floor. She let out a gasp as I pressed myself towards her, attempting to close the gap between us more.

I inhaled her scent, gods, she smelt so good, and tasted even better. I could barely gather my thoughts.

"I hate you," I muttered between our kisses. I hated what she was doing to me. My hand grazed up her thigh and under her skirt and I ran my thumb across her scars.

"I hate you more," she whispered.

"Shut up."

She bit my lip in return and my entire body heated up more than it already was, my heart racing, on the verge of bursting.

I can't breathe.

"I'm going to bloody kill you after this," I said, my breaths ragged.

She nodded with a sigh, leaning her weight more onto me. "After."

I felt so dizzy. Weak. I'd never felt like this before, there were too many emotions for me to comprehend and I didn't understand how Cel was able to bring it out of me. Her mouth parted a bit so I could slip my tongue in. I wanted to get closer, but I couldn't and it was almost frustrating.

I lost control.

"Hyacinth…" She tilted her head back and let out a soft moan. "I… Don't stop, please." Her body turned limp in my arms.

I cursed, moving down to kiss her jaw, licking and sucking on her neck. I couldn't get enough of her.

The door burst open, and I frantically set her down, but she couldn't stand on her own just yet, so I held her up. I had spread glitter onto her. "What are you two doing in here?" the janitor asked.

"Just looking for something to clean up glitter," I explained, reaching and grabbing the first thing I saw, a mop. "I think this will do." *I'm going to stab myself with this.*

The janitor squinted, looking back and forth between us, heavily breathing. Cel quickly recovered from her cataplexy episode, and I released my hold on her.

"I've already cleaned it up and found the trail leading here. Go clean yourselves so you can stop spreading it around the school," he grouched.

I nodded and took Cel's hand, bringing her books on our way out, and handed them to her. Her eyes held onto mine, glowing a soft red. Her lips were swollen, lipstick smudging around her mouth. My body twitched, wanting—needing to do it again.

A fleeting moment, an eternity.

I leaned close to her ear and whispered, "I'll get you back." I lingered close to her for a moment longer, hesitating about what I was going to do next, but I managed to gain control over myself and pull away before leaving in the opposite direction.

I licked my lips, the last bit of her still on it, savouring the taste of her. As I turned the corner, I got a glimpse of Cel. She was crouched down, leaning against a locker, covering her eyes. There was a slight smile on her lips, and she bit down on her bottom one to suppress it. I couldn't help my smirk and cursed.

When I looked in the bathroom mirror, I was completely and utterly mortified. My face was flushed, and her dark lipstick stained my lips. The janitor wasn't stupid, he knew exactly what we were doing. I cleaned myself up, unable to get all the glitter off, but it was good enough. I splashed water on my face, trying to cool myself, and my eyeliner ran. *The one day I wear non-waterproof eyeliner...* With my fingers I rubbed the rest of it off and lined my eyes again.

I shouldn't have kissed her.

I took two pills to distract myself and considered walking to the Great Bridge so I could jump off.

"You're late," the teacher snapped, when I finally arrived to class.

I ignored her and took the seat my friends had saved for me.

"Are you okay?" Iri whispered.

I nodded.

"Your face is so red." Lin snickered with Jamiel.

I covered my mouth with my hands. "I'm just pissed off."

"That's not your pissed off face," Iri commented. "Are you blushing?"

"I just did something," I muttered. "That I really shouldn't have done."

"What did you do to Cel?"

"Nothing," I replied. I should have just skipped this class to fully cool off.

"You've still got lipstick on your piercing," Lin muttered to me with a smile.

I quickly drew my lower lip in and attempted to lick it clean.

Iri went to check on Cel during one of our breaks, wondering what I had done to her. *How nosy.* Luckily, Iri couldn't find her, apparently, she didn't even go to her first class and was seen leaving school.

"You're acting so weird," Jamiel said during lunch.

"Yeah, you're quieter than normal," Lin added, but he seemed to already know what I'd done, though he hadn't told the others.

"And awkward." Iri laughed.

"Drop it," I said, and they listened.

I didn't sleep that night, meditating instead. Clearing my mind of everything and attempting to comprehend this morning's events. Her heavy breathing, her racing pulse, her sighs, her cold, soft skin. The taste of her lips. Now I knew why her mother named her Datura.

Intoxicating.

I tried to focus but my mind kept wandering back to her.

Did she actually want to?

Did I even want to?

Where do we go from here?

***

The next day, Cel wasn't at school, but the day after she was, so I heard, but I didn't see her as she skipped our shared history class and wasn't in the cafeteria for lunch. She avoided me for the next week. Honestly, I didn't know how I would act the next time I saw her.

Niko had also been distant.

"Is there an assignment tonight?" I asked Niko, I hadn't received one since that night I took Cel to the Corpse Killers's territory.

Niko turned to look at me, a look of anger filling his eyes. "You're not getting one any time soon."

I furrowed my brows. "Why not?"

"You know why," he started. "You used Celestine to break an Underworld law of crossing into another's territory."

My eyes lowered to the floor.

He scoffed. "You always talk about wanting to kill her and I should have taken you seriously when you threatened her. I knew you couldn't do it yourself, but I never thought you were pathetic enough to get someone else to do it. I had no idea just how far you'd go, how close you got to getting her killed..." Niko shook his head. "I've never been more disappointed in you, Hyacinth."

I pursed my lips. "I apologised to her—"

"And you think that's enough?" he snapped.

"I..." I hesitated. "I don't know what else I can do."

"You and Celestine were childhood friends," he said. "You loved her so much when you were kids, I thought those feelings would return to you if you were around her again. Clearly, I was mistaken for a fool."

My head began to ache.

"No. You know what?" He looked at me. "I know you are still in love with her. You just can't seem to cope with it, so you think killing her will crush those feelings too."

I'm not in love with her.

Niko's voice began to rise. "Well, let me tell you something, Hyacinth, killing her won't bring back who you were. It won't make things go back to normal—it'll only drag you further from it."

Stop talking.

"Do you know how rare it is to find someone who changes you for the better? Do you understand that not everyone is lucky enough to find love like that?"

My jaw tightened.

"I want you to think about the consequences of your actions and what could have been. I will not be giving you any assignments and you are not to go out for anything except school until I see that you actually feel remorse for what you've done." He picked up his bag, before leaving to pick Cel up for training.

I stood there, trembling, my body on edge. Seeing blood wouldn't be enough to ease this particular craving.

I needed Cel.

I needed her so bad, I felt ill.

Without her powerful presence, the world had turned dull and colourless. An ache settled in my muscles from the absence of her cool touch. Every breath felt shallow, my lungs only wanting to inhale the scent of her. Every sound grated me, because none of them were her voice.

Cel was a drug, and I was addicted.

***

I knocked on Jerome's door and he answered it, rubbing his eyes. "What the hell, Psycho? It's way too early for this."

It was six in the afternoon.

"Come with me."

He released a big yawn, scratching the top of his head bald. "Let me get changed."

I waited a few minutes before he was ready.

"Where are we going?" he asked me.

"House hunting," I said.

He furrowed his brows. "Why? Niko kick you out already?"

"He's about to," I said. I'm eighteen now, legally allowed to buy a house, and I had enough in my personal account to buy a decent one. I always assumed Niko would kick me out the moment I turned eighteen, though he hasn't said anything about it just yet. Now I'm absolutely positive he's going to.

"Huh," Jerome said. "Alright."

We met up with a woman in her early thirties and Jerome took that as his chance to find a wife.

"What are your thoughts on this one?" the woman asked me.

It was a large townhouse on the West side. I don't know what it is about the West, but I preferred the laid-back vibe of it over the suffocating, uptight East. It was also significantly cheaper. The outside of this place looked worn down, but inside had been newly refurbished, almost like a secret hideout in plain sight. There were two stories with five bedrooms and three baths, generously spaced. This was my favourite compared to all the others we had looked at that evening.

"Isn't this a bit too big for you?" Jerome asked.

I squinted at the layout. I don't know why, but I had a strong feeling I would be taking in strays later in life, like Niko had taken me in. Even if I don't, I like the space.

"It's meant more for larger families or for those who want to share with friends," the woman explained.

"I'd love to have a large family," Jerome smirked, winking at the woman. Jerome's resume did not include flirting under skills.

The woman's eyes hardened, but she was working so she couldn't say anything to paying clients.

I asked the woman for more details, the cost, the surrounding area, the plumbing, the electricity, all of it.

"If you get me the down-payment tomorrow, I can have you moved in by the end of the week."

"I'll just pay the whole thing." I hate the thought of owing anyone anything, especially the bank which the government controls.

The woman's face paled. "Oh, yes, of course." She became flustered, not expecting that since we had only been looking at places in the West side.

"Can you pay my rent too?" Jerome joked.

I actually considered doing that for his twenty-fifth birthday. "You can just move in with me."

He laughed, but I wasn't joking. The woman informed me that after the payment went through, she'd give me the keys.

Jerome and I walked back to his apartment, him inviting me to sleep at his tonight. Though Niko has banned me from leaving the flat, I didn't want to be around Niko and his disappointed stares so I accepted. We went through an alleyway and Jerome paused in his steps.

"What's wrong?" I asked.

He crouched behind one of the large metal bins and I followed to see what caught his attention.

It was that orange cat, the one that was once pregnant a few weeks ago. She had her kittens, barely a week old. All of them were beaten senseless. Dead. My heart clenched at the scene in front of me. *How could someone do this?* These kittens were innocent, just trying to survive in this awful city.

A single grey kitten staggered, nuzzling his mother. The only survivor of the horrific murder. His brothers and sisters scattered around, bloodied and motionless.

"Come here, it's okay," Jerome whispered, outstretching his arm for the kitten to come to him.

The kitten meowed, his ears still folded, eyes barely opened.

Jerome carefully picked up the kitten. "She's so cold," he said, holding her close to his chest.

Jerome and I took the kitten to the vet, confirming she was a girl and only six days old. She had an infection in her eye, and they removed it. She was luckier than the others, most likely hid from the murderers. Jerome decided to keep her and named her Borealis. When I left Jerome's home early the next morning, Borealis was curled up on top of him.

***

It was Wednesday when I saw Cel in the hallway, we were both coming from opposite directions, surrounded by our own friends. Her friends were chatting to her, but she wasn't listening.

"Hey, there's Cel." Jamiel nudged me. "You going to get her back for that glitter stunt?"

I waited for her to do something first, but she avoided my eyes as she passed me, like I didn't exist at all. I was suddenly breathing through a straw.

"Cel," Iri called for her, but Cel ignored her, even when her friends were telling her that Iri was trying to get her attention, she just kept walking.

"That was cold," Lin said.

"Did you guys fight?" Iri folded her arms across her chest.

I'd rather it have been a fight than this, at least we could have gone back from that. "No." If we fought, we wouldn't leave each other alone.

"Then, what did you do to her? She couldn't even look at you." Iri squinted at me. "And she won't talk to me."

"Drop it, Iri." I glared at her and she flinched. "Sorry," I quickly said. "Sorry, I didn't mean to do that."

"Are you okay?" she asked, genuinely concerned.

"I'm not sure," I admitted, shoving my shaking hands in my pockets.

My friends exchanged looks with each other, but eventually dropped the topic.

***

When I got home, I locked myself in my room to meditate. I continued even after the sun had gone down, but I couldn't focus properly.

Standing up from the floor, I headed into the kitchen. I was cursing at myself under my breath as I poured myself a glass of water. *Calm down, Hyacinth. Just talk to her, but what would I say?*

"What are you doing up?" I jumped at the voice, spilling a bit of water on the floor. "You have school tomorrow."

I turned to Niko on the sofa, watching a movie with Renee. *How was I so lost in my thoughts I didn't even notice them or hear the movie?*

"I couldn't sleep," I muttered, I hadn't slept properly for a long time now.

"I can see that. What's on your mind?" he asked, gesturing for me to come sit with them. I knew he was only acting nice because Renee was here.

Renee paused the movie.

I didn't go closer, not wanting them to see my face. I pulled my hood up over me. "I think I messed up."

"Why do you think that?"

I shook my head, resting the glass on my lips. "I did something that I can't go back from."

You'd think nearly killing Cel would be the end of our relationship, but because we're both so sick and twisted, kissing each other was the thing to end it all. *How cruel.*

"Who did you kill?"

The relationship I had with Cel. "It's worse than that."

Renee gasped. "I know that face!"

My eyes widened, no way, I have such good control over my face. Are my emotions so strong they're peeking through or am I too tired to fight them?

"He likes someone."

I quickly turned to get more water. "No, I don't." I don't know what I felt for Cel. I don't even tell my friends or Niko and Renee that I like them. The best compliment anyone could receive from me is that I tolerated them and that's as far as I will say Cel was to me. Someone I tolerated.

"Is it Celestine?" he questioned.

"Who's Celestine?" Renee giggled, excitedly.

"Cinth is training her," Niko answered. "They're around the same age. You should see them together." He shuddered. "They're so powerful and she's not even scared of him."

Stop acting like you're suddenly rooting for us. Just last week he went off on me, forcing me to stay away from her.

Renee squealed at the gossip.

"And I've never seen Cinth so protective and gentle with someone before," he added. "More gentle than he is with Ophelia." Renee's cat was cute. I liked her.

My jaw clenched. The amount of bullshit coming out of Niko's mouth. I am anything but gentle with Cel.

"No way!" Renee gasped.

The glass broke in my hand, and they silenced.

"What did you do to her?" Niko asked.

I couldn't say it out loud, it was too embarrassing. Something nobody would expect me to do. I stared at the shallow cuts in my hand, bleeding, and shook my head. "She won't even look at me."

"Did you hurt her?"

I plucked the glass out of my hand. "I don't know anymore." My eyes welled up with tears and I cursed, cleaning up the glass. It was silent for a while and I couldn't take it.

"Can I please... Please," I begged. "Take an assignment?"

"No," Niko said. "You're not taking one until you properly sleep."

That's the excuse you're using in front of Renee?

"I really, really messed up." I threw the glass into the bin and washed my hands. "And I don't know how to fix it."

"Do you want to fix it?"

I let out a shuddering breath, blinking the tears away. "I can't."

Renee embraced me in a hug, and I tensed. "Cinth..." I had no idea she was this close to me. "You're going to be okay. Whatever it is that happened between you two will sort out eventually."

"She won't look at me," I repeated. I should have stopped when she went limp.

"Why don't you tell us what happened, and we'll try to give you some old people advice?"

I let out a small laugh and cursed again. Renee took my hand and led me to sit on the sofa with them, but I couldn't get the words out of me.

"Did you injure her?" Niko asked.

"No," I replied. *I bit her lip, does that count?*

"Did you sleep with her?"

That's a big jump. I felt my face heat up and I covered my mouth with my hand, turning away. "No, gods." But I think I would have done more to her if we weren't interrupted... I should never be alone with her again.

"That's too fast for Cinth," Renee said. *Exactly.* "He probably just kissed her."

How did she guess that so fast?

When I didn't answer, Niko smiled. "Did you?"

Bloody hell, I hate this. "Yeah."

Niko burst into laughter. "Demons below, Cinth."

"Who kissed who first?" Renee leaned closer, a big grin on her face, eager to hear it all.

"I'm not really sure," I muttered. I licked her lips, but she made me lick her tongue and then she pulled me in to kiss her, but I don't know which one counts as who started it.

"But she kissed you back, right?" Renee asked.

I nodded, unable to meet their stares. "I lost control. And I shouldn't have."

"You were following your heart, Cinth," Renee said.

Gross. That sounds so gross.

"You both must really like each other."

"They do," Niko confirmed.

"No," I retorted. "We hate each other."

Niko rolled his eyes. "Clearly."

I shot him a glare and stood up. "Whatever, I was tired of her anyway." *I only want to be around her.*

"No, Cinth, come back," Renee called, as I began walking to my room.

"I don't know what to do," I said, gripping onto the handle of my door. I had to hold back from breaking it.

"She trusts you and she needs you, don't throw her away like this," Niko said.

Why would she trust me?

I shook my head. "I don't even know if she actually wanted it or if it was just her feeling like she had to do it."

"Had to do it?" Renee raised a brow.

"She hasn't been around the best sort of people," Niko briefly explained. "She has that mentality where she believes that when people show her kindness, it isn't free."

Renee's eyes broke. "What? That's—That's terrible."

"It is," I muttered, leaning on my door and sliding down to sit on the floor. "And I think that may be why she did it."

Niko shook his head. "I'm not sure that's true, Cinth. She really does like you."

"Niko," I started. "Cel liking me." I slammed the back of my head on the door. "You know me, I'm not a good person. She sees me as that. She thinks I'm like *them*. I'm familiar to her."

"No." Niko's voice was sharp. "You are not like Silias or whoever else has hurt her, you are nothing like them. Don't you ever think that. Those people are vile."

"Yeah, Cinth, I've known you for years. You're a good person at heart," Renee reassured me. "You just have a hard shell."

"That's not what you thought last week, Niko," I spat at him. "You were so angry, disgusted, and disappointed at what I am. You made it very clear that you don't want me near her anymore."

"I've known you most of your life, Cinth, I know that when you decide that you like someone, you'll protect them with your life, and with Celestine, it's much more different because you *love* her."

Everyone needs to stop throwing that word around like it means anything to me.

"I was angry at you before," he continued, "because I believed that you put her in danger intentionally, but I had a chat with Jerome earlier today and he helped me understand the situation better." He let out a breath. "I know you're struggling internally with your emotions and at that time, so much was happening all at once and I didn't know what to think." He paused. "I know I said that I wanted to see the remorse you have for what you've done and I have been noticing it. You haven't slept, you've barely been eating, and now you're confiding your thoughts with Renee and me, which is very mature of you to do... You've got good in you, Cinth, and I'm sorry that I said otherwise."

I shook my head, I know what I am. I'm a bad person, perhaps not as bad as Silias only because of the limits I've given myself. "Regardless, I'm still mean and harsh with her," I cursed. "And the worst part is that she actually enjoys it when I get aggressive with her."

Renee giggled. "You really found your other half."

"Renee, that's not what I meant," I muttered. "She's been so traumatised, she enjoys being in pain and I've been so traumatised, I enjoy giving it to her." They were the only two living people who knew about my past. "That's wrong, isn't it?"

Niko pursed his lips. "I think you may be overthinking all of this. It's all happened so fast, and this is new territory for you. You need time to process it all."

The thing is, it didn't happen fast. "I wanted to kiss her for so long." *Did I just say that out loud?* "But she's been through a lot, and I don't want to take advantage of her." I still don't know the full story of what she's been through.

"Okay, but look, the fact that you are acknowledging that shows you have control. You haven't lost it like you thought." Niko smiled.

"But I did lose it, Niko, every time I'm around her, it takes all my energy to stop myself." *This was so humiliating.*

"What do you think would help, then?" he asked.

I shook my head, pulling my hoodie further down my face. "I don't know. I think I just need to let go once and I'll have control again."

"No, no, Cinth, you are not going to sleep with her because you think that'll make everything go back to normal," Renee scolded.

"Then, I need to stay away from her." *Though, that has proven to drive me insane.*

Niko rolled his eyes. "Those are two very extreme options."

They're the only options I can think of without killing her. "Did I take advantage of her?" I asked them.

Niko shook his head. "I've seen you with Celestine, you both look so alive around each other. She's really comfortable around you and anyone can see that she likes you a lot."

"If she likes me, then why is she avoiding me?"

"She's probably just embarrassed and doesn't know how to act anymore." Celestine doesn't get embarrassed. "I told you before, her father and I knew you two would find each other again. You've had a special bond since you were kids."

I took a moment to process his words and let out a deep breath. "What is she doing to me?"

They exchanged knowing looks, pursing their lips, before turning back to look at me. "Just relax and wait for her to talk to you," Niko said. "It happened and you can't change that."

"Moira has your back," Renee told me.

No, Moira really doesn't.

I couldn't do this anymore, this was no help. I didn't know why I told them so much. I got up and headed toward the training room, going completely psycho on the punching bag. I was tempted to meet Jerome and go on a rampage, because I needed the release.

Don't feel anything for her.

Let her go.

Cel means nothing to me.

She's a distraction.

Distraction.

A distraction from what?

19

THE MONSTER ISN'T UNDER THE BED

DECEMBER 70 A.D.

I was on a good streak of not getting detention lately. So, on Friday after school, I was able to go to Jamiel's house. Lin was going to meet all of us later as he had tutoring. We hung out, playing a few board games to pass the time before his parents came home.

"Hi Iri and Hyacinth, how are you two?" His mother smiled at us.

"We're good, miss," Iri replied, as I shot her a smile.

"Would you like me to order some pizzas or...?"

"We're going to a party soon," Jamiel said.

"Is there alcohol?"

"Yeah."

His mother laughed. "Best not to have an empty stomach then." And pulled out her phone. "I'll order something. Anything special?"

"Just whatever should be fine, thanks mama!" he said as she left the room.

Jamiel's other mother offered to drive us there and to pick us up if we wanted to.

"Bye mum!" Jamiel lightly pecked his mother's cheek.

"Call if you're not feeling safe," she told us. "I mean it, any of you."

"Thank you," we replied and left the car. It was a large house, with a tall, stoned fence and metal gates.

We entered the house and were immediately offered drinks, even though people usually just brought their own. I pulled out a pill and popped it in my mouth.

I've been feeling extra drained lately, even though I hadn't been doing any assignments and training a bit less. I spent more time meditating than sleeping.

Iri dragged me towards a girl. "This is Poppy," Iri beamed. "She's in the grade below us." Then she leaned in to whisper in my ear. "Please, be nice to her, she thinks you're really cute."

I rolled my eyes. "I don't give a f–"

"Please, you owe me, remember?"

I squinted at her. "This is why you really wanted me to come tonight, isn't it?"

She gave me an innocent smile. "You and Cel are officially done with each other now, aren't you?"

I don't know. We still haven't talked, and she refuses to look at me. Iri had been bitter about the situation as well, knowing I was the reason Cel wasn't talking to her either. At least, Jamiel and Lin weren't giving me shit about it.

"Unless you really do have feelings for–"

I rolled my eyes, letting out an annoyed breath. "I'll give her five minutes." *Hopefully less.*

Iri let out a small squeal. "Thanks, Cinth! I'm going to find Jamiel." Before I could stop her from leaving me alone with this girl, she was already gone.

I stared at Poppy in front of me. She was pretty enough, but everyone seemed a little ordinary after I met Cel.

After I kissed Cel.

I felt my face burn, still in disbelief that we had done that. Thank the gods it was dark in here. Lin knew about it, giving me looks every time someone brought Cel up, but he was waiting for me to talk about it first. Though, I was planning on taking it to my urn.

Poppy leaned towards me and looked up at me through her lashes. "So, are you thinking about going to the formal?"

"No," I said plainly, then I thought about Iri. I needed to be nice and maybe Poppy could distract me from Cel. I cleared my throat. "Are you going?"

She twisted a strand of her hair around her finger. "I mean, I was thinking of going, but I was hoping to go with a date."

"Oh." I shoved my hands in my pocket. I hate talking to girls, minus Iri and Cel. *Get away from my thoughts, you witch.* "Cool."

"You're not going with Celestine, are you?"

"I'd rather not talk about her."

Poppy sipped her beverage, hiding a smile. "Do you not drink?"

"No," I responded. "I don't like the taste." Nor do I like the feeling of losing control over my body, like I did at that one party—*Gods, don't think about it.*

"Alcohol makes me really warm." She unbuttoned the top few buttons of her blouse, revealing more of her large chest. "Do you want to go somewhere else?"

"Not really." My eyes looked around the room boredly, hoping to spot one of my friends to save me. *I can't do this. I thought this would help, but I was so wrong.*

Poppy took my hand and put it on her waist. "Do you want to dance?"

I pulled my arm away from her. "No."

She sighed. "You're really not interested in me at all, are you?"

I met her eyes. "I wasn't hiding it."

Her eyes squinted into a glare. "Kiss me once and I'll let you leave."

My body physically recoiled at her words. "Uh, no." I gave her a weird look. "I'm going to the bathroom." I went around her, and she took my hand and pulled me back to her. I snatched my hand out. "Don't touch me," I growled.

"I'm not leaving you alone until you do. Iri promised you would take me to the formal next weekend. So it's either you kiss me now or you take me to the formal."

"Why would she promise that?" Iri could not be *this* upset with me.

"She said you owed her, and she owes me."

I looked up in search for Iri. *I'm going to kill her.* Instead, I locked eyes with Cel.

She was sitting on top of the kitchen counter, facing us with her legs crossed in front of her. A couple people stood around her, chatting, but she wasn't listening to them. She took slow sips of her drink and looked just a bit more angrier with the shadows casted under her eyes. I didn't know she would be here.

I slithered my arm out of Poppy's grip, but she continued to grab my arm. "Stop it. I'm not going to kiss you and I'm not taking you to the formal."

"You're being so difficult."

"And you're embarrassing yourself."

She sighed and forced my hand on her. "I'm sure if you tried, you'd like me."

I quickly snatched my hand away.

"You–"

I stopped myself. I can't do anything to her, she's a classmate. It's one thing to punch another boy but to harm a girl would be... "Just give me a bloody moment," I muttered. This is why I tried to avoid relationships and touching, it just makes me feel uncomfortable. *Except with Cel.*

Surprisingly, Poppy let me leave, probably thinking I'd come back. No thanks. I walked out of the room and to the kitchen to get some water. The sink was right next to where Cel sat. I turned on the tap, holding a new cup underneath. Before it was even halfway filled, Cel pushed the handle down, stopping the water.

I turned to her. "Really?"

She pretended as if she had done nothing at all, suddenly interested in the conversation in front of her.

I turned the water back on and this time, before she could reach the handle I grabbed her wrist. "Don't you dare."

She gave me this half, amused smile. "You shouldn't waste water," she said. "Don't you know there are people dying of thirst in the West side?"

Like I give two shits about them. "I am going to die of thirst if you don't let me fill my cup."

She let out a gentle laugh, switching legs so she was turned more towards me. "You are so dramatic, Cinth."

My cup was overfilling, spilling all over my hand, so I released her and turned off the tap, downing the entire cup in one go. I set down the cup and looked at her again.

"What are you even doing here?" I shoved my hands in my pockets. "Thought you didn't go to parties anymore."

The last time she was at a party we played spin the bottle, then all those interviews about her came out, dragging her character through the mud, so she had avoided parties and all social gatherings since.

"I was invited," she said. "I wasn't going to come, but I didn't want to go home. Though, after watching you and that girl interact, I'm glad I came." She laughed.

I let out an agitated noise.

"Yeah, I didn't think she was your type." She leaned her weight back on her hand, blinking slowly.

"What do you think my type is?"

Cel gave me a sideways glance. "Not her."

I scoffed. "I don't have a type." *Whatever Cel was, that was my type.*

"Where are your friends? Shouldn't you be with them?" Her head nodded, she could barely keep her eyes opened.

"I'll look for them later, but why don't you want to go home?"

"I'm mad at Silias."

"For what reason?"

"I don't always agree with the things he wants me to do," she answered in a bored tone.

"What did he ask?"

Her mouth opened to speak, but then she closed it. It didn't seem like she would go more in depth with it, so I didn't pester her.

"You've ignored me all week and now you're talking to me normally," I said.

She turned her eyes down. "Not like you really tried to talk to me either."

No, I guess not. "I didn't know what to say."

She shrugged, sipping her drink. "Do you regret it?"

"Do you?"

"I asked you first."

I was afraid if I answered it truthfully, it would scare her away. I don't regret it, but I will if I really had taken advantage of her and if it messes up what we had. Whatever that was.

"No." I finally said.

When we met, all those months ago, I wanted nothing more than to see the fear on her face while I split her insides open. I don't know how we got here or when my view on her changed, when I started calling her Celestine instead of Reaper in my head or when I began feeling like her presence around was normal, but I know that I never wanted to lose this. She gave me parts of myself I thought I lost and things I didn't even know existed.

"Do you regret it?" I asked her in a soft voice.

"I really wanted to do that with you so bad, but." She paused. "You're going to get hurt because of it and I'll never forgive myself for my carelessness."

"Carelessness?" I questioned. "You haven't been very subtle." *She started all this, she drove me to this point. Why is she backing out now? That's not fair to me.*

"Yeah," her voice was low. "I wasn't."

"Isn't whatever the two of you had over?" Poppy sneered, standing close to me and just in front of Cel's legs, attempting to grow the distance between us.

"Gods, you can't take no for an answer," I muttered.

Poppy's face turned red with anger. "You're supposed to be talking to me."

"Don't tell me what to do." Nobody controls me.

Poppy whirled her head to Cel. "And who even invited you? Shouldn't you be at home with mummy and daddy—Oh, wait, you ran away from home to join some street gang. You run out of drugs?"

Oh, now she's done it.

Before I could go off on her, Cel's eyes shifted into something amused, tilting her head back. "What's your name?"

Poppy scowled at her. "Poppy."

"Poppy," Cel repeated, cupping both of Poppy's cheeks in her hand and pulling her close. "I do live with psychopaths who would take crowbars and leave them halfway in the skull of anyone who makes me cry." Her eyes began to well up with false tears, a sudden exaggerated sad expression on her face. "You don't want to make me cry, do you?"

Poppy's eyes widened and her face paled, no longer angry, now scared for her life. "No, I..." Her voice shook, "I didn't mean–"

"You didn't mean to be rude or force Hyacinth to talk to you?" Cel mocked.

"But I thought—"

"You thought?" Cel's eyes widened for a moment, her long acrylic nails digging into her cheeks. "No, Poppy, you must have forgotten, right? You weren't thinking? You're drunk? This is just a silly misunderstanding?"

Poppy let out a couple of sounds, attempting to nod, but Cel's nails etched her face during the movement.

"You're funny, Poppy." Cel roughly pushed Poppy's face away from her, the scratches red and irritated. "But I'm too tired to deal with your shit."

What version of Cel is this?

Poppy gripped onto her cheeks, tears in the corner of her eyes. "Sorry."

"Why are you still here?" Cel spat at her.

Poppy glanced at me for a moment, before quickly rushing away.

What did I just witness? A side of Celestine I had never seen. How many sides were there? Sometimes she was playful, sometimes shy, sometimes reckless, other times a cold, calculated killer. Which of these were just masks, and which were her true self? Or were they all real, and she simply hadn't figured out who she was yet?

I was so lost in my thoughts and shocked by what had just happened, I wasn't able to snap out of it fast enough as she hopped off the counter and walked away.

My phone vibrated in my pocket and I checked my notification, Lin finally arrived and was wondering where I was. It wasn't hard to find them in the other living room.

"Oi, oi, Cinth." Jamiel couldn't stop laughing, "I heard... I heard you–Poppy!" His laugh sounded like a hyena.

There's no way they could have known about the scene with Celestine just yet.

Iri shoved me, causing me to take a few steps back. "I told you to be nice to Poppy!"

"You promised her something I never agreed to," I snapped.

"Well, I may have exaggerated my promise but, come on, she's cute."

"Not my cup of tea."

"Why did you even try to get them together?" Lin asked Iri. "You know him and Cel have a thing going."

"Well, Cel hasn't spoken to any of us for two weeks," Iri argued. "So maybe she lost interest in him."

"Anyways." I rolled my eyes, turning to Lin. "How was tutoring?"

"Oh, Gods." He leaned towards me and the sweet scent of alcohol on his breath tickled my nose. "These guys I'm tutoring, nah, they're not going to pass. They're so stupid, it's shocking. They make Jamiel look smart."

"That's rude!" Jamiel snapped.

I chuckled. "Lucky they have you."

"They should have come to me earlier, there's so little hope left for them." Lin hiccuped.

"Are you already drunk?" I thought he just got here.

"I drank while I was tutoring, I knew I was going to need to catch up." He leaned on me for support, and I helped him stand.

"Iri, go get some water," I said, walking Lin towards the sofas. "Let's sit you down." Iri came back with water, and I forced Lin to drink it.

Lin was the worst drinker, he didn't know his limits nor did he care for them. His bloodline of surgeons all expected nothing less from him. That pressure forced him to study every hour of the day, and the only time he's able to wind down was at parties. It's why he liked to get drunk out of his mind, so for just those few hours, he didn't have to think.

He cupped my cheek and slapped it a couple times with a sloppy smile on his face. "Thanks, man. You're–You're a good friend."

"Right."

Like a switch, Lin straightened his back and stood up. "Eloise!" Quickly, he disappeared into the crowd.

"He'll be fine," Iri said. "How are you going?"

"I'm okay." I leaned back on the sofa. "Go have fun, I'll be here if you need me." I was so exhausted, I needed to sit down.

She nodded and left. I wondered where Jamiel—then saw him, taking body shots off someone and hollering with both his hands in the air. The crowd cheered for him. From the corner of my eyes, I saw Iri making out with the girl she always hooked up with at parties, but they never talked outside of them.

I felt someone staring at me—or glaring and when I turned there was Poppy and her friends gossiping loudly about me. "Why do you even like him anyway? He's always getting in trouble!"

"That's what makes him so attractive," Poppy sighed. "He's so strong and I bet he'd get into fights for me."

Bloody hell.

"You need professional help."

Yeah, she does.

"He's not even that cute!"

How dare they.

"You deserve better, Poppy," another one of her friends said.

"He's so rude."

They continued to insult me, knowing I was within earshot, and I couldn't roll my eyes further back into my head.

"And you know Celestine likes him," one of them said. "Why would you even try?"

Were people scared of Cel like they were scared of me? Since when?

Poppy let out an agitated noise. "Iri told me they were done! How was I supposed to know she's still in love with him when his best friend told me that?"

"Celestine never confirmed that, you know she didn't. Don't get on her bad side." She lightly touched Poppy's cheeks, the scratches still evident. "Or she'll get someone else to hurt you more."

Would she really do that?

"Celestine may have all the boys in school wrapped around her finger, but we all know every girl who isn't also obsessed with her would—"

"Poppy, let's go get more drinks," one interrupted, pulling her by the arm away from the area.

I wondered why they suddenly stopped, when I realised there were others watching them with frowns, their stare following the group as they left. Then, they all turned to look at me and I exited the room quickly.

As I wandered the manor of my classmate, dodging people left and right, I stumbled upon a sanctuary. An empty guest bedroom on the ground floor.

Finally, some peace from the eyes and music.

I allowed myself to fall on the bed and was met with a squeak. My heart jumped out of my throat.

Cel pushed me off her and I rolled off the bed.

I groaned as I made impact with the floor. "Oh, thank the gods it's you. I thought I squished an animal," I exaggerated holding onto my heart. "What are you doing here?"

"I'm taking a nap, what are *you* doing?" she asked, shifting on the bed to get comfortable again.

I got up from my position. "I just needed space. Why are you sleeping at a party?"

"I'm tired," she mumbled, and her breathing became steady.

"Come on." I pulled the blanket off her.

She opened her eyes. "What?"

"You can sleep at mine." I didn't want to be here anymore anyway.

She reached her hand up towards me, and when I took her hand she pulled me down, rolled us over, and got on top of me. "Did you miss me, Cinth?" she asked. Still holding my hand and drawing it closer to her face, brushing her lips lightly against my palm.

Yes. "I hardly noticed your absence."

Cel sank her top two fangs into my palm, drawing blood. I didn't flinch or react to the sting. Her eyes were cold as she gently licked the blood clean, her gaze locked onto mine. "Then stop being nice to me."

"I'm not nice, Cel."

"You pity me," she spat. "Don't."

I furrowed my brows and shook my head. There's a difference between pitying and caring. A fine line, but it was there. "Get off me." I only half meant it.

Her eyes shifted into amusement. "Make me."

I could quite literally throw her across this city if I wanted to. "Someone's going to see us here." I tilted my head back towards the door, which was still open.

She leaned down, planting light kisses on my jaw. "So what?"

"Aren't you tired?" Just as I asked her, she collapsed on top of me, her breathing slow and steady. *Yeah, that's what I thought.* I gently caressed her head. This was surprisingly comfortable and closed my eyes as well.

"Angels above!" someone shouted from the door, and I snapped my head towards them. "Hyacinth and Celestine?" one of our classmates gasped, his words slurred. "I knew it!"

Celestine lifted her head up towards them and I felt the air shift. "You're drunk."

He slowly nodded and left.

She rested her head on my chest again. "Gods, that took more energy than usual."

I bet. "I'm taking you to my place so you can sleep properly, yeah?" I told her in a soft voice.

"We're not supposed to be seen together, Niko will get mad."

"No, he won't."

She pressed her face more into me.

"Let's go."

Cel got up and rubbed at her eyes, smudging her mascara. She followed me out and I found each of my friends, telling them I was leaving. Jamiel brushed me off and Lin was too drunk to comprehend my words.

"You two are speaking again?" Iri asked with furrowed brows.

"It's whatever," I said.

"Sorry, Iri." Cel's voice was soft, doe-eyed and innocent. "I didn't mean to ignore you as well."

I could physically see Iri's heart melting. "Are you okay, Cel?" Iri cupped her cheeks in her hands, worriedly, checking her temperature. "You're so cold."

Cel nodded with a small smile. "I'm just really tired."

"I'm taking her home," I said.

Iri raised a brow. "Didn't know you liked her enough to do that."

I rolled my eyes at her. "Yeah, yeah. Stay safe. Call or text if you need me."

She nodded and said her byes.

Cel was walking so slow out of the house, especially with how tiny she was just making her slower. For every step I took, she used three. So I picked her up and carried her, she wrapped her legs around my waist and her arms around my neck, resting her head on my shoulder. The crisp air entered my lungs and my muscles relaxed. "Did you not take your nap today?"

"Um... I did... Just tired," she whispered. Her body went limp as she fell asleep in my arms and I tightened my grip around her.

Demons were like cats, sleeping longer than they're awake. So, her being narcoleptic on top of it must make it unbearable to stay awake, especially if she doesn't have a proper place to sleep.

People stared at us as I held her, waiting for the train to arrive. When it finally did, I set her down in a seat and she leaned against my arm, still asleep. A few passengers kept their eyes on her, and I hated it. I swore I saw someone shamelessly snap a photo, but I didn't want to overreact in case I was wrong. Not wanting to disturb her, I shifted my leg to block their view. It must be exhausting to have people stare all the time—or maybe she doesn't even notice anymore. Either way, they couldn't seem to look away from her.

***

It wasn't too many stops before I carried her out, and she unconsciously wrapped herself around me again. Eventually, we made it to my place, and I managed to unlock the door without dropping her.

Niko was awake and watching a movie with Renee. "You're home late." He turned noticing Cel in my arms. "What are you doing? What happened?" He ran towards us.

I hushed him. "She's just tired," I explained in a low voice. "She's narcoleptic so—"

"Did anyone follow you?" he whispered in a panic.

"I made sure no one followed us," I reassured, I'm not an idiot.

"Silias is going to hunt us down." He searched for his car keys. "We need to get her home."

"He's asked her to do something she doesn't want to. Silias doesn't need to know she's here."

"Who's this?" Renee asked, coming to our side.

I gave her a small smile. "Hi, Renee. This is Celestine."

She exchanged knowing looks with Niko, before moving behind me to get a look at Cel's face. Renee sucked in a breath, "Demons below." She gently ran her fingers through Cel's hair, needing to touch her to see if she was real. "She looks like a porcelain doll." She turned to me. "I see why you lose control around her."

I felt the prickling heat on my cheeks. "Renee." *Please be sleeping right now.*

Niko stared at Cel's sleeping face on my shoulder, eyes softening. "She takes your room, and you're on the sofa."

"That was the plan." I rolled my eyes at him, as if he thought he had raised an indecent child. I opened the door to my room and carefully set her down. Cel was really knocked out. I took off her shoes and hesitated to take off her jacket. I tried not to make it weird as I did it. *Gods...* She really has so many injuries. Then I pulled my blanket over her.

I brushed my teeth in my bathroom and changed into my sleeping clothes. As I walked out, Cel was still fast asleep. Who would've been able to guess this young, pure face was one of Soulesity's most dangerous killers?

I quietly closed the door to my room and joined Niko and Renee on the sofa, watching whatever movie they were in the middle of.

"Where were you two tonight?" Renee asked.

"A party," I said. "It was boring."

Niko nodded. "This movie's almost finished, then you'll have the sofa to yourself." When the movie finally ended, he turned off the TV and looked at me. "Did Celestine mention what Silias wanted from her?"

"No." I waved my hand in the air, too tired to dwell on it.

He nodded, dropping the subject. "Don't you dare think about touching her."

"Who do you think I am?" I was offended he would even say that. I may enjoy inflicting pain on others, but I don't do things like that.

He squinted at me, glaring.

Renee giggled. "He's a good boy, he wouldn't dare."

I groaned. "Exactly, thank you."

Niko patted my back. "I am not afraid of teaching you a thing or two about consent."

I gave him an annoyed look. "Niko... I'm not like that."

"Sure, Cinth." He rolled his eyes and Renee followed him into his room. "Sleep well."

"Night," I called back, and he closed the door to his room. I cursed, realising I didn't have a pillow or blanket. But I had two blankets in my room and lots of pillows on my bed, so I'd just sneak in and grab them.

I quietly opened my door and closed it behind me, keeping the light out from waking her. I took the spare blanket I kept under my bed and picked up a pillow.

"Cinth?" she whispered.

Shit, I woke her. "Yeah?"

"Don't leave me."

"I'm sleeping on the sofa, I'm not far if you need me."

"I need you." She reached her hand towards me.

"I'm not sleeping with you," I said, sternly. Niko would skin me.

She let her arm fall. "I'm scared," her voice was barely audible.

"You're okay, you're safe here." I looked under my bed. "There are no monsters under the bed," I joked.

"They're not under the bed."

I set down my pillow and blanket at the edge of my bed and went to open my closet. "No monsters in the closet." Closed my closet and opened the bathroom. "None in the bathroom either." I closed the door to the bathroom and went over to gently graze my hand on her head. "You're safe."

Celestine pulled the blanket up to her nose, her head nodding off but attempting to stay awake.

I sat on the floor, leaning against the bed. "I'll sit here until you fall asleep."

She turned to face me and held out her hand, I took it. She was trembling.

***

Blood stained the white snow. My hands were painfully numb, and a heavy feeling settled in my chest. Someone was standing next to me and when I turned to look up, Cel was there— her silver hair and white dress almost blending into the snow.

But she wasn't looking at me. Her wide, fearful eyes were fixed on something else, her brows furrowed as if she were in pain.

What's she looking at?

***

When I opened my eyes, the sun was rising, and I was still holding onto her hand. My heart felt heavy, and it was hard to breathe. A nightmare, but as the seconds went by, the memory of it withered away. I carefully slipped out of Cel's hold and made my way out of my room. Niko was in the kitchen, sipping on coffee, glaring at me behind his mug.

"Did Renee already leave?" I asked.

He grunted in response.

"She was scared to be by herself, but I slept on the floor," I said sleepily. Thank the gods it was Saturday, I could sleep in. I plopped down on the sofa, forgetting to bring the pillow and blanket but I didn't care anymore. I was too tired to get it.

"I know," he growled. "I saw."

I didn't respond and fell right back to sleep.

I woke up to the sound of Cel softly crying in the kitchen. "But it's going to hurt him so bad." I peaked my eyes at the two.

"No, Celestine," Niko's voice was mere whispers. "You're not going to tell him." He pulled her into a hug as she cried harder. I didn't know what was going on and my body was too exhausted to try. I'd just get it out of them later, if I remembered it.

When I woke up again the sun was at its peak.

"Celestine left already, she wanted to thank you for last night," Niko said.

I checked the notifications on my phone, there were a few from my friends debriefing about the party last night. "Are we training today?" I asked, my voice raspier from just waking up.

"Get ready." He sounded angry.

***

Weekend training was always the worst, but today he made it extra difficult. *Definitely angry at me.*

"Another."

I stopped the push ups. "Another set?" I could barely speak. "I just did seven sets."

"If you stopped smoking, you wouldn't be so out of breath," he snapped.

My eyes widened. "How did you—"

"I'm not an idiot, I can smell it on you," he snarled. Though, he didn't know about my drug addiction or maybe he did. "Another."

I shakily stood up and began the first work out all over again. This was just the warm-up, and I already threw up after the fifth set. I was struggling to finish this set and hoped he wouldn't make me do another.

"Trust Celestine and keep her close to you," he warned me. "You'll need each other."

"Why are you being so serious?"

Niko was usually quite the jokester during training and always made them fun, it was almost scary how he was acting.

He didn't answer my question nor give me a break after I finished my eighth set.

"Spar." He took a fighting stance.

My legs shook as I took my stance. Niko lunged at me, his speed was incredible, especially for his age, and in this state, it was hard to keep up.

Niko kicked me down. "Get up, Cinth."

I attempted to stand up quicker this time, but he didn't hold back, kicking me down once more. I cursed. I gathered what little strength I had left and pushed off the ground. Twisting, I swept Niko's legs out from under him and landed on my feet.

"Good," he complimented.

I didn't play nasty, allowing him to stand. We continued to spar some more until he too was out of breath. He finally decided it was time I practised with my bow. "Ten clean shots and then you can be done for the day. Miss one and you're conditioning instead."

I nodded. It should've been easy, but my body ached and trembled and I could feel bruises already forming. I pulled my bow back and just barely hit the middle dot.

He nodded in approval.

"Why have you been training me so much more than usual?" I asked, releasing another arrow.

"Because you need to be ready."

"Ready for what?"

He let out a deep breath. "There's going to be a day, Cinth, where I won't be here," he said. "There's been talks of Stygians rising and you know what comes with that?"

"Angels?" I aimed the final arrow, released and hit the centre.

He nodded. "Angels are ruthless. And Demon Hunters—"

"Demon Hunters?" I cut in, laughing. "That job doesn't exist anymore." It fizzled out decades ago, after the war.

Niko didn't laugh. "They still exist." He turned, grabbed a water bottle, and tossed it to me. "They just call themselves hitmen now." He waited a beat, then added, almost like it was nothing. "My family used to be Demon Hunters."

I caught the bottle but didn't open it. The words didn't register at first. It felt like someone had dropped a rock in my stomach. "What?" I asked, slower this time.

Niko's mouth twisted, like he didn't want to explain but knew he had to. "I grew up being taught Demons were monsters," he said. "But then I met Ender... And he changed everything."

I stared at him. "So, you're one of the Kynigos?"

"Yes," he said simply. "I may be distancing myself from the Underworld, but I'm still a Kynigos. I always will be."

"Do you know who the others are?" I asked, my voice low.

He pondered for a moment. "In due time, they'll reveal themselves to you. The world is currently going through change."

Change.

I wasn't sure if that was a promise or a warning.

"Get yourself cleaned up," he said, as though none of what he'd just dropped on me mattered. "Tomorrow morning's training will be harder."

I nodded, muscles sore, head spinning.

After my shower, I spent the rest of the day meditating in my room.

I heard Renee come in, and they left to go out to eat.

20
OUR BLOOD BIND

DECEMBER 70 A.D.

For some reason, Niko was allowing me to train Cel again, so Monday, after serving detention, Cel met up with me and we walked back to my place. I forgot my bow, but also wanted her to take a nap before we trained. She still wasn't going home, and it looked like she was on her last bit of energy.

"Have you not showered or slept or anything?" I asked.

"God below, I'm not gross," she snapped. "I have a toothbrush and extra clothes. I showered at school this morning and slept in the nurse's office," she said, as if it were obvious.

I nodded, opening the door to the apartment. "Why didn't you come here?"

Cel would be staying with Niko and I soon anyway, so why wouldn't she just come here. Especially with the weather dropping more consistently to negative temperatures, schools and stores would close and winter holiday would begin until it was bearable enough for people to go outside again. Four years ago the holiday lasted four months, the longest I'd ever experienced. While last year was the shortest holiday recorded in centuries, only one and a half months.

She set her bag down and took off her shoes. "Where's Niko?"

I went over to the small note in the kitchen. "Renee's," I replied, going into my room to change and find my bow. When I stepped out, Cel was asleep on the sofa, already in her assignment outfit. *That was fast.* I double checked the assignment we were supposed to do. It wasn't urgent, we could do it later tonight.

Setting my bow back in my room, I went over to her and picked her up. She stirred. "Are you ready?"

"We'll go after you take a nap."

She let out a small breath as I set her down on my bed. "No, I'm fine." She sat up, but I pushed her down. "What?"

"Cel, just sleep for a bit." Falling on the bed next to her, I put my arm over my eyes. "I need a nap too."

She mumbled something and we fell asleep.

***

Standing in the salt flats, two children raced past me in the reflection below, their boots crushing the invisible snow underneath them, laughing and shouting. Two brown braids began at the top of the girl's head, a pale blue bow tying the two strands together, letting the rest curl down a bit past her shoulders. Her dress, the same shade of blue, contrasted her white stockings. The boy chasing her had short black hair, dark brown trousers and a red sweater with a white button-up shirt underneath, the collar peeking over the sweater.

A camera shutter clicked behind them, Oremus lowered the camera, a big smile on his face. "Cinth, Datura," he called. "Dinner is nearly ready. Why don't the two of you come in and clean up?"

My younger self, around nine, walked towards Oremus, but Datura quickly took his arm, pulling him in the opposite direction.

"Datura, wait!" Oremus set down the camera and shuffled for his shoes. "It's dangerous in there!"

I ran, following the children, massive trees appeared around them as we went deeper into the forest, Oremus's shouts smaller. Eventually, the two stopped at a tree, huffing and puffing, their warm breaths fogging in the cold.

"Why did we run?" my younger self asked Datura. "Aren't you hungry?"

Datura swallowed. "Because." She huffed. "You always train after dinner and then I have to go to bed before you finish and then we won't see each other until tomorrow morning and then I go back home before lunch."

My younger self turned towards the direction they had come from. "Do you have to leave?"

"We only saw each other one weekend every month." Cel appeared next to me, her hair dark silver and wearing a white dress, looking exactly like a ghost.

Datura nodded with a pout, leaning back onto the tree closest to her. "It's not fair. We hardly get to play."

My younger self met her eyes. "One day we won't need anyone's permission to see each other."

"When we're older, we'll be so free."

A slight curve formed on my younger self's lips.

"Do you know what Aldring is?" she asked.

"A Demon's coming-of-age?"

"Mama said I'm going to have to choose a partner then, otherwise it's given to me." She nodded. "This Demon named Grey is going to be mine, but I've never met him before."

Something in my head clicked. The reason I beat Grey so bad all those years ago, the last straw I had forgotten, was this. He was going to be Cel's and I could never have her because I was only human. I was and always will be considered weaker than Demons and not good enough for her.

My younger self's face scrunched up. "Grey?"

"Do you know him?"

He rolled his eyes, shoving his hands in his pockets, muttering. "Yeah." He kicked at the snow beneath him.

Datura took his hand. "But I wanna choose you."

My younger self froze, his face heated. "Datura." The redness on his face deepened, avoiding her eyes. "We're going to have to... you know."

She blinked up at him, unbothered. "And?"

His jaw tensed. "You're acting like this is nothing, but it's a huge deal, Datura."

She tilted her head. "Why?"

He glanced away, almost frustrated by how casually she was taking it. "Because it's not just about us. It's about a lot more than that." Something in his eyes changed, a motivation that was no longer spite, but something deeper, something that would drive him longer. "And I don't want to mess it up."

"Cinth! Datura!" Oremus's frantic shouts grew closer to them.

"We should go," My younger self said before they walked back towards Oremus.

"There you are!" Oremus fell to his knees in front of them, checking both for any injuries. "Are either of you hurt?" He rested a hand on their shoulders, his eyes wide.

My younger self shook his head.

"We're okay," Datura replied, taking Oremus's arm, helping the old man back to his feet. "Let's go eat."

He nodded, scolding them as they walked. "You two can't go into this forest, there are dangerous creatures lurking in here."

"Like what?" Datura's eyes brightened with curiosity.

Oremus shook his head. "Many we don't even know about."

The three disappeared behind the trees, before the trees disappeared with them.

"Is this the promise you talked about before?" I asked Cel behind me.

She nodded, and another scene faded into view. It was the same younger versions of ourselves.

My younger self snuck into Datura's bed, getting underneath the covers.

"Cinth," she whispered, her eyes barely opened as she turned to face him. "How was training?"

"It was okay."

She scooted closer, snuggling into him.

My younger self tensed at her closeness and opened his mouth to speak but didn't say anything for a long moment. "Datura."

"Hm?"

"Don't choose Grey. You have to be with me, okay?"

Datura smiled, tilting her head up to look at him. "Will you wait for me?"

He nodded, gently caressing her hair. "Yeah."

She planted a small, short, innocent kiss on his lips. "Let's make a blood bind, then."

His face heated, and he nodded.

Datura took his hand in hers and sunk her fangs in his palm, sucking on it until it was dry. Then she pierced her own palm and gave it to him. My younger self placed his mouth over her wound, sucking on the blood. When they were done, Datura cuddled close to him again.

"I wanna kiss you again." Her voice muffled into his chest.

"Okay," my younger self said.

"But we should wait until we're older, right? Because kissing is something only adults do."

"I guess so."

The scene vanished into the water, and I was alone in the reflection. I looked up to find Celestine standing halfway between the wooden house and me. She nodded at me to follow and I took a step towards her.

***

I startled awake when the door to my room swung open. *Bloody hell.*

"Hyacinth, Celestine," Niko's voice was sharp.

I turned my head to look at him. "We're not doing anything."

"Yeah, that's exactly what it looks like," he snapped.

I glanced down at Cel, who had moved to lay on top of me during our nap. She was awake and staring at him without any expression but if she and I weren't the same, I wouldn't have caught the hint of annoyance on her face.

"You haven't done your assignment," he said.

"We'll do it tonight," I reassured.

"It *is* tonight."

I looked at the window, it was pitch dark. How long were we asleep? I pushed Cel off me and she didn't argue, standing up with me. Then headed out.

The nap drained me, but lucky for us, the assignment wasn't too far, still on the East side. I sighed, thankful I brought my bow. The basement was large and there were around ten people. I drew my bow back, aiming three arrows at the same time.

"You're the only person I know that can shoot three arrows in one go," Cel commented, tying her bandana around her head.

"Probably because I'm the only one in the city who *can* do it." I released my arrows, and they flew through the air, piercing three men, killing them instantly. Seven to go.

Cel jumped down, a couple crates below shortened her fall. I watched as she took down two men, so quick they didn't have time to process her moves. Then shot three more arrows before coming down to her side. We had one each. I took my butterfly knife and slashed the centre of the last man's chest open before turning back to Cel to see her mouth covered in blood. "Did you get hit?"

"No." She licked the blood off the palm of her hand like a cat.

Cel seemed calmer, blood being a release for both of us — a quiet understanding that needed no words.

I nodded, stuffing my knife into my pocket. "Let's get out of here." I noticed her uncertainty. "You're still not going back to Silias, right?"

She nodded.

I used my thumb to wipe the bit of blood off her chin. "So, you're sleeping at mine."

"Is it really okay with Niko?"

I rolled my eyes. "Yeah."

We walked back in silence until Cel finally spoke. "What are your thoughts on Stygians?"

"What do you mean?" I asked.

"Like—" she gathered her words. "Do you think there's more Stygians should have, or should they be grateful for what they have now?"

"It's not really my place to give my opinion on that," I said, glancing at her. "Since you're Stygian, what do you think?"

"Ignatius and Paxon often talk about how they're afraid and tired of trying to fight for how it used to be, but Silias constantly reminds me that this comfort is temporary—it's fragile. Keeping the effort takes more than all of us realise, one wrong move and everything could come crashing down."

"And who do you agree with more?" I asked.

"Well, I'm not sure. Ignatius and Paxon must know what they're talking about because they've experienced the war and the Angels, but I also think they may be a bit blinded by their fear to push for better." She paused for a moment. "So, what do you think?"

I took a moment to process. I hated Silias with every atom in my body and the thought of agreeing with him hurt my soul more than anything.

"I would never settle."

We got back to the apartment as Niko was cooking dinner. "Celestine, are you hungry?"

"I just ate."

Niko noticed the blood on her but didn't say anything.

"Oh, Cinth, you're back." Renee emerged from Niko's room, her hair in a bit of a mess. It was obvious what they were just up to. Her gaze rested on Cel, wide eyed as she quickly patted her hair down. "Hi, Celestine, I'm Renee."

"Niko's partner," Cel said, giving her a polite bow.

Renee nodded with a smile, stepping closer to her, then gasped. "Wow." This was the first time she was seeing Celestine awake. "Your eyes..."

Cel gave her that smile of hers and I held my breath, my heart beating a bit too hard over something as simple as a smile.

"I–" Renee couldn't find the words to speak, nor could she look away. "Are you injured?" Renee finally asked her.

Cel shook her head.

"I heard you and Cinth were close," Renee teased. "You're staying over, right?"

"Um." Cel looked to Niko.

"Yeah, Cel, you're staying," I said and Niko nodded in confirmation.

"After you get cleaned up, would you like to watch a movie with us?" Niko asked her.

Cel's brows twitched in a moment of confusion. "I..." she hesitated. "I'm a bit tired."

"You can use my shower and sleep on my bed," I said. "I'm going to eat first."

She followed me into my room. I found her a shirt she could borrow and handed it to her.

She nodded her thanks and headed inside the bathroom, while I went to eat with Niko.

"You're sleeping on the sofa," he said.

I let out a small sigh. "Yeah, okay, but we didn't do anything, Niko." I should have never told him we kissed. It only complicated things.

He rolled his eyes, setting down three plates of food.

"She's staying with you two to train during the holidays, is that right?" Renee asked.

Niko nodded. "We'll be moving into the dojo for the holidays."

"Are you excited, Cinth?" She glanced at me with a teasing laugh. "It'll be in just a couple weeks."

Living with Cel was something I thought would be far away. Honestly, it's likely Silias would *suddenly* change his mind about it all, especially since Niko and I are still training her.

"I have a feeling I will be entirely sleep deprived this winter," I said.

We continued to chat until we finished dinner.

"Are you going to watch the movie with us?" Renee asked.

I shook my head. "That nap I took earlier only made me feel more tired, I'll move to sleep on the sofa when you two are finished."

Renee nodded. "We'll try to keep it down."

"It's fine," I reassured, taking their plates with mine and putting them away, cleaning a bit of the kitchen. I headed over to my room to find Cel already asleep on my bed, when I went to my bathroom, I noticed she had her toothbrush drying on the side of the sink. I placed it in the glass with mine, brushing my own teeth before hopping in the shower. I finished my nightly routine and put on some pants and a hoodie, before joining her in bed, scrolling through my notifications.

I purposefully kept the door opened so they knew I was serious about how Cel and I weren't going to do anything. I could hear the movie they were watching, it was their favourite that they'd seen a thousand times before and was a part of their many inside jokes that I understood but didn't find as funny as they did.

Cel shifted, wrapping her arms and legs over me, kissing my neck.

"Sleep, Cel," I told her, feeling my body heat up. "You must be exhausted."

"Not really." She didn't stop.

"The door is open," I warned, but she didn't shy away like I thought she would. Instead, she moved to sit on top of me, brushing her lips against my jaw. I set my phone down and pulled her closer to me, meeting her lips. It was even better this time. No hesitation, no uncertainty.

Just us.

I bit her lip. "Sleep," I muttered.

"After," she replied, slipping her tongue into my mouth.

"Hyacinth, Celestine," Niko's voice was sharp at the door, but neither of us could stop nor did we really care, even if it was Niko. "You said you weren't going to do anything," Niko growled.

I caved.

I could hear Renee giggling from behind him. "Just leave them alone, Niko. They're teenagers."

I pushed Cel away, barely hiding my amusement. "You told me to do this."

"No. I told you to follow your—"

"So, what?" I interrupted to save myself from cringing at his words. "Staying in control never gave me this."

"Gods, I hate your soul, Cinth." Cel rolled her eyes at me.

"And I hate your entire essence, Cel." I moved my grip up to her hands and intertwined our fingers together. "I hate that no matter how hard I try, I can't stay away from you."

Her eyes softened at my words. "I hate that you're the only person I ever want to give everything to." She rested her forehead on mine, and we closed our eyes.

"Are they trying to say love?" Renee asked Niko.

"I think so."

We ignored them and Cel melted back into me.

I heard Niko muttering under his breath about our indecency and Renee reassuring him that we'd be fine as the door closed.

I didn't know what I was doing, honestly, I just knew I craved more. I liked the way she kissed me, the way she breathed and gasped, the way her eyes glowed a soft red—it was intoxicating. It should have scared me, how easily I gave in, how completely she pulled me under. But with her, I didn't care.

I never wanted this to end.

We stayed like that, close and breathing together, our heartbeats slowly syncing. I pressed a soft kiss to her hairline, my fingers brushing lightly against her cheek, as if trying to memorise the feel of her. Exhausted but content, I pulled her a little closer, and soon we both drifted into a deep, peaceful sleep, wrapped in the quiet of the moment.

***

I was back in the salt flats once again. Cel took my hand leading me towards the wooden house.

"Where are we?" I asked.

Our steps rippled the still water beneath us, my reflection with my arm stretched out, but Cel wasn't mirrored below.

"A place between the living and the dead." Cel released my hand, carefully opening the door. It creaked and groaned on its hinges.

"We're not in a dream?" I asked.

"Somewhat. Our bodies stay in the living realm, but our souls are here."

"How come your hair is silver and your clothes are different from the ones you sleep in?" My clothing always matched what I was wearing in my sleep and when I met Jerome here, he was the same, so logically, hers should too.

"You ask too many questions, Cinth."

We stepped through the threshold, met with the same endless maze of hallways that I had been to before. The grandfather clock stood by the door, the long hand ticking between 6:06 and 6:07. Paralysis stood before us and it froze me in my tracks.

"Hyacinth." Paralysis's voice was strained, hissing.

***

I woke up to the door of my room open, Niko must have checked on us throughout the night, but I knew he hadn't seen anything to worry about. I tilted my head up towards the clock on my side table.

"Cel," I nudged her. "Classes start in an hour."

"Oh," she sighed. "Can I skip today?"

"No." I laughed getting up. "You skip school too much."

"For a bad guy, you go to school too much," she snapped back.

"Niko bargained with me that if I get decent grades and never skip school–unless I was too injured to go–I can get detention all I want and he won't get mad at me." I laughed. "Besides, who said I was a bad guy?" I mean, I am but...

She laughed, sat up, and turned to me. "Aren't you and I villains?"

I furrowed my brows. "Villains? That's a bit extreme," I said. "The world isn't black and white. We're good guys in some situations." Very few, but I'm sure there's some. "And bad guys in others."

She tilted her head. "I like being the bad guy."

"And why is that?" I asked, curiously, heading over to my closet to find my uniform.

"It's more fun." She gave me a smile.

I chuckled. "For someone who likes to play bad guy, you like to be praised a bit too much."

She threw a pillow at me.

We finished getting ready and Cel skipped breakfast to leave first. We couldn't be caught being near each other, not at this hour.

School went on as normal, I didn't really see Cel except in passing.

"You seem really chill today, Cinth," Lin commented as we found a spot on the landing of the stairs to sit and chat, Jamiel got too cold to stay outside.

"Yeah," Jamiel said. "Less like you hate the world."

I shrugged. "I don't know, it just feels like things are going okay."

"Did something happen?" Iri asked.

Cel happened. I shook my head, not answering.

"That's good," Iri sighed, leaning against the wall, stretching her legs out. "I'm so tired today, I was up all night studying for physics."

"Demons below, I completely forgot!" Jamiel exclaimed.

"Would you have studied if you remembered?" Lin asked.

"No." Jamiel laughed.

I managed to not get detention today, a rare occurrence that's been happening a lot lately and I assume the teachers think I'm planning something big.

"Are we training today?" Cel asked me at my locker after school.

I shook my head. "No, Niko wanted to have a chat with me." I glared at her. "Probably because of you."

She laughed, walking off. "I'm not sorry."

21
NIKODEMUS KOLDEN

December 70 A.D.

I got home to Niko saying his goodbyes to Renee, not leaving a single part of her skin without at least one kiss from him.

She couldn't stop giggling. "Niko, I have to go." *She's been here a lot lately.*

"I love you, Renee. So much."

"I love you too, Niko, but I really need to get back to Atlas, I was supposed to be at the store two hours ago."

"Okay, okay." He continued his kisses. "I love you."

She pushed him away, but he kept pulling her back. This was gross. I'd just wait in my room, I wanted to shower anyway.

When I got out, Niko was waiting for me. "Put this on." He had set down a black suit with a black tie on top of my bed.

"What's the occasion?" I asked. I've only worn a suit a few times in my life. "Aren't we training?"

"We're going somewhere nice," he said. "I have some news I want to share with you." With that he left me to change. Before we stepped out, Niko tightened my tie, but I loosened it again right after. He gave me a disapproving look. "Must you always try to look cool?"

"I am cool," I joked.

We went to a restaurant in the East side. "Do you remember when we first met?" Niko asked me.

"Barely," I admitted. Out of pure and utter rage, I had locked my foster family in a room and set fire to their home.

"You were covered in soot," he chuckled. "I thought you came from working at a factory."

I shook my head, poking my food with my fork. "Why are you bringing this up?"

"Because I want to tell you what I saw in you," he said.

"A scared little boy?" My tone bored. "You felt sorry for me and took me in, isn't that the story?"

He couldn't help his smile. "Yes, well, you were definitely scared, but I knew you were a fighter and I remember that there was this... Something in your eyes I didn't understand at the time." Niko looked at me. "When I learnt you murdered your foster family because you were sick of the mistreatment, because you wanted revenge, I knew that this was a boy who was going to change this city and that he was willing to do it anyway he could as long as it was efficient."

"Well, sorry to disappoint," I muttered. I haven't done anything that changed Soulesity for the better. I am a menace to these streets.

"No, Cinth, I don't want you to think I've ever been disappointed in you–horrified, yes, sometimes you do things a bit out of my comfort zone–but regardless." He took a breath, gathering his thoughts again. "You are a powerful, smart, independent man. You've worked so hard to become what you are now. And I know when you mature further, you're going to understand and figure out who truly is evil and be the only one with the courage to do something about it."

I am a wicked soul, he had so much confidence in me to be good, but it's not what I wanted.

"I know you think you're a bad person, a villain, that you've the blackest of hearts, but I see you, Cinth. I see you pat animals with the gentlest touch, I see you play along with the imagination of children, I see you protecting Celestine from everything you can. You are still so young, you do not know who you are just yet and that is completely normal and fine."

"What if..." I started, "what if I *want* to be bad?"

He shook his head. "I know you're going to be bad in your own way."

Niko's eyes kept staring at something behind me, but before I could turn to finally look he said, "I know your birthday was a few weeks ago." He pulled out a small box from his pocket. "But I wanted to give this to you now."

He slid the box across the table, and I caught it before it could fly off. I opened the box to reveal a beautiful silver watch inside, "Niko, this is..."

"Maybe now you won't be late to class," he mocked.

I rolled my eyes, strapping the watch over my wrist, "I'm not going to want to be there any less."

He chuckled. "Happy birthday, Cinth."

Niko had only given me two presents in my life. My butterfly knife for my tenth birthday and now this. Usually, if I wanted something, I'd get it with my own money, so I never asked for anything. I didn't want a watch, but I did need one.

"And," he added, "with Celestine, I really mean it, trust her with your soul."

"Why are you saying this?"

"Have you figured out who her father is?"

"Ender." I was a fool. Everyone knew but me. I was only thankful he was dead, because if Ender were still alive, he would eat me, *slowly*, for the things I'd done to and with Cel.

Niko nodded. "Poiesis created Demons in Phobus's image, humans in Moira's, Selkies in Archaeia's and Angels in her own. She created seven of each to start with."

"Poiesis was the Goddess of the Ether, Goddess of creation," I started. "Phobus the God of the Netherworld, the God of death. Archaeia the Goddess of the Sea, the Goddess of archives. Moira the God of the Surface, God of fate."

Niko nodded.

"Each of the seven original Demons had been given one trait from Phobus that would be passed down to their children, Valorous, Ego, Temptation, Sly, Callous, Sadist and Fury," Niko explained. "Every Demon after was a descendant of one, rarely two of the seven original Demons. Zuriel a descendant of Temptation, a seventh generation Demon. Ignatius, a descendant of Ego and Temptation, a fifth generation Demon. Paxon a descendant of Valorous, third generation Demon. But Ender was a descendant of three; Sly, Sadist, and Fury. A second and third generation Demon and pureblooded. He was the most powerful and respected Demon who ever lived."

Ender was Phobus's favourite Demon.

"I know all this, Niko," I said. I knew how powerful the Demons who lived after the Reckoning were and I knew just how eminent Ender was since his birth.

Niko continued. "I need you to understand. I need you to listen carefully to everything I'm telling you."

I sighed, circling my finger over the rim of my glass. I was not here for a history lesson, but had no choice.

"Ever since female Demons were killed, powers have been watered down with every new generation and with every child, so, the first sibling is stronger than the second and so on. From what I know, Ender had only one child before Celestine who was killed in the Reckoning. His name was Finlay."

The stories of Finlay were legendary, but it was his heart that led to his demise.

"Celestine may be mixed with human blood, but with her father being Ender, it's not a wonder why or how she is already so powerful, but you must swear to keep her powers secret."

"Doesn't Silias already know?"

"If they knew, they'd be using her, don't you think?"

I nodded in agreement. "Right. But, Niko, why are you telling me all this?"

"Because soon you'll have to decide whose side to be on."

"Why do I have to choose a side? Why can't I stay out of it—" I paused. "Is this because you think I'm that stupid prophecy that's written in the Book of Ice?"

"It's not just written in the Book of Ice, Cinth, it's in the Sky Scrolls, the Deep Archives, ancient tomes, sacred scripts — every religious text."

"But I'm not Phobus's son. You can't possibly believe that I could be—"

"I know," Niko reassured. "But Celestine is definitely the other half."

"You don't think it's Bernadette?"

"Celestine is playing the part of a weak little girl. Of course Bernadette and the others think it's her, but it's not. I need you to protect Celestine until she finds the child of Phobus."

"What's going to happen when they do eventually meet?"

Niko shook his head. "I don't know, nothing is written after."

I stared at my half-eaten food, cold now. I turned my head up to meet Niko's eyes. "So, is this what I've been training for? Is this why you chose me, why Ender favoured me?"

He released a breath. "The day you first met Ender was also the day I learnt about Celestine's existence. He told me everything soon after."

I took a sip of my drink.

"He favoured you because you reminded him of his son, Finlay."

It didn't fully answer my question.

"But yes, we trained you so that you would one day be powerful enough to protect Celestine."

"I'm just a weapon, a pawn," I spat. "This whole time, you've just been using me?"

"No, you're more than that." His voice held firm. "Hyacinth, I've raised you like my own son, I never want anything to happen to you, but Celestine is important—"

"I know, I get it."

"Please, Hyacinth—"

"Niko. I *will* protect Cel, but not because you raised me to, but because I genuinely care about her. I never want anyone telling me what to do or how to live my life. You raised me to be a killer, you gave me the ability to fight and the skills to survive. I'd die before anyone lays a hand on Cel, but it'll be bloody hard to kill me."

Niko let out a relieved breath. "I was afraid I had turned you to hate her again."

"No, Niko, you were right," I said. "It was never hatred I felt." I realise that now.

He gave me a smile and stood up from his seat. "Come on."

I followed him through a door, and we headed up to the rooftop of the restaurant where no one else was. The sun was blocked by the Ether Kingdom, the grey clouds heavy around the city. Niko released a slow, deep breath as he stared at the view. "I want to retire." He pulled out a ring from his pocket. "And ask Renee to marry me."

I gave him a smile, ever since he met Renee, Niko had grown softer.

"It's a bit soon isn't it? She's only been waiting eight years."

He laughed. "Yeah, well, we were discussing things about how this would all work and," he paused, nervous to say his next words. "We wanted to officially adopt you and live with us."

My eyes widened. "Adopt me?" Light snow began to fall from the sky, the flakes attaching to Niko's hair.

"I do consider you my son already and we do live together, but I wanted to make it official."

"Are you serious?"

He laughed. "Of course. The papers are being processed as we speak."

I didn't know what to say. I thought for sure he was going to kick me out. I thought he was tired of me. I thought I was going to be on my own again. But Niko wanted me. Renee wanted me.

They're *choosing* to be my family.

"I love you, Cinth." Niko extended out his arms with a big smile and I stepped into his hug.

I wish I had said it back.

He was wet and something sharp poked me in the chest. *What is that?*

"Are you good?" I laughed, as his weight fell onto me. "Woah, what is going on with you?" I knelt down from the sudden heaviness as he collapsed onto me.

I pushed him off, turning him over, and cold dread sank into my bones. An arrow pierced him directly in the heart. Blood. His glazed eyes stared blankly up at the sky and I looked up to find the source, the killer, but I couldn't see anyone on top of any of the buildings around us. It came out of nowhere.

I turned back to my mentor, my father figure for the past decade, his eyes already glazed over and his body quickly growing as cold as the air around us. The world seemed to fall away, tilting under the weight that suddenly crushed my chest. Silence swallowed everything. The man who guided me, protected me, was gone.

***

A light layer of snow covered the both of us by the time someone came up to the roof. I couldn't process the words they were saying as they rushed over to Niko, shouting things to what I assume was a few others behind us.

I didn't move when paramedics picked Niko off the snow, covering him up with a white sheet. A police officer crouched down next to me. "Hi, my name's Xander. Could you tell me what happened?"

I wasn't able to respond, I just stared at the indent in the snow in the shape of what once was Niko's body and the red that stained it. *Niko's blood.* My fingers were blue, but I couldn't feel it. I couldn't feel anything.

"We need to get you inside, you're freezing." There was a long silence as he waited for a response from me. When he realised I wasn't going to move, Xander asked me, "was that your father?"

Father?

"Do you have anyone I can call for you?"

Renee.

She's going to be so heartbroken.

"Leave him alone," another officer said, "he's in shock."

Xander turned back to me, he scribbled something onto a note and handed it to me. "When you're ready, call this number. We'll have him cremated for you."

Cremated. That's what they do in Soulesity when someone dies so that Demons don't eat their corpses.

When I didn't take it, he slipped it into the front pocket of my jacket and patted me on the back. "You're going to be okay. We'll find the people who did this."

No, the police are incompetent jokes. *I'm going to do it.* I finally stood up, feeling almost too calm.

"What's your name?" Xander asked.

I met his eyes, and he flinched. "Vulture," I said in a low voice.

Their eyes widened at the name. "Don't tell us... That was... Nikodemus Kolden."

I didn't reply, I just walked over to the edge of the roof and jumped off it, landing on the snow covered pavement.

EPILOGUE

He stabbed his target in the neck, a quick and easy death, and the man crumbled to the ground. When he lifted his head up, two police officers stood at the other end, horrified expressions on their faces.

He cursed under his breath.

"Stop—Stop right there!" one of them shouted, while the other used his intercom to call for backup and an ambulance.

He darted in the opposite direction as they chased him, turning left and right and right again, trying his best to lose them.

As he sprinted through the crowd, he shoved a man out of his way. Normally, he never spared a glance at who he pushed aside, but this time something made him look back. It was an elderly man, balding with greying hair clinging to the sides of his head, his deeply etched wrinkles telling the story of a long life. Behind his thick glasses, his eyes were wide with fear—terrified of falling, of breaking his hip, or worse. He looked like his late father.

He stopped abruptly, guilt shooting through him, and reached out. Grabbing the old man's arm and the back of his head, he softened the impact, carefully lowering him to the ground. His own mouth hung open in shock, struggling to process the moment. But the sound of approaching officers, their whistles sharp in the air, snapped him back to the present.

Glancing back, he saw someone rushing to help the old man up, and thankfully, it seemed no harm had been done. No time to dwell. He whipped back around, taking a sharp turn into a narrow alley—and crashed right into someone. Dead viola flowers burst into the air as he tumbled to the ground.

He groaned curses.

The police shouted in the distance. The person he had bumped into pushed him into the door she had come out of and hid him behind a few boxes placing a finger to her lips. Then she went out to pick up the flowers that had fallen onto the ground and the man covered his mouth to keep from breathing so hard. "You, miss!" the police shouted, out of breath. "Did you see a man run past?"

His heart dropped when she replied. "Yes, officers."

Feeling instantly betrayed, he pulled out his knife, ready to strike and escape. His legs trembled with adrenaline.

Instead, she pointed down the alley. "He knocked me over and continued down there," she said in an exaggerated annoyed tone.

"Thanks, miss." They gave her a polite nod and continued sprinting down the alley.

He took a few more moments to breathe before getting up to help the woman with the flowers. "I'm sorry about your flowers," he said.

"Don't worry, I was throwing them out," she reassured.

He finally looked up at his saviour, shocked to find a young woman with glasses staring back at him. She was unexpectedly beautiful, with freckles dusting her cheeks and withered viola flowers tangled in her dishevelled hair. Dirt smudged her dress, but even in that disarray, she seemed radiant. His heart raced—not just from the running. "Why did you help me?"

She met his eyes and gave him a smile but didn't answer. Instead, she pointed at the dark red stains on him. "Blood?"

"It's paint," he blurted out, but it was stupid of him to lie, she saw the police chasing after him. He put his face in his hand and bit his tongue, wishing he didn't say anything at all.

She gave him a sad smile. "As long as it's not yours."

He didn't understand why she was being so nice, there was nothing forcing her to help him. "Uh, so, um." His eyes looked everywhere but at her, a blush creeping up his face, before resting on the sign of the florist. "You work here?"

It was just another stupid thing to come out of his mouth, as she was wearing an apron with the florist logo on it.

"Yes." She giggled with a light blush across her cheeks.

He offered his hand to help her stand. "Are you injured?"

Her soft hands took his calloused ones. "Nothing that won't heal." She gave him a small bow. "My name is Renee."

He politely bowed back. "Nikodemus."

CHARACTER INDEX

Apex

- Hyacinth (Hi-uh-sinth) - The Vulture: Hitman. If you're his victim, you're already dead.

- Datura Celestine Vicary (Datch-uh-ruh) (Seh-les-teen) (Vik-car-ee) - The Grim Reaper: Kokkino clan's assassin. She leaves no witnesses.

- Jerome - The Jack of Spades: Serial killer. He leaves his victims looking just like him.

- Bernadette - The Siren: Mov clan's princess. She knows everything about everyone.

- Peter - The Mercury: Ex-university professor. He knows chemicals like he's reciting the alphabet.

- Neha - The Silver Lining: Vigilante. Justice seeker.

Other characters

- Nikodemus Kolden - Hitman and mentor to Hyacinth.

- Galinthias Zika-Vitalis - Hyacinth's best friend.

- Jamiel Dawoud - Hyacinth's best friend.

- Iri Donatoris - Hyacinth's best friend.

- Renee - Nikodemus's partner.

- Symeon - Third best hitman in Soulesity.

- Kahlik - Fourth best hitman in Soulesity.

- Octavius Gautier - The lighthouse keeper's son.

- Thessaly Zorlu - Octavius' partner.

- Elijah Voss - Inner circle of the Corpse Killer Clan.

- Aaliyah - Leader of the Corpse Killer Clan.

Kokkino clan

- Silias - Leader.

- Rayne - Second in command.

- Oremus - In charge of finances.

- Leo - Twin of Sterling, inner circle clansmen.

- Sterling - Twin of Leo, inner circle clansmen.

- Datura Celestine Vicary - Inner circle clansmen.

Gods and Goddesses

- Poiesis - Goddess of the above, Goddess of creation.

- Moira - God/Goddess of the land, God/Goddess of fate.

- Archaeia - Goddess of the sea, Goddess of archives.

- Phobus - God of the below, God of death.

Four surviving Demons after the Reckoning and their children

- Ender - Kokkino clan

  ○ Finlay (Deceased)

  ○ Datura Celestine Vicary

- Zuriel - Mov clan

  ○ Bernadette

  ○ Wystann

  ○ Sylvester

  ○ Steiner

  ○ Flint

  ○ Callan

- Paxon - Prassino clan

  ○ Mica

- Ignatius - Hriso clan

  ○ Grey

  ○ Albion

The Vicary Family

- Senator Eugene Vicary - Father of Ren Vicary.

- Senator Ren Vicary - Father of Vasos and Marigold Vicary.

- Delilah Vicary - Mother of Vasos, Datura and Marigold Vicary.

- Vasos Aspen Vicary - Eldest Vicary child.

- Datura Celestine Vicary - Middle Vicary child.

- Marigold Cassia Vicary - Youngest Vicary child.

Want to be in the loop of events and the next books in the series?

Sign up for Nova's newsletters on her website www.novakardinalis.com

Tiktok and Instagram @novakardinalis

Found an error or have something to say?

Email b.novakardinalis@gmail.com about it!